The Man Who Wasn't Beckham

A Crooked Lake Mystery

Robert W. Gregg

ISBN 0-7414-4463-1

Cover photographs courtesy of Steve Knapp.

Published by:

PUBLISHING.COM

1094 New DeHaven Street, Suite 100
West Conshohocken, PA 19428-2713
Info@buybooksontheweb.com
www.buybooksontheweb.com
Toll-free (877) BUY BOOK
Local Phone (610) 941-9999
Fax (610) 941-9959

Printed in the United States of America

Printed on Recycled Paper

Published March 2008

To the three wonderful generations of my family.

Acknowledgment

to Dr. Melissa Brassell, forensic pathologist,
whose advice regarding the probable condition
of the body in the ravine was invaluable

PROLOGUE

Among the attractive natural features of New York's Finger Lakes region are the gorges that channel snow melt and storm waters off the hills and down into the lakes. These ravines of irregularly layered shale vary from a defile no more than a few feet wide to spectacular glens that enjoy status as state parks and attract tourists from far and wide. The most impressive of these gorges drop hundreds of feet from their points of origin, following tortuous paths that present ever-changing vistas. Deep pools of water accumulate where boulders have scoured out the soft rock. Steep, nearly vertical banks send water cascading over moss and fern-covered cliffs. Shaded corners harbor dense thickets of brush and trees, anchored to the ground against the falling water by stubborn root systems. Fallen trees create transient bridges across these gashes in the earth, until they, too, are eventually swept downhill by the occasional storm that turns a trickle of water into a flood.

Near the north end of Blue Water Point on Crooked Lake lies a ravine of modest size, too narrow and not steep enough to impress the state fathers who create state parks, but large enough to attract those who wish to escape from summer's heat in its cool, winding course through the woods above the lake. For much of the year, this ravine, which bears no name on any map, is quiet, its pools mostly still, its scattered waterfalls only thin curtains of intermittent spray. As winter's snows melt and April's showers herald the arrival of spring, though, the ravine becomes dramatically greener and wetter. Water tumbles more rapidly down off the hill and into the lake, leaving the pools deeper and the shale and sandstone floor of the ravine slipperier. Over the course of many years, of many centuries, the very contours of the ravine will change as water and the things it carries grind away slowly at the walls and bottom of the ravine.

But speculation about geological change of such magnitude was not on the minds of two young boys as they ventured into the ravine on a chilly spring day. They were in search of

1

crayfish with which to go fishing. What they did not know was that they would find not live crayfish, but the body of a very dead woman in a large pool of water at the bottom of a steep bank some distance up the ravine from where it empties into Crooked Lake. A woman who appeared to have fallen to her death from the top of the bank — or had she been pushed?

CHAPTER 1

"Mom, I'm going up the ravine!"

The voice came from the kitchen of an old, well weathered, but still attractive cottage on Blue Water Point. The message was intended for Lisa Keyser, who was making beds on the upper floor of the cottage, and she quickly abandoned her chore and hurried downstairs.

"Do you really have to?" Lisa knew that this was a silly question, that her son would announce that of course he did, and that she would acquiesce in his plan after telling him to be careful. She was a chronic worrier, and she worried that her hyperactive boys would do something foolish that would lead to an accident, resulting in a broken leg or the need for stitches.

"Aw, come on, Mom. It's okay. Billy's already gone, and I promised to bring cookies for lunch." Darrell Keyser was stuffing a handful of chocolate chip cookies into a Ziploc bag as he spoke.

"You know I don't want you climbing up any of those banks. Just stay down on the level." Lisa had never been up the ravine, but had heard enough stories that she had formed a fairly accurate picture of its topography. "You should really put on your sneaks. Those flip-flops are no good in the ravine. Come on, do it for your mother."

Darrell reluctantly changed shoes, assured his mother that he and his brother would take care of themselves, and raced out the back door, slamming it behind him.

It was a chilly and windy morning on a weekend in late April, much too early in the season for swimming in the lake, but otherwise no deterrent for two young boys enjoying their spring break from school, visiting grandparents and escaping from the confines of city living. The ravine was always an adventure for two budding naturalists, collecting salamanders and minnows and catching the occasional glimpse of a fox or deer. In warmer weather, they would strip off their clothes and take a dip in one of the pools. Not today, however. The water would still be icy cold, and in any event, they were hoping to find a few crayfish for fishing. Billy and Darrell Keyser made their way quickly up the ravine.

"Gonna go climbing?" Darrell asked his older brother as he jumped across a suddenly deeper slot in the bed of the ravine. Their mother would disapprove, but there would be nobody around to watch, and what she didn't know wouldn't hurt her — or them.

"Don't know. Maybe." Billy was supposed to be his brother's keeper, or so his mother told him, but in fact he was the less responsible of the two boys, the greater risk-taker.

They came to a stretch of the ravine where the serrated shale formation rose sharply on either side of the stream, making it difficult to maintain footing. The boys, one after the other, grabbed onto the branches of overhanging trees and pulled themselves along the ridge until they came again to more even ground. Just beyond a sharp bend in the ravine, a fallen tree lay across their path.

"There it is," Billy said as he ducked under the tree. It appeared that the ravine had come to an end. Behind them it had been mostly level, the grade barely noticeable. Some fifty yards ahead of them rose a steep bank forty or fifty feet high. Bushes crowded the bank on both sides, and between them a thin sheet of water made the rock look like a wet, misshapen blackboard. Near the far corner of the bank, a more turbulent stream of water poured over the ledge, cascading down the bank and into a large pool that had been carved out of the soft shale below. Above the bank, the ravine would continue for another mile or so, a funnel through which water on the hills would find its way to Crooked Lake.

But this was as far as the Keyser boys would go that morning. Whether they would have been tempted to try the treacherous climb to the top of the bank, and whether they would have confessed to doing so if their mother had asked them, will never be known. Their morning's adventure came to an abrupt and altogether unanticipated end when they reached the pool at the base of the bank. And it did not end with Billy's bucket full of crayfish.

"I bet we get a dozen," Darrell called out as they scrambled the last few yards up the ravine to their goal. By this time, both boys' shoes were soaking wet, their feet cold, but neither seemed to care.

"Are you kidding? We'll be lucky to find any. I'll bet it's too cold for 'em." Billy was remembering that they usually found crayfish in the lake's warm shallows in the summer.

Whether there were any crayfish in what the boys had come to call "Grandpa Brock's Pool" quickly became moot.

"Hey, look at this." It was Darrell who had reached the pool first, and who was thus the first to realize that something was wrong.

The boys squatted on the edge of the water, staring down into the bowl, which tumbling rocks and falling water had created at the foot of the bank. It was roughly seven feet across at its widest point, and was now full of water to a depth of something like four feet. What the boys saw in Grandpa Brock's Pool was a body, unmistakably human, entirely submerged except for a hand that broke the surface of the water at a corner of the pool where a large rock had become lodged.

"What's he doing in there?" It was Darrell who asked the question.

"It isn't a he, it's a she. Can't you see her hair?" The body was lying face-down in the water, and Billy's certainty that it was a woman could well have been misplaced. Men have been known to wear their hair long, and the body was fully clothed. What could be seen from the edge of the pool was a body clad in jeans and a corduroy jacket that came below the waist, so that with the hair below the collar and boots on the feet, it was impossible to see any skin or flesh. Except for the hand. Otherwise, the boys could have been looking at a department store mannequin or a test dummy.

"What happened?" Again, it was Darrell's question.

"I guess she fell," was Billy's answer. He looked up at the bank, and for the first time since he had heard their mother tell them it was dangerous to climb it, he realized that maybe she knew what she was talking about.

Darrell got up and went over to a pile of brush and tree limbs that had washed down the bank and collected at a corner of the ravine near the falling water. He pulled out a branch, came back and started poking with it at the body in the pool.

"Hey, don't do that," Billy snapped at him. "What do you think you're doing?"

"She's dead, isn't she? I just wanted to see what she looked like." But the branch was waterlogged and broke apart as he tried to move the body. It quickly became apparent that if they were going to get a better look at the body in the pool, they would have to get into the water and turn it over with their own hands. But in spite of their curiosity, neither of the boys was anxious to touch the body.

Darrell tossed the broken tree limb away and walked around to the other side of the pool and into the mist that dampened the air around the waterfall, but the different vantage point gave him no better a view of the body.

"That hand looks funny," he said. Indeed it did. It was a deadly white, and there was something about the skin that made it look more like a sponge than a normal human appendage. "There's something wrong with it. What do you think we ought to do?"

Billy had decided that it was time to justify his mother's hope that he would show some maturity and take care of his younger brother.

"I think we'd better go tell Grandpa."

"You afraid to tell Mom?"

"Of course not. But she wouldn't know anything about dead bodies. She'd probably think we made it up." Billy had no idea how their mother would react to this particular bit of news, but he figured that she might see it as evidence that the boys ought to stay out of the ravine. Grandpa would get the story first.

It was clear to both of them that they would not be collecting any crayfish that morning. They didn't want to muck about in the pool, and getting back to the cottage and alerting the family to the discovery of a dead person in the ravine took precedence over searching for bait to go fishing.

The trip up the ravine had not taken the boys as long as it usually did. The trip back took even less time. They burst into the kitchen only forty minutes after setting out for the ravine, shoes soaked, hands dirty, cookies uneaten.

"Grandpa?" Billy hollered in a voice that could be heard all the way down to the Brocks' dock.

But it wasn't the senior member of the Brock household who materialized from somewhere in the cottage.

"You're back!" Lisa Keyser sounded relieved, and then immediately annoyed. "Stop right there! You've got to take those shoes off. You know we don't bring mud and stuff into the house."

The boys knew the drill full well: no shoes in the cottage. But even painfully learned lessons could easily be forgotten in the excitement of the morning's events.

Shoes off, they headed for their grandparents' living room.

"Where's Grandpa?" Billy inquired.

"He and Grandma went down to Southport to do some shopping. Why do you need to see him?"

"Oh, nothing really." It was while he was debating with himself whether to tell his mother about what they had found that Darrell solved the problem for him.

"Guess what we found?"

"How would I know what you found?"

"Well, it was a dead woman, right there in the ravine. Drowned in that big pool where the crayfish are."

Lisa never knew quite which of Darrell's stories to believe. Not that he exactly lied to her, but he had a tendency to sometimes say things that she didn't find credible.

"Now what kind of a story is that?" his mother wanted to know.

"It's true. Ask Billy. We saw her. Or maybe him. Billy's sure it's a woman. Anyway, the body's still up there, lying in that pool. You know, at the bottom of that bank you don't want us to climb."

Mrs. Keyser looked at Billy, who shrugged.

"Yeah, it's true. We don't know what happened, but she's in that pool. And she's sure dead. That's why we came back so fast, to tell Grandpa about it. And you. What are you going to do?"

She wasn't sure. She wasn't at all eager to go into the ravine to verify the boys' story. But if it were true, and she had now heard it from both boys, the authorities had to be notified. Already she found herself worrying about what effect this discovery of a dead person would have on their young minds. Not a good beginning to their weekend at the lake, she thought as she reached for the phone.

CHAPTER 2

Sheriff Carol Kelleher could hear the phone ringing before she got to the top of the stairs in the county office building. It had rung five times before she reached the door. Where did Ms. Maltbie go, she wondered as she leaned across her desk and picked up the phone.

"Sheriff's office," she said, reflexively assuming the role of her secretary rather than inviting speculation that Cumberland County law enforcement was understaffed.

The woman on the other end of the line started to say something, but then appeared to be interrupted by someone. The sheriff heard her telling that someone to be quiet. Moments later, the problem apparently resolved, the caller started to tell the sheriff about what her sons had discovered in the ravine on Blue Water Point.

"I think I've learned something that the sheriff ought to know about," she said. "There seems to be a dead person over here. My boys tell me that they found her while they were looking for crayfish to go fishing with. I don't know whether I've got the story straight. You know how kids are, but—"

The sheriff broke into this rambling monologue.

"This is the sheriff," she said. "You are reporting a death, is that right?"

"Yes, at least I think so."

"Where are you?"

"Oh, of course, you'd need to know where this happened. We're over on Crooked Lake. I'm calling from Blue Water Point on the West Lake Road."

No, not again, the sheriff thought. It had been — what? — only seven, eight months since she had spent the better part of two weeks on Blue Water Point trying to track down the killer of the owner of one of the area's largest wineries, and falling into what had become an unusual and ultimately frustrating relationship with one of the residents of that point.

Carol Kelleher pushed that thought aside.

"Please, let's take things in order. First, with whom am I speaking?"

"My name is Lisa Keyser. I'm the mother of the two boys who tell me they found a body. It's up a ravine near here."

Keyser. The name sounded familiar. Hadn't there been two young boys named Keyser she'd met during the previous summer's investigation of that murder on Blue Water Point?

"Okay, Mrs. Keyser. Now suppose you tell me about this. You say your sons found a body. Have you seen it? I mean are you able to verify what your boys have told you?"

"Well, no, not exactly. But they seemed so sure about it, I thought I'd better call and report it."

"Indeed you should have called. I appreciate that." Her memory bank now activated, Carol remembered that the Keyser boys — what were their names? — had had rather vivid imaginations, not to mention a penchant for misrepresenting facts when she had questioned them about what they had seen the night of the murder. If, that is, these were the same boys.

"You said something about a ravine. You are telling me that your sons found someone, someone they claim is dead, in a ravine. And that the ravine is on Blue Water Point. Is that right?"

"Yes. It's one of those gullies that empty into the lake, and it's not far above us — runs under the West Lake Road between here and West Branch."

The sheriff did not have a mental map of the many ravines that channel water into Crooked Lake, and she was not familiar with the one Mrs. Keyser was describing. But she had a pretty good idea of where it was, and was sure she could find it with no trouble. And find it she would, as soon as she had told her caller what she should do — or, more importantly, what she and her sons should not do.

"Have you told anyone about what your sons found? Or have they told anyone?"

"I don't think so. Well, I haven't, and I think they came directly back to the cottage from the ravine. So, no, I guess nobody knows but us."

"Good. Don't talk to anybody about this. And make it very clear to the boys that they are to stay at the cottage. Keep them off the phone. The last thing I need is to have the neighborhood aware that there's anything unusual going on up in that ravine. We'd have a crowd of curiosity seekers on hand before I could get over there. You do understand, I'm sure. Nobody's to know until I come by. I should make it sometime within the next hour. Tell the boys I need to talk with them."

"Yes, Sheriff. I'll see that they stay here." Lisa Keyser made it sound as if keeping them there would be no easy task, but there was nothing the sheriff could do about it if the boys' mother failed to do so. Carol would have to move quickly if she expected to be only the third person to see a dead body in the ravine at the north end of Blue Water Point on this morning in April.

———

Sheriff Kelleher wanted a colleague with her on this mission. Deputy Sheriff Bridges was on leave, so she checked the duty roster to see who else among her small staff was where. Barrett looked like the best possibility, and she reached him on his car phone.

"Jim, Kelleher here. Look, I just got a call from someone over on Blue Water Point saying that there's a dead body up a ravine near where they live. I'm heading over there to check it out. I want you to meet me there — just drop what you're doing and get over there as fast as you can. No reason why you can't do it right now, is there?"

Assured that Officer Barrett wasn't in the process of writing a ticket somewhere else, she gave him his instructions.

"I don't picture this particular ravine, but it sounds like it's right at the north end of Blue Water Point. I don't believe we can miss it. No idea whether there's a pull off on that stretch of West Lake Road; just park on the shoulder if you have to. And wait for me if you get there first."

It was twenty minutes and change later that the sheriff turned onto the West Lake Road. She had spotted several places where water trickled down exposed shale at the side of the road in the general vicinity of Blue Water Point, but they were too small to qualify as ravines. About a hundred yards north of the gravel road that led to the cottages on the point, the road passed over a gully that looked as if it might be the ravine Mrs. Keyser had described. She slowed down, trying to get a better look. This must be it, she thought, and at just that moment, Officer Barrett's car came around a bend in the road ahead of her. They waved in acknowledgment, and both pulled as far off the road beyond the ravine as the narrow shoulder allowed.

"This had better be it," the sheriff said as she climbed out of her car. She realized that she had neglected to ask how far up the ravine the boys claimed to have found the body. Not that they would have been able to give a precise estimate, but she wasn't in the mood for a hike of who knows what distance in what might be the wrong ravine.

As it turned out, it was the right ravine, and the trip didn't take the two officers long. It had been many years since Carol had done something like this, probably way back in her high school days or earlier. In spite of the purpose that had brought her to this spot, she found herself enjoying her surroundings as they worked their way upstream. It was easy to see why the Keyser boys had been attracted to it.

There had been no mention in the brief phone conversation with Mrs. Keyser of just where the body had been found. She was annoyed with herself for not asking. When they came within sight of the high bank, she shared that annoyance with her colleague.

"I sure hope we find it this side of that bank. Do you think you're up to climbing up there if we have to? It looks pretty vertical to me, and I don't see any good place to climb. Can't see any obvious toe holds. All that moss'll make it damned slippery." Like their mother, Carol thought it looked like a dangerous place for two young boys.

Officer Barrett wasn't ready to comment yet on the problem of climbing to the top of the bank. Nor did he have to. They both saw the body as soon as they got to the pool.

"Jeez, look at that, will you," Barrett said. "Ugly fall, looks like."

"I think that's an understatement," the sheriff said, looking up at the ledge from which the victim must have fallen. No way it could have been a freefall, she thought. While the bank was steep, it rose at an angle of much less than ninety degrees. Anyone falling down from the top would inevitably hit the rock wall several times before landing in the pool at its base. Which would mean that the victim of this fall would show a lot of bruising and possibly broken bones. Unless, of course, the body had been in the pool so long that it would no longer be possible to tell just what had happened to it during the fall. Not that it mattered. The two or three rocks in the pool were large enough, and the pool was shallow enough, that breaks and bruises could have been incurred

11

there as well on the bank. Carol found herself wishing that Cumberland County had a coroner with medical credentials. Tom Liberti was a good man, but his election to the post had had more to do with his politics than any skills that would be relevant in a case like this. But she'd have to call him anyway and get him out here to examine the body; then she'd have to wait until an autopsy had been performed before she would know what had happened to the woman in the pool. And when.

Unlike Darrell Keyser, the sheriff was sure that it was a woman. To another woman's eye, that was obvious. Still, Carol wanted to have a look at her face.

"Let's see if we can't turn her a bit," she said to her colleague. "I don't want to move her, just rotate the body enough so we can see the face under all that hair. Okay? Just be careful."

Being careful wasn't easy. Officer Barrett had to wade into the pool, which was slippery as well as cold, and he wasn't wearing waders or even rubber-soled shoes. Nonetheless, with the sheriff's help, he was able to change the angle at which the body lay in the water. He pushed the wet hair back, revealing what had been a human face.

"That's enough," Carol said, and Barrett eased the body back to something like the position in which they had found it.

"Looks like she's been in the water for a long time." Carol had no firsthand knowledge of such things, but she knew that this was not the face of someone who had died within the last few days. A few weeks? A month or two? She couldn't say, but she suspected that they were dealing with something that had happened at least as far back as early spring or late winter. She wondered what happened to bodies immersed in cold water for such a period of time.

"It's a puzzle, isn't it? Winter lasted forever, and spring's been nasty. Why on earth would somebody be climbing up this bank by herself on a cold day, snow probably still on the ground? I know people do crazy things, but I just can't imagine any sensible person hiking up this ravine back then." Or even now, she added to herself.

"Well, maybe she wasn't a sensible person," Barrett said. "Maybe she was one of those physical culture nuts, you know, the ones who go jogging and stuff like that all year long, never mind the weather."

And that's probably the way it was, Carol thought. But now there were more important things to do than speculate on why this particular woman had been in this particular place on a date still to be determined — if that date could be determined.

"Look, I've got to go down to the lake and talk to those kids who found the body. Hate to do this to you, but you'll have to stay here until the coroner's office gets somebody up here. And an ambulance. They'll need a body bag, and I'm going to suggest a couple of husky guys to help you. Getting her down out of the ravine isn't going to be a picnic."

The sheriff realized that she was leaving the unpleasant stuff to Officer Barrett, but she wanted to be the one to talk to those kids. Besides, their cell phones wouldn't work from where they were. Too hemmed in by the surrounding hills and overhanging cliffs. She'd need to get out of the ravine to make her call to Liberti.

Sheriff Carol Kelleher left her partner sitting on a rock near the waterfall, his only company the lady in the pool, and headed back down the ravine toward West Lake Road.

———

As she turned onto the gravel road that served Blue Water Point, the sheriff felt a tightening in her chest. There, stretching out ahead of her, were all of the cottages whose denizens had been the focus of her investigation the previous summer into the murder of John Britingham. Most prominently among those cottages was Kevin Whitman's. Now shuttered and obviously unoccupied, it was a painful reminder of her mixed feelings for the man who had reported the crime, gradually insinuated himself into her investigation, and then, at its conclusion, become her lover. It had all happened quickly, and for all practical purposes, it had ended just as quickly when he packed up and returned to his home in the city to resume his duties as a professor of music at a local college. That had been just after Labor Day. And here she was, eight months and three seasons later, driving past his lake cottage en route to a meeting with neighbors who had discovered a woman's body in a ravine less than a quarter of a mile up the road.

No question about it, she thought, as she pulled in behind the cottage next to Whitman's. These were going to be the boys she remembered from the previous summer. Young, small, full of misinformation.

It was the anxious mother who opened the door.

"So glad you're here," a harassed Lisa Keyser said as she welcomed the sheriff. "The boys have been nagging me to go out ever since we talked. They don't seem to see why it would matter if they told people."

"Sorry it's been a problem, but it's better that they didn't. Anyway, I'm Sheriff Kelleher. I think I remember your sons from last summer. It's Billy and Darrell, isn't it?"

She had been wracking her brain for the names, and Mrs. Keyser confirmed that her memory had served her well.

The Brocks had lit a fire in the fireplace to take the chill out of the spring air, and Carol joined three generations of the family around that fire and promptly tackled the problem of the body in the ravine.

"So, you seem to have had another experience with violent death," Carol began, addressing the boys. "I'm really sorry about that. Why don't you tell me just what you saw and what you did."

So Billy and Darrell recounted their morning's adventure, with Billy doing most of the talking and Darrell interrupting when he thought his brother had left something out. It was all pretty much what the sheriff had expected, and this time it had the ring of truth.

"I'm surprised that you're here at the lake. School isn't out for the semester, is it?"

Lisa answered for the boys, obviously concerned that the sheriff might think she had pulled them out of classes to let them go wandering up a Crooked Lake ravine.

"Oh, no. It's their spring break. We took advantage of it to visit my parents. Their grandparents," she added, by way of including the older couple in the conversation.

"I see. By the way, do you all come up here to the lake often? I mean, were you here earlier, say back in the winter or earlier this spring?"

"Just once. It was Presidents' Day weekend, just a short visit."

"Did you spend any time in the ravine back then?" The sheriff's question was intended for the boys.

"Absolutely not," Lisa again spoke for her sons. "There was snow on the ground, and I'm sure the creek would have been iced over. It would have been too dangerous to be in the ravine.

No, Bill and I — Bill's my husband — we wouldn't have allowed it."

Carol considered the fact that the ravine had indeed proved to be a dangerous place. Whether because of snow and ice, she did not know.

After eliciting a mumbled apology from Darrell for having tried to move the body, she decided that she had learned all that she could from the boys. They wouldn't like it, but she also had to insist that they stay away from the ravine for the rest of the day. Bad enough that they had been the ones to discover the woman in the pool; she didn't want them also to witness the removal of her body from its resting place in the ravine.

The sheriff pulled out of the Brocks' driveway and headed back to West Lake Road. Slowly. She found herself staring at the Whitman cottage, wondering just when his college semester would end, when he would be coming back to the lake. The more immediately important question, of course, was the identity of the woman in the pool, but for a fleeting moment all she could think about was the man who had discovered a dead man on his dock the previous summer, the man whose next-door neighbors had just discovered a dead woman in a nearby ravine. Too much violence for one normally quiet point on a normally quiet lake. But the cases had nothing in common. The first had been murder. This one was an accident, a tragic fall. Or was it?

Sheriff Kelleher brushed that thought aside. The cause of death would be a no-brainer this time. She wouldn't need Kevin Whitman's help in closing the case of a woman who had foolishly gone hiking alone up a ravine on Blue Water Point, lost her footing, and fallen to her death.

CHAPTER 3

Just two weeks remained of the spring semester. Two weeks and four days before he could pack and head back to the lake for the summer. Kevin Whitman stared at the pile of term papers on his desk, the last best thoughts of students in his "History of Opera" course. He hoped that those thoughts would be original, but suspected that too often they would be patched together from ideas cribbed from various Web sites on the Internet. Kevin enjoyed teaching. He had always found satisfaction in working with his students, encouraging their interest in music and culture, counseling them about career choices. But he hated grading papers, and at the moment he was stalling, postponing the inevitable.

It was while he was debating with himself whether to tackle the papers today or when he was more in the mood, perhaps tomorrow, that the telephone rang. It was a welcome interruption.

"Hello, Whitman here."

"Kevin? This is Carol Kelleher."

"Carol!" The pile of ungraded papers suddenly lost its importance. "You've made my day. I love you! You can't imagine, well, maybe you can, but — hey, how are you?"

"Are you all right?" Carol was obviously confused by this torrent of words. "You don't sound like yourself. But I'm glad you're glad to hear from me. Really, I am."

Kevin wasn't about to tell the sheriff of Cumberland County that he had been in a funk because of 25 ungraded term papers. Or that he loved her because she had given him a reason to temporarily forget his students. He realized that he hadn't been in touch in nearly a month, that he hadn't told her often enough that he loved her. Or thought he did. Suddenly, all the old questions came rushing to the surface.

"Let me apologize for not calling," he said, then added "or writing," and offered what probably sounded like a lame excuse. "I know people think academic life is just one extended vacation, but my dean had me working overtime on development of a new curriculum this spring."

"No apology necessary," Carol said, not entirely sure she meant it. "Things have been hectic up here, too. But I didn't call to revisit our relationship issues. I thought you'd be interested to know that there's been another mysterious death on Blue Water Point."

Kevin was relieved to think that this was not going to be a conversation about their relationship. They both knew it was an unusual one, and neither knew what to do about it. It had begun the previous summer when he had found a dead man on his dock early one August morning and become her unlikely partner in the investigation of the man's death. And then, to the surprise of both, they had become lovers. For one week. He had had to return to the city and his position on the faculty of Madison College. She had had her own responsibilities as sheriff of Cumberland County. They had seen each other only twice over the months that followed. She had visited him in the city in late fall and shared his small apartment and his bed over a three-day weekend. Seven weeks later, he had made a trip back to the lake. His cottage had been buttoned up for the winter, so he had stayed with her in Cumberland. It had been an uncomfortable two days. Whereas they had enjoyed the anonymity of the big city, Carol had been uneasy about the gossip that she feared would spread when people realized that their sheriff was spending the night with a strange man in her own home. She worried about it a lot, they talked about it a lot, and the result was that it had not been an enjoyable visit. They had not seen each other since.

But now Carol was on the phone. And talking about another death on Crooked Lake.

"You've got another murder?" Kevin shifted mental gears, setting aside his mixed feelings about their relationship, focusing instead on this news flash from the lake.

"No, nothing as dramatic as that," Carol said. "We found a woman up in that ravine at the north end of your point. Looks like she fell from the top of a ledge. Landed in one of those pools that form in the ravines. She's been dead for heaven knows how long — maybe a month or more. We'll get the autopsy report in a couple of days."

Kevin was about to ask why she had called to tell him this, but caught himself and rephrased his question.

"I thought I was only called in on murder investigations." He had intended it to sound jocular. Somehow it didn't come off quite like that.

"That's right. You are." But her tone of voice said she wasn't in the mood for banter. "Look, we have no idea who this is. No identification on her. I assume we'll find out eventually, but I was hoping you'd have an idea. She may not be anyone from around your part of the lake, maybe not even from the upstate area. But it would appear that she got there on foot — no car, no bike, nothing like that. So I thought I'd ask if you know anyone from around there who's in the habit of hiking up the ravines. A woman. Age hard to tell without the autopsy report, but I'd guess in her thirties. She's about five-foot-seven or so, dark hair."

This was the businesslike sheriff he remembered from their first meeting the previous summer, not the woman who had fallen into his arms the night they had wrapped up the Britingham case. Okay, he thought. Better play it her way. For now.

"But Carol," he said, "I'm never up there at the lake in the winter. You say she must have died — when did you say, a month ago? That would be in March, maybe earlier. I can't imagine anyone being up any of those ravines at that time of year, but what do I know? Anyway, I don't think I've been in the ravine more than two or three times, ever. So I don't pay much attention to what my neighbors do. The Keyser kids, of course. When they're not in the lake, chances are they're in the ravine. And I think Jim Stuart likes it. He's a botanist or something like that, seems interested in mosses and lichens, or maybe its toadstools. But you said it was a woman, and Jim's wife is short. And blond. No, I guess I can't help you."

"I didn't think you could, but no harm asking. We'll probably know soon enough."

It looked as if this conversation had come to an end. Was that all Carol had called about? Kevin waited a moment, giving her a chance to say something more, hopefully something more personal. The silence suggested that neither of them was ready to hang up.

It was Kevin who broke the silence.

"I've only got two more weeks to go before end of term," he said. "Can't wait to get away. There's nothing to keep me down here, so I expect to move back to the cottage by Memorial Day at the latest, hopefully by mid-May. It'll be good to get back to the lake. You know what I mean — I've really missed you."

He hoped Carol had really missed him. That she would welcome him back into her life. That they could put the long winter of separation, the tentative phone calls, his unsatisfactory visit to Cumberland in February behind them.

"I know. It's been hard. Kevin, I don't think I can talk about this right now. I hope you understand. When you get to the lake, give me a call. I do want to see you. And if I learn anything about our mystery woman, I'll call you right away. Okay?"

"You know it is. I'd be disappointed if you didn't," Kevin said. Their relationship had begun during an investigation of a mysterious death on Crooked Lake. If it took another mysterious death, he'd be a willing participant in her investigation, even an eager one.

"I promise," she said. "Bye, now."

The phone back in its cradle, Kevin contemplated the pile of term papers. His enthusiasm for the task was even less than it had been before the sheriff's call.

CHAPTER 4

Sheriff Kelleher had spent the better part of the afternoon worrying. She had never been one for second guessing herself, but now she was unhappy with the way she had handled the telephone conversation with Kevin. Why had she been so cold, so impersonal? It wasn't his fault that his job called him back to the city so soon after they had found themselves falling in love. Nor was he to blame for the fact that she hadn't thought it appropriate for him to stay with her in Cumberland. The problem was quite simply that she was here and he was there, many miles apart, with the telephone an unsatisfactory substitute for a face-to-face relationship. Especially at this stage of that relationship.

And why had she called him? She had asked if he knew anyone on or around Blue Water Point who made it a habit to spend time in the ravines which emptied into Crooked Lake. But she hadn't expected him to provide a helpful answer to her question. After all, she had no way of knowing whether the dead woman was from that area. And if it turned out that she was, what were the odds that Kevin would know anything about who among the many people in the area frequented a ravine near his cottage? Not good.

No, to be completely honest with herself, Carol would have to admit that she had called Kevin for more personal reasons, using the discovery of the woman in the ravine as an excuse to get back in touch with him. But when he answered the phone, she had suddenly had second thoughts about what she was doing. And made a mess of what should have been a pleasant chat between two people who were soon to become neighbors — and lovers? — again.

She debated calling him back, thought better of it, and turned her attention to the matter of the identity of the woman in the ravine. The woman who had almost certainly been dead for weeks. The woman whose absence for all of those weeks had occasioned no missing person report. And that was strange. This unknown woman must be known to someone. Someone must have noticed that she was missing.

The sheriff could think of two reasons why she'd heard nothing about a missing woman. The first and certainly the most obvious was that she was not from the Crooked Lake area. Somewhere, someone had reported that a spouse, a relative, a neighbor had gone missing, but that somewhere could be in Vermont or Michigan or New Mexico, and word would not have reached Cumberland County, New York. Which would mean that whoever reported the missing person did not know that she was going to be in the vicinity of Crooked Lake, and that that bit of useful information had not come to the attention of whatever authorities were investigating her disappearance. Carol had already contacted the police in local villages as well the editors of area newspapers, but had come up empty. She had placed calls to neighboring jurisdictions, and initial responses had been equally negative. Which meant that the woman was probably from some place farther away.

But if so, why was she in the vicinity of Crooked Lake? Had she been visiting someone or on her way to visit someone? If so, why had that someone not reported that she was missing? Maybe she had just been traveling through, yet her presence in the ravine suggested that she knew the area. It was highly unlikely that a stranger to the lake would suddenly go walking up what looked from the road very much like an ordinary gully. Moreover, there had been no car nearby.

The sheriff was feeling frustrated, which led to thinking about the other reason the woman's disappearance might not have been reported.

What if the fact that she was missing was being concealed? What if someone had not wanted her to be found? In such a case, there would have been no missing person report. And that could mean that she was not necessarily from some place far away from Crooked Lake. She could even be a neighbor of Kevin's, which Carol had seemed to suggest when she asked him who among his acquaintances hiked in the lake's ravines.

Why would someone who knew that the woman was missing not have filed a missing person report? The obvious answer was that that someone had something to do with her being missing. Which led to the possibility that she had not been the victim of an accidental fall, but had instead been pushed to her death from the top of the high bank in the ravine. If that were the case, the sheriff would be facing a second murder investigation in less than a year. To the best of her knowledge, John Britingham's death the previous August has been Cumberland County's only murder in at least eight years. She very much hoped that the death of the mystery woman would not make it two murders in less than a decade.

Carol pushed the thought aside. Better to wait for the autopsy report, which might well tell her who the woman was and how she had met her death. Or then again, maybe it wouldn't. She'd think about Kevin Whitman instead.

———

Down in the city, Kevin was thinking about Carol Kelleher. Like her, he had not been happy about their telephone conversation. They had discovered, months ago, that they were not telephone people, and so they had not called each other a lot. There had been e-mails and the occasional letter, but it had become increasingly clear to both of them that they were drifting further apart.

The prospect of another summer at the lake cottage held out hope that they would come back into each other's lives, that they could rediscover the pleasures they had enjoyed so briefly the previous August. And Kevin knew that he would be returning to the lake before the end of May. Suddenly that seemed like an eternity away.

The evening after Carol's call about the news of the mystery woman in the ravine, Kevin was toying with an uninspired frozen dinner. His mind was not on whatever it was he was eating, nor was it on the talking heads on the six o'clock newscast, who were providing evidence that the state of the nation left something to be desired. He pushed away from the table and went to the desk in his study. He knew what remained to be done before the end of the semester, but he needed to verify dates on the university calendar. Perhaps he could leave for the lake sooner than he had planned.

No such luck. Commencement was sixteen days away, and he was expected to be there. His dean was a bear on the subject; moreover, he had promised to present a prize to one of his best students as they sent her off to face the real world, which meant that he wouldn't be moving into the cottage for close to three weeks. And that wouldn't do. Kevin decided that he simply had to see Carol, not in three weeks, not even in one week, but right away.

Much as he didn't like to, he picked up the phone and dialed Jennifer Laseur's number. Jennifer was his graduate assistant, a talented and attractive young woman who made him very nervous. It was widely known that there were two great loves in her life. One was the German violinist Anne-Sophie Mutter. A violinist herself, Jennifer had recently accepted a scholarship to Julliard, where she would hone her considerable skills until she could be compared favorably with the international star who was her inspiration. The other love of her life was Professor Kevin Whitman. This was apparent not only to his colleagues in the music department, but to students and faculty all across the Madison College campus. That Kevin did not reciprocate Miss Laseur's affection did not seem to dampen her interest in him. When she wasn't practicing the violin, she camped in his office, or found excuses to call him at home, or surprised him at his favorite after-hours watering hole. And she had apparently let it be known to more than a few people that they had a special relationship. She was too honest — or at least too prudent — to fabricate details of that relationship, but she had dropped enough hints that colleagues who might have been expected to know better had asked him about it. Or, in some cases, kidded him about it.

Kevin knew Jennifer would be delighted by a spur-of-the-moment request for her assistance. She would almost certainly be willing to put the violin back in its case for a week to do his bidding, no small compliment in view of her goal as a musician. But all Kevin needed was someone to cover for him in the last class of the semester and to proctor the final exam. Jennifer would do so gladly, and she would handle these modest assignments with panache. She would also, undoubtedly, weave the story of his request into her idyllic conception of their relationship. Or at least she would if he didn't tell her he needed her help because he had to leave town to visit the woman with whom he thought he was in love.

But there was no need to mention Carol Kelleher to Jennifer Laseur. It would not be fair to Carol, and it would be cruel to Jennifer. Let her think whatever she likes, he thought. She's my assistant, and all I'm doing is asking her to do some of the things that assistants are paid to do.

He was relieved when Jennifer did not answer the phone, enabling him to leave a carefully worded message on her voice mail and sparing him a breathless assurance of just how happy she was to be able to help him out. She would call back promptly, of course, but for the moment at least, he could concentrate on his dinner, now that he had made the decision to spend a few days at the lake. There wouldn't really be time to put the cottage in shape, but he could turn on the water, make up the bed with fresh linens, and stock the refrigerator. He hoped that Carol could be enticed down from Cumberland. He would sound interested in her mystery woman; he might even come up with an idea or two regarding that woman's presence on Blue Water Point. But Kevin wasn't making this hastily arranged trip to the lake to help the sheriff with a case of accidental death in a ravine. He was doing it because he needed to see her, to talk with her, to demonstrate how much he missed her. To bring their relationship back to where it had been in those exhilarating days at the end of the previous summer.

Kevin put the dinner dishes in the sink and went into the bedroom to start packing.

CHAPTER 5

The clock on the wall of the conference room in the Cumberland County Sheriff's office read 9:23. The Monday morning meeting of Sheriff Kelleher's small cadre of officers had come to a close. Armed with assignments for the day, they drained their coffee cups, buttoned up their jackets, and headed for the parking lot and their patrol cars. A raw wind greeted them as they left the building; spring had officially begun over a month earlier, but it was little in evidence on this late April day.

Deputy Sheriff Sam Bridges lingered after the others had gone.

"You didn't give us much about the lady in the ravine," he said to the sheriff. "I'm sure the guys are wondering what's up. Want to tell me what you're thinking?"

She had told them that their inquiries of regional authorities regarding missing women had turned up nothing and that the autopsy report was not yet in her hands, but she had not been drawn into speculation about the matter. Her own thoughts were too muddled, and she didn't want any of her officers to be in a position to pass along those muddled thoughts to what would surely be a curious public.

"Look, at this stage of the game it's all just guesswork. I'd rather not start guessing until we have a bit more information. Maybe the autopsy will tell us something, maybe it won't. But let's hope it does; then we take it from there."

"Do you think there's any chance her death wasn't an accident?"

"Guesswork, Sam, guesswork."

"What are the odds we'll learn anything important from the autopsy? Can't imagine it'll tell us who she is." Sam gathered up his things then paused at the door, where he posed another question. "Ever seen 'em do an autopsy?"

"No, and I don't plan to. If I'd known you were interested, I could have arranged for you to watch Doc Crawford do this one."

Deputy Sheriff Bridges was making it very clear that he had no interest whatsoever in observing an autopsy when the phone rang.

Ms. Maltbie was at her desk, but Carol beat her to the phone. She had half expected Crawford's report on the autopsy that morning, and her hunch proved correct.

There was a brief exchange, and then the sheriff cupped her hand over the phone and spoke to Sam.

"You'd better get moving. Doc says that this will take a bit — *complicated* is what he calls it. So why don't you get going on that stolen tractor case — I'll fill you in later on Crawford's report."

Sam's face reflected his disappointment, but he gave the sheriff a thumbs-up sign and disappeared out into the parking lot.

"Okay, Doc, what've we got?" Carol's tone of voice said that she feared that the answer would be "not much."

It took the better part of thirty-five minutes for the area's resident medical examiner to spell out for the sheriff what the autopsy told him and what it didn't tell him. And why.

The bottom line was indeed not much, or — depending on whether one was inclined to be a glass-half-full person — quite a bit. Sheriff Kelleher spent the better part of the next two hours mulling over the results of the autopsy and thinking about how she could — and should — act on them.

It was apparently not possible to determine with much precision just when the woman in the ravine had met her death. Doc Crawford was of the opinion that she had been in the ravine for some time, probably weeks. But the icy water would have slowed the process of decomposition, so he could not say with certainty whether the relatively good condition of the body meant that the death was fairly recent or that it was attributable to the fact that she had been immersed in cold water for a longer time.

Nor was the cause of death clear. Had the woman died as a result of trauma from the fall down the bank? Had she drowned in the pool at the bottom of the bank? Inconclusive, was Crawford's verdict. The lungs were water-logged, as was what he called the sphenoid sinus in the skull, but apparently that did not prove that she had drowned; she might have been killed by the fall, with the water seeping in during her lengthy immersion in the pool. There were broken ribs and a fractured arm, plus numerous bruises still visible on the body; while they had almost certainly been incurred in the fall, they did not prove that the fall had killed her.

"Tell you what I think," Crawford had said. "She could well have been unconscious when she landed in the water and then drowned without regaining consciousness. We'd have to know what happened that day to say for sure it was death by drowning, and it doesn't look like we'll know that unless you figure it out in your investigation. Or should I say until you figure it out?"

Sheriff Kelleher had sighed audibly. She hoped to discover what had happened up in that ravine on an unknown day in late winter or early spring; if she failed, it wouldn't matter much whether death was by drowning or trauma suffered in the fall.

It was after telling her what he couldn't tell her that Doc Crawford surprised her with two pieces of information he had deliberately saved for last. The old rascal, Carol thought.

The first might or might not help her investigation, but it just might open up new avenues of speculation. The woman was more than three months pregnant at the time of her death.

Of much greater interest was the fact that the woman had been wearing a t-shirt under her jacket and blouse that bore the name of a soccer camp.

SOUTHSIDE SOCCER CAMP
HOME OF THE DAN RYAN KICKERS

The officers who had removed the woman's body from its resting place in the ravine had not found a pocketbook or purse, and her jacket pockets had been empty. They had not poked around further in her clothing. Officer Barrett had thought it best to leave that task to the medical examiner, and Officer Grieves, a rookie, was only too glad to defer to his more experienced partner's judgment. But even if they had discovered the T-shirt, neither of the men would have had any idea where in these United States the soccer camp was located.

Nor did Sheriff Kelleher, but she realized that those nine words might well provide a clue to the identity of the woman. There would be hundreds of soccer camps across the country. There would be dozens of places called the Southside in cities large and small. But there wouldn't be nearly as many soccer teams bearing the name Dan Ryan. Who was he? The Kickers' coach? The founder of the camp, or the benefactor who anteed up money for uniforms and balls? A local boy who had made good in the world of professional soccer?

It would take time, maybe a lot of time, to pinpoint the location of this camp, but now they at least had something to go on. The sheriff was giving some thought to how they might proceed in their attempt to locate the soccer camp, and hence the area from which the woman had come, and then a scowl crossed her face. What if the t-shirt had nothing to do with the woman's place of residence? Weren't people always sporting t-shirts picked up in their travels? She remembered seeing her deputy sheriff on an off-duty day wearing a sweatshirt with Notre Dame emblazoned across the front. She knew that Bridges had never attended Notre Dame; she had been surprised, and then doubtful, that he had ever even visited its South Bend, Indiana campus.

No, they would pursue the location of the Southside Soccer Camp, but it might well turn out to be a dead end. It was while the sheriff was downgrading the possibility that the t-shirt would help them identify the woman in the ravine that she had another thought. Was it likely that this woman would be a soccer player? Carol had never played soccer or paid much attention to the Mia Hamm phenomenon and the late and lamented women's professional soccer league. But those women were surely younger than the woman whose identity she was seeking. Or were they? And just how old was the woman? She realized that she had failed to ask Crawford that question. She had been making the assumption that she was in her thirties, but was now aware that she had been doing what she had warned Bridges about, guessing. The fact that she had been pregnant wasn't much help; it only meant that she was somewhere between puberty and menopause.

The sheriff would call Doc Crawford back, but the momentary wave of excitement with which she had greeted news of the t-shirt had already begun to fade. Mystery woman, who are you? she asked herself.

CHAPTER 6

Kevin had left his apartment just ahead of nine o'clock in the morning, which meant that he was driving in the opposite direction of rush-hour traffic into the city. It also guaranteed that he would arrive in Southport in time to pick up some staples on his way to the cottage, and have an hour or two to put the place in shape for what he hoped would be a reunion of sorts with Carol Kelleher. Of course, she would have her own duties to contend with; he didn't expect her to take a vacation from Cumberland County law enforcement. But there would be the evenings, and maybe, if he handled things right, a night or two in the cottage.

As he drove the last few miles up Crooked Lake's West Lake Road, Kevin began to worry that it might have been better to call her and tell her he was coming. He had decided that she would respond better to surprise, but now that he was almost back at the cottage, he wasn't so sure that this had been a good plan. What if she were tied up with a problem that would keep her at the office or at the scene of some crime? Crimes were supposed to be rare in this bucolic upstate area, but they did occur, as he had discovered the previous summer. Or worse, what if she had plans for the evening with somebody else? Kevin had let himself assume that Carol led a private, monastic life, that there were no other men that interested her — or were interested in her. But why had he made that assumption? She was an attractive, intelligent woman. And if he were honest with himself, he would have to admit that he really didn't know her well enough to know whether there might be other men in her life. By the time Kevin pulled into the gravel parking apron behind his cottage, the excitement he had felt when he left the city had turned into a gnawing anxiety.

Whether that anxiety was warranted or not, Kevin knew within ten minutes that he would be seeing Carol that evening. Before unpacking the car, he had called her office, and miracle of miracles she was at her desk and — more importantly — amenable to dinner.

"I worried that you might be tied up," he had said, "but I guess this is my lucky day. Let's meet out at the Cedar Post — you know where it is, right?"

Of course the sheriff would know the Cedar Post, probably had eaten there dozens of times. They agreed on seven o'clock, and Kevin, now breathing more easily, went about the business of putting the cottage, closed since September, into shape.

———

"So what are you doing on Crooked Lake?" Carol asked. "I thought you said you would be doing the things you professors do for a few more weeks. You didn't get fired, did you?"

"No, I've got tenure." Kevin entered into the banter, pleased to sidestep more personal conversation. They had managed a table for two not far from the crowd at the bar, and had to raise their voices to be heard above the noise emanating from several guys who were trying to get the bartender's attention to set them up with another round.

"You don't look bad." Carol was taking stock of the man across the table, the man who had helped her solve the most important crime since she had become Cumberland County's sheriff, the man who had become her lover for one magical week the previous summer. "Pale. Yes, quite pale — city pale, much in need of some of our Crooked Lake sun."

"Are you kidding? There's no sun up here. What happened to spring? Almost the first of May, and it's cold — I mean really cold."

"Yeah, a real bummer. But you take what you get. Probably means we'll have a summer-long heat wave." The sheriff took a sip of her beer, fiddled with her fork, and studied Kevin. "I really am surprised to see you, you know. And I mean it, you don't look bad."

"Is that damning with faint praise?" Kevin asked, a smile on his face. "I was hoping maybe I looked good."

"Don't get too eager, mister." Carol found herself laughing out loud and a couple of the guys at the bar turned to see what was going on. What they saw were two people in the process of shedding weeks of worries about their personal relationship. Neither Kevin nor Carol was ready to talk about it, but it was obvious to both of them that the evening wasn't going to be as awkward as they had feared.

The Cedar Post was a simple, undistinguished place on a back road north of West Branch, but what it lacked in upscale amenities was compensated for by its invariably friendly, informal atmosphere. Moreover, on this night a robust log fire added to the welcome warmth of that atmosphere. It was still a good month before Memorial Day and the annual influx of summer residents on Crooked Lake, so the crowd consisted almost entirely of locals, most of whom were old friends or acquaintances.

The sheriff and the professor considered the steak sandwiches, but ultimately settled on Buffalo chicken wings. When had he last had that for dinner? Kevin wondered. Certainly not since last summer. It was only a few hours since he had arrived back at the lake, and already he found himself looking forward to the many little things that made summers at the cottage such a welcome respite from the academic wars and city life. Little things like Buffalo chicken wings. And one other thing, he thought, one very important thing — the woman sitting across the table from him. This year there was a whole summer ahead of them, not just one short week.

"You haven't told me yet how you happen to be here," Carol said. "I didn't expect to see you until sometime around Memorial Day. Let me guess. You've had a brainstorm about that woman we found in the ravine, and figured it'd be easier to talk about it over chicken wings than over the phone. Right?"

Kevin had already decided that he'd talk first about Carol's mystery woman, even if he had nothing to say that would help her bring that particular case to closure. Then he would find a way to segue into a discussion of the real reason he had made this impromptu trip to Crooked Lake.

"I don't know that I'd call it a brainstorm, but I haven't been able to get it off my mind. You have a way of doing that to me — you know, taking me away from things I ought to be doing and involving me in your job. I love teaching, but I think I'm beginning to like sleuthing almost as much."

"Can you really just walk away from your classes like that and come up here to play detective?"

"There are some things you don't know about the academic life, Carol. One of them is that professors are notoriously independent creatures. Another is that many of us have graduate assistants, bright young things who are supposed to cover our backs when we decide to do something like fly off to Prague to give a paper or drive up to Crooked Lake to help a beleaguered sheriff. I happen to have one of those assistants, and he is meeting my classes and proctoring my exams. So here I am, sharing your table, guilt free."

He hadn't planned to tell that one small lie. It just came out that way — *he* is my assistant, not she. Did he, at some unconscious level, not want Carol to know that back in the city there was a young woman named Jennifer Laseur who was taking his classes for the week and probably spreading the word that Professor Whitman just couldn't manage without her? No matter, Carol would never know Miss Laseur. Or care about her.

"Sounds like a nice life. All I have is one deputy sheriff and six overworked and underpaid officers, this in a county almost the size of Rhode Island. No trips to Prague for me."

"Well, we don't pay our assistants much either. They gripe about it all the time. Anyway, that's how it happens I'm here. I thought I might go wandering up that ravine, take a look around. You haven't got it cordoned off, have you?"

Carol was surprised at the question.

"No, my men gave the area a thorough going over the day after we found the body. Nothing. Not a thing that could tell us anything about her. What did you think you might find?"

"No idea." Which was true. Kevin had spent a good part of the drive to the lake thinking about the sheriff's mystery woman, but it had been a futile exercise. She would be someone he didn't know, someone he'd never seen, someone he'd never heard of. Better to find out what Carol had learned about her from the autopsy.

"Anyway, now that we're talking about the woman in the ravine, why don't you tell me what you know? I'm assuming you have the autopsy report, and I don't have to tell you I'm curious. She's not from around Blue Water Point, is she?"

"What makes you say that?" Carol asked.

"Just a hunch. Besides, you'd have told me right off the bat if you'd discovered that she's a neighbor of mine."

"The medical examiner's report was a real disappointment. I thought medical examiners were magicians, that they could tell you just about everything you wanted to know about your corpse de jour. Guess I've been watching too much of that forensics stuff on TV."

A harried waitress chose that moment to serve the chicken wings, squeezing between their table and the happy beer drinkers at the bar. One of guys had been eyeing her as she approached, and she almost lost her tray trying to fend off his unwelcome hand. Kevin turned away from this sorry little episode in the battle of the sexes, his thoughts on the sheriff of Cumberland County.

Why this feigned interest in an unknown woman who had foolishly gone climbing up a dangerous rock wall, when his real interest was in the woman sitting across the table from him in the Cedar Post?

"You know, Carol, this is crazy. Here we are talking about an accidental death as if it were the biggest news of the year. No, I'm not saying it isn't sad. These things always are. But your business is crimes and misdemeanors, and I'll bet you've had a few of those recently. And all of them more important to the state of law and order in Cumberland County than the woman in the ravine."

Carol shook her head.

"I thought you said you were curious. Don't you want to know what the autopsy tells us?"

Kevin admitted that he did, and after placing an order for two more beers, he sat back and listened as the sheriff filled him in on Crawford's report.

She doled out the information much as the medical examiner had, saving the t-shirt for last. Kevin had not found it particularly interesting and had listened in silence as Carol laid out the details, such as they were. The t-shirt elicited a different reaction.

"Well, there it is," he said. "Your woman was from Chicago."

"Chicago?"

"I'd bet you money on it. You said the shirt says 'Southside Soccer Camp' and refers to a team called 'Dan Ryan.' Put 'em together and you've got Chicago."

"Pardon me, smart guy, but why Chicago?" Carol's expression said that she wasn't ready to accept Kevin's conclusion so readily.

"Ever been to Chicago?" he asked, but didn't wait for her answer. "It's got a big area, well known, called the Southside. That's where the White Sox play baseball. But the clincher is Dan Ryan. The expressway coming into Chicago from the south is called the Dan Ryan. Now how many Dan Ryans do you think there are, Dan Ryans in the Southside?"

"How would you know about an expressway in Chicago?" She still sounded skeptical.

"Professional meetings. Academics are always going to professional meetings. My association had its last one in Chicago, and like a damn fool, I drove."

"But this doesn't prove that the woman is — was — from Chicago. People pick up t-shirts from all over when they travel. You probably have, too."

"Sure, from places like Paris or Yellowstone. Or they wear shirts promoting their favorite team. I see 'em up here a lot in the summer. Buffalo Bills. New York Yankees. One of the guys over on my point has a Pittsburgh Steelers shirt, wears it all the time. But who runs around in a Dan Ryan Kickers t-shirt? I mean, who ever heard of the Dan Ryan Kickers — except maybe someone from the Chicago Southside? It's got to be something that belongs to people who play in that league, go to that camp. Which means whoever's wearing it comes from Chicago."

Carol was obviously considering Kevin's logic.

"Maybe. But this woman doesn't look like someone who'd be attending a soccer camp. We don't know her age for sure, but I'm sure she's past the soccer camp years."

"Okay, you don't know for sure. But I'd start concentrating on Chicago. I'll bet she's from there. She could have picked up the shirt even if she didn't play for the Kickers — or go to that soccer camp. At least it gives you some place to start. Better than the whole US of A, or even upstate New York."

The conversation drifted off in other directions. It was 9:20 when Carol announced that she had to be going.

"There's a problem I've got to get busy on early tomorrow. Even more urgent than the mystery woman, if not as interesting. Have to be up by six at the latest, maybe 5:30. So I'm afraid I'd better shove off. Sorry to cut the evening short, but you know how it is."

Kevin wasn't particularly interested in knowing how it is. He would have been willing to sit and talk until the Cedar Post closed, or better yet continue their conversation back at the cottage. But whether Carol did indeed have business to see to early in the morning or only wanted an excuse to postpone the inevitable discussion of their personal relationship, he knew he would have to be understanding.

The bill settled, they were getting into their coats when one of the men at the bar intercepted them.

"You're the sheriff, aren't you?" His voice was slightly slurred, not surprising in view of the fact he and his buddies had been downing beers since Kevin and Carol had arrived and probably for some time before that.

The sheriff looked at the man. She had been vaguely aware of him all through dinner, but had no idea who he was.

"Yes, I'm afraid I am." She favored him with a brief smile and turned to leave.

"I think I know something about that woman they found on Blue Water Point," he said. "You know, the body in that ravine."

CHAPTER 7

The sheriff's first reaction had been to pursue the matter then and there at the Cedar Post. If this stranger knew something about her mystery woman, she had wanted to find out what it was and to do it now, no matter how late the hour. But it didn't happen that way. He claimed he had to get back to his home right away, and would prefer to come by her office in Cumberland the next day. It wasn't clear why going home was suddenly such an urgent priority, especially after killing several hours at a local bar, but Carol reluctantly agreed to a meeting at 10:30 the following morning.

It was at 10:47 that the man from the bar, now identified as Carl Thompson, walked into the sheriff's office, apologizing profusely for his tardiness. Carol had had a few moments of anxiety, fearing that she might have let a potentially important source of information get away. Perhaps he had approached her the previous evening while high from the consumption of too many beers, only to have second thoughts when sober. But her worries were now moot; Carl Thompson, still breathing hard from what had apparently been a strenuous effort to make his appointment on time, was standing across the desk from her.

"Ah, Mr. Thompson," she said as she got up to shake his hand and offer him a seat. "Can I get you some coffee?"

"Sure, that would be great. Nothing in it, thank you — just black."

Carol relayed the coffee order to Ms. Maltbie, then settled into her chair for what she hoped would be an informative chat with this man who seemed to know something about the woman they had found in a ravine on the west shore of Crooked Lake.

"So tell me, how do you happen to know about this woman? I mean how did you know we'd found her body?"

"It's been on the local radio station. You don't get much news — mostly music, you know, that golden oldies stuff. But I guess it's a big enough story that they keep mentioning it every time there's a news spot."

And that's the way it would have been, Carol thought. The weekly *Cumberland Gazette* hadn't been published since the discovery of the body, and her office hadn't yet put out a call to the public for help in identifying the body. But the fact that a dead woman had been found in a ravine north of Blue Water Point was no secret. Carol had been in touch with area authorities, and by now those first contacts would have generated many conversations and much speculation across the entire upstate area. Perhaps Carl Thompson would be only the first of many to come forward with information about the woman in the ravine. She hoped so.

"You said last night that you know something about this woman whose body we found recently. We'd love to hear it. Do you know who she is, or should I say who she was?"

"Not really. Not if you mean do I know her name or anything like that."

"Well, why don't you then just tell us what you do know."

Thompson looked thoughtful as he reached for the coffee cup he had set down on the edge of the sheriff's desk. Carol had the distinct impression that he was trying to decide how to say what he had come to say.

"I saw her back in — oh, let's say early March. Not exactly sure of the date, but it was the better part of two months ago. Saw her at the Cedar Post, same place I ran into you last night."

"Let's back up a bit, Mr. Thompson. How do you know that a woman you saw in the winter is the same woman we just found up a Crooked Lake ravine?"

"I suppose I can't be a hundred percent sure, but it figures, doesn't it?"

No, Carol thought, it doesn't figure. No pictures of the woman had been released yet, and the word circulating was that she was probably in her thirties, had dark hair, and was of average height and build. It was a description that could have fit lots of women. The sheriff said as much to Thompson.

"Yeah, but here's a woman who's not from around here, she comes into the Post, she looks like the dead woman — well, pretty much like her. Don't you have a photo? I'll be I could tell you for sure if I saw her picture."

The sheriff didn't want to discuss with Thompson the problems involved in creating a presentable photograph of the dead woman, and she didn't have a good sketch artist on her staff. She chose to focus on the woman he had seen at the Cedar Post back in the winter.

"We don't know that the woman's not from this area. But I'm interested in the woman you met at the Cedar Post. Tell me about her."

Carol had decided that Thompson would be one of those men who regularly make a mental inventory of the attractive women in any room where they happen to be. There must have been something about the one he had seen at the Cedar Post that had made a lasting impression. Or at least an impression that was still fresh after a couple of months.

"There are two things," he began. "She was asking someone if he knew of a guy — someone she was trying to find, didn't know where he lived."

"Do you remember the name of the person she was asking about?"

"Becker or Beckman, something like that. It was kind of noisy, and I didn't hear her real good."

Too bad, Carol thought, imagining Thompson straining to overhear what was said, probably trying to find a way to engage the woman in conversation himself.

"And the other thing?"

"Now that was more than a little interesting. This guy comes up, offers her a drink — he was really hitting on her. She wasn't biting, but he wouldn't let it go. Kept pushing, you know, one of those guys that can't imagine a babe who's not impressed with his line. She tried to get up from her stool and he took hold of her arm, still thinking, I suppose, that he could talk her into whatever he had in mind. That's when it happened. She threw her drink in his face. Now that was something to see, his face and jacket all covered with beer. Looked just like he was foaming at the mouth."

Thompson was obviously having a good time remembering the episode at the bar.

"What happened after that?"

"Nothing. Well, nothing that I know of. Everybody was sort of surprised. She just grabbed her coat and walked out the door. The poor guy went to the men's room — never did see him come back to the bar."

"Know who the guy is? You know, maybe a regular at the Cedar Post, somebody you've seen around?"

"I might have seen him, but I'm not sure. He's nobody I know," Thompson said. "I'll bet the bartender over there would be able to give you a name."

"Do you remember who was tending bar that day?" Carol doubted that he would.

"Sure. It was Ginny Smith."

Of course, she thought. Ginny Smith, the pretty, pleasant, and buxom woman the Cedar Post had probably hired precisely because she was likely to generate more business, especially from the male population in the vicinity of Crooked Lake. Carol would have a talk with Smith at her early convenience.

"So this woman you saw at the Cedar Post was a stranger, looked like our description of the dead woman in the ravine, was asking about someone whose name you can't remember, and threw a drink at a guy who was making a nuisance of himself. All very interesting — provided that she and the dead woman are one and the same. Otherwise, it just adds up to another fun night at the bar."

Thompson started to protest, but the sheriff cut him off.

"Look, I'm not saying your information isn't important. We don't know much of anything about the woman, so what you've told us may give us something to go on. I'm just sorry you can't be certain that your woman in the bar is our woman in the ravine — but then, how could you be?"

As Thompson got ready to leave, Carol asked one final question.

"I don't suppose you ever saw the woman again, did you?"

"No," he answered, sounding regretful that he couldn't say he had. "From what I hear, she was dead not long after that night, so I guess I couldn't have seen her again."

Left to ponder the significance, if any, of what she had learned, Carol almost immediately found herself wishing she might discuss it with Kevin Whitman. Which reminded her of the way she had come to feel the previous summer, and of the way in which Kevin had gradually become her partner in the investigation of John Britingham's murder.

The previous night, after dinner at the Cedar Post, she had decided against going back to the cottage with him. Much as she had wanted to continue the discussion of her mystery woman, she did not feel ready for the inevitable conversation about their personal relationship. She was not sure which of these conflicting feelings would win out tonight. Or which she wanted to win out.

———

Kevin had called her at the office shortly before noon. The time had come, he had decided, to be more direct. He did not know that Carl Thompson had left only a few minutes earlier, and that his call came at a most propitious time. When he broached the subject of dinner at the cottage, Carol surprised him by readily agreeing to the idea. He had expected resistance, and had prepared what he hoped would be a persuasive argument.

"Wonderful," he said, and meant it. Kevin suddenly felt better than he had for many weeks, maybe months. "I was afraid you'd have some reason for saying you couldn't do it."

"I could possibly think of one or two, but the truth is I want to talk about my mystery woman and don't think I'm in the mood for another meal at the Post. You have anything in your fridge?"

"Don't expect a gourmet dinner, but yes, I ran into Yates Center this morning and picked up a couple of T-bones and things. You'll even have a choice between beer and a pretty decent red wine."

"Sounds good. Is six okay?"

"Of course. Come on down sooner if you can get away."

And so it was that Carol and Kevin sat down together at the Blue Water Point cottage for the first time since the previous summer. They ate Kevin's steaks, drank his wine, and talked on into the evening about what they knew and didn't know about a woman whose body had been discovered less than a mile from Kevin's cottage by two young boys just four days earlier. And how they might best go about tracking down her identity and explaining how she came to be lying in a pool of icy water in a ravine close to 700 miles from the Dan Ryan Expressway. The year before, it had only been with some reluctance that Carol had acknowledged Kevin's role as her partner in the investigation of a murder on Crooked Lake. He now was once again assuming the role of her partner, this time without any objection from the sheriff of Cumberland County.

They both finessed the larger issue of where their personal relationship was going by not talking about it, but at sometime around eleven o'clock, Carol did accept the pair of pajamas that Kevin offered her, only to leave them lying on the floor at the foot of the bed when the bedside light was turned off.

CHAPTER 8

Kevin had neglected to close the curtains tightly the night before, and it was the light that streamed through the gap that finally awakened him from a sound sleep. After a fleeting moment of temporary confusion, he knew where he was and who was in the bed beside him. Except that when he turned over, the bed was empty.

No alarm had been set, but Carol had obviously been awakened by an inner clock that told her it was time to get up and head back to the county seat and her duties as sheriff of Cumberland County. Had she kissed him goodbye before leaving? He smiled at the thought as he stepped into his slippers, picked up his robe, and headed for the kitchen. She had not made herself breakfast, but she had left a note on the kitchen table.

"Thanks for dinner. I liked dessert best."

Kevin frowned. There had been no dessert. But the frown quickly vanished, along with his literal reading of Carol's note. He knew he had made the right decision in coming back to Crooked Lake.

They had talked the previous evening about the many things that needed to be done if they were to identify the woman in the ravine. And they had arrived at a rough division of labor. It was, of course, the sheriff's job, and she had colleagues who could be assigned the tasks of talking with the bartender and seeking information from Chicago police regarding a missing woman who seemed to have something to do with a local soccer club. Carol might even do these things herself. But she had been only too happy to enlist Kevin's help, and he was more than ready to be her partner in another investigation. He realized that it had been her growing confidence in his ideas and his judgment that had led to their warm personal relationship, not the other way around.

Today he would do two things. He would make the trip up the ravine to see for himself where the woman had fallen, and while there he would poke around — in search of what, he wasn't quite sure, but there just might be something that had escaped the attention of the sheriff's men. And then he would tackle the task of determining whether there were any residents of the area whose name was Becker — or Beckman, or something like that.

———

It was another cold, blustery day, and Kevin had to scrounge around in a couple of closets before he found outdoor gear appropriate for this nasty spring weather. He did not remember owning the jacket he was putting on, and he doubted that the boots had been worn in several years. He hoped that when he returned to the lake after college commencement later in May, spring would finally have arrived. At least today the ravine would look much like it had when Carol's mystery woman met her death, or so he imagined.

The hike up the ravine was uneventful, and in something like twenty minutes, he arrived at the foot of the bank the sheriff had described. It had been a few years since he had been there, but it looked familiar. The pool of water in which the woman's body had been found was now empty except for a boulder or two and a broken branch from a hemlock tree.

Kevin surveyed the tall bank ahead of him. He didn't think that he was up to trying a direct ascent. Too steep and almost surely too slippery. That would have been a problem for the woman, too, which meant that she had probably left the ravine bottom some distance back and worked her way along the earthen wall, using low-hanging tree branches to pull herself, yard by yard, to the top of the bank. It would have been rough going, but not nearly so dangerous. He would now do what he imagined she had done.

It didn't take him long to become aware of how out of shape he was. His boots were soon covered with mud, and his face bore the marks where tree limbs kept slapping his face. When he reached the top of the bank, he used a small but sturdy tree to brace himself, then looked down to where he could see the pool of water. No question about it, the fall could have been fatal. If the woman had survived it, she would have been badly hurt. What on earth had she been doing up here? he wondered.

Above him, the ravine continued its course up the hill. Had the woman gone further up the streambed before returning to the bank from which she had fallen? He had no way of knowing. If he was to search for evidence of her presence in the ravine, it made more sense to concentrate on the rim of the bank and on the path she had presumably taken to reach it. Kevin had no idea of what if anything he might find, but he pictured himself as a tracker, even if he knew perfectly well that he had no special skills in that field. And although he didn't know the sheriff's people, he suspected that their skills were not likely to be better than his. So for another half an hour, Kevin poked around carefully in the brush and in the moss and the mud, first at the top of the bank and then along the path he had used in his climb.

By the time he reached the bottom, he had discovered four things which were not a part of the natural order of things, and hence might — just might — be of importance to the sheriff's investigation. The first was an old, empty, and much battered beer can, trapped in a tangle of tree roots. It was in plain sight, which led him to believe that the officers who had searched the area had not taken his route to the top, but had instead climbed up the steep side of the bank. If so, he was impressed with their climbing skills, but not with the thoroughness of their search of the ravine.

It was the other three things that gave him the feeling that his morning had been well spent. One was an unusual, odd-shaped button, attached to a short length of thread, in a dense thicket of unfamiliar bushes some thirty feet down the path from the rim of the bank. Another, Kevin's discovery of which was wholly serendipitous, was an artificial fingernail of the kind worn by some women. It had been almost completely buried in the mud. Moreover, it had obviously been pressed into the mud by someone's boot. Kevin had noticed boot marks with a waffle shaped sole pattern at several places along the side of the ravine. None of them were sharp or complete, and to his untrained eye the marks looked old. But it was when he bent down to examine one of the better boot prints that he spotted the fingernail. Initially it had looked like nothing more than a tiny piece of wood, but lying in his palm with the mud scraped off, it was obviously a fingernail.

As Kevin headed back to the cottage, he was feeling very pleased with himself. In his jacket pocket were a button and a fingernail, and in his mind was a picture of the imprints somebody's boots had left along the south side of the ravine at the north end of Blue Water Point. It was possible that none of this had anything to do with the woman whose identity they were seeking, but it should be an easy matter to determine whether her jacket was missing a button and whether the one he had found was a match for others on that jacket. Moreover, if she had been wearing artificial fingernails, it was unlikely that she would have lost them all in her hike up the ravine, which meant that it should be easy to determine whether the one in his pocket had belonged to her. The boots should be no problem either. There weren't many prints, but the ground had been sufficiently protected from rain runoff in enough places that those prints could be matched with the woman's boots.

Kevin's feeling of satisfaction with his morning's adventure slowly ebbed away as he ran these thoughts through his mind on his way back down the ravine. What if, as he had assumed, the button, the fingernail, and the boots all turned out to belong to the mystery woman? So what? They already knew she had been in the ravine. They might now know that she had reached the top of the bank by a somewhat circuitous route, but what did that tell them? It would not bring them any closer to finding out who she was.

By the time he reached his cottage, Kevin found himself considering a different explanation for the button and the boot prints. Suppose they belonged to someone other than the woman. What if she had not been alone on her trip up the ravine? But he did not like where that line of reasoning took him, for it meant that in all probability there was someone somewhere who knew what had happened to her. Or perhaps had been responsible for her death.

No sooner had this scenario crossed his mind than Kevin dismissed it — or tried to. The color of the button was very much like that of the branches and dead leaves around it; it could have been there for a year or more, unnoticed by hikers in the ravine. He had been lucky to spot it. As for the boot prints, they could have been left at almost any time while the ground was damp. He realized he was jumping to conclusions, on the basis of what — a fertile imagination? An unconscious desire to turn a tragic accident into another murder mystery?

He'd show Carol the button and the fingernail, and he'd tell her about the boot prints, but he would be careful not to make any claims for the significance of any of those things. Chances were that she would send one or more of her officers back into the ravine for another look. Maybe they'd take molds of the boot prints. Did they have the means to do that up here in the rural hinterland of upstate New York? He didn't know, and for the moment didn't care. It was the sheriff's problem. His job was to put facts on the table, not to deconstruct them. Not yet.

————

The second task that Kevin had set for himself had to do with the man the mystery woman had been looking for, the man whose name Carl Thompson had heard mentioned weeks ago in the Cedar Post. Of course, the woman Thompson had overheard might not be the mystery woman, and he hadn't been sure of the man's name. It had been something like Becker, a relatively short name that suggested German roots.

This search, unlike the one that had occupied his morning, would be sedentary. He would sit down with the phonebook — a small volume that covered all of the villages in the area of Crooked Lake as well as the cottages around the lake. It would be a tedious chore, and there might well be other more efficient ways to find whether there were people with a name like Becker living in the area. But Kevin was not in the mood to make a circuit of local town and village offices to peruse their records, so after a simple lunch, he settled into his favorite chair and started through the phone book.

It was a boring task, as he had known it would be, but by the time he finished he had discovered that there were quite a few people living in the area — or at least quite a few people who had phones — with names similar to the one Thompson had overheard. There were four Beckers, two Beckleys, one Beckham, a Boecklin, a Buckner, and seven Barkers. There were even more Deckers and Bakers, plus a few other names that just might have been spoken at the Cedar Post that night, although they struck him as marginal candidates. Kevin prepared a list, complete with addresses and phone numbers, and found himself hoping that the sheriff might turn up somebody who had been at the Cedar Post that night, somebody who remembered more precisely the name of the man the woman had been looking for. Otherwise, it was going to take quite a long time to contact and speak with all of the people on his list.

In any event, he would not be the one to have to track down Becker or whatever his name was. For one thing, he would be going back to the city in a couple of days. For another, he was sure that Carol would want any questioning of all these men to be done by one of her officers. Why, after all, would a summer resident on Crooked Lake be asking questions of any of them regarding an unknown woman who had mentioned a name that might or might not be theirs? No, this would be a task for the sheriff's department.

CHAPTER 9

Sam Bridges, the Deputy Sheriff of Cumberland County, pulled out a stool at one end of the bar in the Cedar Post. It was not quite five o'clock, and the place had not yet begun to fill up with the usual end-of-the-working-day crowd. Sam watched the woman behind the bar as she went about the business of cutting the fruit that would join the olives in mixed drinks for the few customers who preferred them to beer or wine. She was an attractive woman who appeared to be in her thirties; she was wearing a low-cut blouse and sporting a creative tattoo just above her cleavage. He was a faithful husband, but he found it hard to keep his eyes off the bartender, as did many of the regulars at the Cedar Post. Ginny Smith, for that was her name, was well aware of her status as a featured attraction at the Post, but she never let the attention go to her head.

"Hi, Sam," she greeted him cheerfully in a husky voice that seemed to add to her allure. "Isn't it a bit early for you law enforcement types to be hitting the pubs?"

"Never too early if it means I get a chance to talk with you," he replied, enjoying the good natured repartee. He had come to the Cedar Post on this day and at this hour because Sheriff Kelleher had asked him to. They had finally had a discussion of what she had learned about the woman whose body they had found in the ravine. It wasn't much, but it did include the fact that someone who might have been that woman had had an unpleasant altercation with an overly aggressive man at the Post a couple of months earlier. The sheriff wanted to learn more about that episode, and the person most likely to know more about it was Ginny Smith. She had called the Post to find out when Ginny would next be on duty, passed the information on to Sam, and told him to pursue the matter with the buxom bartender. She knew that Sam would be pleased with the assignment, and so he was.

"What're you having?" the bartender asked, knowing full well that Sam always ordered his favorite draft beer.

"The usual. Today I get to drink on duty. How about that?"

"The sheriff know about this?" she inquired.

"Oh, yes." Sam maneuvered his stool closer to the bar. "Truth is, I'm here because I need to ask you a question or two."

Smith looked surprised, then nodded her head, pointing down the bar to where another customer was waiting for service.

Having set the other man up with what he had ordered, she returned to Sam's end of the bar, his beer in hand, and gave him one of her patented smiles.

"So what it is that you want to talk to me about?" She hoped that it would not be personal; she liked Sam, and didn't want him to spoil a good relationship by asking her — or telling her — something he might later regret.

"I'd like you to think back — oh, maybe two months ago, give or take a week — and see if you remember a night in here when there was a bit of a rumpus. There was a woman here at the bar and some guy was coming on to her. Word has it that she got pissed with him and tossed her drink in his face. Does that ring a bell?"

The bartender hadn't known what to expect, but the question made it clear that Sam was wearing his lawman's hat.

"Look, this isn't a fancy place, and our customers aren't always on their best behavior. You know that. We've had to ask a few to leave, not often, but every once in awhile. Do I remember problem nights? Sure. And I think I remember the one you're talking about."

She went down the bar to pull a couple of drafts for newcomers, thinking as she did so about a night in early March. Trouble, on those rare occasions when it occurred, was usually between two men. In this case, it had been between a man and a woman. A woman she had never seen in the Cedar Post before.

"I doubt that I could give you an exact date," she said as she resumed the conversation with Bridges. "But it was the night we had that late snowfall, the wet one that knocked down wires along the lake. You could look it up, but I think it was around the first or second of March, not much later."

"Sounds about right," Sam said. "So what happened?"

"I'm not really sure. It was busy, and I wasn't paying much attention. But voices were raised, and then all of a sudden the noise stopped — like something happened that shut 'em up. I didn't see it, but this guy at the bar said 'Did you see that? She threw her drink at him,' or something like that. I could see that one of the guys had water or beer or whatever running down his face and chest. And then he bolted for the restroom. It all calmed down pretty fast — we didn't have to do anything. The place was sort of different after that — volume less than usual, if you know what I mean."

"What about the woman?"

"There was a woman in the middle of this group of men, including the one who'd been spritzed. She must have been the one who threw the drink. Everyone stepped back, maybe afraid they'd get it, too. Anyway, she snatched up her coat and hightailed it out of here. Never saw her again."

"Had you noticed her before? Know who she is?"

Sam hadn't learned anything yet that the sheriff hadn't learned from the Thompson man. He hoped Ginny Smith could put a name to the woman in the bar, or at least give him a better description than Thompson's. But it wasn't to be.

"Sorry, Sam. Sure, I was aware of her — this isn't that big a place. But it was crowded, and she never asked me for a drink. One of the men must have gotten it for her. From back here she looked, you know, just ordinary. No, I don't quite mean that."

It was obvious that the Cedar Post bartender didn't want him to think that she was measuring the other woman against her own physical appearance.

"She was average height, maybe five-five or -six. Dark hair, pretty face, probably in her thirties. When I got a good look at her, she was putting on her jacket, and it was one of those bulky things. Couldn't really tell about her weight, but she looked liked she had a good figure. Wish I could be more specific."

So they were right back where they were after the sheriff's conversation with Thompson. Still the mystery woman.

"So you didn't talk with her?"

"No, I'm afraid not."

"She's supposed to have been overheard asking someone if they knew of a guy around here named Becker, or something like Becker. You didn't hear that?"

"Yeah, I think I did. Like I said, I was too busy to follow all of the conversations around the bar, but I remember a name like that being tossed around. And I don't think it was Becker. How about Beckham?"

"Beckham?"

"Yes, like that British soccer star, the one who's married to Posh Spice."

Posh Spice? Did people really have names like that? But if Smith was sure of the name, it could simplify their search for the man the mystery woman was seeking.

"You sure the name was Beckham? Not Becker?"

"No, but I'm pretty certain. I follow the sports news, you know. My son plays soccer in that league they have around here for high school kids, and Beckham's a big name in soccer. So when I overheard the name, it just clicked."

Sam had not known that Ginny Smith had a son, much less a teenage son. For no reason he could have explained, he found that news depressing. But he now did have at least one bit of potentially useful information for the sheriff. No name for the woman, not a very specific profile of her appearance, but a name for the man for whom she had been looking.

He pulled out his wallet and asked for the bill.

"Would you like to talk with the man your woman threw her drink at?" she asked as she returned his change.

The deputy sheriff almost choked as he drained his beer glass. Why had he not asked her about the man who had caused the trouble at the Cedar Post those many weeks ago? It was such an obviously relevant line of questioning, and it had never occurred to him. Thank God the bartender had saved him from a dressing down by Sheriff Kelleher.

"I was going to ask you if you knew him," Sam said, but he doubted that she believed him.

"I thought you would," she said, as a smile spread across her face. "Anyway, he's someone who's in here a fair amount, and I'm not surprised that your woman found his attentions irritating. When you talk with him, I wish you wouldn't say I said anything critical about him, but his name is Phil Chambers. He's from somewhere around West Branch. He's about your size, curly brown hair, looks like he's trying to grow a mustache. I think he works at one of the marinas, but I'm not sure. You'll find him, that is, if you need to ask him any questions."

Sam thanked her for the information, trying not to look overly grateful.

"By the way, if he drops in anytime soon, would you like me to tell him you're looking for him?" she asked.

"Please don't do that." Sam didn't want to compound his failure to ask about the man called Chambers by having him alerted to the sheriff's department's interest in him before Sam or one of his fellow officers came knocking on his door.

CHAPTER 10

It was nearing 9:30 on yet another chilly spring evening, and the sheriff and the professor were enjoying a cup of after-supper coffee in his cottage on Blue Water Point. The conversation had covered many things, but not the problem of what to do about their relationship. It was as if both of them had decided to pretend that there was no problem and to simply enjoy each other's company, at least for the present and hopefully for the summer ahead. It was so much easier to talk about the identity of the mystery woman than it was to talk about the fact that their very different careers and responsibilities made a long-term relationship difficult. Or impossible. It was their third evening together since Kevin had returned to the lake, and the second at his cottage. This time Carol had brought a small overnight bag, complete with nightie and toothbrush. Kevin had suggested that she call the cottage her home away from home; it was as close as they were to come to a discussion of living together.

"How much longer do you think you can finesse those papers that are waiting for you?" Carol asked. "I'll wager that there aren't any elves down there, secretly grading them for you."

"Oh, maybe two more days," he said, knowing that there was no way he could — or should — ask Jennifer Laseur to grade the papers for him. "That should give us time to discover the identity of the woman in the ravine and wrap up your case."

Of course neither of them thought it likely that they would solve in two more days the case that had been Kevin's excuse to come back to Crooked Lake before the end of his semester at the college. But they were having fun sharing the results of their days' endeavors and discussing next steps. It seemed like old times, although a few weeks the previous August hardly qualified as old times.

After listening to Kevin's account of his adventure in the ravine that morning, Carol suggested that he might benefit from more regular exercise — preferably not in the ravine. She took custody of the button and the fingernail, said she would try to determine whether either one belonged to the mystery woman, and promised to send one of her men back to the scene of the accident to look at the boot marks. In the meantime, there didn't seem to be much point in speculating further. They moved on to other things.

The sheriff had spent a good part of the day trying to link the dead woman in the Cumberland morgue to a missing woman in Chicago. It had been a frustrating experience. It took some time to get through to the office in that city that handled missing persons reports. After listening to a recording of a surprisingly long menu of options, she finally got to speak to a real person. And that person had explained, as if to a novice where such matters are concerned, that almost all missing persons are young people, usually adolescents and mostly girls who had run away from home. Carol found the tale of missing teenagers sad and depressing, but she was looking for an older woman, probably in her thirties, and said so to the man in Chicago. After a considerable period of time during which he left her on hold, the man came up with some figures as to the number of open missing person reports, together with statistical support for his claim that most such cases involved young girls. There had been a few cases involving older women, but they were typically much older, and in most instances were presumed to be victims of Alzheimer's who had simply wandered off somewhere.

There were only two cases which sounded remotely promising, and Carol had made notes of the relevant details. One of the two she was inclined to dismiss out of hand because it was nearly a year old. The other case had been reported only a week earlier. The sister of a missing woman had filed the report and had apparently had some misgivings about doing so. She wasn't sure the woman had really gone missing; it was just that she had been out of touch for much longer than usual and hadn't left any kind of a message. But the woman's sister had left a photograph with the authorities, a picture which she admitted was rather dated. According to the man on the phone, the picture was not much help — the woman was seated, so it was hard to tell about her height, and she was wearing one of those tent-like beach robes which made it impossible to hazard a guess as to her weight. Moreover, she had blond hair.

"Looks like a dead end," Carol said. "Of course, our woman may not be from Chicago at all. That soccer t-shirt could well be a red herring, something she picked up somewhere else."

"Possibly, but I'm not ready to write off a Chicago connection. Maybe no missing person report was filed on her.

Suppose she lived alone, didn't have many friends, had a habit of traveling — you know, one of those persons who pretty much stays out of sight, does her own thing without telling people what she's up to. There must be lots of those."

"That could be. But let's assume you're right about her being from Chicago. I'd still like to see that photo of the woman on the beach, decide for myself if she looks at all like our mystery woman. The blond hair doesn't mean much. Lots of women dye their hair from time to time. Anyway, it's all we've got right now, so I asked them to put the picture through — it's probably on my computer by now."

Carol looked pensive.

"I want to talk with this sister, the one who filed the report. I'll call her, but what I'd really like to do is go out there, meet her, get into the missing woman's home if I can. Problem is, we're short staffed and there's a lot on my plate beside the woman in the ravine. I'm not even sure our budget could cover a two or three day trip to Chicago."

"So how about letting me go to Chicago? Off budget. I've got a friend on the Northwestern faculty. It'd give me a chance to see him as well as the sister of a missing lady."

"I can't believe I'm hearing this," Carol said. "You're going to play Sherlock Holmes while your students wonder where their teacher has gone? I love your interest in Cumberland County law enforcement, but aren't those ungraded term papers your first priority?"

Kevin knew she was right, but he was once again feeling the excitement he had experienced the previous summer as he became caught up in the sheriff's investigation of the Britingham murder.

"I'll work it out. You don't have to worry that I'll let the kids down. Maybe I can put in an all-nighter, just like most of them do — you know, grade papers until dawn if I have to."

"I thought you once told me that student papers too often read like they've been written in the middle of the night on a caffeine high. And now you're going to do the same thing? Okay, how you handle your end-of-term problems is your concern. But maybe nobody needs to go to Chicago, at least not yet."

Carol was having second thoughts about her next step, and they concerned the man named Beckham. If indeed his name was Beckham.

"It occurs to me that we may be able to learn more about our woman from that guy she was looking for out at the Cedar Post," Carol said. "Bridges says his name is Beckham."

"Assuming that the woman who was looking for him was our woman," he interrupted. "We still don't know that. She may no more be the lady in the ravine than the missing woman in Chicago is."

"I know. But what if this Beckham does know something about her? It's an easier lead to follow than traipsing off to Chicago. So don't make a plane reservation until I talk to him. I'll do it tomorrow."

In spite of his doubts, Kevin knew that she was right to pursue the Beckham lead first. Beckham. One of the names he had dredged out of the local phone book. One of more than thirty. What a waste of time.

"You say that your deputy knows it's a Beckham we're looking for. How does he know that? I ruin my eyesight working my way through the telephone directory, picking out every name from Becker to Decker, and now you tell me it's somebody named Beckham we're looking for."

"Sorry about that," Carol said, not sounding terribly sorry. "Frankly, I didn't have a lot of confidence in the memory of the bartender at the Cedar Post. Or even that she would have heard the name, what with all the noise and her being busy. Anyway, we don't know for sure that the man's name is Beckham. The bartender might have heard it wrong. Bridges says she's into soccer and knows a lot about a soccer star named Beckham, so maybe she unconsciously turned Becker or something else into Beckham."

"Now there's a coincidence for you," Kevin said. "Or is it? Your mystery woman turns up dead in a t-shirt advertising a soccer camp, and several weeks before that she is heard asking if anyone knows the whereabouts of a guy who has the same name as an internationally known soccer player. Maybe your woman was a soccer groupie."

"Yeah, and maybe this local Beckham is a cousin of the famous one. I think it's getting late and we're letting our imaginations run wild. Too much coffee."

Yes, Kevin thought, it is getting late. The log he had put into the fireplace had burned down to a flameless orange glow, and he realized that it was about time to put the puzzle of the woman in the ravine on hold. Whether he went to Chicago or not, there would only be one or two more nights with Carol before he returned to the city and the pile of term papers in his office.

"Let's have a nightcap," he said, and headed for the liquor cupboard in the kitchen. The sheriff kicked off her shoes and tucked her feet under her in the nest of pillows on the couch. A contented smile lit up her face. She'd think about her mystery woman tomorrow.

CHAPTER 11

It was taking the sheriff longer than she had anticipated to locate 2100 Turkey Hill Road. She had traversed the full length of the road from the village of Yates Center to the county line without spotting it. It was now late in the day, and it was probable that she had simply missed some side road in the gathering gloom. Carol turned around and headed back in the direction from which she had come, driving more slowly this time as she looked for post office boxes or other signposts along the way. The road was paved in places and then abruptly shifted to gravel. She wondered at the explanation for this patchwork road surface, and caught up in that thought, she almost missed the discolored mailbox that announced the entrance to the driveway leading to the house at 2100.

The house was a trailer, and it was set well back from the road; like the mailbox, it was dingy and much in need of a coat of fresh paint. The pickup truck at the side of the trailer was much brighter. Either it had just recently been purchased, or its owner had lavished more attention on it than he had on his trailer.

Carol had not informed Dennis Beckham that she was coming to see him, and she was relieved to find him at home. Bridges had offered to talk to Beckham, but Carol wanted to conduct this interview herself. She had worried that the trip might turn out to be a wild goose chase, but the presence of the pickup truck and the light coming through the trailer's windows made it likely that the man her mystery woman had been seeking was inside. Unless, of course, it was the man's wife. The sheriff hoped that would not be the case, but thought she could handle it if need be. Or hoped she could. We'll soon find out, she thought.

The man who came to the door was tall and dark haired and had a bad scar on his right cheek that was hard to ignore. He also looked surprised to see her.

"Hello, Mr. Beckham — you are Mr. Beckham, aren't you?"

"Yes, Dennis Beckham. And you, the uniform — you the police? What's the matter?" He sounded anxious.

"Nothing that I know of," the sheriff said. "I'm looking for information, trying to find someone. I've been asking around, and now here I am at your place. Mind if I come in?"

The man named Beckham stepped aside and let her into the trailer. It was considerably neater than she had expected in view of its external condition.

"What is it you want?" he asked. There was something in his manner which suggested either that she had interrupted something important or that he found her presence uncomfortable.

"If you don't mind, I'll take a seat. This will only take a few minutes." The sheriff wasn't sure whether it would take a few minutes or half an hour. It all depended on what Beckham had to say — or didn't choose to say.

"In the first place," she went on, "I'm the sheriff of Cumberland County, as you may have guessed. We've been investigating a rather puzzling case. Have you heard about that woman whose body was discovered recently in a ravine over on the west side of Crooked Lake?"

"No, I don't know anything about that." Beckham shook his head as if to emphasize his lack of knowledge of the area's biggest news story. "Why would you be asking me about it?"

So, Carol thought, we get right to the point.

"Well, it seems that this woman — and we haven't been able to identify her yet — that she may have been asking around for someone with your name. She was overheard one night in a local bar asking if anyone knew someone named Beckham. We've been checking, and it seems as if you're the only Beckham in Cumberland County, or, for that matter, this part of the Finger Lakes region."

She paused for a moment to let this information sink in.

"So you see," she said, "it makes sense for us to talk with you, to see if you know anything about a woman who obviously didn't know where you live and was trying to find you."

Carol decided that Beckham did indeed look uncomfortable.

"But I told you, I don't know anything about this woman," he said, sounding defensive. "Are you suggesting that I might have had something to do with the fact that she's dead? That's ridiculous. I can't for the life of me imagine why some woman was looking for me. Maybe it was somebody else."

The sheriff had not, of course, suggested that he had had anything to do with her death. But the implication was implicit. She could understand his concern.

"You're right, of course. It could have been someone other than you she was looking for. Names do get confused sometimes. But I think you can understand why I thought I'd better ask you some questions. After all, Beckham isn't that common a name."

"Don't I know," he said. "There's a guy who's big in soccer, guy named Beckham, like me. I don't know how many times people have asked me if I'm related to him. It's crazy. I'd never heard of him until someone first asked me if we were related."

"Okay. You're not related to David Beckham. And you don't know this woman I'm asking about. Are you married?"

It was a direct question, nothing subtle about it, and Beckham was quick to grasp where the sheriff might be going.

"No, not anymore. And I don't spend my time chasing skirts. If you think I had something going with your woman, you're wrong. Haven't even had a date in over a year. That's a good one, isn't it — a date, at my age."

Beckham sounded bitter. His social life had obviously been on hold, and he didn't seem happy about it.

"Well, then, is there a chance that this woman, the one we found in the ravine, might be your ex-wife?"

There was a moment of silence, as Beckham considered her question.

"My wife?" he asked. "But why would she —"

He didn't finish his thought.

"It doesn't make sense, does it?" The sheriff thought she knew what he was going to say. "Surely your ex-wife would know where you live, that is unless you recently moved. So she'd know where to find you, wouldn't have to go asking around for you."

"Maybe, but I'm not sure," he said. "And I haven't moved since the divorce. She's just weird."

Everybody is probably weird in some way, Carol thought, but the man on the couch across from her clearly had something else in mind.

"I don't know just what you mean when you say your ex-wife is weird, but I'd say it would be weird for someone to be asking for an address at which she herself had lived, and probably not that long ago. Am I right, the divorce was fairly recent?"

"Yeah. About eighteen months ago." He didn't volunteer more information, so Carol pursued the matter of the ex-wife's weirdness.

"Okay, so why do you say she's weird? It's not a word most people would use in describing their spouse — even their ex-spouse."

"You'd have to know Annie, be around her awhile," Beckham said, his tone of voice suggesting that the sheriff would not want to know her or spend time with her. "She had a way of doing crazy things. She used to disappear, leave home for days at a time, never tell me she was going. Then she'd come back and act as if everything was just fine. It was no use trying to get her to say what she'd been doing, where she'd gone. She'd just go all cuddly, tell me not to worry. Since the divorce she's been doing the same thing. I think she's lived in three, maybe four places. Not that I try to keep track of her, but I know she's been a wanderer. In fact, I have no idea where she's living now. Wouldn't you say that's kinda weird?"

For all the sheriff knew, the woman had some kind of mental problem. There were a number of possible explanations for her behavior, but at the moment Carol was more interested in whether the ex-wife, in her recent wanderings, had come back to Crooked Lake, tried to make contact with her former husband, and died in a pool of icy water in a ravine not twenty miles from where she was now sitting.

"Mr. Beckham, what does your wife look like?" She was careful to use the present tense.

"Oh, she's attractive enough," he replied, obviously not wanting to leave the impression that his standards hadn't been very high. "I haven't seen her recently, so I don't know whether she's put on weight or not, but she had a pretty good figure. Average height, around five-five. Dark hair. Fair complexion. Is that helpful?"

Yes and no, the sheriff thought.

"I think you should see the woman we found in that ravine," she said. "It's not a very pleasant business, but I'd like you to let us know whether it's your wife or not. The body's in the morgue, and I'm afraid she's not going to look as good as she did in life. But you should be able to identify her — that is, if she was your wife."

Or, Carol was thinking, even if she was not your wife and you and she had been in some kind of relationship. But if that had been the case, it was unlikely that he would identify her for the sheriff.

He had obviously been reluctant to view the body, but could hardly refuse to do so in the circumstances. So when Carol finally left the trailer and headed back toward Blue Water Point and the supper Kevin had promised would be waiting, she had elicited Dennis Beckham's agreement to meet her at the morgue at his earliest convenience. That meeting might help to solve the mystery of the woman in the ravine. On the other hand, it might accomplish nothing.

Carol chose to think about other things, such as the fact that Kevin would soon be heading back to the city, probably tomorrow. And that got her to thinking about the inescapable fact that he would always be heading back to the city. This week. Next fall.

CHAPTER 12

The man who wasn't Beckham looked at himself in the mirror as he wiped the last remnants of shaving cream from his face. Everything's going to be okay, he said to himself, but for the first time in many weeks he felt uneasy.

The *Cumberland Gazette* had just published its weekly edition, and the lead story concerned the discovery of a woman's body in a ravine on the west side of Crooked Lake. The story indicated that the discovery had been made several days earlier. If there had been talk of it on Crooked Lake, he had not heard it. A flu bug had been going around, and he had caught an especially virulent case of it. He had tried to tough it out, but eventually had decided to do the prudent thing and go to bed. It was on the morning of his third day of self-imposed bed rest that he got up and retrieved the paper from the mailbox on the road behind the cottage.

The story in the *Gazette* suggested that the sheriff's department did not know the woman's name. Which meant that they had probably sought the public's help in identifying her. But who from around Crooked Lake would have known the woman? No one, as far as he knew. So whom would they be questioning? The logical place to start would be homes and cottages in the vicinity of the ravine. But he lived not that far from the ravine, and nobody had come to his door or called to inquire if he knew the woman's identity.

He tossed the paper aside and went back into the bedroom, thinking of the implications of the fact that no one from the sheriff's department had asked him about the identity of the woman in the ravine. Perhaps the sheriff was not all that smart or efficient, and was simply not investigating the case systematically. Or perhaps she had already learned who the woman was and had chosen not to go public with that information just yet. But how could that be? Barring a coincidence too rare to be believable, there would be no one other than himself in the area who knew her. And he was confident that he had left no means of identifying her on her body. He had carefully tucked her wallet and the odds and ends he had removed from her clothes into an old folder and stuffed it under his mattress. No, he could not imagine that the sheriff knew the woman's identity and for reasons of her own had declined to share that information with the local paper.

But he could not shake off the feeling that something was wrong. He sat down on the bed and started to inventory what he knew and what he didn't know. The woman's name was Sandra Rackley, or so she had told him. She was from Chicago, and had been quite open about where in the big city she lived. She had said she was divorced, although that could have been a lie; she might well have wanted him to think that there was no husband to worry about. Not that it mattered to him. It had been a fun evening and the sex had been good, but he had assumed that that was it, nothing more. When he left the next morning, he had not expected to see the woman or hear from her again.

And he hadn't, not until a cold, nasty day in March when she had suddenly appeared out of nowhere at his cottage door. He had been shocked to see her, as well he might have been considering that he had never given her his address and had used a false name. To be sure, he had mentioned in passing that he was from somewhere around a place called Crooked Lake, but he had been deliberately vague. And he had come up with a phony name on the spur of the moment. He had been skimming through the sports section of a Chicago newspaper and the name of a British soccer star much in the public eye had caught his attention and stuck in his mind, so for that one night in a midtown Chicago hotel he had become D.B. Beckham. He had no idea what the D.B. was supposed to stand for; he just fancied the way it sounded.

He remembered all too well her story of how she had found him. It had been pure chance. He had been filling his gas tank in Yates Center when she pulled in to the same service station. She told him that she was stopping to ask for directions, but when she spotted him climbing into his car only a dozen yards away from her, the need for directions suddenly became moot. He had not heard her call his name, perhaps because he did not remember that he was supposed to be someone named D.B. In any event, she had followed his car out of the station, around Crooked Lake, and down the West Lake Road, anxious not to lose sight of him on this trip over unfamiliar roads. She had almost missed him when he turned off the road just above Blue Water Point, but managed to turn her car around and arrive at his home only moments after he had parked and gone inside.

He could still recall how he felt when he opened the door to find her standing on his back porch. Surprised, yes. And immediately worried. Worried about why she had gone to what must have been a great deal of trouble to find him, worried that someone would see her and wonder who she was and why she had come to his house. He didn't like the idea of her walking into his life, and he didn't want to become the subject of local gossip. He had hustled her into the house, knowing that he would have to figure out how to get her to move her car. And do it quickly. Of course, none of the cottages nearest his own were occupied. They were owned by summer residents who would not be settling in at the lake for several more weeks. Nonetheless, this part of the lake was home to a number of year-round residents, and someone was bound to notice that he had a visitor. A woman. He would need to act fast.

But Sandra Rackley did not want to be hurried. He recalled the alacrity with which she had made herself at home.

"Boy, you are one hard man to find," she had said as she stepped past him into the house. "Do you know that I've been looking for you for two days? I've been driving all over the place, going through telephone directories, trying to find a D.B. Beckham. Nothing, no Beckhams. And then just this morning I came across one in a phonebook over in Yates Center, a Dennis Beckham, lives on Turkey Hill Road. I was going to ask about how to get to the Turkey Hill address when I spotted you. Right there in the Chevron station. You must not have heard me, so I followed you here."

He wasn't sure which bothered him most, her seemingly interminable monologue or the information that someone actually named Beckham lived in the area.

"I wondered how you happened to find me," he started to say, only to be interrupted.

"You're not Dennis Beckham, are you? I mean, I've only seen an address and number for one Beckham. And this road — Turkey Hill? It didn't look very hilly to me. I'm confused."

It was time for some creative lying, and he was good at it.

"No, my name is D.B., like I told you. And this isn't Turkey Hill Road. You didn't find me in a phonebook because I've got an unlisted number. The other guy Beckham is no relation. I don't even know him."

Sandra started again to regale him with her account of her effort to find him, but this time he cut her off.

"Do you mind my asking why you are here?" It was a blunt question. She could be in no doubt that he was not exactly pleased to see her.

"Would it be okay if I had a drink? Scotch if you've got any, otherwise vodka."

The last thing he wanted to do was to give her an excuse to stay longer, but if he wanted her to answer his question it was obvious that he'd have to come up with the drink. He quickly produced a short scotch on the rocks, and repeated his question.

"Look," she began, "this will probably come as a surprise to you. I've been hoping you'd be pleasantly surprised, but I suppose that's asking too much."

She paused, as if to gather her courage.

"I'm pregnant, and I'm sure it's yours."

He had been shocked to find her at his cottage door, but her matter-of-fact, unadorned explanation for her presence in his home on Crooked Lake landed like a blow to the solar plexus.

"Are you sure?" It was a question that must have been asked thousands of times by thousands of men when confronted with this news. He realized that he was stalling, buying time in which to collect his thoughts, to decide on how he would handle a dangerous situation he had never anticipated.

"Yes, I'm absolutely certain. Before I met you I hadn't been to bed with a man in almost a year. You probably thought I was just an easy lay, one of those women who hop into bed any time an attractive guy invites them up to his room. Well, I'm not. And I wasn't that night either. You were being helpful — no, it was more than that, you were being kind. You seemed to be someone special, and — well, it just happened."

He remembered the circumstances. He had been walking in Grant Park, and she was jogging down the path toward him when a guy chasing after a frisbee crashed into her. She had been knocked to the ground and the guy and his frisbee partner had mumbled an apology and kept right on with their game. He had helped her to her feet, and when it appeared that she had twisted and possibly sprained an ankle, he had suggested that they could go to his hotel room just across the way and put some ice on it. There had been no ulterior motive. He really had wanted to help her. But one thing led to another — ice on a well-turned ankle, her acceptance of an offer to shower and clean up, the sight of her in a sports bra and spandex shorts, supper at a sandwich shop around the corner, conversation that included a pleasant riff on the troubles of the Cubs and the Bears, and ultimately unplanned but very satisfying sex.

But now he did not want to be helpful or kind, and sex was the furthest thing from his mind.

"I remember," he said, not wanting to give the impression that it was a memory he treasured. "Anyway, I'm sorry it turned out like this. I assume you're going to have an abortion, right?"

He rated the chances of this assumption being correct at about one in a hundred. And he was right.

"No, I can't do that. I'm a good Catholic girl. I may have disappointed my church, but I would never have an abortion. It's against God's law."

At the moment he was totally uninterested in God's law. He only wanted to do whatever had to be done to get Sandra Rackley and the unplanned child she was carrying out of his life.

"So what is it you propose to do?"

"Well, I was hoping that you might help me again. Maybe if you and I could spend a little time together, we'd come up with something."

She had not come out and said it in so many words, but it seemed clear to him where this was heading. She was going to try to move in with him, sweet talk him into marrying her or at least into living with her and raising the child together. In all probability, if things didn't work out, he would be expected to agree to contribute to the child's upbringing.

Suddenly, a day that had looked like any other was turning into a nightmare. Sandra Rackley, she of the one-night stand in Chicago, was making herself comfortable on his couch and proposing a very different life than the one he had been looking forward to.

They could sit there in his living room and discuss this like civilized adults. The day might end with drinks and supper. She probably hoped it would end in bed. He would have nothing to do with any of this. But he had to be careful. He had to avoid sharp words, not issue an ultimatum, try to sound reasonable. He had to pretend to be concerned, to be willing to discuss that which he had no interest in discussing. Better to do this away from the too-comfortable ambience of the cottage. Better out in the cold, bracing fresh air. It was then that he had an idea, only partly formed.

"Sandra," he had said, hating to use her name but hoping that doing so would send the right signal, "why don't we get out of the house. It's stuffy here. I know of a great place where we can talk about this. You're an outdoor person, I remember. There's a beautiful ravine down the road a bit. This isn't the best season, but there's a great waterfall not far above the road. We could sit there, enjoy the scenery, maybe have some good thoughts about your problem — no, let's call it our problem. I just wasn't expecting to see you today, or hear about the baby. This is all so sudden. I guess I'm a bit confused, need to clear my head, start thinking about the future. What do you say?"

Sandra Rackley had readily agreed. At his suggestion, they had taken her car, which he parked off the road near the ravine. It turned out to be a relatively brief trip. The discussion of their problem had come to an end when Sandra fell from the top of the bank into a pool of icy water. He knew the minute he reached the floor of the ravine and got to the pool that she was dead. He had collected her personal belongings, walked back to the car, and drove off into a relatively deserted part of the countryside above the lake where an old abandoned barn provided a perfect hiding place for the Ford rental car. The walk back to the cottage was slightly less than three miles, every step of which had made him feel better about a day which had been going very badly.

It was now close to two months since that nerve-wracking day in early March. Recalling that day, reviewing what he had done and how he had done it, reassured him that he had no reason to fear that the discovery of Sandra's body would put the sheriff on his trail. He had overlooked nothing. He was safe. He decided that he was finally over the flu, that he would go back to work the next day. The man who wasn't Beckham went to the refrigerator and took out a tall beer.

CHAPTER 13

Kevin had given Jennifer Laseur access to his office computer shortly after she had been assigned to him as his assistant. He had figured that it would enable her to help him with the busywork of the course, including responding to students asking questions they should have been able to answer had they read his syllabus carefully and attended his classes regularly. He trusted her enough to know that she would be suitably polite in her communications with students and administrative staff, and that she would refer to him any messages that required his unfiltered response.

But on the morning of the last class day of the semester, Jennifer Laseur opened a message that Kevin would have preferred that she not read. It was from the sheriff of Cumberland County, to whom he had said goodbye just before eight o'clock that morning before heading back to the city. Carol rarely e-mailed him, and when she did she always used his home address. But on this day he had said he was going directly to his office, and in view of the urgency of her message, she had chosen to contact him on campus. She had tried to reach him via his cell phone, but being one of those people who take seriously the admonition not to talk on the phone while driving, Kevin had not turned it on. Thus it was that Jennifer found herself reading the following message when she turned on Kevin's computer at 9:15.

Hi, Kevin — Tried to contact you before you'd put too many miles between here and there, but it didn't work. I did a dumb thing — left my gun in the cottage. I'm sure it's in its holster, probably under your robe, which I dumped on the bedroom chair. I know I can pick up another one, but can you believe that I've become attached to a sidearm I've never had to use? Anyway, any chance that you have an emergency key to the cottage tucked away somewhere — you know, under a mat, in a window box? I'd like to get the gun today — don't want to wait until you're back at the lake if I can help it. You can phone or e-mail me at the office — not to worry, Maltbie knows all about us (I think she's privately tickled). Loved these last few days — looking forward to the summer. Carol.

Jennifer had no idea who Carol was, or Maltbie either, for that matter. But she was disturbed by what she had read. Obviously some woman named Carol had left a gun in Professor Whitman's summer cottage and wanted to get it back right away. More troubling was the implication that this Carol was more than a casual acquaintance of the professor. She had referred to his robe hiding the gun. And in the bedroom. What had she been doing in his robe and his bedroom? And she had "loved these last few days" — what did that mean? What had there been to love about them? And then there was the reference to more such days over the course of the summer. It suddenly occurred to Jennifer that her professor might well be living a private life of which she knew nothing, a private life that involved some woman in upstate New York. A woman named Carol. A woman who carried a gun.

Jennifer stared at the computer screen, her imagination in overdrive. Had Professor Whitman asked her to cover for him so he could spend time with another woman at his summer home upstate? How well did he know this other woman? What kind of relationship did they have? Why would she be wearing a gun? She had no answers for the questions that multiplied in her mind, but she would have to find answers. She knew she wouldn't be asking him those questions. Too direct an approach, one not guaranteed to elicit honest replies. The more she thought about it, the more she became convinced that she was not the only woman in her professor's life. Jennifer didn't think that she could accept that. Something would have to be done.

But there was a more immediate problem. Professor Whitman would know that this Carol woman's message had been opened. And he would know that she had opened it and read it. It was while she was thinking about how she could finesse his questions about the message that she had what she considered a brilliant idea. She could simply delete the message! He would never know, at least not until Carol, whoever she was, asked him why he had not replied to her urgent message. He would claim, of course, that no such message had been delivered. Whatever the outcome of that discussion, he would never know that Jennifer had read the message; and just possibly, the other woman would be annoyed with him. The thought brought a smile to her face.

————

Sheriff Kelleher was initially surprised and then mildly irritated that Kevin had not called back. He had had plenty of time to reach the city, get to his office, read his e-mail. She had busied herself with paperwork and a couple of relatively minor problems, not wanting to tackle any of the more pressing issues on the day's agenda, including the matter of the woman in the ravine, until she had heard from him. But it was now past noon, and she didn't want this to be a wasted day. So she turned her attention to the Chicago woman who had filed a report that her sister was missing — or might be missing.

The photo had been as unhelpful as the Chicago officer said it would be, but so far the missing person report from a woman named Lacey Morton was the sheriff's only lead, so she took out her cell phone and punched in the number she had been given by the Chicago office.

"Hello, this is Lacey." Happily, the person on the other end of the line was the one Carol had hoped to speak with. Carol had worried about what kind of message she should leave if Mrs. — or was it Ms.? — Morton were not at home, and she was relieved not to have to contend with that problem.

"This is Carol Kelleher," she said. "I'm the sheriff of Cumberland County in New York state. Do you have a few minutes? I'd like to talk to you about a missing person report you filed awhile back."

"Oh, my. Is it Sandra? Has something happened to her?"

"I don't know. That is why I'm calling. Apparently you have a sister, a Sandra Rackley, who is missing, and we are trying to discover the identity of a woman here in my jurisdiction. We have no reason to believe that this woman is your sister. But I'd like to ask you some questions, if I may."

Carol knew that there was no way to spare the Morton woman the anxiety her questions would arouse. But she tried not to sound as if she were conveying bad news. After all, she had no idea whether the woman in the ravine had been Mrs. Morton's sister.

"I am calling from a small town in a rural area of upstate New York near a body of water known as Crooked Lake. Several days ago, a woman's body was discovered close to that lake. We have been unable to identify her, and we are not suggesting that she is, or was, your sister. But when we learned that you had reported that your sister was missing, I thought it might be a good idea to talk with you."

"I don't understand," Mrs. Morton interrupted. "What makes you think this woman might be Sandra?"

"Actually, I hope I can rule out that possibility. But the woman was wearing a t-shirt that had lettering advertising a soccer camp on Chicago's Southside and carrying the name of a local soccer team named the Dan Ryan Kickers. When I talked with the police in Chicago, they mentioned that you had reported your sister missing, so I thought it best if I spoke with you. I need to ask you some questions about your sister."

"Of course," Mrs. Morton said, her voice betraying her fears.

"First of all, I suppose, is whether she had any friends or acquaintances in the Crooked Lake area. Whether she ever talked about visiting out here."

"I really don't know. We've never been close." Her tone of voice suggested that she was regretting that they had not been closer. "She certainly never talked about that lake, whatever its name is. I didn't know she'd ever been to New York. Well, the big city, of course, but I gather that you're not from around there."

"Did she, let's say back in February or March, talk about taking a trip?"

"You think that's when she came to your area?"

"The woman whose body we found appears to have come to Crooked Lake at about that time."

"We don't see each other more than two or three times a year. I'm pretty sure we haven't talked to each other since Christmas, and that was just one of those 'hello, how are you' conversations."

"If you saw so little of each other and talked so rarely, how does it happen that you filed a missing person report? I mean, how did you know that she was missing?"

There was a long pause. Mrs. Morton was either trying to remember why she had made the report or concocting what she thought was a better explanation of it than the one she had given the police.

"Well, it had to do with Terry," she finally said. "That's Sandra's son. He doesn't live with his mother — she kicked him out of the apartment months ago, took away his key to the place. Anyway, he called me, asking if I could help him get into the house. Said he wanted to pick up some stuff he'd left there."

Another pause. Inasmuch as Mrs. Morton had not explained what this had to do with filing of a missing person report, Carol pressed her further.

"So what happened?"

"Well, I wanted to honor Sandra's instructions not to give Terry a key, so I told him I would go to the apartment and collect what it was he wanted. It was when I got there that I realized that things weren't quite right. It smelled — you know, one of those odors that tell you there's food spoiling. Things were neat enough — Sandra was always neat — but the garbage can under the sink hadn't been emptied and the refrigerator had stuff in it that was going bad. This wasn't like my sister. And it meant that she had gone away without taking care of things, gone away quite a few days before. Oh, and the mail had piled up. So you see, I was worried, worried enough to call the police. Of course, Sandra is funny about taking off without telling anybody, so my report might just have been a false alarm."

But then, as if remembering why the sheriff was calling, she added something to the effect that it now looked as if her sister was dead.

"Please, Mrs. Morton, we don't know that. But what you're telling me takes me to a couple other questions. You've mentioned that your sister has a son. I want to hear more about him — his age, for example, why he isn't living at home, whether he plays soccer. I know that this sounds irrelevant, but bear with me."

"I suppose what I tell you about Terry will tell you something about Sandra. Is that it? Well, Terry is now 21. She had him when she was only 15, and the father just disappeared. Our mother was alive at the time, and she helped take care of Terry until Sandra was old enough to get a job and move out on her own. But my sister and Terry just never got along. By the time he was an adolescent, he was like most boys that age, only worse. He was lazy, always angry, paid his mother no respect. Used to hang out with his friends, come home if and when it pleased him. Eventually Sandra had had enough. He was through school, capable of holding a job, spending most of his time at friends' homes anyway, so she kicked him out — told him to try being a man. Believe me, it was unpleasant, but Sandra wasn't backing down. Now he's working in a store that sells video games, that kind of stuff. Seems to be okay — well, more or less."

"What about soccer?" the sheriff asked.

"I don't understand. Is that important?"

"Like I said, the woman we found back in New York was wearing a soccer t-shirt. It was our first clue that she might have been from Chicago."

"Oh, I'm sorry. I forgot about that. Sandra didn't play soccer or anything like that. But Terry did. She got him involved in a Southside club when he was in high school. Figured it might help straighten him out. Turned out he was actually pretty good at it, but it didn't make much of a difference in their relationship. I suppose —"

Mrs. Morton paused, as another thought occurred to her.

"If your woman was wearing that soccer t-shirt, that must mean she's Sandra. Is that what you're thinking?"

"It does make it more of a possibility, yes. But we still don't know. I wonder if you'd be able to come to Cumberland — that's where I work — and take a look at the body. Then we'd know — you'd know — whether the woman is your sister. Or if you can't, perhaps your nephew could do it."

It was obvious that Mrs. Morton was reluctant to view the body of a woman resting in the Cumberland County morgue, a woman who might be her sister. But in the end she agreed to do so.

"If it's between Terry and me, I guess it'd better be me."

They discussed making arrangements, and then Carol raised another question.

"I know this has been hard for you, Mrs. Morton. I'm really terribly sorry to be doing this. But there's one more thing I need to ask about. Well, maybe two things. Did your sister ever mention a man named Beckham or something like that?"

"Who's he?"

"The woman who might be your sister was heard asking around the Crooked Lake area for someone with that name."

"Oh, dear." Mrs. Morton was obviously trying to figure out why this might be important. "No, I'm sure I never heard of him. Like I said, we don't talk much. Was he someone she was involved with? I mean dating or something like that?"

"I have no idea. I was hoping you might know. One more question, then I'll let you go. Do you know whether your sister is pregnant?"

"Goodness gracious, no. There haven't been any men in her life since Terry was born. No, that's not quite true. I think she recently started to get in touch with dating services, you know, those online things. So I guess she may have been seeing men. But she never talked about it. Are you thinking that this man Beckham made her pregnant?"

"The woman whose body we found was pregnant — around three months pregnant. Beyond that, we can only speculate. We don't know that the woman is your sister. So we don't know that your sister is pregnant. And if the woman turns out to be your sister, we still don't know who the father is. Or would have been. Look, let's not jump to conclusions. The first step will be for you to view the deceased. If she isn't your sister, you still have a problem to solve, but I'll leave that to you and the Chicago police. And wish you luck. Again, I'm sorry to complicate your life like this, and I look forward to seeing you in Cumberland."

The sheriff gave the woman her number and address and hung up the phone. It was too bad that Mrs. Morton didn't have a closer relationship with her sister, one that would have elicited more satisfactory answers to her questions. But Carol still found herself more and more inclined to the view that the body in the morgue in Cumberland was indeed that of Sandra Rackley.

CHAPTER 14

Sheriff Kelleher was frustrated and it showed. She had been impatient with Sam Bridges, her capable, if somewhat unimaginative, deputy, and she knew that she had unfairly criticized him for the way he was handling a relatively minor case. Her problem, she realized, had something to do with the fact that after a week she still did not know the identity of the woman in the ravine, not to mention whether she had accidentally fallen to her death or been the victim of foul play. Moreover, she had to acknowledge that some of her frustration had been caused by Kevin's failure to call her. It was just one more reminder that no matter how much she enjoyed his company at the lake, their relationship was more complicated when he was down in the city. Which he was for nine months out of the year.

After three nights at Kevin's cottage, she was back in her own digs, cooking her own dinner. An old standby tuna casserole that should suffice for two or three meals was now in the oven and would not be ready for another hour. Carol uncapped a beer and sat down with her cell phone, hoping to find out why she hadn't heard from Kevin. He answered on the second ring.

"Kevin," she said, determined to get right to the point, "what have you been doing down there? I left a message at your office this morning, and never got a call back."

"I don't understand. There was no message from you, either at the office or here in the apartment. What's up?"

"No, I'm the one who doesn't understand. I sent it while you were still en route, figured you'd be in touch as soon as you got to campus. I needed to know how I could get my hands on a key to the cottage because I left my gun there. So why didn't you call?"

"Well, looks like we've got another mystery on our hands. There was no e-mail from you, just three or four messages about college business. Are you sure you didn't plan to contact me and then got busy and forgot?"

Carol was not pleased with this suggestion.

"Come on, Kevin. My attention span isn't that short. I really needed to get into the cottage."

On the other end of the line, a disagreeable thought suddenly took shape in Kevin's mind. Damn it, he said to himself, I'll bet that Jennifer saw the message and deleted it.

"I'm sorry you haven't heard from me, but I've got a hunch that my assistant may have deleted your message. I can't think of any other reason why it's not there. If it isn't too late, you can find a key on a hook under the back porch, just a bit to the left of the steps."

"I'll stop by first thing tomorrow," Carol said, somewhat mollified. "But I really felt naked without my gun all day today. I'd convinced myself that you'd just plunged right into grading your papers, ignoring my S.O.S. You're sure you didn't do that? You're not just making excuses, are you?"

"Absolutely not," Kevin replied, concerned that she could even have imagined such a thing. "I'll talk to my assistant in the morning. Can't imagine why he would have deleted it, why he never mentioned it to me."

Actually, Kevin could readily imagine why Jennifer might have deleted the message and not mentioned it to him. In all likelihood it would have said enough to tell her that there was another woman in his life. Jennifer would not be happy to learn that. She would immediately have started to speculate on the nature of his relationship with this other woman. And she would not have wanted him to know that she knew about her. He wondered how she would handle this newly acquired knowledge. While he hadn't given the matter any thought before, it now occurred to him that his assistant, with her misplaced conviction that they enjoyed a special relationship, might well have been transformed into a jealous woman.

Carol was now ready to move on to other things. Kevin would deal with Jennifer tomorrow. Or try to.

"So have you finished those papers?"

"Most of them. I still have seven to go, and then I have to draft a final exam. And make it to one final faculty meeting in the morning. Did you learn anything new about your mystery woman today?"

"Yes, and that's another reason why I'm calling. I know that you can't move back to the lake until after finals and commencement, but if I remember what you said about your calendar, you could get away again for two or three days this coming weekend. Is that right?"

"If it means several more bonus days with you, absolutely — I can make it by Friday evening." Kevin had not planned on going back to the lake until later in May, but he was delighted to hear that Carol was anxious to see him again even sooner.

"We talked about you going to Chicago, remember? About you maybe getting into the house of that woman who was reported missing, the one who just might be the same one we found in the ravine. Well, I've had an interesting conversation with the person who filed the missing person report. She's the sister of the woman who's gone missing. I didn't learn anything that qualifies as proof that the two women are one and the same, but I think there's a reasonably good chance that they are."

Carol proceeded to fill Kevin in on her conversation with Lacey Morton.

"Now, what I want to propose is that you go to Chicago, meet with the Morton woman, and go through her sister's place with a fine-tooth comb, looking for anything that might help us figure out what could have brought her to Crooked Lake. Morton has a key to the place, and I'm sure she'll be willing to let us in. I'd much rather that we tackle the apartment than leave it to Chicago's finest. They'd be professional, I'm sure, but we've got a better feel for what's likely to be important. I know I'm asking for you to pay for the trip — our limited budget doesn't cover trips to Chicago, but I promise to do what I can to reimburse you."

Carol had no idea what Kevin's financial situation was like. She knew that he would be willing to take the trip, but she hoped that she was not being too presumptuous in asking that he cover its costs, at least for the time being. Kevin in turn was disappointed that what Carol was proposing would not bring them together at the lake again, but he was pleased that she really needed his help on her most puzzling case. They agreed that he would fly directly from the city, a far more efficient and less costly plan than coming back to the lake and using the small regional airport nearby.

Once again, Kevin Whitman would be serving informally as a deputized member of the Cumberland County sheriff's department, much as he had briefly the previous summer when Carol Kelleher had let him become a participant in the investigation of the murder of the owner of the Silver Leaf Wine Company. In that case, he had tried to persuade her to let him play a role, and she had reluctantly agreed. This time, she had asked him to play a role. It was still an ad hoc arrangement, but it was clear to both of them that now they really were a team.

CHAPTER 15

Cumberland County is a relatively quiet part of the state. Small towns, family farms, parts of two of the state's beautiful lakes, many acres of grapes on the slopes above those lakes, tertiary roads with light traffic. The statistical record makes it clear that crime is low, which accounts for the fact that the county budget for law enforcement is modest. Which means that the sheriff's department is small, its officers not handsomely compensated. On most days and for much of the year, these resources suffice to preserve law and order in the county without great difficulty. But on occasions, such as heavy winter snows and surges of holiday traffic, Sheriff Kelleher's staff is stretched thin and some cases receive less attention than they should.

The sheriff faced just such a day early in May. There had been the theft of several computers at the central school; a bunch of kids had gone for a nighttime joyride on the old Braxton Road with unhappy consequences; two cars had been involved in collisions with deer; a refuse truck had lost its load, necessitating the rerouting of vehicular traffic on the outskirts of Southport; a long-simmering dispute over responsibility for the collapse of a house under construction had turned nasty; and for no apparent reason, more drivers than usual had seen fit to ignore local speed limits. The result of all this was that the file on the woman in the ravine lay unopened on Carol's desk for more than 48 hours.

When she focused again on that case, it was because two people arrived at her office with the announced purpose of viewing the body. The first was Dennis Beckham. He had promised to come by the morgue and see if the dead woman was his ex-wife, but he had failed to call to set a day and time for doing so. It was not convenient to set aside what she was doing, but Carol had no choice but to accompany him to the morgue. She watched him closely as the attendant pulled down the sheet to reveal the face of a woman too long dead and too long submerged in water. She had expected him to say something quickly — she is my former wife or she isn't. Instead, he stared for almost a minute, his own face expressionless. She doubted that his problem was that he wasn't sure. Perhaps the shock of viewing someone now dead, someone in this condition, had produced this moment of paralysis.

But after what seemed like an eternity, Beckham turned to the sheriff and said, quite simply and in a dull voice, that the woman was not his ex-wife.

"All right. Have you ever seen her before?"

This time there was no hesitation.

"No, never. She doesn't look like anybody I ever met."

He left the morgue, thinking his own thoughts. She wished she knew just what he was thinking. And whether his answer to her second question was the truth or a lie. She had assumed that he would say something more equivocal, something like "I don't think so." But his "no, never" had been emphatic.

The second person to view the body was Lacey Morton, and her presence in the sheriff's office later that afternoon was not a surprise. Once she agreed to come to Cumberland to see if the deceased was her sister, she had decided at the urging of the sheriff to do it right away. "No point in putting off such an unpleasant task," she had said, and had then promptly made flight arrangements. Officer Grieves had taken time off from his investigation of the stolen computers and picked her up at the airport, and now she was walking with Carol down the block to the county morgue.

Carol had not expected the body to be that of Beckham's wife, but now she was even more certain that it would prove to be that of Mrs. Morton's sister, Sandra Rackley. That would take care of one part — a very big part — of the mystery she had been grappling with ever since Mrs. Keyser had called her to report what her boys had discovered. But she didn't much like the thought that she was asking Mrs. Morton to identify the body as that of her sibling; even if the two had not been close, it would not be pleasant for her.

For the second time within four hours, Carol watched while the face of the woman in the ravine was uncovered. And for the second time within four hours she watched the face of the person standing next to her in the morgue as the sheet was pulled down. Unlike Dennis Beckham, Lacey Morton did not hesitate.

"I'm afraid that's her," she said. "She doesn't look quite as bad as I'd imagined, thank goodness. But that's my sister. How long did you say she's been dead?"

"We aren't exactly sure, but it's been a week since we found the body, and the medical people say she had probably been dead for anywhere from five or six weeks to two months before we found her."

There were no tears, but the Morton woman looked sad.

"What's so awful about this — aside from her death, that is — is that I didn't really know her better. I never really cared, yet now I feel as if I should have been there for her. I once offered to take Terry in and try to raise him when it became obvious that Sandra couldn't cope. My kids were all grown, and I could have done it. Well, I think I could have. But she wouldn't listen to me. In fact, I think she resented my offer, like it was a criticism of her. Anyway, we drifted even further apart after that. To think, the last thing I did for her was to take out that smelly garbage after she disappeared. She never knew I did it."

Carol put an arm around the woman's shoulders and steered her out of the building and into the street, where they could see that the sun was shining for the first day in almost two weeks.

"Please don't blame yourself, Mrs. Morton. We all make our own lives, and it seems as if your sister did, too. We still don't know why she was here. Or how she happened to be up in that ravine over by the lake, so far from Chicago. But I'm determined to find out, and we'll let you know what we learn."

Later, after discussing what Mrs. Morton wanted to have done with Sandra Rackley's body, Carol broached the subject of Kevin's pending visit to Chicago.

"I'm going to ask one of my people to go out to Chicago, and what I'd like him to do is spend some time in your sister's apartment. I'm hoping that we can find something that will help explain her presence on Crooked Lake. I'd very much appreciate it if you'd lend him the key to the apartment for a day or two. He's a conscientious, professional man, and I'm sure he'll take good care of the place, leave it just as he finds it. It may prove to be a wild goose chase, but it's always possible that there are messages on the answering machine, letters, notes that your sister made — I'm not sure just what, but I think we'll have a better feel for things if we can look around in what was her space. Do you understand?"

"Of course I do," she replied. "Why don't you have your man call me when he gets in, or better yet, let me know when he expects to be there and I can meet him at the apartment."

Carol was relieved that Mrs. Morton would cooperate so readily. She also thought that Kevin would have loved the build up she had given him.

"One other thing. You'll have to let the police know that you've found your sister, but there's no reason for them to get involved. This is our case, not theirs. I don't think that there will be any problem, but if they sound as if they want to investigate your sister's death, please have them call me."

After handing Mrs. Morton over to Officer Grieves, Carol headed back to her office. She glanced at her watch. It was 4:10. Now that she was focusing again on the death of the woman in the ravine, it might be a good idea to spend the rest of the afternoon pursuing another of the loose threads in that case. They now knew that the mystery woman in the ravine was one Sandra Rackley. What they did not know was what she had been doing in that ravine so far from home. Or whether it was Sandra Rackley who had thrown her drink at Phil Chambers one night at the Cedar Post.

CHAPTER 16

It was late in the afternoon, but there was still time to drive down to the lake and pay a visit to Chambers at Cobb's Marina.

All of the sheriff's fellow officers were engaged elsewhere, but she had wanted to be the one to talk with Chambers anyway. And so, more convinced than ever that the woman who had so dramatically rejected his advances was Sandra Rackley of Chicago, Carol climbed into her car and headed for Crooked Lake and the marina.

She tried to imagine how Chambers would have reacted to what happened at the Cedar Post that night in early March. From what she had heard, he had a rather good opinion of himself, especially when it came to the fairer sex. As Ginny Smith had recreated the events of that night for the deputy sheriff, he had singled out the Rackley woman and done his best to convince her that she should join him in whatever it was that he had in mind for later that evening. In view of his alleged reputation, it was likely that he would not have taken her rejection seriously. He had apparently persisted, even after it had become apparent that she was not interested. And then had come the ultimate "no," a splash of whatever it was she was drinking right in his face. He had hastened off to the men's room to clean himself up, and she had stalked out of the Cedar Post.

What had happened after that, she did not know. But she could well believe that Chambers had been both embarrassed and angry. Angry because he had been embarrassed in front of a lot of other people, and angry because he had been rejected. How would he have handled that anger? The embarrassment she could understand. She couldn't think of anyone who would simply shrug and laugh off something like that. Rejection was another matter. Perhaps there were men — even women — who were so self-impressed, so confident of their appeal that they would find rejection by the opposite sex virtually inconceivable. She didn't know any. But she didn't know Phil Chambers. What if he were that vain? What would he have done? He would be steamed, that went without saying. But would he have bothered to seek out the woman again? And if he did, what would he have said? Would he apologize? Unlikely. Resume his pursuit of her? Conceivably. Strike back at her? Carol was having a hard time picturing such a scenario. She could imagine verbal anger. Anger that took physical form was another matter. She realized that she was speculating about the possibility of Chambers killing Rackley. No, she said to herself, don't go there. She'd talk with Chambers with an open mind. And probably find stories of his vanity much exaggerated.

Cobb's was one of many marinas on the lake that catered to the needs of residents and vacationers. It stored boats over the long winter season. It serviced them over the summer months. It sold accessories and replacement parts. It enabled boat owners to gas up. It rented boats of various descriptions to short-term visitors. In effect, it contributed to the boating culture, which was a main reason so many people found the lake an attractive place to live and to vacation. Cobb's Marina was located several miles north of Southport. It was neither one of the largest nor one of the smallest marinas, but it had a reputation as the one that handled many of the largest power boats to be found on the west fork of Crooked Lake.

The busy season had not yet begun, and Sheriff Kelleher parked her car in a largely empty lot near the network of docks at the base of the drive into the marina. Only about a third of the berths along the docks were occupied, and her eyes were drawn to one that contained one of the most impressive boats she had seen in all her years in this area. It was not only an unusually large boat for a body of water as modest in size as Crooked Lake; it also spoke of wealth. She found herself thinking that there couldn't be more than half a dozen permanent residents of Cumberland County who could afford a boat like that. Must belong to a very well-heeled summer resident.

Carol walked over to the building, which looked like a combination marine products store and office. A stocky man with close-cropped gray hair was doing something at a computer behind a desk in the corner, and she asked him where she could find Phil Chambers.

"I think he's down at the dock working on the Slavin boat," he said. "You can't miss it — it's much the biggest boat out there."

She retraced her steps, heading for the boat she had been admiring as she drove in. The closer she came to it, the more impressive were its dimensions. It looked as if it could sleep a family. It was also obvious that it had been immaculately maintained. Carol did not particularly appreciate ostentatious displays of wealth, but she had to admit that she was impressed.

Spread across the stern in bold letters, black against the white of the hull, were the words *Second City*. Like many of the boats on the lake, this one had been named by its owner. Unlike most owners, this one had not chosen to name the boat for a beloved spouse or for the pleasures of a carefree life. Second City. Wasn't that one of the names by which Chicago was known?

She dismissed that thought and looked around for Chambers. Neither he nor anyone else was in sight, on the boat or on the dock. It would have been possible for her to use a short set of stairs and step out onto the boat, the better to find him if he were below deck. Instead, she leaned over a rail and called his name.

A few seconds later, a face appeared from somewhere off to her right. The smile that it wore when it came into view disappeared immediately, replaced by a look Carol associated with people spotting the uniform and realizing that their visitor was an officer of the law. Did this account for the change in Chambers' countenance? Or did he have a guilty conscience, and might it have something to do with the late Sandra Rackley?

"Hello," she said cheerily. "I'm Carol Kelleher, the local sheriff, and I hope you're the man I came to talk with. Would you be Phil Chambers?"

"That's me," he said, clearly trying to anticipate what it might be that the sheriff wanted to talk with him about. "What's the problem?"

"Well, Mr. Chambers, I don't really know if there is a problem. Can we talk somewhere? I'll come aboard if you like, or we can go somewhere else — maybe that bench at the end of the dock, or to my car."

She gestured back toward shore and the official car, which stood out in the nearly empty parking lot.

"The bench is a good idea. Mr. Slavin doesn't like people using his boat." He quickly added that he hadn't meant to imply that the owner would disapprove of the sheriff being on his boat, but Carol acceded to the suggestion that they sit on the bench. Chambers climbed up and over the rail and walked with her down to the end of the dock. He was shorter than she had pictured him, but good looking in a man-boy way under a shock of curly brown hair. She doubted, however, whether he would ever be able to grow a decent mustache. When they had made themselves comfortable, she got right to the point.

"I'm sure you won't be surprised to hear that there's been some talk around the lake about an incident you were involved in several weeks ago out at the Cedar Post."

Chambers looked decidedly uncomfortable. And, she thought, perhaps a little bit frightened.

"Oh, that," he said. "It was a long time ago. I'd forgotten all about it."

No, Carol thought, I'll bet you haven't forgotten it.

"But is it true that you had an argument with a young woman and that she threw her drink at you?"

"Yeah, that's about what happened. It wasn't a big deal, just a misunderstanding. I didn't do anything — she's the one that lost it. Anyway, I never gave it another thought. Why are you asking me about it now?"

"It seems that the woman who threw her drink at you disappeared shortly after that evening. You've probably heard that a woman's body was found in one of the lake's ravines recently. We are exploring the possibility that that woman was the same one that you had an argument with in the bar."

Carol paused, letting this information sink in.

"I don't get it," Chambers said. "What has this got to do with me? Like I said, I never saw her again. Why do you think she was the woman that was found up that ravine?"

What I think, Carol said to herself, is that you might have been angry enough that you tried to pursue the issue. And that you might possibly have had something to do with her death. But what she said to Chambers was something quite different.

"The woman from the ravine is now in the morgue in Cumberland. I would like you to come over and take a look at her, see if she is the same woman who threw the drink at you."

Phil Chambers relaxed visibly. And then, almost as quickly, he sounded agitated.

"Well, of course I'll do it if you think it will help. But like I said, I only saw her for a few minutes one night a couple of months ago. And I certainly couldn't tell you who she is, even if I recognized her."

"All I'm asking is that you tell us if you recognize her. We're not interested in your argument with her. Happens all the time. So just come over to the morgue, take a look, and tell us yes, she's the woman, or no, she's not."

Carol preferred to have Chambers view the body the following morning, and said so. She offered to tell his boss that he would be taking time off at her request, but he obviously preferred to provide his own excuse, one which would not mention either the sheriff or the incident at the Cedar Post.

When Carol pulled out of the marina parking lot, she left an anxious Phil Chambers doing whatever it was he was doing to the wealthy Mr. Slavin's oversized powerboat.

CHAPTER 17

Kevin's knowledge of Chicago was limited to hotels in the Loop and in the vicinity of Michigan Avenue. He had attended professional conferences in those areas on several occasions, but he had usually spent more time in the conference hotel lobbies and coffee shops than he had taking in the sights of the big city. Once he had been able to get a ticket to a Cubs baseball game, and he had walked down to the Art Institute to spend quality time with the impressionists two or three times. But he was totally unfamiliar with the area south of Hyde Park, and that was where Sandra Rackley had lived and where Lacey Morton would be meeting him. So he had taken the el from O'Hare into downtown Chicago and then hailed a taxi for the trip to Rackley's apartment building.

Carol had called him before he left for the airport and made some suggestions regarding things he might look for when he searched the apartment. She had also told him about her meeting with Phil Chambers, and passed along the news that Chicago had surfaced once again in the investigation, this time in the form of a large, elegant boat named *Second City*. Chambers looked as if he might throw up when confronted with the woman's body at the morgue, but he had sucked it up and told the sheriff that she looked vaguely familiar and might be the woman who had thrown a drink in his face at the Cedar Post. Whether the woman was only vaguely familiar because of partial decomposition or because Chambers had his own reasons for not wanting to sound sure about the identification, she didn't know. Before hanging up she had said that she'd like Kevin to meet with Chambers, see what he thought of the man. Needless to say, Kevin was pleased with this request for his opinion. We really are a team, he thought.

The taxi pulled up in front of an old and not especially distinguished building, and Kevin paid the driver what he thought was a rather steep price for the ride. Mrs. Morton must have been watching for him from a window in the second floor apartment because she appeared at the entrance to the building almost as soon as he punched the button next to Rackley's name.

"You're Mr. Whitman?" she asked, but stepped aside to let him in before he answered.

"Yes, and you're Mrs. Morton. Thanks for taking the time to help us — and for letting me into the flat. I didn't know your sister, of course, but I am so very sorry about her death. Maybe I'll learn something that can help us to understand what happened."

The woman looked more tired than in mourning over the loss of a sister.

"I hope so. I can't believe she's dead, or that it happened in a place like that. I mean, nothing wrong with your part of the country, but it's so strange her being there. I never heard her mention it. Not that we talked much."

Mrs. Morton was beginning to ramble, so Kevin decided to take charge.

"You're very kind to let me in, but I think the sheriff said that you'd be willing to leave the key with me. There's no need for you to stay. I don't know how long I'll be taking. This evening may do it, although I'll probably also want to be here in the morning. I reserved a hotel room in any event."

"It wouldn't matter if you slept here tonight, if you need to stay over," she said. "I don't know how Sandra left her bed, but there's a spare room, used to be Terry's. I don't mind, and I'm sure she wouldn't have."

It was a strange offer, Kevin thought, but he told her that he'd spend the night at the hotel.

She showed him into her sister's now empty apartment, then hovered at the door as if afraid that too quick a departure might look rude. It was nearly three o'clock when he was at last alone.

Kevin surveyed the living room. It was immediately apparent that Sandra Rackley had been an uncommonly neat and tidy person. The room had been furnished modestly, but those furnishings were immaculately clean and polished. It looked as if everything had its place and was in its place. The effect was pleasing, even to a bachelor who didn't usually think much about such things. He wandered through the apartment, and what he saw elsewhere confirmed the impression made by the living room. In the end, his search of the place might reveal little of interest to the sheriff, but it was obvious that the search would be relatively simple. No problem of disorganized files, of stuff piled high on desks and in corners, of drawers overflowing with evidence of a disorderly life.

Kevin decided he would begin in what should be the most promising room, a small study that had probably been son Terry's bedroom before he had been sent packing. A single day bed occupied most of one wall. Between a tiny closet and the room's only window stood a desk, on which were a computer monitor, a printer, a small lamp, and a pile of unopened mail. A file cabinet nestled under the windowsill, and a chair which looked very comfortable filled the corner opposite the door. Unless Rackley had hidden things under the cushions of the couch or the chair, the only place he would need to search would be the desk and the file cabinet.

The mail was old; it would presumably include many unpaid bills. Mrs. Morton, in addition to throwing out the garbage, had put a hold on further deliveries of her sister's mail; otherwise she had left things in the apartment as she found them back in March. Kevin went through the mail, tossing the catalogs and junk mail in a wastebasket and scrutinizing the bills for any evidence of what Sandra Rackley had been doing and when. A Visa bill told him that she had purchased an airline ticket on a date around the time Sandra had presumably come east to Crooked Lake. None of the other Visa charges or bills told him anything that seemed helpful. By the time he had opened the last piece of mail, he realized that there had not been a single personal letter. Perhaps she communicated with her friends exclusively by e-mail.

But that turned out not to be true, unless she had few friends. Accessing the e-mail messages proved to be easier than he had expected, but not very rewarding. Like the snail mail, the handful of electronic messages shed no light on what she may have been doing, or with whom, in the months preceding her fatal trip to Crooked Lake.

The bedroom was even more of a disappointment than the study, and Kevin dispensed with the bathroom, kitchen, and a linen closet quickly. When he moved back to the living room, he was convinced that there would be no need to revisit the apartment the following day. The only items in the living room that didn't count as furniture were several shelves of books and a trio of magazines on an end table by the couch. He dutifully leafed through the magazines and then turned his attention to the bookcases. The titles were a mixed bag, heavy on fiction — some of it surprisingly high brow — and much of the rest biography. He recognized a few of the titles, had never heard of most of them, and was surprised to find a history of the Peloponnesian War at the far end of one shelf. It was while he was speculating on what had led Ms. Rackley to the latter subject that he noticed a number of thin volumes with dark blue spines bearing no titles or authors' names. He pulled one out and turned it over. The cover was blank except for a taped-on 3 x 5 card with "Summer 2005" written on it in red ink.

Kevin opened it and was immediately aware that he was looking at a diary or journal. The frustration that had been building up as he worked his way through the apartment vanished in an instant. He quickly pulled several of the other blue books from the shelf. They looked identical except for their dates. There were journals for "Autumn 2004," "Winter 2004/2005," "Spring 2005." Kevin went back to the shelf and took out the rest of the copies of what was obviously Sandra Rackley's diary.

"Yes!" he said aloud to himself as he found the ones that interested him most: "Autumn 2005" and "Winter 2005/2006." By the time he had assembled all of the thin blue books, it was clear that the journal had been started in 2002, that it was organized by seasons of the year, and that it had been written in an unbelievably perfect hand that would have cheered the heart of his elementary school teacher of penmanship.

Kevin wondered if there might be more of the blue books somewhere else in the apartment, although he couldn't imagine where that somewhere could be. He'd take another look before he left, but for the moment he was grateful that he'd found what should be the most valuable volumes — those that covered the recent months when Sandra Rackley had become pregnant and decided to take a trip to Crooked Lake.

He retreated to the comfortable chair in the study and began reading what the Rackley woman had written, beginning in September of 2005. Her notes were organized chronologically, as he had expected. Some of the entries were banal, such as one from late September that announced the welcome loss of seven pounds, courtesy of the bathroom scale. There were a number of comments on shopping excursions, although it did not appear as if any big ticket items had been purchased. If the Rackley woman had had a social life, she had chosen not to mention it in her diary. More likely there had been no social life. That would square with what the Morton woman had told Carol and what he had discovered in going through the mail.

But wait. On October 17th was an entry that concerned a man named Karl.

> "Another disappointing evening. His name is Karl, and we did the usual, had dinner at a restaurant in the Loop. He's pleasant enough, and he can keep a conversation going, but there's no real spark. He didn't want to talk much about his life or his ex. I'm not sure what he gets a kick out of. Just a nice, bland guy settling into middle age. I'm about ready to give up on these Web sites that promise a new man in your life. Lacey would say my standards are unrealistically high, but I'm not going to give up my freedom just so there's someone around to help keep the bed warm."

Kevin thought that Sandra Rackley had sounded pretty sensible. That was exactly the way he had felt until last summer when Carol Kelleher had come into his life. If the Rackley woman had lived, he would have urged her not to give up. Maybe the next one would have been the right one. But no. Unfortunately, there was a good chance that the next one had very definitely not been the right one.

The pattern established in the first pages of the diary changed very little as he read on. By the time he reached December, he was beginning to feel depressed. There had been one more stab at a blind date, and it had gone even less well than the one with Karl.

Kevin knew that the woman in the ravine, now known to be Sandra Rackley, had been three months pregnant when she died. And she had presumably died sometime in early March, give or take a week or so either way. This made her journal entries after Thanksgiving critically important. He doubted that she would have written so candidly about unsatisfactory dinner dates and then not mention a sexual liaison.

He turned a page to the entry dated December 3rd. And there it was.

"How should I begin? Last night was one of the strangest I've had in ages. And one of the best. I met a man in Grant Park and — I can't believe I'm writing this — we spent the night together in a hotel. It was all quite accidental. I was jogging and some kid knocked me down chasing a frisbee. This man — his name is D.B. Beckham — helped me up, we got to talking, and he walked me back to his hotel. Not sure why I did it, but he was being real nice. Anyway, he let me take a shower to clean up — can you imagine showering in a strange man's hotel room half an hour after meeting him? One thing led to another — in this case that old cliché is the only way to put it — and after supper we went to bed. It wasn't what you'd call a great fuck, but it's been a long time and I'm not complaining. And that's all. He went on to whatever he's doing this morning and I came back to the apartment. Just a one-night stand. But, hey, I needed that."

Kevin was feeling like a voyeur and not liking the feeling, but he managed to push that aside, reminding himself that they were looking for an explanation for Sandra Rackley's ultimately fatal trip to Crooked Lake. And he knew, or was pretty sure he knew, what was coming next. Somewhere within December's journal entries there would be a paragraph — maybe a page or more — telling him that she was pregnant. Of course he was right. Just before Christmas the following entry appeared.

"I've been afraid of this for over a week, but now I know. Dr. Ober confirmed it. I'm pregnant. Pregnant again after more than 20 years! I swore that it would never happen. How could I have been so stupid? Of course it's that nice man who rescued me in Grant Park. And what am I supposed to do? I'll never see him again — don't really have any idea who he is. I spent about three minutes thinking about an abortion, but that's not me. God would never forgive me. Maybe I'm meant to pay for my screwed-up life — a mother

at 15, no husband, a failure with Terry, not much
of a family, no close friends, and now sex with a
total stranger. What a mess!"

The journal entries in the weeks after the one announcing
her pregnancy were devoted almost exclusively to what had
obviously become the most important issue in her life. There was a
brief mention in passing of a lonely Christmas and a not very
successful New Year's Eve party involving people she worked
with at an insurance company office. In early February, she had
apparently tried to take her mind off her problem by joining a
book club sponsored by her church. But it was the fact that she
was pregnant — and that she didn't know what to do about it —
that dominated the last volume in Sandra Rackley's journal.

Entry after entry revealed a woman worrying ineffectu-
ally. There was no evidence that she had ever revisited the thought
of an abortion. Nor was there evidence that she was trying to
formulate a plan. There wasn't even an indication that she had
discussed it with her sister. It was as if she were unwilling or
unable to take control of her life. At one point, she actually said as
much, using the words of an old pop tune, "Que Sera, Sera."

And then came an abrupt shift in tone in an entry dated
February 24th.

"I thought again about Beckham last
night. Not sure if it was a dream. Maybe I was
half awake. Anyway, woke up telling myself I had
to see him. He'll know what to do. Or will he?
What do I know about him? Nothing. But he's got
to know. After all, it's his child, too. Maybe we
could be a family. Did I really write that? I don't
even know if he's married or not. For all I know
he hates kids, beats his wife, works for the mob.
Whatever. I've got to see D.B. Beckham."

Two days later, another entry made it clear that Sandra
Rackley was serious about pursuing the man who was responsible
for her condition.

"Made a reservation today, leave on
Thursday. It won't be easy, but I feel pretty opti-

mistic. Wish he'd been more specific, but the AAA says that lake he talked about doesn't look very big. There don't seem to be any big towns in the area, so how hard can it be finding a man named Beckham. I hate to change planes, but you can't go direct from O'Hare or Midway to that rinky-dinky airport. It should be a nice change of pace driving those rural roads after the downtown traffic here. No idea how long it'll take. 3 days? A week? Don't know, but I'm out of my funk."

There was but one additional entry, the last one Sandra Rackley would ever write in her journal.

"Off to the airport. Daddy, here I come."

CHAPTER 18

The sheriff had been too busy to go back to Kevin's cottage, locate the spare key under the porch, and let herself in to collect her gun. But now it was a new day, and she decided to take a ride over to Blue Water Point and pick it up. For the first time in what seemed like weeks, the sun was out and the temperature had climbed to a respectable 64 degrees. Perhaps spring was really making a belated appearance. Carol was enjoying the drive.

It was shortly before 9:30 when she pulled up at the cottage. There had been a time when she worried about what the neighbors would think when they saw her car in Kevin's driveway, but she had now been there so often that she no longer gave it much thought. Somehow it was different than the gossip that would start circulating were Kevin to park regularly in her driveway in Cumberland. Especially if he did so overnight. In any event, Blue Water Point was quiet this morning. Most of Kevin's neighbors were already at work or had not moved back to the lake for the season. As she climbed out of her car, she could see only three cars up and down the point, and the closest was five cottages away.

Carol found the key where Kevin had said it would be and let herself into the kitchen. He had turned the heat down before he left for the city, with the result that it was no warmer inside the cottage than out. She stepped into the hall and started to adjust the thermostat before she remembered that all she was there for was to pick up her gun. There was no one there to see it, but Carol Kelleher smiled a broad smile and turned the thermostat to 70. She decided to make herself a cup of coffee and stay for awhile. Why not? She could do what she had planned to do this morning at the cottage as well as at the office. What she had planned to do was spend some quiet time systematically organizing her thoughts about the Rackley case, and Kevin's study would offer a perfect environment for doing so.

Once the coffee was percolating, Carol took a quick tour of the cottage. She had seen it all before, several times, but never by herself. Now she found herself thinking about it as if it were her place as well as Kevin's. What changes would she wish to make if it were their decision, not just his? And she was surprised with herself. For much of the winter and early spring she had been conscious of distancing herself from Kevin, of rethinking the wisdom of a close relationship with this man who had come into her life in the unusual circumstances of the previous summer. And here she was mentally refurnishing his cottage as if it were hers as well as his.

When she got to the study, she looked at the desk with its drawers full of — of what? What might she learn about this man whose bed she had shared just two nights earlier if she were to poke around in his desk? And in his file cabinet, his dresser, his closet? Carol had to acknowledge that she was tempted, but thought better of it and went back to the kitchen to get her cup of coffee. If they were to get to know each other better, much better, it would have to be by mutual agreement, not surreptitious snooping.

It was going to be the warmest day of the spring, but she wished it were even warmer. Then she could move out onto the deck and tackle her day's agenda with the lake as a backdrop. But it was the study where she settled down and turned her attention to the woman in the ravine, a woman who now had a name, but about whom there was so much more to learn.

What did she know? That the woman's name was Sandra Rackley. That she had lived in Chicago. That she had been unmarried. Lived alone. Had a son recently out of high school who lived on his own (no love lost between mother and son). Was three months pregnant when she died. According to Kevin's report, she had had a one night stand in early December with a man named D.B. Beckham. Had come to Crooked Lake looking for Beckham in early March. Had had an altercation with an overly aggressive local named Phil Chambers. Had somehow wandered up a ravine north of Blue Water Point and had died from a fall in that ravine.

There were a few other things that she knew, but could not be sure of their relevance. One was that there was a man named Dennis Beckham living in the area, although he claimed that he knew nothing about the Rackley woman. Another was that Kevin had found a button and boot sole marks that weren't Sandra's on the path he believed she had used when she climbed the bank in the ravine (she ignored the finger nail, which obviously did belong to Rackley). She knew, via Kevin's report, a few things about D.B. Beckham, such as that he had been in Sandra's thinking a nice man. But how good a judge of character was she? In view of the fact that he had failed to use a condom and that he had apparently not divulged much information about himself, Sandra's "nice" might be a serious misreading of the man.

What she didn't know about her was arguably even more important than what she did know. And much the most important thing she didn't know was whether she had met her death in an accidental fall or through foul play. If the latter, it would mean that somebody had accompanied her up that ravine. In their phone conversation the night before, Kevin had seemed to be coming to the conclusion that Sandra Rackley had been pushed to her death. No, that wasn't quite true. It was more that he thought they should pursue the investigation as if they might have a murder on their hands. Or, if not a murder, a case in which someone had witnessed Rackley's accidental death and then had not reported it.

The sheriff had no idea where to begin such an investigation. The only people she had met who might warrant her attention were Dennis Beckham and Phil Chambers. Of the two, Chambers was the more likely. He had admitted meeting Rackley, had been the target of her ire in the now infamous bar incident, and could conceivably have harbored a grudge. But there was no evidence that he had turned a grudge into an act of violence.

Beckham was in the picture only because he had the same name as the man with whom Rackley had had sex in Chicago back in December, the man she had come to Crooked Lake to see. But the Beckham with whom she had met called himself Dennis, not D.B., and he had claimed to know nothing about a woman named Rackley. His inability to identify the body had seemed genuine.

Carol sighed, acknowledging that she would have to keep an eye on both Chambers and Beckham. In all probability they had had nothing to do with Sandra Rackley's death, but she was in no position to trust their protestations of innocence. Not at this stage of her investigation.

Her coffee cup was empty. Time for a refill. She had come to the difficult part of the brainstorming exercise on which she had embarked. Did Rackley ever meet the man she had come from Chicago to see? Who was that man? Was his name really Beckham? What did the D.B. stand for? Why had that man, whoever he was, gone to Chicago in the first place? Was there a man in the area of Crooked Lake who had had a personal or business reason to be in Chicago in early December?

The more she pondered these questions, the more daunting her task looked to be. How does one go about the business of finding out who from around Crooked Lake had traveled to Chicago in the late fall? The area was relatively sparsely populated, but it was still home to thousands of people. And she could not even be sure that Sandra Rackley's Beckham was a resident of the area. He had apparently told her that he was, but she could think of reasons why that might have been a lie. Yet even if it was a lie, Beckham had to have known that there was a Crooked Lake.

Carol realized that this line of reasoning was taking her nowhere. She shifted focus. The woman had rented a car. Where was it? Had she returned it? But that made no sense; it would have left her with no means of getting back to the lake. Unless she had met Beckham, they had returned the car to the airport, and she had subsequently used his car. She would have to contact the Budget rental car agency at the airport and ask them if the car had been returned. Kevin had made no mention of the agency communicating with Rackley, inquiring about the car, and surely someone at Budget would have wondered what had happened to it.

Carol reached for the small phonebook, looked up the phone number of the Budget agency at the airport, and dialed it. A woman's voice answered after the second ring.

"Good morning, Budget Rent A Car. How may I help you?"

"Hello," Carol said, and got right to the point. "This is Sheriff Kelleher. We're looking into a matter involving a woman who rented one of your cars back in early March — it would have been around the 4th or 5th. Her name is Sandra Rackley. I wonder if you can tell me when she returned the car."

"Well, that's interesting. I don't even have to look this up in our records. She never brought the car in, never contacted us about it. It's a pretty big deal here — can't remember anything like it before. We tried to get in touch with her, eventually sent her a letter at the address she'd given. That was a few weeks ago—let me check."

The woman at Budget left the phone to check the file. When she got back on the line she reported that the letter had gone out on the 3rd of May. Which meant that it was probably being held at a post office in Chicago, thanks to Sandra's sister.

"When she picked up the car," Carol asked, "how long did she say she'd be needing it?"

"I'm looking at the paper now," the woman answered. "There's no return date. Jack - he's the one who handled this back then - made a note that she wasn't sure just how long she'd need the car for. Said she was looking for someone, might take a few days, maybe a week."

"If she didn't specify when she'd be back, why did you write to her about it?"

"We have a very small fleet of rentals, Sheriff," the woman said, somewhat defensively. "It just seemed like an unusually long time, and we needed the car back on the lot. Still do."

That made sense, Carol thought. Writing to Rackley at her Chicago address didn't. How could she have been expected to receive such a letter unless she'd decided to drive the rental car all the way back home, which was highly unlikely. But there was no point in criticizing the agency. There would have been no other way to reach her.

"Have you notified the police in your jurisdiction about a missing vehicle?"

"As a matter of fact we did, just last week."

Carol thought that if it had been her company, she'd have done it much sooner. She'd have to get in touch with the sheriff of neighboring Torrence County where the regional airport was located. She had no idea what had happened to the car, but in view of what had happened to Sandra Rackley and where, she knew that she would almost certainly be assuming primary responsibility for a search for the missing vehicle. Her colleague over in Torrence would understand.

"One final question," she asked the woman at Budget. "Can you give me the details on the car? My people are going to have to help in the search for it. We'll need to know everything about it."

Carol made notes of the data on the missing car, and was about to hang up.

"Has something happened to the woman who rented the car?" the woman at Budget wanted to know.

"Yes, I'm afraid so. She's dead."

CHAPTER 19

The semester had ended at Madison College, and the students had vacated the dorms and scattered around the country for a summer of job hunting, a leisurely hiatus before the next academic year, or whatever their respective plans and circumstances called for. Members of the faculty were not far behind, only too glad to have graded their last batch of exams until the fall semester. One of the faculty members who made a hasty exit from campus was Kevin Whitman, who headed for his summer residence on Crooked Lake the day after commencement.

Few of the departing students knew anything of Professor Whitman's summer plans. Some of his faculty colleagues knew of those plans, but gave them little thought, preoccupied as they were with their own agendas. One member of the Madison College community who knew of his summer plans and had given them a great deal of thought was Jennifer Laseur. Miss Laseur, who had served as his graduate assistant during the just completed academic year, had devoted many an hour over the last few days to thinking about her mentor's other life in upstate New York, the life that he was about to resume.

Her focus on that other life had begun when she had read an e-mail addressed to him by a woman named Carol. It had been clear that Carol had some kind of close relationship with Kevin. She had obviously spent time in his cottage on the lake and had left a gun there. Jennifer had tried to read between the lines, and in doing so had concluded that Carol had probably spent the night in the cottage, which could only mean that she and Kevin had slept together.

It had only been with the greatest of effort that Jennifer had not asked her professor who Carol was. Instead, she had deleted the message and acted as if she knew nothing about it. Carol, whoever she was, had probably queried Kevin as to why he had not responded to her message. She had pictured him telling Carol that he knew nothing about such a message. But he had never mentioned either Carol or the e-mail message to her, with the result that, on the surface, Jennifer's relationship with Kevin was just as it had been for many months. How things really stood might be another matter. And Jennifer was determined to find out just how things stood.

She tried to rid her mind of images of Kevin and this woman sharing a cottage, sharing a bed. But those images wouldn't go away. So, in spite of a regimen that required practice on her violin for as many as four hours a day, Jennifer started to lay plans for a visit to Crooked Lake. She had never been there, and had never even given much thought to where it was or how to get there, but she now turned her attention to the geography and logistics of doing so. She had bought and studied a map and had calculated that she could make the trip in a little more than a half day's drive. She knew that Kevin had a cottage on Crooked Lake, but she had no address and the lake appeared to have sixty or more miles of shoreline. Her search of his computer and his office files failed to turn up the address, not to mention any useful information about his life at the lake. No matter. It looked like a rural, small town environment, one where somebody — probably many somebodies — would know a Kevin Whitman and where he could be found. She was confident that she could easily learn his address without letting anyone know that she was even in the vicinity.

Jennifer was not planning to knock on his door and surprise him with her presence. But she was determined to shadow him and discover who this Carol woman was.

It was the following day that Jennifer pulled into a parking spot along the town square in Southport. There was a public phone on the corner. Hopefully it would have a directory. It did, and although it was old and dog-eared, the page with Kevin's phone number and address had not been torn out. Jennifer made a mental note of the address, climbed back into her car, and headed up the lake.

This was not her kind of country. To be sure, it did have a kind of quaint charm, but Jennifer was a city girl and found it hard to imagine why anyone would wish to live here. Why would the man she was so enamored of be among those who liked it? Maybe it was because Carol lived here. She refused to consider the possibility that Kevin might actually enjoy it for the non-city attributes she found so distasteful.

She paid close attention to the numbers on mailboxes as she got nearer to Kevin's address. But because Blue Water Point and the cottage she was seeking lay down a gravel road that branched off the main road, she didn't realize she had gone too far until the numbers on the mailboxes told her so. It didn't take long to rectify the error, and she soon was driving slowly past the cottage where Kevin spent his summers and Carol had left the gun.

There was no car at the cottage. She would like to have parked and looked around, peering into windows and otherwise getting the lay of the land. But if she did so, he might pull in, see her car, and then she'd have some explaining to do. Or neighbors might see her and ask him who the woman was who was snooping around the cottage. She would need to be careful. And patient. He might be back in fifteen minutes, or it might be five hours. There was nothing to be gained by sitting in her car for heaven knows how long. Better go into town, have lunch, come by the cottage again later. It might take a couple of days, but at some point she would pass the cottage when he was there. But then what? Wait until he left and follow him? Jennifer had begun to realize that her quest for information about someone named Carol might be a wild goose chase. Yet what other course of action was there? Her mission was too important to abandon just because it would take time. She would drive back to Southport and rent a motel room.

But Jennifer Laseur was in luck, although she didn't realize it at first, when she swung by the cottage for the third time that day. At a quarter to five that afternoon, his car was in the driveway. And next to it was what looked like a police car. She stopped several cottages away and studied the scene. It was indeed a police car, and the lettering on the vehicle proclaimed that it belonged to the Cumberland County Sheriff's Department. This made no sense to her. Was Kevin in some kind of trouble with the law?

There were no cars at any of the immediately adjacent cottages, so she decided she could stay where she was for a few minutes and see what, if anything, happened.

She didn't have to wait five minutes. The back door of the cottage opened and Kevin came out in the company of an officer in uniform. And the officer was a woman! Jennifer's pulse quickened. The two talked for a minute, and then Kevin pulled the officer to him and gave her a hug and a kiss that seemed to last forever. Okay, she thought, maybe ten seconds. Just as bad.

The police car had left, Kevin had gone back inside. Jennifer sat behind the wheel, slumped down in the seat. It was all too clear. The gun belonged to an officer of the county sheriff's department. That officer was a woman. That woman's name was

Carol. And Carol was more than just a friend of Kevin's. Friends share quick hugs when saying goodbye. This had not been the usual goodbye hug.

It took Jennifer less than an hour to learn the name of the woman Kevin had been kissing on the back porch of the cottage. A call to the listed number of the county sheriff's office had elicited the information that the only woman on the force was the sheriff herself. And that her name was Carol Kelleher.

Later that evening, Jennifer stopped into Jack's Tavern in Southport for a beer. She wasn't hungry, but she needed a drink. The odds were that Kevin wouldn't show up at the tavern that evening, but she positioned herself at the end of the bar so that she could watch the door and make a quick exit if he should happen to walk in. She made small talk with the bartender, eventually working into the conversation a question about the sheriff.

"Hear your sheriff's department is run by a woman. No glass ceiling up here, I guess. What's the word on her?"

"Oh, she's doing great. Everyone loves her," he replied enthusiastically. "People still talk about how she wrapped up that murder of the owner of the Silver Leaf Winery last summer. Some lady, Sheriff Kelleher."

"I thought I heard someone say she's dating one of your summer residents. That'd make a nice story, wouldn't it?"

"You know how it is, small town, lots of people fancy themselves as matchmakers. Especially when it concerns an eligible woman like the sheriff. I don't know anything about her private life. None of my business. But there's been talk about some professor. Seems they got to know each other during that murder I mentioned."

Jack Varner, the owner-bartender, smiled at Jennifer Laseur and shook his head as if to say that he didn't really approve of the Crooked Lake gossip mill.

Jennifer was glad that the mill was working. But she didn't like the gossip. Nor the evidence that she had a rival for Professor Whitman's affection. Something has got to be done about that, she thought. And I'll have to do it.

CHAPTER 20

They had shared a quick hello late the previous afternoon, but it was not until the following morning that the sheriff and the professor had a chance to savor the fact that they would actually be living within a short few miles of each other for the better part of the next several months. The long winter of separation was officially over. Even if the calendar served to remind them that Labor Day would come around once again, both Kevin and Carol were less caught up in a sense of urgency than they had been fifteen days earlier when he had dumped end-of-semester duties on Jennifer Laseur and rushed back to the lake.

They were having a celebration of sorts on Kevin's beach. It was still a bit chilly, but spring was definitely in the air. He had dragged two lawn chairs out from under the deck and set them up near the water's edge, where they were watching a pair of wood ducks bobbing along a dozen feet off shore.

"I love those ducks. Don't see too many of them — it's usually just mallards," Kevin said. "It won't be long before we'll be seeing families of little ducklings. I always worry the bass will nab them. They start off as six or seven, all following the mother duck, but then one by one you notice that the brood is getting smaller. Nature can be downright unpleasant sometimes."

This was a side of Kevin that Carol had not seen before.

"I didn't know you were a sentimentalist," she said.

"Only where ducklings are concerned," he replied with a wry smile. "Actually, I think I'd call myself a romantic. Didn't know that, did you? But I am. I could sit here and take in that hill across the lake for hours — well, maybe not for hours, but just look at it. It's been a late spring, but you can almost see it changing from gray to green as we watch. Just looking at it is like listening to Brahms' second symphony, and that's romantic."

"Which reminds me, where's the canoe?" Carol asked.

Ah, yes, the canoe, Kevin thought, remembering the night the previous summer when their relationship had taken a decisive turn. What if there had been no canoe? What if there had been no canoe ride on a quiet late August evening? Would they still have become lovers?

"It's under the deck," he said. "I'll take it out when we put the dock back in the water. Probably next week."

Carol's smile told him that she, too, remembered that night in August.

"Good," she said. "Just let me know when you're ready. I want the first ride of the season."

But then she changed the subject.

"Officially, you know, I came over here this morning to talk about the Rackley case. Maybe we should put ducks and canoes on hold. Okay?"

"Sure. Kevin Whitman, deputy sheriff, at your disposal."

"Very funny, Kevin." Carol reached across and gave him a good-natured punch on the shoulder. "You've been arguing that I'm looking at something other than an accidental death. Convince me."

Much as he would have preferred to reminisce with Carol about that magical evening in August, he also enjoyed discussing the problems she faced as the sheriff of Cumberland County. And he knew that she was on duty.

"It's just a hunch, you know. But I'm having trouble picturing this woman's death as one of those unfortunate, freakish accidents. I know you'd like it to be that way. Sad, yes, but better than having to track down someone who killed her and left her up there in the ravine. Anyhow, I'm skeptical. Let me tell you why."

Carol was afraid that Kevin actually preferred that it had been murder. He had found a new avocation the previous summer, that of amateur sleuth, and he might well want to spend his vacation from the academic grind helping her catch the killer. But she had come by the cottage to talk with him about the case, and she would hear him out.

"First," he began, "we know why Rackley was in the area. Her journal tells us that. But we don't know why she was in the ravine. I mean it's one thing to come to Crooked Lake. She apparently had good reason for wanting to do that. But it's quite another to go wandering up a ravine. There's nothing in her diary to suggest that she knew anything about this part of the country. Her sister tends to confirm that. So it's a safe bet she knew nothing about the ravine. Which suggests either that she just stumbled on it and took a hike, or that someone who did know about it took her to it. Do you like the first option? I don't. She's here to find a guy named Beckham, and she's preoccupied with the fact that she's pregnant by him. That doesn't sound like a woman who happens upon some oversized gully and decides to put her reason for being here on hold so she can go exploring."

Kevin was warming to his task. Carol listened, her expression noncommittal.

"So doesn't it seem likely — more likely — that she had met someone, let's say Beckham, and had gone to the ravine with him? Of course, it wouldn't have to be Beckham. Maybe it was this guy Chambers. Or any one of a number of people we don't know about, people she met while she was looking for Beckham."

Carol started to interrupt, but Kevin reached over and put a hand on her arm. This was his story.

"I know, you're going to ask me why Beckham would have taken her up the ravine. Maybe he wanted to show her the countryside. Maybe he thought she'd enjoy the waterfalls. Or maybe she'd told him she was pregnant, and he couldn't cope with what he feared would be the consequences. So he figures the ravine would give him a place to kill her. Out of sight, away from other people — and good odds that no one would find her for a long time."

"That's a horrible scenario, Kevin. I have trouble picturing a man who would rather kill a woman than take responsibility for having made her pregnant. But I suppose it's possible. I would rather believe that she fell by accident and that he suddenly found himself with a way out of his problem."

"If that was the case, he'd still be a pretty nasty piece of work," Kevin said. "Why not call the police, report the accident, act distraught — you know, make believe you're heartbroken to have lost the love of your life in such a tragic way."

Carol was shaking her head.

"No, he wouldn't report it," she said. "He'd probably figure that we'd suspect him, and that would lead to an autopsy, a DNA test, proof that he was the daddy, and voila, he'd be in deep trouble. And he'd have been right, we would have suspected him."

"Of course, her companion in the ravine could have been somebody else," Kevin suggested. "Are you ready to write off Chambers?"

"No, not yet. In fact, I'd like you to talk with him, see what you think of the guy. I'm sure you could come up with some reason to chat him up. I still think it's possible he was so angry about what happened at the Cedar Post that he couldn't let it go.

What if he tracked her down, lost control, and killed her? Pushed her off that bank in the ravine? Do I think it happened that way? No, probably not, but given what I've heard about Chambers, he could be our man. I've wondered —" Carol stopped in mid-sentence, remembering that there was no evidence that Sandra Rackley's death had not been accidental. "Damn it, Kevin, now you've got me thinking I have a murder on my hands."

"Well, I wouldn't be surprised if you do," he said. "Want to talk about the car? The rental car the woman was driving? That's another reason I think her death was no accident."

"The car bothers me, too. What's your take on it?"

"You've got more information on the car than I do, but I think we have to start with the fact that it was rented in early March and never returned to the agency at the airport. What's that now, two, going on three months? It would surprise me if it isn't somewhere within an hour's drive of where we're sitting. Have you looked for it?"

"Started to," Carol answered. "But it won't be easy. It's not like it's a canary yellow Mercedes with New Mexico plates. Just a gray Ford Taurus, nothing distinctive about it. My men are keeping their eyes open. In all probability, Rackley parked it somewhere near the ravine that day, took her fatal hike, never came back. So the car probably sat there for awhile. But where did it go? Somebody must have moved it. There's no record of anyone calling to report an abandoned car."

"Don't you suppose that Beckham or whoever killed Rackley moved the car? Probably did it that very day. He wouldn't have wanted to leave it there, drawing attention to the possibility that there was someone up the ravine. In fact, one of the reasons I think the woman was killed was because there was no car where logically there should have been one - no car and no car keys on Rackley."

"She could have walked to the ravine," Carol said. "Remember, she was an active woman. She met Beckham while she was jogging, didn't she?"

"I suppose she could have made it on foot, but I doubt it. And if she did, I'd bet she didn't come from miles away. The weather wasn't what you'd call walking or jogging weather. If she walked to the ravine, chances are it was from someplace around here. Maybe she'd found her Beckham, and it turned out he lived in a nearby cottage. And her car was parked there."

"Are you suggesting that Beckham was a neighbor of yours? We've checked it out — there's no one named Beckham living anywhere near Blue Water Point. Just that guy up on Turkey Hill Road."

"I know," Kevin said. "Which could mean that Sandra Rackley's Beckham wasn't really Beckham at all. The man she met in Chicago might have given her a phony name. Lots of guys probably do just that. It'd be a good way to keep a one-night stand from turning into a big problem."

"Are you making this up as you go along?" Carol asked.

"Of course," he replied with a straight face. "But seriously, it makes sense, doesn't it? We don't know what happened. To Rackley. To the car. Or whether she ever met this Beckham she was looking for. And if she did, just who he is. But if we make the assumption that her death wasn't accidental, I think we'd soon find ourselves looking for a false Beckham. And looking for him not far from that ravine."

Carol knew that it was a big assumption. But if she simply closed the case, treating Sandra Rackley's death as an accident, she would be forever haunted by the thought that a murderer just might be living among them.

"All right," she said, "as of this morning, I'm conducting a murder investigation. And looking for a man who may or may not be Beckham."

CHAPTER 21

The man who wasn't Beckham was sitting in a corner of Woody's Barber Shop in Southport. While waiting for his turn in the chair, he was reading the latest edition of the *Cumberland Gazette*. Or skimming it, looking for information on the status of the investigation into the death of a woman whose body had been found several weeks ago in a ravine north of Blue Water Point. This was still the biggest news story on and around Crooked Lake, and the editor had given it pride of place on the front page. There were also two feature articles concerning the case, as well as five letters to the editor that offered opinions on the case by local residents. But the man who was waiting to have his hair trimmed was disappointed by all this journalistic attention to the death of one Sandra Rackley.

It was obvious that the *Gazette*'s editor was catering to the public's understandable interest in the case. But it was equally obvious that he and his staff had little hard information to share with the public. Although the paper now had the name of the woman who had lost her life in the ravine, for the most part it was simply rehashing what had been reported the previous week. And offering unattributed speculation as to what the woman had been doing in the area. The man who wasn't Beckham paid particular attention to the letters to the editor, hoping that one or more of them might tell him something that the *Gazette*'s unimaginative staff couldn't. They didn't, and he decided that he would have to use other means if he were to learn what course the sheriff's investigation was taking.

He had already been pursuing other means ever since his recovery from the flu bug. He had developed the habit of dropping in at Jack's Tavern and taking his lunch at Ida's Luncheonette over in Cumberland or at the Waterside Diner in Southport, always positioning himself at a counter seat where he could overhear nearby conversations. On occasion he had launched such conversations himself, expressing sadness over the tragedy in the ravine or wondering aloud what might have brought this woman to Crooked Lake. He thought that he had done it well, that he came off as a naturally curious citizen of the local community. Which he was, of course, except that his curiosity was the product of a well-founded concern that the ongoing investigation might lead to him. And that was something he was determined would not happen.

He had learned more from these informal conversations over coffee and beer than he had from the *Gazette*, but what he had learned was more about what various of his fellow citizens were thinking about the case than what was on the sheriff's mind. Once or twice he had suspected that a rumor might have had its origin in an off-the-cuff remark by someone in the sheriff's department, but he had been unable to confirm those suspicions. The only rumor that had legs was that Rackley was pregnant, and he was in a position to know that that rumor was true. Or at least, he was quite certain that it was true. It had crossed his mind after her death that perhaps she had lied to him about the pregnancy, hoping to use it as bait to trap him into marriage. But the more he thought about it, the more certain he became that Rackley had indeed been pregnant and that her death had spared him a terrible dilemma. And now that she was dead, he could not afford to have his liaison with her become public knowledge.

So far, nothing had come to light to suggest that he had anything to do with the Rackley woman. But he had remained hyper vigilant, ever on the alert to any hint that something had happened, something been found, something been said, that might arouse interest in him. There had been the occasional night when he had awakened in a cold sweat, momentarily fearful that his role in Rackley's life and death would somehow be revealed. In the bright light of morning, those fears always ebbed away. But he hadn't been able entirely to lay them to rest.

That evening, while watching a not very believable cop show on TV, he found himself thinking about the ironical fact that there was another man named Beckham living on Crooked Lake. A man whose name, unlike his, was really Beckham. He had learned a great deal about that man in the last week. It hadn't been difficult. By a remarkable coincidence, the man's initials were D. B., the very ones he had chosen when talking with Sandra. He had chosen them because they were the soccer star David Beckham's initials; the man who lived on Turkey Hill Road north of the lake had those same initials because his first name was Dennis.

Beyond that, he and Dennis Beckham had little in common. Dennis was a moderately attractive man who was approaching middle age, ran an appliance store in Yates Center, had recently been divorced, lived alone in a trailer on that back road, drove a bright red pickup truck, seemed to enjoy bowling, and was something of a loner. At no time had he spoken with him, but he had made it a point to observe him at close range in his store and elsewhere around the lake. He decided that Dennis Beckham might possibly be someone Sandra Rackley would have found appealing. Provided, of course, that they had ever met, which was extremely unlikely inasmuch as she had lived in Chicago and he didn't seem to be the traveling kind.

No matter. A plan was taking shape in the mind of the man who wasn't Beckham. What if something could be found that would seem to link Dennis Beckham to Sandra Rackley? It could start a line of investigation that might not hold up in the long run, but then again it might. At a minimum it would focus the sheriff's department's attention elsewhere. And he thought he knew just what the necessary red herring could be.

He retrieved the manila folder from under his mattress and took out Sandra's wallet. It had dried out, of course, since he had taken it from her jacket pocket in that pool in the ravine. But the cards and bills and a few other odds and ends were no longer in pristine shape, which was just fine in view of what he was planning to do. He had been through the wallet before, but he sat down at the kitchen table, emptied it, and went through everything again. His inventory of its contents told him that there was nothing that could incriminate him. Then he poked around in the utility room until he found an old pair of gloves. He put them on and proceeded to wipe away any prints that might remain on the wallet and its contents.

The man who wasn't Beckham was feeling pleased with himself. Much more so, he thought, than Dennis Beckham of Turkey Hill Road would be feeling in a few days. At first, he had had trouble figuring out how he could use Rackley's wallet to make the sheriff pay attention to Dennis. He couldn't actually plant the wallet in the man's trailer, but even if he could, he didn't see how he could get the sheriff's department to find it there. And then one day he had an idea. It came to him as he was driving home from Yates Center and suddenly had an urgent need to relieve his bladder.

He was so excited by this idea that he almost wet his pants before he reached his own driveway. Turkey Hill Road went right by Beckham's trailer. It would be a dark road at night, and not heavily traveled. The perfect place for a man to stop his car and step out to take a leak. And discover a lost wallet in the brush beside the road. Of course he would not need to make the trip, pretend to relieve himself, pretend to find the wallet. It would be sufficient to mail it to the sheriff's office, together with a note explaining that he had found it and, like the good citizen he was, was trying to return it to its rightful owner.

He promptly set to work putting his plan in motion. The wallet would need to look as if it had been lying beside the road for quite some time. That necessitated rubbing it in dirt, creating what he thought was a shabby, well worn appearance. Then he sat down at the computer and crafted a note for the sheriff's office.

To whom it may concern:

I do not know whether your department handles lost-and-found inquiries, but I am sure you will know what to do about this wallet I found last night.

I was driving on Turkey Hill Road when I suddenly had to take a leak very badly. I know it isn't nice to do it by the side of the road, but it was an emergency. Anyway, this wallet was lying there in the weeds by the roadside, right where I stopped the car. As you can see, I did not remove anything from the wallet. It is just as I found it. I hope you are able to find the owner.

A conscientious citizen.

He had no intention, of course, of signing his name to the note. As he typed the words "a conscientious citizen," he chuckled to himself. He was a conscientious citizen. He hadn't stolen the cash or credit cards in the wallet, he wasn't asking for reward money, he obviously wasn't interested in getting credit for his good deed, and he sounded appropriately apologetic about relieving himself in a public place.

He would go to the post office in the morning, buy one of those small mailers, and send the wallet on its way to the sheriff's office. And then watch as the minions of the law closed in on Dennis Beckham.

CHAPTER 22

Three men who lived on Crooked Lake had been in Chicago during the first week in December, some three months before Sandra Rackley's body was discovered in a nearby ravine by two young boys. The reasons for their presence in the windy city were as disparate as their jobs, their personalities, and their life stories.

One of these three men was Tom Carrick. At thirty something, there was nothing about him that would make him stand out in a crowd. Average height, average build, soft spoken. His most interesting feature was a streak of white in an otherwise brown head of hair. Tom had not lived in the area long, with the result that he knew relatively few people and was in turn not known to many. That he was living on Crooked Lake was in itself an interesting story.

For a period of a dozen years, Tom had been employed in restaurants in Chicago. He had started with minor jobs in the kitchen, but a combination of hard work and natural talent led eventually to the position of sous chef in one of the city's best known eateries. He mostly kept to himself and thus had few friends, but he was respected by his co-workers and was recognized by both the manager and the chef as a comer, someone who would in time become the head chef in a three-star restaurant.

But Tom's gradual rise to a position of prestige in his chosen field came to an abrupt end one day when he was arrested for peddling marijuana. There had been no particular reason why he had become a smalltime bottom feeder in the drug business. He didn't need the money, and he was not himself a serious user. He had become involved with a colleague at the restaurant in what he remembered as an "adventure," but carelessness and sheer bad luck had landed him in trouble. The result was a conviction and a two-year term in jail.

It had been a sobering experience. Not only had he lost his job, he also had lost the opportunity to attend Cubs games at Wrigley Field and Bulls games at the United Center. For two long years he suffered not only from the ignominy of incarceration and the blow to his culinary aspirations, but from the inability to watch his favorite teams perform. Nor did his situation improve upon release from prison. He quickly discovered that his skills in the kitchen were not wanted anywhere from the city's Gold Coast to the Loop.

Frustrated and increasingly desperate, he had sought out the restaurant manager for whom he had worked as a sous chef. He pleaded with him for help in putting his life back on track, and somewhat to his surprise, his former boss was willing to lend a hand. Rocky Lando believed that Tom Carrick was not a basically bad man. He also knew that he had real talent. While his days in the Chicago restaurant business may have been numbered, there might be opportunities elsewhere. It took about three weeks, and then one day Rocky called him and reported that he knew of a place in upstate New York that had advertised for a chef. With a letter of recommendation from his former manager in hand, Tom traveled to Southport and to the Hilltop, reputedly one of the better restaurants in the area.

The setting was far from ideal, but Tom was in no position to be choosy. He decided that he could live for awhile as a large fish in a small pool and accepted the Hilltop's offer of a contract, and set about the task of turning a place with a "great ambience/average food" reputation into the top dining spot on Crooked Lake.

While Rocky Lando had praised Tom's culinary skills, he had also mentioned his brush with the law. As a result, the new chef at the Hilltop started work there on a short leash. Frank Ascola, the owner, was willing to take a chance with a chef so highly regarded by a major restaurateur in a city the size of Chicago. But he wasn't about to put up with another misstep. So he made it clear to Tom that he would be fired in an instant should he do anything to harm the image of the restaurant on the hill above Southport. And he spelled out just what might constitute harming the Hilltop's image.

Tom had no intention of repeating the stupid mistake which had cost him his job and his freedom in Chicago. Within a matter of a few weeks, the word was out that the Hilltop's menu had changed, and changed for the better. People came to see whether the rumors were true, and because they were, people kept coming to the Hilltop.

While he was glad to be back at the task of creating a menu and putting good food on the table, Tom was less than happy with life outside of the Hilltop's kitchen. Initially he had stayed in a motel, but by the beginning of the new year, he had found a rental property on the West Lake Road and moved in. The price was steep, and the cottage would have to be furnished sparely until he was in a position to buy more furniture. It was not a large place, but even so Tom made use of only the first floor and quickly realized that he might have been better off in an apartment. He didn't really miss his former wife. She hadn't stood by him after his arrest, and before he had been in jail a month, she had filed for divorce. But he quickly realized that he missed a companion, someone to talk with after work and, yes, someone to go to bed with.

The more serious problem, however, was that Crooked Lake was a long way from a city large enough to host a professional sports franchise. Chicago had been home to the Cubs and the White Sox, the Bears, the Black Hawks, and, most importantly, the Bulls. But Southport was a tiny place, boasting a population of little more than a thousand people. The nearest city with a professional team was Buffalo, and it was a long drive away. Moreover, he was not particularly interested in that city's Bills and Sabres because his real love was basketball. So he had to content himself with following the Bulls from afar, and even that wasn't easy inasmuch as televised Bulls' games were a rarity.

Tom found himself becoming more and more restless. Not naturally gregarious, he wasn't making friends, and he had failed miserably in his one effort to establish a relationship with a local woman. But one afternoon in November he dropped in to Southport's pharmacy-cum-gift-shop, and while waiting for a prescription to be filled, was perusing the titles on the store's magazine rack. The one that caught his eye was the annual edition of a preview of the professional basketball season, a season that was already several weeks underway. He plucked it from the rack and turned to the analysis of the Chicago Bulls and their prospects. The analysis was followed by a summary of the team's home schedule.

The idea of going back to Chicago to take in a Bulls game had not seriously entered his mind. Too far, too expensive. But as he read down the list of home games, he came to a stretch of three in one week in early December. And what games they were! The Phoenix Suns, the Dallas Mavericks, the Los Angeles Lakers — three of the best teams in the league, all playing at the United Center in one week. He knew just where he would be on those nights if he were still living in Chicago. Unfortunately, he thought, I'm living in no-man's land, the better part of 700 miles from Chicago.

The woman at the cash register called out his name, telling him that his prescription was ready. It wasn't until she had called him a second time that he heard her. He was thinking of the Bulls, and an idea was taking shape in his mind: maybe he could see those games. He took the magazine with him to the counter, paid for it and the prescription, and set off for his car across the town square. Instead of going to the Hilltop to take charge of preparations for dinner, he headed up the West Lake Road and his cottage. He would call the Bulls' ticket office and see if he could still get tickets for those three games.

When Tom entered the Hilltop's kitchen later that afternoon, he was in a better mood than any he could remember since coming to Crooked Lake. Yes, tickets were available. No, they weren't especially good seats, but he had taken them gladly. It would be an expensive week, what with plane tickets and a hotel room. He would have to tighten his belt for a couple of months, defer buying that chair and ottoman he had taken a fancy to. But to watch his Bulls in action again — well, that made it worth every penny he'd be spending.

There was only one problem, and it was an important one. Mr. Ascola would almost certainly not be amenable to giving him a week off to watch basketball games. Not only would Mr. Ascola refuse his request, he would not like it that the request had been made. Tom knew how tenuous his position as Hilltop's chef was. The owner had been pleased with the changes that Tom had wrought in the menu and in the compliments from the restaurant's patrons, but he was still not an easy man to deal with and on several occasions had reiterated his warning that he would tolerate no misbehavior on the part of his chef. Of course, taking leave to attend a basketball game is a very different matter than trafficking in a forbidden drug, but Tom doubted that Mr. Ascola would appreciate the difference.

Tom had ordered the tickets without giving much thought to how he would handle his request for a week off. Now he had to come up with an excuse that would not place his relationship with Mr. Ascola and the Hilltop in jeopardy. The excuse he chose to use was that his mother was ill. His mother did in fact live in Chicago, and he might actually go and visit her between games while he was there. She was not ill, at least not as of their last telephone conversation. But he could think of no reason why Mr. Ascola would call her or otherwise check up on her physical condition. In fact, the excuse he planned to offer for his trip to Chicago would probably reach a sympathetic ear. The owner of the Hilltop was himself a member of a large Italian family, and he and his wife were known to have six children. Mr. Ascola would in all likelihood approve of a son who would want to visit an ailing mother.

And indeed he did. Permission to go to Chicago was granted without a question raised. Tom actually felt a bit guilty when Mr. Ascola expressed what sounded like genuine concern for Mrs. Carrick's health. And when the time came to head for the airport, Tom had done all he could to make sure the kitchen would function smoothly in his absence. He would, of course, have to remember to steer clear of conversations about the Bulls and be prepared to report on his mother's condition. But he was confident that he could do so. And that no one at the Hilltop or elsewhere in the area of Crooked Lake would ever have reason to know that he had enjoyed a week of basketball on the shores of Lake Michigan.

CHAPTER 23

Garrett Larrimore closed his office door. His last patient had left five minutes earlier, and his receptionist had just followed him out into the small parking lot next to their building on Willow Street. Garrett sank into the chair behind his desk, took a deep breath, and absentmindedly leafed through the papers in his To-Do basket. He had no intention of doing anything with any of those papers, but the day was over, and he wasn't ready to go home. He wondered if he would ever really be ready to go home at the end of a day attending to the orthodontic needs of the residents of Crooked Lake. Home should be a place where he could take off his shoes, pour a drink, relax, and share the news of the day with his wife. But Garrett Larrimore's home was not like that, and had not been for many a long month.

His wife had left him the previous May. A Memorial Day present to herself, she had said as she walked out of his life. Garrett was not sorry to see Janet leave. She had become increasingly negative ever since they had moved to the lake from suburban Washington — negative about the absence of what could be called a social life, negative about what she referred to ad nauseam as a cultural desert, negative about the quality of local restaurants, negative about the cold and snowy winter weather. Even negative about him. Indeed, she had complained about almost everything he said or did; it was if she were determined not to forgive him for resettling in this god-forsaken place.

In the last weeks before Janet ended their relationship, she had substituted silence for chronic complaining. Garrett preferred the silent treatment to the constant carping that had preceded it, but it hadn't made home a pleasanter place to be. Nor did her departure. The house still seemed somehow unwelcoming, even claustrophobic. Janet's ghost was a constant presence, and Garrett was forever looking for reasons to leave the house and stay late at the office.

Habits developed during the months when they were drifting further apart were hard to put aside. He had found reasons to go out of town for a weekend, even for an entire week. There were limits to how often he could do this while maintaining his practice in Southport, but he had slowly mastered the art of justifying his absences to his patients. And they seemed to be tolerant of his constantly changing schedule, in part because he was the only orthodontist in town, but also because he was good at what he did and didn't overcharge.

Now as he sat at his desk, not yet ready to return home and prepare another dinner for one, he started thinking about getting away for awhile, about once again putting some distance between himself and Crooked Lake. Maybe it was time to think seriously about a permanent move. Why had he ever believed that they would be happy up here? He knew that the move to the lake had been his decision, and that he had not given much serious thought to what it might mean for Janet. He had been frustrated by the hectic pace of the metropolitan area, by the dreadful traffic, by the impersonality of life there. He hadn't cared whether he ever went to the theater or a concert, so the thought of losing Washington's cultural advantages was never a factor in his decision. Himself a small town boy during his formative years, he imagined that the move to the lake would be something like a return to a fondly imagined time and place. But his nostalgia had been misplaced, and Janet's instant dislike of the lake had turned what had seemed to be a good idea into a nightmare.

Obviously he could not decide at that very moment to pack up and walk away from a practice which he had only begun a little over a year earlier. But he could get away for a week. No, he had to get away for a week. He had to be someplace else, someplace where he would not constantly be reminded of the things that had gone wrong with his life. Someplace where he could recharge his batteries. Garrett was ready once again for a temporary change of scene. The only question was where he would go.

It was then that serendipity came to the rescue. While he was idly rummaging through the professional mail that had piled up on his desk, he came across a notice about a conference for orthodontists. He belonged to the American Association of Orthodontists, which members of his profession automatically joined, but he had rarely attended their annual meetings. But one such meeting was apparently scheduled to take place in early December, just a few weeks away, in Chicago. He picked the brochure out of the stack of mail and scanned it for details. It was a second notice, intended for those who had not already registered, announcing that rooms were still available at the conference hotel and inviting him to fill out the enclosed form and mail it in with his registration fee.

Garrett knew very little about Chicago, and it was not a place he would have picked for the trip away from Crooked Lake that he so badly needed to take. But it offered one obvious advantage: he could go there without having to come up with some spurious reason for the trip. His patients could hardly question their orthodontist's need to attend a conference in his professional field. Of course, the conference would only last two and a half days; the brochure made that very clear. But none of his patients would know that. He needn't say anything to anyone about the duration of the conference. All he would have to do would be to have his receptionist reschedule appointments for a week. The only person who might make a fuss about rescheduling would be Phyllis Warren. It would be the third time in three months that he had postponed an appointment to work on her son Peter's bad bite, and she had grumbled about it the last time. Of course, rescheduled appointments would create a badly overcrowded calendar when he returned to Southport, but he was sure he could manage that. It would be a small price to pay for the week he was already contemplating.

By six p.m. he had booked his flight, filled out the reservation form and written a check, and dropped them in a mailbox up the street from his office. He decided to celebrate by having dinner at the Hilltop. That would be infinitely better than rewarming the leftover chili in his refrigerator, and it would mean that he would not have to face the cheerless house on the West Lake Road for at least another two hours.

CHAPTER 24

Mel Slavin was sitting in the backseat of the taxi, his briefcase on the seat beside him, the *Chicago Tribune* spread across his lap, as they made their way through traffic down Michigan Avenue. But he wasn't reading the paper. His mind was on the meeting he had just come from with his lawyer, and he was in a foul mood. That bitch isn't going to get one cent out of me, he thought. That bitch was his wife, Sarah Slavin, and she was suing for divorce. And his very well paid lawyer, Marvin Branson, had better make sure she didn't get one cent. He wasn't sure who made him angrier at the moment, greedy Sarah or overly cautious Marvin.

Mel was a wealthy man, well able to make it possible for Sarah to continue living the life to which she was accustomed. But it was a matter of principle. It was her doing, that affair he had had with the Dancy woman. She had driven him to it with her incessant nagging, her stupid friends, her increasingly weird tastes. God, he thought, she's a real bird brain. Mel must have been muttering under his breath, because the driver turned his head and asked if he was all right. He mumbled something that sounded like 'yes' and turned his attention back to Marvin. His lawyer had said that there was no way he could prevent a settlement in her favor. Okay, he said grudgingly to himself, so she'll take a chunk out of my hide. But damned if she's going to get the boat, not *Second City*.

The boat was not the most valuable of Mel Slavin's possessions, but it was by far the one he valued most. The cruiser had become his home away from home, a getaway based at a marina on Lake Michigan south of the Navy pier. Once upon a time, he and Sarah had used it for overnight cruises on the lake, sometimes going as far as Holland on the Michigan shore across the lake or anchorages on the upper peninsula north of Chicago. Those days were over, but he still enjoyed taking the day off and heading out to where the shoreline disappeared and he could once again feel as if he ruled the world. Now Sarah was demanding that the boat be part of the divorce settlement. He had to come up with a plan that would foil her, which would let the boat be his retreat into sanity after the trauma of the last few months.

The taxi pulled up in front of the hotel that he had chosen as the bunker from which he would launch his counterattack on Sarah and her battery of lawyers. He paid the driver and decided he would have a drink before retreating to the sterile room that had been his temporary home in recent weeks. He took a seat at a table in the corner of the bar, ordered a scotch on the rocks, and opened his briefcase. In addition to papers related to his business pursuits on the Board of Trade, it contained the accumulated personal mail of the last two days, now delivered to his office rather than to the Lincoln Park address. He went through it quickly, finding nothing that might take his mind off Sarah and Marvin. Nothing, that is, until he came upon one of the periodic newsletters from Auburn University's alumni association.

Mel Slavin had not been a conscientious alum. He had regularly ignored solicitations for contributions to this building fund or that scholarship program. He hadn't even followed closely the fortunes of his university's football team, although he was vaguely aware that the Tigers were typically among the nation's elite. But he took time to skim the newsletter, especially the section devoted to what members of the various graduating classes were up to. The report on his class, that of 1965, was relatively brief. The names meant nothing to him until he came to the following paragraph.

> Steve Wilder sends word that he has relo-
> cated to the Finger Lakes area of upstate New
> York, where he and wife Beth now have a home
> on Crooked Lake. He reports that what lured him
> away from Florida after all these years was the
> opportunity to take over a historic site and convert
> it into an elegant resort. He also tells us that both
> the Wilder boys are now in college, a reminder of
> how quickly time passes. If any of Steve's class-
> mates find themselves in the area, he wants you to
> know that you are welcome to stop by. Drinks will
> be on the house, he says.

Well, I'll be damned, he thought. Steve Wilder. Haven't thought about him in years. And then memories of the days when they were fraternity brothers at Auburn came flooding back. Not only had they been fraternity brothers, they had been close friends and a couple of pranksters who spent more of their time horsing around and making mischief than they had in attending classes. Mel remembered a time when they had snuck into the Deke house on the Alabama campus in Tuscaloosa and stolen a miniature cannon. Those were the days. Wonder why we drifted apart? I'd like to see him again.

It was then that he focused for the first time on the major news in the brief paragraph about the Wilders. They were now living in what was called the Finger Lakes area. Some place called Crooked Lake. An idea popped into Mel's head. I wonder, he thought, what kind of lake that is? What if it's big enough for a boat the size of *Second City*? What if I could hide her away on this Crooked Lake? Sarah and those snooty lawyers of hers would never be able to find her. After all, who'd ever heard of Crooked Lake?

Mel was now excited. He'd get Steve's phone number, call him, reminisce about the good old days and the crazy things they had done. And if his lake turned out to be more than a pond, maybe he could talk Steve into reliving the fun and games of their college years, at least for a few days, while they moved *Second City* from Lake Michigan to Crooked Lake. Of course he wouldn't want to leave it there indefinitely, not on what was surely a small lake in what was surely the middle of nowhere. But it could be a great place to store it until the divorce settlement had been finalized.

Later that evening, Mel Slavin punched in 411 on his cell, obtained Steve Wilder's phone number, and leaned back on the bed, listening to a phone ringing in upstate New York.

"Wilder residence." It was a familiar voice. Mel thought he would have recognized it even if he had not known who was on the other end of the line.

"Steve, how are you? And what in hell are you doing in upstate New York? This is Mel Slavin, remember me?"

"Mel? I don't believe this, after what — must be a dozen years or more."

"I know. I've intended to call, just never did it. What's that old cliché — you know, the road to hell is paved with good intentions. Maybe it isn't hell, but whatever. Anyhow, tell me what was it lured you up north?"

"How'd you find me?" Steve asked. "Bet it was that alumni newsletter. So you know I've gone into the restoration business. It's the new me. Job bored me, and I heard about this place from a colleague down there. Took a trip, liked the area, thought the challenge would be fun. And I'd salted away enough that I could afford to throw the dice. So far I haven't regretted it. And neither has Beth."

"How'd you like it if we got together again? And I mean soon?"

"That's be great. What's on your mind?"

"You're not going to believe this, but hear me out," Mel said. "My wife and I are getting a divorce. No love lost, to put it mildly. She wants everything I've got, and frankly, I've got a lot. There's one thing I'm determined she won't get — a really neat boat I use out here on Lake Michigan. Yeah, that's where I live, in Chicago. Anyway, it occurred to me when I read about you living on a lake that maybe I could move the boat to your lake. She'd never be able to get her hands on it there. And so I was hoping you could help me pull off one of those stunts we used to be so good at, sneaking the boat out of here and hiding it down there."

"You've got to be kidding, Mel. Moving the boat won't solve your problem. It'll still be part of your assets. Your wife's attorney won't let you get away with it."

"Maybe, maybe not," Mel argued. "But I'll be making it hard for her. Indulge me, okay? I guess my first question is whether your Crooked Lake would be a fit for my boat. How big is it?"

"We're getting into hypotheticals, aren't we? Okay. The lake is about 20, 22 miles long. Never more than a mile and a half wide. Has a funny Y shape. And it's pretty deep; I'd say around 175 feet."

Mel was relieved to hear that recital of Crooked Lake's dimensions.

"Well, it won't be Lake Michigan, but it'll do. I assume that there are marinas where it could be stored."

"Quite a few. There's one only a few miles down the lake from where we live. By the way, just how big is this boat of yours?"

"Not that big by Great Lakes standards, but I imagine it would be one of the biggest on your lake. It's got a pair of heavy-duty diesel inboards."

"How do you propose to get it here?"

Mel was encouraged. Steve wouldn't be asking all of these questions if he wasn't willing to help.

"Put it on a trailer, drive it out to your place," he said. "That's how I thought you could help. You could drive out here and we'd form a convoy. That's how they do these wide-load jobs, I think."

"They do, but there's sure to be a limit on how big a boat you could move by road. I don't know what the regs are, but I'm sure there will be restrictions on how wide in the beam it can be. And high — remember those overpasses."

"I suppose so," Mel said, "but where there's a will, there's a way. Let's say I can get a permit; will you do it? It'd be like old times."

"It might depend on what you have in mind. Good God, we haven't even talked in years, and here I am agreeing to some fool plan to lug a monster boat halfway across the country."

Good, thought Mel.

"Look, it's nowhere near halfway across the country, and she's not a monster. It'll be fun. You're a real buddy, Steve."

They talked for another quarter hour, and Mel promised he'd start making the arrangements. Before ringing off, the two men were discussing the challenge of moving *Second City* as if it were an adventure.

When Mel Slavin fell into bed at 11:20, he had convinced himself that he had outwitted the bitch.

CHAPTER 25

When Kevin Whitman returned to Crooked Lake to settle in for the summer, he had never heard of Tom Carrick, Garrett Larrimore, or Mel Slavin, which meant that he knew nothing about the fact that the three men had either lived in Chicago or had reason to travel there. Sheriff Kelleher's knowledge of these men was only slightly greater than Kevin's. She had at least heard of Slavin, inasmuch as she had seen *Second City* and spoken briefly with Phil Chambers about him. And it was because Carol had urged Kevin to meet Chambers that he first became acquainted with what he and the sheriff were soon to think of as the Chicago connection.

For Kevin, the previous summer had begun with a plan to write an article on Puccini for an opera magazine. By Labor Day that article had been forgotten, preempted by the Britingham murder case and his budding relationship with the sheriff. This summer, it was obvious that if he were to write another article on some aspect of opera it would have to wait until the Rackley case had been wrapped up. Murder, if that was what it was, came first.

It was nearly a week after his return to the lake, and he had not opened either his briefcase or his laptop. He had spent that week putting his cottage in shape and stocking the larder, but mostly in reviewing with Carol the status of the strange case of the woman whose body had been discovered in a ravine not far north of Blue Water Point. Now the day had come to deliver on his commitment to take a drive down to Cobb's Marina for a talk with Phil Chambers, the man at whom Sandra Rackley had tossed her drink so many weeks before. And the man who was working on a boat named *Second City*.

The slips at the marina had already begun to fill up with boats as people returned to the lake and removed them from storage. It was a busier place than it had been when Carol had met and talked with Chambers. The day was sunny, and Kevin took a minute to walk out to the end of the dock with the fuel pump at its end to survey the lake and breathe in the fresh air. He was pleased to be back. He would have to talk with Mike Snyder and get him to help in putting his dock back in the lake. It would still be a couple of weeks before he would be going swimming, but the water looked inviting. He squatted down and dipped a hand in the lake. Still pretty cold, but maybe he'd try the water sooner than he had planned.

Carol had described Chambers to him, but none of the men he could see from the dock seemed to fit her description. All of them were probably boat owners, but how would he know? He walked back to the office to inquire about Chambers, but found it temporarily empty. Frustrated in his plan to meet the only man from around the lake who admitted talking to Rackley, he headed back to the docks and the slips, looking for a boat bearing the name of *Second City*. Carol had said it was quite large for Crooked Lake. Kevin was not interested in power boats, and had paid little attention to those of his neighbors and those that sped past his cottage towing water skiers or otherwise doing what such boats were equipped to do. But he didn't see any boat that looked to be unusually large. He walked along the docks, examining the names proud owners had given their boats. After several minutes and a dozen boats, he concluded that *Second City* was not at Cobb's Marina.

It had begun to look like a wasted morning, but he would go back to the marina office and see if anyone had come in. Anyone who could tell him if Phil Chambers was working that day, and where he might find the owner of *Second City*. This time he was in luck.

"Yeah, Phil's in today," was the proprietor's answer to Kevin's first question. "He's out doing a test run with the Slavin boat. That'd be *Second City*. He should be back pretty soon."

Okay. Two birds with one stone. Kevin would wait. He wandered back down to the waterfront. This time he noticed something he'd missed earlier. There, among the half dozen cars and pickup trucks in the parking lot, was a car with Illinois plates.

Kevin knew better than to jump to conclusions prematurely, but the car from Illinois prompted the obvious thought: *Second City*'s owner was probably from Chicago. The boat's name was therefore not the product of some odd whim of the owner's; it merely reflected the fact that the boat's home was Chicago. Of course, there might be a totally different explanation for the name of the boat than for the presence at the marina of a car with Illinois license plates, but if it was only a coincidence, it was an interesting one. The morning, it appeared, had not been wasted after all.

Kevin learned nothing more during his wait for the return of *Second City*. Nothing other than the make of the Illinois vehicle — a BMW — and something about its driver's habits — neat and tidy. Instead of the newspapers, coffee cups, and miscellaneous odds and ends cluttering the interiors of most of the other cars in the lot, the BMW looked as if it had just come from the dealer's showroom. If the car belonged to the owner of *Second City*, Kevin was prepared to bet that the boat would be in comparably immaculate shape.

It was slightly after ten o'clock that he spotted a large power boat rounding the shoreline of the wooded hill that bisected Crooked Lake roughly halfway between Southport and the towns that lay at the north end of its two arms. The boat moved at a moderate speed as it headed for Cobb's Marina. Whoever was at the wheel was clearly not trying to test the boat's limits. He was simply bringing her into dock.

This was surely *Second City*. It was larger than any of the other boats at the marina, one of the larger boats Kevin could recall from his summers on the lake. Not so large as to invite disbelief at its presence on Crooked Lake, but large enough to cause speculation that it might be capable of cruising among the Virgin Islands. Or that it would be at home anywhere on the Chesapeake Bay. Even the Great Lakes.

Whoever was driving the boat brought her in to a slip with accomplished skill. His task was made easier, of course, by the fact that the berth was at the end of the dock and by the absence of any wind. But Kevin, who had no experience in docking any boat larger than a canoe, was impressed nonetheless. As he watched, a man who resembled Carol's description of Phil Chambers stepped out of the boat and onto the dock. He busied himself with ropes and soon had the boat securely fastened. Satisfied that all was well, he headed for shore.

Kevin walked quickly down to the beach and met the man as he left the dock.

"Phil Chambers?"

The man who had brought the big boat in had seen Kevin approaching. His face registered the look of someone who was wondering who this stranger was and what he wanted.

"Yes, I'm Phil. Something I can do for you?" Perhaps the stranger was another boat owner in need of his help.

"I'm Kevin Whitman — live up the West Lake Road a bit. I was just looking around, and I saw that boat you brought in – saw you coming across the lake. She's really impressive. I don't think I've seen one like it on the lake before. Where'd it come from?"

Chambers was used to people asking about *Second City*. He was obviously enjoying his role as caretaker of the big boat. And answering questions about her.

"'Mr. Slavin brought it down from Chicago awhile back. It's really something, isn't it? My own boat's mostly for fishing," he added with a deprecating laugh. "It looks like a toy beside this one. Anyway, I never thought I'd get a chance to take a boat like this out on the lake."

Kevin was mildly amused by this frank talk by a local guy who'd had what sounded like the lucky break of a lifetime when the owner of *Second City* tapped him as caretaker of his boat. If, as Carol had reported, Phil Chambers thought of himself as irresistible to women, the opportunity to be seen at the helm of *Second City* must have seemed like a heaven sent gift. Kevin wondered if Chambers had had any woman of his acquaintance onboard the boat. The thought had surely occurred to him. For all he knew, Chambers had picked someone up and taken her for a ride that very morning while over on the east arm of the lake and out of sight of Cobb's.

"How'd it happen that the owner moved the boat down here from Chicago?"

"I don't know," Chambers replied. "I brought it up, but he didn't seem to want to talk about it, so I let it go. Just figured he moved here, liked the boat, didn't want to sell it."

And that's probably the way it was, Kevin thought. But he pursued the point.

"Lives around here, does he?"

"I guess so. Like I said, Mr. Slavin doesn't talk much. About himself, I mean. Just boat talk."

"So I take it he doesn't stay on the boat, right? It looks like it's big enough to sleep several people."

"Yeah, it's got nice sleeping space, living space. I think he'll stay on her come summer. He hasn't said so, but he's had me looking into some stuff for the cabin. Right now he's not down here at the marina much. I suppose it sounds funny, me not knowing much about him, not even seeing him more than once or twice a week. But he's got a lot of confidence in me."

Chambers was obviously enjoying Slavin's confidence and the resulting opportunity to give the boat a spin now and then.

Kevin had come to the marina primarily to form an opinion of Phil Chambers. He hadn't given a lot of thought to the owner of *Second City*. But now an idea was taking shape in his mind.

"I'm a bit of a boat fanatic, you know," he said, surprised at how easily the lie came to his lips. "I don't have Mr. Slavin's money, so I'm not looking to buy a boat like his. But I try to take in the boat shows. Went to a big one down in Annapolis last year. That was a great weekend, let me tell you."

Kevin realized he was overdoing his alleged love of the power boat culture. Better get to the point, he decided.

"What I'm getting at," he said, "is that I was hoping you'd let me come aboard *Second City*, take a look around. I wouldn't think Mr. Slavin would mind — probably be pleased to know people are impressed by his boat."

But Chambers wasn't sure he agreed with this assessment of Slavin's willingness to open the boat up for inspection.

"Well, I'm not sure. I've got the impression he doesn't like the idea of people poking around on the boat. He's pretty fussy. Let me talk to him. I'd like to take you aboard, but I'll need his okay first. Why don't you check back with me in a few days?"

Kevin was disappointed, but he agreed to let Chambers pursue the matter with the owner. "Tell me," he said, changing the subject, "aren't you the guy that's supposed to have had that run in with a woman at the Cedar Post back in March?"

He knew that Chambers would not be pleased to be reminded of that night. Carol had told him as much. But he was nonetheless surprised at the change that came over the man.

"Not again." He said it quietly, more in resignation than in anger. "Why is it everyone keeps bringing that up? It was nothing, and I mean nothing. And it was a long time ago. I'm so sick of it."

And indeed he did sound sick of it. Kevin thought he'd better drop the matter or he might lose Chambers' help in getting him onboard *Second City*.

"I'm sorry, Mr. Chambers," he said, adopting the tone of someone who regrets a social faux pas. "I didn't know it was a sore point. It just occurred to me that I'd heard your name in connection with something, and then it came to me it was that business at the Post. It must be a pain to have to listen to that stuff all the time."

Kevin regretted that he'd had to abandon a discussion of the Cedar Post episode, but Chambers seemed to be mollified.

"Glad you understand. And, yes, it has been a pain."

They brought the conversation to a close, and Kevin headed back to his cottage. Phil Chambers returned to the dock and his work on *Second City*. It was later that morning that something occurred to him, something that bothered him. This Kevin Whitman with whom he had been talking had greeted him by asking if he was Phil Chambers. Which meant that Whitman had been looking for him, that he had known who he was. What was Whitman's interest in him? Was it just a matter of using him to get aboard Slavin's boat? Or was it something else? Phil was unaccountably nervous.

CHAPTER 26

The sheriff sat at her desk, staring at a dirty wallet. She had read the note that had come with it, and had gone through its contents enough to satisfy herself that it belonged to the late Sandra Rackley. Now she was trying to make sense of this unanticipated surprise in the morning's mail.

Carol was disinclined to take the note at face value. It was possible that the person who had mailed the wallet had indeed found it by the roadside while relieving himself. But there was something about the note that troubled her. In the first place, there was no hint that the finder had opened the wallet, searching for the owner's identity even if he had not intended to remove credit cards or cash. That would have been the natural thing to do. Instead, the writer of the note had tried a bit too hard to sound like a good citizen. And then there was the frank reference to taking a leak. Wouldn't anyone purporting to be such a good citizen have finessed the circumstances in which the wallet had been discovered? Or at least found a more dignified euphemism for the act of urinating at the side of the road?

Carol did not believe that the wallet had so innocently come into the possession of the person who had mailed it to her. But she forced herself to pretend that it had. If so, there was a certain logic to it. The wallet was found on Turkey Hill Road. Dennis Beckham lived on Turkey Hill Road. Sandra Rackley had been looking for a man named Beckham. She might well have been on Turkey Hill Road on her way to or from a meeting with Beckham. As for the wallet being on the roadside, she could have accidentally dropped it as she got out to check something on her car. A malfunctioning windshield wiper? A nonfunctioning headlight? No, it was entirely possible that the note was an honest statement of how and where the wallet had been found.

But some gut feeling told Carol that that was not the case. It was simply too convenient. She had suddenly come into possession of evidence that pointed to Rackley having found Beckham and presumably met with him. If that hadn't happened, who would have wanted the sheriff to believe that it had? The answer, of course, was someone who was responsible for her death. The note and the wallet would focus her attention on Beckham and hence away from the real guilty party.

Whether her surmise was right or not, Carol knew she would have to pay Beckham another visit. She would need to develop another line of questioning, a more probing approach, one that wouldn't let him get away with vague answers to her questions. And that would be easier said than done.

Carol was glad that she had exercised extra care in examining the note and the wallet. She had used kleenexes to hold them and to extract cards and cash from the wallet. She had done so more from force of habit than from any thought that they might contain fingerprints that would be useful in getting to the bottom of the Rackley case. In any event, they would now have the opportunity to check for prints. She'd have that done right away.

The arrival of the package containing the wallet had been the day's first surprise. The second was the report that there were no prints. None on the note, none on the wallet, none on any of the credit cards, the driver's license, or other windows into Sandra Rackley's life. Not even any on the bills which had not been stolen by the conscientious citizen who had found the wallet. So much for that story, she thought. Her hunch had been correct. Whoever had sent her the wallet had taken the trouble to remove all prints, his own, of course, and necessarily Rackley's as well.

Carol briefly debated canceling plans to pay Dennis Beckham a return visit, but she ultimately decided she'd better talk with him. It appeared that someone was trying to frame him, or at least trying to get the sheriff to concentrate her investigation on him. Perhaps that made another talk with him more rather than less necessary. She would go back to the Turkey Hill Road trailer again that evening, just as she had planned to after the package arrived.

———

The sheriff deliberately repeated the mistake she had made on her first trip to see Beckham. It gave her an opportunity to scrutinize both sides of Turkey Hill Road. She could see that it would indeed have been possible for the wallet to lie unnoticed for a long time in the brush that crowded the road on both sides. Assuming that Sandra Rackley's wallet had been lost somewhere along that road, something she now doubted.

Beckham was expecting her, and he was obviously nervous to be facing more questions from the sheriff about something he had repeatedly claimed to know nothing about.

Carol had decided to approach the matter directly.

"Mr. Beckham," she began after taking the same seat she had occupied at their first meeting, "I have received in the mail a wallet belonging to the woman who was looking for you. The one we talked about before. The one who died in that fall in the ravine. What is interesting about this, as I'm sure you will appreciate, is that the wallet was found by the side of the road near here — on Turkey Hill Road. How do you suppose that happened?"

Beckham looked puzzled.

"I don't get it. Like I told you before, I never knew this woman. What would her wallet be doing on my road?"

"That's what I'm asking you, Mr. Beckham. It looks like she lost it close to here, and I wondered if she was on her way home or somewhere after meeting with you."

This was clearly an alarming idea.

"But she didn't meet me." He leaned forward in his seat to emphasize the point. "Never. I don't know anything about her. Why are you trying to make it so we saw each other?"

"Maybe she wasn't coming from your place," Carol said in a patient voice. "Maybe she was on her way to your place when she lost her wallet. I'm just having a hard time figuring why the wallet was found practically in your back yard. Especially when we know she was here at Crooked Lake because she'd been told that this is where you live."

Dennis Beckham was becoming increasingly agitated.

"What am I supposed to say, Sheriff? I can't help it if some woman was trying to find me. She must have gotten things mixed up — it wasn't me she was looking for."

"That's possible, of course," Carol said, ready to change the subject. "This may sound like a strange question, but is there anyone you know who may have it in for you — anyone who might want me to think that you knew this woman?"

Her question quite obviously came as a surprise to Beckham. His expression made it as clear as words would have that the idea had not occurred to him.

"No, absolutely not. I get along with people. Really, I do. Can't think of anyone I've had angry words with. Well, not since high school."

He had apparently recalled some old unpleasantness, but quickly brushed it aside to emphasize his belief that he had no enemies.

"I don't mean to sound like a saint," he said with the barest hint of a smile, "but you could ask down at the store. I guess I'm kind of a pushover."

Carol had known a couple of people who were pushovers and were unpopular, but she was prepared to believe Beckham's self analysis.

"Okay, but we still have a puzzle on our hands, don't we? Either you knew this woman better than you're letting on, or someone wants me to think you did. Anyway, I've got to go now. But I'll be back. I intend to find out why that wallet was found up here in your neighborhood."

If it was found here at all, she thought as she climbed into her car.

CHAPTER 27

The sheriff now knew that the woman whose body had been found in the ravine was Sandra Rackley. Although the evidence for it was only circumstantial, she was also virtually certain that Ms. Rackley's death had not been the result of an accidental fall, which meant that she was looking for a murderer. And then there was one other thing: the car that the woman had been driving, the car that so mysteriously had disappeared. Kevin had convinced himself that whoever had killed the woman had hidden the car, and Carol had agreed that a search for it should be a high priority. So the small cadre of her officers was devoting a substantial portion of its time as they cruised the area roads to looking for the missing 2005 Ford Taurus.

They had made it a point to drive along seldom used back roads, many of them little more than dirt tracks. They had scoured every corner of every parking lot within miles of Crooked Lake. They had stopped many a recent model Ford Taurus, checking documentation and serial numbers in case the driver had changed plates. And they were frustrated.

Carol had been in touch with fellow law enforcement officials in neighboring jurisdictions, and had been assured of support in her search for the missing vehicle. Every time her phone rang, she had experienced a momentary surge of hope that someone somewhere had found the car or had at least spotted it on the highway. That hope had been repeatedly dashed.

It was nearly a month since the discovery of Sandra Rackley's body, and Deputy Sheriff Sam Bridges was parked on a counter stool in a Dunkin' Donuts shop in Yates Center. It was the beginning of yet another day in a job which consisted largely of routine patrolling of county roads, watching for speeders and ready to help motorists in trouble. The search for the missing rental car had become something of a contest for Sam and his fellow officers. They had started a pool and had kidded each other about their respective chances of being the one to win the small pot. Sam had gone along with the game, but was privately of the opinion that the car would eventually turn up in some place far removed from Crooked Lake.

Having polished off his second donut, he paid up and set off on his daily rounds. On this particular Thursday he was scheduled to stay in the vicinity of the lake, looking into a complaint about an abandoned car on the West Lake Road. Unfortunately, this car was a ten-year-old Honda, not a recent model Taurus. He hoped that he had been persuasive in his argument that the complainant should be patient.

Later, after he had addressed a number of other minor problems that he had either resolved or put on hold, the day was drawing to a close. Sam set off for home by way of a back road that served as a short cut to the main road back to Cumberland. He was looking ahead to a good dinner and a cozy evening with his wife. It was somewhere near the junction of county road 26 with the road to Cumberland that he passed an abandoned farm.

The small complex of buildings sat some fifty feet off the road. All of the windows of the house appeared to be broken out; the door that was visible from the road was hanging from one hinge. The barn was in worse shape than the house. One or more heavy snows over the years had caved in the roof, damaging a supporting wall, so that the building looked decidedly lopsided. The ramp that once had allowed farm machinery to move into and out of the barn was now a bed of weeds and rocks. What had once apparently been a pen for cattle had disintegrated into a jumble of rotting wooden posts and fallen fences. A former owner had started to erect a silo, but it stood unfinished beside the barn, a sad reminder of yet another failed venture on the hill above the lake. Even a big old maple tree near the house looked to be dead or dying.

Sam found himself wondering about the presence of these abandoned farms. One could not drive two miles over the back roads above the lake without encountering one or more of them. What had happened to their owners? Why were they left to decay untended? Why had no one thought to dismantle them, if not to rebuild, at least to sell off the lumber and furnishings? He wondered who possessed title to the land on which they sat. By the time he had reached the Cumberland road, Sam had begun to think of other things. Such as that missing rental car.

He pulled his car over to the side of the road and sat there for a minute, pondering the idea that was taking shape in his mind. Abandoned farms. The missing Ford Taurus. Might it be possible that a car could be hidden somewhere on an abandoned farm?

Perhaps in a ruined barn? Turning his car around at the intersection of the two roads proved to be easy inasmuch as there was no other car in sight. It was barely more than a mile back to the farm about which he had been musing only moments before. He turned off the road and drove about two car lengths before it became apparent that he would do better on foot. The approach to the barn was cluttered with junk and fallen limbs from the maple tree. He made his way carefully over the uneven ground and up the ramp to the barn. The entrance to the barn was not wide. The door could not be budged along its rusted track.

Sam thought that the opening, while not wide enough to admit a tractor or other large piece of farm machinery, might be wide enough for a car. He walked into the barn and into darkness, relieved only by a small amount of late afternoon light coming through a hole in what was left of the roof. No sense in stumbling around in the dark, he thought. Better get the flashlight.

Armed with the light he always carried in his glove box, Sam surveyed the barn's interior. There was considerable space, more than the view of the barn from outside had led him to believe. That space was filled with various pieces of old farm machinery and implements. Sam, who did not come from a family of farmers, had no idea what most of them had been used for, nor did he care. What attracted his interest was a car at the very back of the barn, where it was almost hidden from view by a tractor. At first he had not been sure it was a car. It had been partially covered by a dusty, tattered piece of canvas. In the dark it would have been invisible. But the flashlight picked up a wheel and part of a fender. The hubcap was a bright silver, itself a shining light in the otherwise gloomy barn.

Sam followed the beam of his flashlight to the car. It had taken considerable skill to maneuver it into the corner where it now sat beside the tractor. It would not have been easy, but with the car's headlights on it would have been possible for a good driver. And Sam was thinking that Sandra Rackley's killer had been a good driver. He pulled the canvas tarp off the car, revealing a vehicle which was obviously of more recent vintage than anything else in the barn. They could stop looking for the Taurus. He had memorized the number on the license plates of the missing rental car, and this car's plates were a match.

Back in his own car, Sam called the sheriff. It was now late enough in the day that he doubted she would be in the office, so he tried her home. No luck. Rather than leave a message, he decided to try the number she had given him the previous week, the number of a Kevin Whitman. It was common knowledge in the office that the sheriff was seeing quite a bit of this man. Sam was of the opinion that his boss should be getting married, but he wasn't sure how he felt about the fact that she was probably sleeping with this Whitman person. It was none of his business, of course, but he didn't think it looked good. At least she was doing it at his place, not hers. Not in Cumberland, less than a mile from the building with the words Cumberland County Sheriff's Department over the entrance in bold black letters.

———

Sheriff Kelleher felt very much as her deputy did about having Kevin stay overnight in her house in Cumberland. She had decided some time ago, however, that she could live with a compromise solution to her problem. She didn't wish to stir up gossip about her private life that would reflect negatively on her office. But she did want to spend time with Kevin, as much time as she could manage with her busy schedule. And that meant the occasional night, which of course meant that they would be sharing a bed. Their relationship had progressed well beyond any discussion of who should sleep on the couch.

Carol was smiling at the thought just as the phone rang. It was Kevin who grabbed the phone.

"Hello, this is Deputy Sheriff Bridges. Would the sheriff be over there by any chance?"

Kevin looked across the room at her, comfortably ensconced on the couch. He was less bothered that Bridges knew where to find her than that what had promised to be a pleasant evening might now be at risk.

"Why, yes, as a matter of fact she is," he answered. "Just a minute."

Carol mouthed the word *who*. Kevin covered the phone and said it was the deputy sheriff.

She was as unhappy with this interruption of their evening as he was. They hadn't even started dinner yet, much less gone on to dessert. But she took the phone from him.

"What is it, Sam?"

"I think I have some good news. I've found the Rackley woman's rental car."

Carol's mood shifted instantly from disappointment to excitement.

"Are you sure? Where is it?"

"Yes, I'm sure — matches the description we've got of it, and the plates are definitely the ones we've been looking for. It's tucked away in an abandoned barn not far off the West Lake Road. Know that old shortcut to Cumberland from south of Blue Water Point? Well, that's where it is. I'm over there right now, and I thought you'd want to know right away."

Amazing, Carol thought. It's been right here near the ravine all along. Probably not more than three miles from where I'm standing. She looked at Kevin, who was silently trying to ask her what this obviously important call was all about.

Carol held the phone to her chest and told him that the car had been found.

"This is big, Sam. Look, we're not in a good position to do anything about it tonight. But I don't think we should leave it there without someone to keep an eye on it. Someone might have seen your car, come back to check out what's going on. Or maybe the person who put it in the barn comes by now and then to see if it's still there. No, I want an all-night watch on the place. Sorry about that. Who's been off during the day?"

"Barrett, I think."

"Yes, that sounds right. Okay, I want you to call, get him over there to relieve you. But stay until he gets there. By the way, are the keys in the ignition?"

"I don't think so. It's hard to see into the car in this light, but I can't see any keys."

"Okay, another mystery. Please tell your wife I'm sorry if I messed up your dinner hour. I'll go over there in the morning, and I'd like you to come along. We'll see what this car tells us about our murderer."

"It is murder, for sure?" Sam asked.

"I'm not a betting person, Sam, but if I were, I'd say yes."

Kevin was relieved that Carol would be staying the night, not rushing off on law enforcement business. But he was also excited by the discovery of the rental car. She gave him such details as Bridges had passed along, with emphasis on the fact the car had been hidden within walking distance of the cottage.

"This calls for a drink," he announced. "What'll it be?"

"Beer. Whatever you've got that's cold," she said. "You know, I hope Sam doesn't think I'd rather spend the evening with you than get cracking on the Rackley case. He didn't say so, but something in his voice gave me the impression he wished I'd said I'd come on over to that barn. Now, tonight."

"I doubt it. What good would that have done? Anyway, you've got the best of both worlds, right? The cottage tonight, then a five minute ride, max, in the morning."

"I hope so. Anyway, it won't be long before we take that car apart — figuratively speaking, that is."

"Maybe literally," Kevin suggested. "Let's hope there are at least some good prints, but frankly I don't think you'll find any. Anybody who'd go to the trouble of removing fingerprints from dollar bills in a woman's wallet isn't going to leave them on the steering wheel of a car."

Gradually the conversation shifted back to more personal matters, dinner was cooked and served, and Kevin and Carol retired to the bedroom for what would be their last night together for several weeks. Neither of them realized that at the time, of course.

CHAPTER 28

Cumberland County law enforcement personnel were out in force the next morning. Four uniformed members of Sheriff Kelleher's team were gathered around a locked car in the abandoned barn west of Blue Water Point when the sheriff herself arrived. Kevin was not with her. Both of them thought it better not to make his informal role in her investigation of Sandra Rackley's death too obvious. Moreover, there was no point in encouraging jokes among the men about their boss and this man in her life having made the morning's trip from bed to barn.

The officers may not have had at their disposal all of the state-of-the-art equipment that their colleagues down in the city had, but they knew how to open a locked car without a key, and they did it quickly. Carefully, their hands gloved, they went through the car from glove box to trunk. And found nothing of interest other than the paperwork for the rental, and it only confirmed what they already knew. Going over the car for fingerprints took quite a bit longer, but they found nary a one, not even a partial. Kevin had been right. Whoever had hidden the Taurus had been exceedingly thorough.

Carol gave Bridges the task of contacting the rental agency and the somewhat more time-consuming business of arranging to get a replacement key. Moving the car so that it could be hooked up to a tow truck was difficult, but not impossible, so by noon it was on its way to Cumberland where it was destined to receive an even more thorough going over. Before heading back to her office, Carol called and passed along to Kevin the fact that the car was unfortunately free of prints. Just what was it that she now knew that she hadn't known or assumed before Sam's discovery of the Taurus? Not much, she thought. In fact, to be completely honest about it, the answer was nothing.

———

Kevin had not expected that any fingerprints would be found on the rental car. He had been sure that the door handle and the steering wheel would have been wiped clean. He had hoped that there might be a few prints elsewhere in places the man who had killed Rackley and hidden the car had touched, but they were clearly dealing with someone who was leaving nothing to chance. Not a print on the wallet. Not a print on the car.

Like Carol, he had decided that the discovery of the car had not been of much help. It had initially seemed like an important breakthrough, but the more he thought about it the more its importance faded. Kevin was feeling frustrated. It might be a good idea, he thought, to put the investigation into Sandra Rackley's death on hold for awhile, to turn his attention back to opera and the piece he was supposed to write for publication in the fall issue of *Opera News*. It wasn't his investigation in any event. Perhaps he should leave matters of law enforcement in this corner of upstate New York to the sheriff's department. To Carol Kelleher. He'd help out if she asked, but he didn't need to let the Rackley case become an obsession.

It was while he was mentally reordering his agenda that his neighbor Mike Snyder called.

"Kevin," the familiar voice boomed out over the phone. "You said you'd like my help putting your dock back in the water. How about today? I took the day off to get my annual physical, and it went much faster than I expected. So I've got most of the rest of the day. Want to do it?"

In his preoccupation with the woman in the ravine, Kevin had almost forgotten the dock.

"Why, sure. If you think the water's not too cold."

"I've got a wetsuit. You can use it if you want to. You know me — I'm supposed to be tough, one of those all-weather guys. No, I don't think we'll have a problem."

If Mike was willing to tackle the job in water too cold for casual swimming, why should he argue with him? Kevin was only too ready to accept the offer of the wetsuit.

It was just after two in the afternoon that they set about the task of moving the dock sections to the beach and into the lake. It was hard work, harder for Kevin, who quickly realized that he wasn't in as good shape as Mike. But after three quarters of an hour of manipulating the sections into place and aligning the dock with the cottage to Kevin's satisfaction, the job was finished.

They had changed into dry clothes, and by way of thanks for help with the dock, Kevin invited Mike in for a beer. After no more than two minutes of pleasant banter, Mike raised a question that had obviously been on his mind.

144

"You got a problem of some kind?"

"Problem?" Kevin didn't know what he was talking about.

"I don't want to sound nosy," Mike said, sounding nosy, "but there's been a police car over here several times since you came back. Sat there behind your cottage all night once. Gloria thinks it may have been there overnight other times, too."

So, Kevin thought, the neighbors are noticing that the sheriff's been spending time at my place.

"I guess you're right," he said. "Belongs to our sheriff."

He left it at that, interested to see how far Mike would push for more information.

Mike looked as if he were going to out wait Kevin. It didn't work.

"I'm sorry," he said. "It's none of my business, I know. But I was worried that you might be in some kind of trouble. And there's been another car parked here a few times, a Buick, I think it is. I know it's been here overnight, three, four times. Gloria said I should ask you about what's going on."

Kevin' face broke into a smile. Gloria might well have been curious, but he was sure that Mike was equally eager to know "what's going on."

"I'll let you in on a secret," he said, guessing that what he was about to tell Mike was no secret to his neighbor. "Both cars belong to the sheriff. Her name is Carol Kelleher, as I'm sure you know."

Sure you know, Kevin was thinking, because she treated you as a suspect for awhile during the investigation of the Britingham murder the previous summer.

"Anyway, I'm having what they used to call an affair, and the sheriff is what they used to call my significant other. Does that surprise you?"

Mike now looked embarrassed.

"I'm sorry," he repeated himself. "I didn't know. Well, I'd heard a rumor — you know how it is, people talk, usually don't know what they're talking about. It just didn't seem —"

Mike let his thought trail off. Kevin found the situation amusing. Mike could hardly be blamed for being surprised to find his neighbor cohabiting with the county sheriff. After all, his relationship with Carol had not begun until days before he moved back to the city in September, he had never discussed it with Mike, and he had only been back at the lake for two weeks. But armed with local gossip, Mike had decided that he had to satisfy his curiosity about this new development in Kevin's life.

"Look, I'm trying to be discrete," Kevin said. "I'm not making a big thing of it. But I'm not pretending that Carol and I aren't spending time together. She's a big girl and I'm — well, I'm a 39-year-old bachelor. We get along. But you say you've heard people talking. What are they saying?"

Now it was Kevin who was curious. Was his relationship with the sheriff a big story around the lake? He couldn't imagine why it would be, but he knew that small towns were notorious as incubators of gossip. And Crooked Lake was only a somewhat elongated version of a small town.

"Like I said, people sort of latch onto little things." Mike hemmed and hawed for a moment, trying to find the best way to put it. "I don't think it's as much about you sleeping with her — oh, I'm sorry, I didn't mean that —"

Kevin interrupted. "Yes, you did, and it's all right. Stop saying you're sorry. I guess if I wanted to discourage rumors, I'd tell her not to park back of the cottage."

"Well, okay, if it doesn't bother you. Sure, people are interested in what you and she are doing — you know, after dark. Hell, this place is one big rumor mill. Anyway, everyone knows who she is, but not many people know who you are. So I hear lots of questions about you. Who's this Kevin Whitman? Where did he come from? Is he her type? As if anyone really knows what her type is. I think you're going to become a local celebrity. Ready for that?"

"Probably not. But I'll cope, as long as the *Gazette* doesn't come asking for an interview."

"You know what the latest rumor is?"

Kevin had no idea and wasn't sure he wanted to know.

"There's talk that you've been put on the sheriff's payroll. Sort of an undercover agent in charge of the investigation into the death of that woman they found up the ravine. What do you make of that?"

"Can't imagine who thought that one up."

"So you're not working undercover for the sheriff?"

"Of course not," Kevin said, a hint of exasperation in his voice. "Good grief, I'm a professor of music. Do people up here think I'm ex-FBI or something?"

"I'll bet someone had trouble with the idea of the sheriff in a romantic relationship, so he came up with the undercover agent theory."

Kevin wasn't buying Mike's explanation.

"Pretty weird theory, if you ask me."

"Maybe, but I heard you were grilling Phil Chambers down at Cobb's Marina. Asking questions about somebody's boat. Trying to get Phil to talk about that business out at the Cedar Post. What's that all about?"

"Where'd you hear this?" Kevin was ready to dismiss gossip about his relationship with Carol. After all, it was true, and he hadn't tried very hard to hide it. But why would anyone think he was the sheriff's undercover investigator? Even if he was, in a manner of speaking.

"Got it from Phil himself. He's got some idea that the sheriff put you up to it — that you're working for her."

Kevin didn't say so, but he found this information disturbing. For Mike's benefit he laughed at the idea that Chambers thought he was working for the sheriff. But he wasn't amused. He hadn't realized that he had been so obvious when he spoke with Phil Chambers. For the first time since returning to the lake, Kevin worried that he might, with the best of intentions, be impeding Carol's search for Sandra Rackley's murderer.

CHAPTER 29

Ms. Maltbie rapped on the door and, pushing it open, got the sheriff's attention.

"Mail just came, and I think this one is for your eyes only," she said, handing Carol a single page typed note, together with the envelope in which it had come.

Carol could not recall her secretary ever using that expression before. The note must be out of the ordinary. She leaned back in her chair and read the following message.

Dear Sheriff Kelleher:

I have hesitated about writing this letter. But as a dedicated feminist, I am proud that our sheriff is a woman, and I would not want your image tarnished by a scandal. Although you presumably regard it as a private matter, your relationship with a Crooked Lake resident named Kevin Whitman is no secret to many of your fellow citizens. What you may not know is that Mr. Whitman, who lives for much of the year in the city, is romantically involved with a woman down there. I happen to know that this is not a casual affair, but a very intense relationship. He regularly spends many a night with this woman, and rumor has it that they are contemplating marriage.

It could become awkward for you professionally, not to mention personally, if it became widely known in our area that the man with whom you are keeping company is about to be married to another woman. The resulting gossip could undermine the fine job you are doing as head of law enforcement in our county.

This may be none of my business, but I am sincerely concerned that your relationship with Mr. Whitman could jeopardize your career. Whatever you choose to do, please know that you have my very best wishes.

An admirer.

Carol put the letter down on her desk and stared for a moment at the opposite wall. Then she picked it up and read it through again, but a second reading did nothing to change the first impression it had made. It was all very straightforward, even if the writer's rationale for the message was patently disingenuous. Kevin Whitman — her Kevin Whitman — stood accused of leading a double life. If true, he was treating her shabbily, using her for his transient pleasure while his real interests lay elsewhere. If true. But why would someone be making these allegations if they were not true? Carol found herself counting the weeks — no, the days. How many had there been since she had met him, since she had first gone to bed with him? Very few. They had spent less than a week together after Labor Day at the end of the previous summer. Then one weekend in the city, and one in Cumberland over the next seven months. And now three weeks in May. She knew no one who was part of his other life, his real life, down in the city. No one at the college where he taught, no one with whom he shared nights at the opera, no one with whom he shared the occasional drink and dinner. He was a charming and a bright man who fancied himself a detective. And he was good in bed. But she had to admit that she really knew next to nothing about him. If she were asked to write his biographical profile, it would probably come in at fifty words. Or less.

Summer on Crooked Lake suddenly looked much bleaker than it had only minutes earlier when she had been anticipating with pleasure another night at Kevin Whitman's cottage.

———

"I think you should look at this," Carol said, handing Kevin the letter as she sat down on the couch. She had debated calling and canceling her plan to join him for the evening. But she knew that she had to confront him with the message from the "admirer," and she couldn't do it over the phone. So she had traded the official car for her old Buick and driven over to Blue Water Point. On the surface, nothing had changed. The setting sun gave the cottage a warm late spring glow. Whatever Kevin had cooking in the oven smelled good. And he was looking unusually sharp in a maroon turtleneck, beige slacks, and loafers. It was hard to believe that this man with whom she planned to spend the night was actually intimately involved with another woman. But the letter she had given him to read said otherwise.

"What is it?" he asked, a quick glance at the signature — or lack thereof — telling him nothing.

"Read it." Carol tried to keep her voice in neutral.

Kevin read it. It took him less than a minute. He handed it back to her and scowled.

"This is absolute nonsense," he said. "It's all a lie. Who on earth did it come from? There's no name. Any address on the envelope?"

Carol had expected him to dismiss the message, whether it was true or not.

"No, no address. I thought maybe you could tell me who wrote it — who might have written it. It had a city postmark — that's your world, not mine."

"But it sounds as if the person who wrote it is from around here — talks about 'our' sheriff."

Carol didn't choose to comment.

"You surely don't think there's anything to it," Kevin said, aware from her tone of voice and now her silence that she might think just that.

"How would I know? You've spent the better part of eight months in the city since last summer. I have no idea what you've been doing with your time. Or with whom."

"But Carol," he protested, "this isn't me. You know me. I wouldn't do something like this to you. Except for you, I've hardly talked to another woman since my divorce. Just colleagues at the university. This letter, this — it's insane."

"What kind of women are these colleagues?"

"What?" Kevin looked at her as if she had lost her mind. "Come on, Carol. I can't imagine who is supposed to be having an affair with me because there is no affair. Not with a faculty colleague, not with anyone."

Carol started to say something and then stopped. She had noticed the change in Kevin's expression. It was obvious that something had occurred to him.

"Wait a minute," he said. "I think I may know who wrote that letter."

He got up and walked over to the kitchen door.

"If I'm right, you're going to have a hard time believing this. How'd you like a drink while I tell you?"

"No, I'll pass on the drink. I'm already having a hard time believing any of this. Just sit down and tell me."

Kevin resumed his seat, wondering just how he would explain Jennifer Laseur's infatuation with him.

"You remember I told you I had a teaching assistant, the one who took my class when I came up to the lake a few weeks ago. Well, she thinks — I'm not sure how to put this — let's say she's got a crush on me, fancies that we've got some kind of special relationship. It's all in her head. I've never encouraged her, but with her it's like an obsession. So I can believe she'd be jealous of you. I'll bet that she wrote the letter and that she's the woman I'm supposed to be having an affair with. If I'm right, then she's really sick, and I mean sick enough to need professional help."

It was clear to Kevin even before she said anything that Carol was not satisfied with his explanation of the letter. She was now mad.

"I'm leaving, Kevin," she said as she got up from the couch. "Enjoy your dinner."

"But why? What's wrong?" he asked.

"What's wrong is that you can't get your stories straight. You told me your assistant was a guy. Remember? Now it turns out it's a girl. A girl with a crush on you. A girl you've never mentioned to me. And I think I can see why."

Kevin got up to head her off as she headed for the door.

"Carol, this is crazy. We've got to talk."

"I can't. Not now. Please let me by."

He did as she asked and watched, stunned, as she closed the door behind her.

CHAPTER 30

It had been a bad night. Kevin had slept, but only fitfully. He had tried to get his mind off the letter and Carol's reaction to it, but nothing had worked. Not a novel, which he had started twice before tossing it aside. Not TV, which rarely interested him anyway. Not a couple of beers, which only woke him up to use the bathroom. And once awake, he had had trouble getting back to sleep. Tired, cross, and discouraged, he called it a night shortly after six in the morning.

The weather, as if ordered up to dampen his already bad mood, had turned unpleasant overnight. The rain hadn't started, but it was on the way. The skies were gray, and a gusty wind was pushing waves down the lake and snapping the flags on his neighbors' docks. In spite of the weather, Kevin slid into a windbreaker, poured himself a cup of coffee, and headed for the beach. He picked up one of his Adirondack chairs and carried it out to the end of the dock, where he sat to sip his coffee and watch a few swallows, up early as he was, skim across the water in search of insects on which to feed.

He let his mind wander back to the previous August, when at an hour not much earlier than this, he had returned from a swim to find a dead man on his dock. A dead man lying almost exactly where he was now sitting. It was the shocking beginning of what was to be one of the more exciting experiences of his life. It was an experience that had brought the sheriff of Cumberland County into his life, initially to regard him as a suspect in the death of John Britingham, then to welcome his contributions to her investigation of the crime, and ultimately to become the woman he loved and hoped one day to marry.

But now a simple one-page letter had come between him and the sheriff. Between him and Carol Kelleher. His thoughts were muddled. One minute he found himself worried about his relationship with Carol. No, worried was much too mild a word. He was in a state of near panic at the thought of losing her. But in the next minute his thoughts turned to Jennifer Laseur, his assistant at the college and the person he suspected of having written the letter.

There was no proof that Jennifer was responsible for the malicious letter. But who else could it have been? He could think of only a few close colleagues at the college who even knew about his relationship with the sheriff, and he couldn't imagine any of them composing and sending such a letter. It was possible, of course, that in spite of the city postmark, somebody from the Crooked Lake area had written it. He was aware that there were local people who knew — or thought they knew — that he and Carol had been spending time together. Mike Snyder had confirmed that. And the letter left the impression that the writer was from the upstate area. But with the exception of a few good neighbors on Blue Water Point, he knew of no one from around the lake who had any knowledge of the life he led in the city. And so, by a process of elimination, the letter writer had to be Jennifer Laseur.

He had never mentioned Carol to Jennifer, much less discussed his relationship with the sheriff with her. Yet there was the mysteriously missing e-mail from Carol, the one asking for the whereabouts of a key to his cottage so that she could retrieve her gun. He had concluded that Jennifer had opened it and then deleted it so that he would not know she had seen it. Carol's message would have disturbed Jennifer, even if it had not contained language suggesting intimacy. It would have told her that there was another woman in his life, a woman who may have spent the night in his cottage. And knowing something of his role in Jennifer's fantasy life, he could well imagine that she would not rest until she had discovered who that other woman was. She was a smart girl. It would not have taken her long to identify Carol as the sheriff of Cumberland County, and she had probably invested more time and effort in gathering information on the sheriff's extracurricular activities. Damn it, he thought, why doesn't the girl concentrate on the violin?

The problem, of course, was what to do about Carol and Jennifer. He had made a silly mistake in referring to his assistant as "him." Carol had remembered, and was now assuming that he was hiding a relationship with Jennifer. Why had he lied about his assistant's gender? He hadn't even thought about it — it had just come out that way. Perhaps subconsciously he had thought Carol would be uncomfortable — even jealous? — if she knew his assistant was a young woman. And now, now that she knew the truth, she was indeed behaving as if she were jealous. No, he thought, that's not right. In fairness to Carol, she was behaving as if she were angry with him because he had lied to her. He could hardly blame her.

Somehow he would have to talk to Jennifer, convince her that what she had done was hurtful to him. And to Carol. Which would mean he would have to be brutally frank and tell Jennifer that there was no room for her in his life. He had avoided doing that for months, hoping that she would wake up to reality and forget her sophomoric infatuation with him. Now it might be too late.

Ideally, he would persuade Jennifer to apologize to Carol, owning up to her authorship of the letter and confessing that it was all a fabrication. But the more he thought about it, the less likely it seemed that she would do anything of the kind. Even if she could accept the truth that he was not interested in her romantically, she would probably find an apology too painful and humiliating. If Jennifer would not apologize, it would be up to him to convince Carol that the letter was a lie. And his effort to do that the previous evening had been a disaster, which didn't augur well for his ability to change her mind about him. What could he say? He tried to think about how to approach the subject, but no idea that occurred to him seemed promising. He felt trapped, trapped by a young woman's crush on him and his own little white lie.

Maybe he could do something which would change her mind about him. No, not flowers. Not poetry. All of the usual "let's kiss and make up" gambits were too puerile for a 40-year-old college professor. He quickly amended that thought, correcting his age to 39. No more lies, he thought, not to her, not to himself. But what if he could do something which could help her bring the Rackley case to closure? Something really big, like identifying the woman's killer.

Of course, it had only been a couple of days earlier that he had been telling himself that he ought to be less involved in Carol's investigation of that crime. Mike Snyder's story of rumors about him having become an undercover investigator for the sheriff had convinced him that it was time to back off. Yet now he was thinking of becoming even more involved. And he would have to do it without Carol's permission. He doubted that in her present frame of mind she would want him as a partner. Even a partner at arm's length.

On a cloudless morning, the sun would have made its appearance above the hill across the lake. Not today. It was beginning to mist and Kevin was aware that his windbreaker was becoming damp. His coffee was cold. He got up and headed back to the cottage.

Later, over toast and eggs, he turned his attention back to the matter of what he might do that would put him back in Carol's good graces — and Carol back in his bed. He soon found himself thinking about the Chicago connection, the question of whether there were people in the area of Crooked Lake who might have been in Chicago and had sex with Sandra Rackley back in early December. People who might have killed her when she came to Crooked Lake in March.

Who might such people be? What citizens of the lake area would have reason to be in Chicago? He started making a mental list. There could be former residents of the Windy City who had gone back to visit friends. There could be locals who had never lived in Chicago but who had relatives there, sons or daughters in college at Northwestern or DePaul or the University of Chicago. He'd have to look it up, but there were probably at least a dozen institutions of higher learning in that city and its environs. There could be people who had business there. He tried to think of businesses that might necessitate such a trip, but gave it up. He'd brainstorm that later. There was a lot he'd have to do later, unless he got lucky. This search for the Chicago connection was going to be difficult. The more he thought about it, the more he found himself thinking about six degrees of Kevin Bacon. At least he wouldn't have to worry about everyone in the area. He could concentrate on the adult men.

The one person he knew of who very probably had Chicago ties was the owner of the *Second City* down at Cobb's Marina, a man whose car had Illinois license plates. Kevin wondered how easy it would be to locate all the cars in the vicinity with Illinois plates. Not easy, he decided. He couldn't just drive up and down the lake and into the nearby towns looking for such cars. Nor would it be a very sensible way to use his time. The Illinois plates were probably irrelevant anyway, a red herring. Odds were that Rackley's killer had registered his car right here in Cumberland County. But he would have to follow up on his plan to talk with Mel Slavin. It was time for him to get in touch with

Phil Chambers, see if he had laid the groundwork for getting him aboard the *Second City*.

Later that morning, Kevin called the marina hoping to speak with Chambers, but he wasn't there. Probably out on the lake on the *Second City*, the man who answered the phone said. Kevin decided against leaving a message. He'd try again later, maybe even drive down to the marina. Now what, he wondered. Actually doing something to track down Rackley's killer was going to be much harder than simply making a list of people who might have had a reason to be in Chicago in December. He felt stymied.

Without a plan, Kevin spent much of the rest of the morning in a funk. He had no interest in tackling the essay he had promised to write for *Opera News*. He slipped the Domingo recording of Verdi's *Otello* into the DVD player and sat down to enjoy the haunting first act duet, music that gave no hint of the tragedy which lay ahead for the Moor and Desdemona. But he was restless and was soon pacing about, only half paying attention to the music.

Kevin's thoughts kept coming back to Carol and Jennifer, to Sandra Rackley and Chicago. He finally turned the opera off and went back to the study to try Chambers again. It was while he was searching for the notepad on which he had written the marina's number that he saw an unopened envelope addressed to him in the small pile of the previous day's mail. He knew why he hadn't opened it. His mind had been on Carol, and a routine communication from his professional association didn't interest him. Kevin hadn't even attended the association's annual conference last year, and had given no thought to attending this year. He was about to pick up the phone when an idea occurred to him. There was another reason why someone from the area might have visited Chicago, he thought. He might have been going to a professional conference. Chicago is a convention city, a city that probably hosts the meetings of many organizations. What if someone from the area had been in Chicago back in December for the purpose of attending such a meeting? And while there had met the ill-fated Sandra Rackley in Grant Park?

Not likely, he thought, but worth an inquiry. He would contact the Chicago Chamber of Commerce, which presumably would be able to tell him what organizations had convened there in December. That would be the easy part. Whether any area residents belonged to those organizations would be much harder to establish, but trying to find out would be infinitely more sensible than hunting for cars with Illinois license plates. At least he would be doing something, and that would be good therapy for his bad mood. He'd get on it that afternoon.

Feeling slightly better about things, Kevin dialed the marina again.

CHAPTER 31

There were more things for the sheriff of Cumberland County to do as the Memorial Day weekend approached than massaging her anger with Kevin Whitman. Unlike Kevin, she had a job that demanded her attention, and fortunately for her frame of mind, that job had suddenly become much more demanding. It even threatened to put her investigation of Sandra Rackley's death on the shelf for the time being.

She had, of course, thought about Kevin and his other life off and on all night, and like him, she had not slept well. But when she climbed out of bed the next morning, she told herself that the ball was now in his court, and that she would neither call him nor spend another minute thinking about this abrupt and unexpected end to their brief affair. If he had something important to say, something that made sense, she would listen. Until then, whenever then turned out to be, she would concentrate on being an effective sheriff at what was always a challenging time of the year.

The evidence that it was going to be a challenging time was everywhere to be seen. More cottages were occupied each day. More cars were on the roads. More boats were on the lake. More people were calling about some problem — vandalization of property over the winter, disputes about property lines, questions about matters such as the level of the lake and septic tank inspections, which were not her responsibility and had to be referred to the proper jurisdictions. That morning had brought a call of the sort she expected would become much more common as the summer season progressed. It concerned the jet ski menace.

When she had been growing up in the area, no one had heard of jet skis. Now they were ubiquitous — loud, fast, and apparently a load of fun for the many people who owned them. But the people who operated them, mostly teenagers and somewhat older guys who weren't quite ready to abandon their teenage ways, kept on doing stupid things. Bridges had come into her office that morning with a report that two skiers had collided somewhere north of Southport. Moreover, they had collided within fifty feet of shore, having ignored the rule that was designed to protect swimmers and their docks and floats. And they had obviously been going much too fast for the circumstances. Carol hoped that an investigation would not also lead to evidence that the operators were underage. There were always complaints about kids on jet skis. The previous summer, one complainant had reported a nine-year-old whipping around in what were supposed to be figures of eight in front of her cottage.

But rarely did anything come of these episodes except the occasional warning. Things would calm down for a few days, and then a rude or thoughtless operator and an especially sensitive neighbor would be at it again. In the case at hand, the need to spend a handsome sum to repair their crafts might serve as the best deterrent to future grandstanding. In any event, she would send one of her men down to the scene of the imbroglio.

The clock on the wall said it was 11:50. Where had the morning gone? Carol wondered. She hadn't had time to think about the Rackley case, much less do anything about it. And she was hungry. Did appetite increase when things went bad? Was it one of nature's coping mechanisms? She hadn't brought a sandwich from home, and she didn't think she could tolerate another bad lunch at the Rustic Inn. It would entail a slightly longer lunch hour, but Carol decided to drive over to the Cedar Post.

As she made the turn to go north on West Lake Road, she realized that she had not eaten at the Post since her dinner with Kevin at the end of April. The dinner that marked the beginning of another summer in each other's lives. Had she unconsciously thought about having lunch there because of her falling out with Kevin? She doubted it. She just wanted a decent lunch, but she couldn't shake off the thought that it was at the Cedar Post that they had rekindled the excitement of sharing ideas about a criminal investigation. And she remembered how quickly her mixed feelings about their unusual relationship vanished that evening. They had again gone to bed together the very next night. Well, not this time. She'd settle for a medium-well buffalo burger.

The parking lot was fairly crowded, but there were a couple of places out back. Carol took one of them and walked into the Post. It was bustling as usual, but there were a few seats at the end of the bar, and inasmuch as she was dining alone, Carol headed in that direction.

"Long time, no see," was the cheerful greeting of the woman behind the bar as she turned her attention to Carol.

"I'm afraid that's true," Carol replied, smiling at Ginny Smith, everyone's favorite bartender. "How've you been?"

"Great. Money's tight, what with my two youngest in braces. But what else is new?"

Carol liked Ginny, but continued to be surprised that she earned her living behind a bar. Smart, happily married, raising what was reputed to be a nice family. Why pour drinks for a living? The story seemed to be that she had taken the job at the Cedar Post because it let her work at convenient hours when she was raising young kids, and now that they were older and self-sufficient after school, she had stayed back of the bar because she liked it. Liked the informal camaraderie with the customers, liked the tips. Or so it was said. Carol could believe that it was true. Today she was glad to have someone pleasant to talk with.

"Not much," she answered Ginny's query about what else was new. It wasn't true, but she had no intention of discussing personal matters. At least not her own. "You've got kids in braces? I can't believe they're that old."

"Neither can I. The girls are 14 and 12. And Josh is 17. It's enough to make a gal feel her age. Am I right, you don't have kids?"

"Afraid not. I'm not even married. But you know that."

"Yeah. No secrets around here. But I do hear that you've been seeing a guy who lives down the lake. Talk is he's a nice person. Good looking, good talker, good personality. I don't like some of the gossip people bring into the bar, but I'm always happy to share the pleasant stuff."

This wasn't the direction Carol had wanted the conversation to go. Yes, Kevin was good looking, if not exactly handsome. And she had to agree that he was a fun conversationalist and had a winning personality. Unfortunately, he might also have been two-timing her, and that tended to cancel out all his virtues.

Ginny had taken note of Carol's silence.

"I hope that wasn't out of place, my talking about this guy," she said. "None of my business. But I hope it works out. Maybe one day you'll be getting braces for your kids."

The conversation shifted to other things, including a brief mention of the Phil Chambers business. And then Ginny was off to tend to the needs of other customers. Carol ate her burger in silence, pondering the two conflicting pictures of Kevin Whitman that Ginny had unwittingly churned up in her mind. She had said to herself that she wouldn't give another thought to him, and here she was inviting indigestion by doing just what she had said she wouldn't do.

———

It was 2:30 p.m., and she hadn't gotten anything done. It seemed as if everything she turned to ran into some problem or other. Calls weren't answered. A file was missing. A man who had a two o'clock appointment failed to show up. Even the ever-reliable Ms. Maltbie had gone home sick. Carol was frustrated. The hell with it, she said to herself. I've got to get out of here, take a deep breath.

Just then, Bill Parsons came into the office. She saw less of Bill than most of her fellow officers, and that was because he spent most of his time patrolling Crooked Lake in a boat, keeping an eye open for problems and reminding lake residents of the rules of the road by his presence.

"Hi, Bill. Got a problem?"

"As a matter of fact, I do, Sheriff. Robby had a call, something about his kid getting suspended from school for fighting, and he had to take off. You know we have that 'two men in the boat' rule, so I parked it up by West Branch and thought I'd see what needed doing here."

Carol suddenly knew what she was going to do with the rest of her day.

"Let's go. I'm going to be your partner for the rest of the day. I've been going stir crazy here. Anyway, I haven't been in the patrol boat since last summer. It's about time I get to see what you're doing, burning up all that gas cruising up and down the lake."

She gave Bill her best smile, grabbed her jacket, and followed him out the door to his car.

It was a little more than half an hour later that Officer Parsons backed the boat away from the dock with a practiced hand and turned it south down the west arm of the lake.

"I'm not checking up on you, you know," Carol said. "It's just that I was getting a headache and needed to get out of the office."

"I understand," he replied, letting it go at that.

Bill Parsons was the oldest officer in the sheriff's department. He'd been with the force for many years before Carol had come aboard, and had cultivated a reputation as a taciturn, soft-spoken lawman who had good people skills. She'd never had a complaint about him, and had pretty much left him alone to do his thing. His thing had been cruising the lake in an old but serviceable boat with the word *Sheriff* in large red letters adorning both its port and starboard sides.

The early morning wind out of the north had calmed down and the clouds were beginning to break up. Other than in emergencies, Bill never pushed the boat to its top speed. And its top speed was nothing special, which meant that he was never tempted to chase power boats whose drivers were behaving irresponsibly. This afternoon they motored along at a moderate pace toward Southport.

"Things look different from the water, don't they?" Carol said. "I'm not sure I recognize that area over there."

She pointed to a built-up stretch of shoreline, dominated by two large white homes with lawns that sloped down to the lake.

"Arrowhead Point." Bill played the role of tour guide.

"Oh, sure, I should have guessed," Carol said, getting oriented. "Any idea why it's called Arrowhead?"

"They say somebody was digging out for a new foundation a long time ago, found some old Indian arrowheads. Don't know whether that's true or not."

"Could be." Carol knew that the area had been inhabited by Native American tribes long before the Europeans had moved this far in from their settlements along the coast. But it didn't matter. Arrowhead it had been for as long as she could remember.

They passed several other points which Bill identified as they passed. Off Crowder Point, he turned the boat in toward shore to talk with a man fishing from a dock. Did he have a license? Well, no, not yet, he'd just arrived yesterday and had planned to get one as soon as he could. Okay, but do it right away. Bill had not written the man up, hadn't even asked for his name. Nor had he seemed to worry about how the sheriff would view his handling of this infraction of the law.

Carol had only smiled to herself. She'd have done the same thing.

A few minutes later they passed a spot where the flow of water off the hillside had carved a channel, pushing the shoreline a bit further out into the lake. Carol was pretty sure it was the mouth of the ravine in which Sandra Rackley's body had been found.

When they passed what she recognized as Kevin's cottage a little more than half a mile further on, she knew she had been right.

Carol had joined Parsons in the boat to forget a bad day, not to be reminded of her problems. She willed herself to think of other things.

It was while she was thinking of other things that Bill broke the silence that had lasted since they passed Blue Water Point.

"See that big boat over there?" he asked. Carol recognized Cobb's Marina and spotted the *Second City* at dock.

"I know, it's the *Second City*. I've been trying to figure out what it's doing here on Crooked Lake."

"I just don't get it," he said. "It's not just that one, but all these big, fancy boats you see more and more of. New, big, lots of power, lots of chrome. Have to cost a fortune. Why do people buy 'em? Showing off their money, I suppose. Didn't used to be this way. People had fishing boats. Power boats were the right size for this lake. But now these things. All this wealth. Where'd it come from?"

Bill shook his head, obviously displeased with what was happening on a lake he had lived on and loved for decades. Carol could sympathize with his feelings, but she knew that she would have to make time to get back to the marina to talk with the owner of *Second City*. Too big for Crooked Lake, but more importantly, a boat with a name that suggested a Chicago connection. And that took her back to Sandra Rackley.

The sheriff and Kevin Whitman may have gone their separate ways, but their thoughts at that very moment were surprisingly similar.

CHAPTER 32

Trying to keep his mind on something other than Carol, Kevin had tried several times to reach Phil Chambers by phone and had finally driven down to the marina. The *Second City* was there, but no one in the shop or on the docks seemed to know where he was or when he was due to return. Stymied on that front, Kevin returned to the cottage and put through a call to the Chicago Chamber of Commerce, hoping to obtain a list of associations of one kind or another that had convened in the Windy City around the first of December.

It quickly became apparent that this was not a routine request. He had first been told by a recorded voice that he should listen carefully because their menu had changed. He had listened, but none of the options promised useful information. Eventually, repeated requests to speak with a human being paid off, and he found himself speaking with a woman who sounded eager to help him but proved to be a disappointment. She didn't know whether they kept that kind of information, and didn't seem to know who might know. Kevin patiently asked for her supervisor, and after a twelve minute hiatus, found himself speaking with another woman. This one allowed that the chamber might have a list of conventions and conferences held in Chicago as far back as late fall. It might not be a complete list, she said, but it would probably cover all the big ones.

But having provided this promising piece of information, the woman started asking questions, questions that suggested she might not be willing to divulge the information Kevin was seeking.

"What do you need this for?" she asked.

Kevin hadn't expected the question, and he fumbled for an appropriate response. The truth was that he was looking for a convention that somebody in the Crooked Lake area might have attended late in the previous fall. A somebody who might have met a woman while in Chicago. A woman he might later have murdered. Kevin tried to imagine how such an explanation would sound to the woman on the other end of the phone line. She would probably think he was crazy. At a minimum, she would want to know on whose authority he was seeking this information, and how would he answer that question?

He chose to deal with the problem by pretending it was not a problem.

"I just assumed that the Chamber would be the best source of information about conventions in Chicago."

"We probably are, but I'm not sure we can rustle up that kind of information unless we know why you need it. I mean it would take some time. Is there some specific group or organization you need to know about?

Oh, come on, Kevin said to himself. You must have it all right there in some computer file. Just print it out and I'll tell you where to send it.

What he said to the woman was that it was a police matter. He'd risk Carol's wrath rather than abandon his quest for information that might — or might not — be of use in identifying Rackley's killer.

They sparred for a minute or two, Kevin providing some judiciously edited information about the case and the woman at the Chamber reluctantly agreeing to respond to his request. It might take some time, but she said she'd do it.

Secrecy, he thought, venting his irritation on the empty room after hanging up the phone. The government, banks, businesses, you name it — always wanting to know everything imaginable about us, but never wanting to divulge anything to us. Kevin could appreciate the importance of privacy, but why on earth should whether XYZ had met in Chicago in December be privileged information?

Unable to locate Phil Chambers and forced to wait several days before he would have the report from Chicago's Chamber of Commerce, Kevin decided to take a break from the day's frustrations by going out to dinner. His years of bachelorhood had accustomed him to dining alone, and he hadn't been to the Hilltop in almost a year. Word circulating around the lake was that the kitchen had improved. He'd give it a try.

Kevin changed to something slightly more upscale than the jeans and sweatshirt he had been wearing, and headed out at five o'clock for an early dinner.

The parking lot at the Hilltop was less than half full. He pulled into a spot not far from the restaurant's entrance, and as he did so, he noticed a car several spaces to his right. What caught his eye was the rear bumper of the old Pontiac. It had two colorful bumper stickers, one on either side. The one on the right contained a Chicago Cubs logo. Its companion spoke to the owner's interest in the Chicago Bulls. A man for all seasons, Kevin thought. The Cubs in summer, the Bulls in winter.

It was not until he was climbing out of his car that the realization that the bumper stickers proclaimed a Chicago connection kicked in. He had been interested in the Illinois license plate on Mr. Slavin's car down at Cobb's Marina; now here was another vehicle that got his adrenaline flowing. It had New York plates, to be sure, but it was unlikely that many New Yorkers would be strong supporters of two Chicago teams.

Kevin wasn't quite sure what to do. He wasn't in the mood to wait around until the car's owner came out of the restaurant and then follow him home, wherever home might be. That might not be for another hour or so. And the owner might be from some place out of the area, so that following him — or her — home might take him to Rochester or Elmira or heaven knows where. Kevin took a piece of paper from his wallet and wrote the car's license number and make and color on it.

But he ate his dinner quickly. Too quickly to really savor it and form an opinion as to the quality of the Hilltop's food. There was, after all, a chance that the car would still be there. And if it belonged to someone who lived on or near the lake, he could follow it home. He had nothing else to do that evening. Carol wouldn't be coming over.

When Kevin returned to the parking lot, the car with the Cubs and Bulls bumper stickers was still there. He slid in behind the wheel, slumped down in the seat, and began a vigil the duration of which he could not guess. He told himself he'd give the owner of the car until dark, although he doubted he'd need to wait that long. Once again he was playing at being a detective, and he was enjoying it.

It was just after 7:15 that a man suddenly appeared beside the car with the bumper stickers. Kevin had been watching the entrance to the Hilltop, observing people going in and coming out. This man had obviously come from another direction. Kevin could see no other entrance, but then it occurred to him that there would be a place for deliveries, probably around in the back. And that could be the door used by employees. Perhaps the man now getting into the other car worked at the Hilltop. If he did, he almost certainly lived someplace relatively close, not in Rochester or elsewhere out of the area.

Kevin started his engine. The other car backed up, turned, and pulled out of the parking lot. Kevin followed, doing his best not to alert the driver to the fact that he was being tailed. The Pontiac went down the road toward Southport and then turned north along the West Lake Road, Kevin a couple hundred yards behind but close enough that the car was always visible except briefly on sharp curves. They passed Cobb's Marina. They passed Blue Water Point. And then the car with the Chicago bumper stickers disappeared. It had turned off to the right on the lake side of the road.

Kevin slowed down, looking for a place where the other car had exited. He realized that he was only a short distance north of Blue Water Point and not more than half a mile above his own cottage. He remembered the area as one he had passed numerous times in his canoe. There were three, maybe four, small cottages tucked close together with barely forty feet of lake frontage each, sharing a common steep driveway. The car he had been following was nowhere to be seen because it had gone down that drive and was now below the level of West Lake Road.

Kevin drove a bit farther until he found a spot to turn around, then headed back to his own cottage. There was no point in following the owner of the Pontiac down that steep driveway to one of those cottages. What would he say to him? When were you last in Chicago? Do you know a Sandra Rackley? No, he'd need to give a lot more thought to how he'd approach the man. And barring the possibility that the man had been visiting a friend rather than going home, he'd be near at hand, and Kevin thought he'd be able to manufacture some excuse to talk with him.

Later that evening, while trying to find something to occupy his mind and hence avoid worrying about Carol, Kevin found himself thinking again about bumper stickers. Wasn't he making too much of something which probably had a much less sinister explanation? What if the owner of the car had purchased it secondhand and it was already adorned with evidence that a previous owner had a thing about the Cubs and the Bulls? But even if that were true, wouldn't those bumper stickers suggest that the transaction had taken place someplace in or near Chicago? Why, on second thought, would that have to be the case? A lot of people, people from every corner of the country, could be displaying their affection for the Cubs. After all, many people seem to have an affection for a chronic loser, and the Cubs were certainly chronic losers — no World Series appearance since 1945, no World Series championship since 1908. And the Bulls, they had become a household name from coast to coast because of Michael Jordan's heroics.

I'm becoming obsessed with this business about a Chicago connection, Kevin thought. What, after all, are the odds that two bumper stickers are a clue to murder? But then there's the fact that the car bearing those bumper stickers belongs to someone who lives virtually within shouting distance of the ravine where Sandra Rackley's body was found. Coincidence? Yes, probably. But what if it isn't?

Kevin set aside the novel that he had conspicuously not been reading for the last half hour. Time to pack it in. Maybe a good night's sleep would help. If, in Carol's absence, he could get a good night's sleep.

CHAPTER 33

"I don't understand this stuff."

Deputy Sheriff Bridges was sitting across the table from the sheriff in the squad room. He put down the note that had prompted his remark, pushed his chair back from the table, and walked over to the soft drink dispenser.

A bottle of Coke in hand, he resumed his seat.

"I mean it," he said. "Why can't the sexes get along?"

Sam was not aware that his boss and Kevin Whitman were having a problem. What was bothering him this morning was that a woman had called and asked that the sheriff's department do something about a man who was stalking her.

Carol pushed the reminder of her troubles with Kevin out of her mind and asked her deputy what was on his mind.

"It's a stalking case," he said. "This woman called, wants us to put a stop to it. I set up a meeting for one o'clock. She said it'd be easier if she could come by on her lunch hour. Do you want to sit in?"

"No, you handle it. Just be patient; remember, matters like this often boil down to she said, he said. Maybe we can deal with it without having to get a court order."

"Do you want to know who the stalker is?"

"No, why should I?"

"Well, I'll tell you why," Sam replied, a slight smile replacing the irritated look he had had when decrying the battle of the sexes. "The complainant is a woman named Karen Lester. The complainee, if that's a word, is Philip Chambers."

"Chambers? Phil Chambers?"

"That's right. I thought you'd be interested."

"What's he supposed to have done?" Carol asked, now considerably more interested.

"Don't know much. The Lester woman just said he'd been pursuing her for several weeks, wouldn't let her alone. She's coming over to give us the details."

"So. This guy the Rackley woman threw a drink at is now accused of annoying another woman. Sounds like there may be something to the popular line that he won't take no for an answer."

"Do you think he went after Rackley and killed her?"

"No, Sam," Carol said firmly. "No point jumping to that conclusion. We have no idea whether he ever saw her again after that night at the Cedar Post. We don't even know whether this story about him being a stalker is true. Let's see what the woman has to say. When did you say she's coming in?"

"One," Sam said, looking at his watch to see how much time they had.

"Why don't you do the talking — you know, ask her about the details. When, where, what he said, whether he got abusive, ever threatened her. How she reacted, what she did to discourage him. I'll try to be a fly on the wall, but you know me."

Sam knew the sheriff very well, and he fully expected her to take over the questioning of Karen Lester. Probably sooner than later.

It was shortly after one when they sat down again, this time with the young woman who was complaining about Phil Chambers. It was quickly established that she was 22, not that many years out of the Yates Center high school, and was working as a check-out clerk at the local supermarket. She had moved out of the family home and into an efficiency apartment on Randolph Street back in November. She was a reasonably attractive blonde who wore her hair in a pony tail which bounced when she shook her head. No resemblance to the late Sandra Rackley, who among other things had been many years older.

Miss Lester started to walk them through a litany of complaints, but before she had gone beyond an April phone call, Sam interrupted her.

"Let's start at the beginning. When did you meet Mr. Chambers?"

"I'm not exactly sure, but it was around the first of spring."

"First of spring according to the calendar or by the weather?"

"Oh, I meant the date. That would have been March 21st, wouldn't it?"

Sam nodded. He made a note on a pad that was open in front of him.

"Why don't you tell me about that first meeting. Where did it take place? What did you do?"

Miss Lester looked puzzled.

"I thought this was about him stalking me. Do you need to know all of these other things?"

"I'm afraid we do," Sam said. "We just need to know something about how he knew you, why he would have been bothering you."

"Oh, I see. Well, it happened at Jacob's, you know, the supermarket. He started talking to me — I remember that someone behind him in the line asked him to please move on. Anyway, he asked when I got off work, I told him, and he was there when I clocked out."

"And then —?"

"Well, we went out that night. He took me down to that tavern in Southport. Jack's, I think it is. We had a couple of beers, danced a bit. That's it."

"That's all?" Sam asked. "Didn't he take you home?"

"Oh, of course."

Come on, girl, Sam said to himself. Don't make me pull it out of you.

"Okay, you and Mr. Chambers arrive back at your apartment sometime that evening after some beers. And some dancing. Then what? He go on home? Did you sit around and talk? Did you make out?"

Karen Lester blushed. And twisted around in her chair, as if to see if the sheriff were still sitting in the other corner.

"I don't want to talk about this, but I suppose you know what happened. Yes, we did make out."

"You mean you had sex with him, is that right?"

"Yes. It was stupid of me, I know. But he seemed kinda nice, and he wanted to."

Carol watched the now uncomfortable complainant while Sam made notes. It was clear to the sheriff where this was going. She wasn't sure whether to feel sorry for Miss Lester or be angry with her.

"Now, please tell me whether you went out with Mr. Chambers again. And how often," Sam added, feeling fairly certain that they had gotten into a relationship before things went sour.

"I think it was just two more times. No, I know it was twice, once that same week, and again a week later. We did the same stuff, a few drinks, danced a little."

"And sex? Did you go to bed with him again?"

"The first time. I mean the first time after that first night. Which makes two times in all. But not the third time."

"Why not?" This was, Sam figured, a critical question.

The young woman looked at her hands, which were knotted together on the table in front of her. But when she spoke, she seemed more relaxed than she had at any time since her arrival.

"I knew that what we were doing was wrong. He was too old for me. And he was so pushy about the sex. He didn't really like to talk. We'd get back to the apartment and he'd want to get me out of my clothes almost before the door was closed."

Both Sam and Carol could readily imagine how it had been.

"Anyway, I told him I couldn't keep doing this, that I didn't want to see him again. I was nice about it, you know, nothing unpleasant, just tried to make him see it my way."

"And I take it he didn't like that?" Sam asked.

"Well, at first he just tried to kid around, said I didn't mean it, everything would work out fine. But when I wouldn't let him kiss me, when I didn't change my mind, he started to get upset. He said some nasty things, then he apologized, said he didn't mean it. It was maybe an hour before he left."

"And it was after that the stalking started?" Sam asked.

"Yes. He called the next night, apologized all over again. Asked if he could come over. I said no and he hung up. A couple of nights later, he called again. Same thing. And then the calls started coming, almost every night. He'd ask how I was, tell me he loved me, wanted to see me. It got to the point where I'd ignore the phone. But it would keep on ringing. He's even called in the middle of the night, one, two in the morning."

"Have you seen him since that third date?"

"Oh, yes. He seems to shop at Jacob's almost every day now. I try not to notice that he's there. Sometimes he comes down my aisle, says hi. Other times he sort of stands off to the side and stares at me. It's scary. What finally made me call your office was that he came to the apartment this weekend. When I answered the bell, he pushed the door open and just came right in. He didn't do anything. He sat on the couch, giving me that stare. I didn't know what to do. I told him to leave, and he finally did. I think he was there for about ten minutes."

"I wish you'd gotten in touch with us before this, Miss Lester," Sam said. "There's no reason why you have to put up with this kind of behavior. We're going to do something about this Chambers guy."

Carol, who had not interrupted as Bridges had expected her to, finally spoke up.

"Deputy Bridges is right," she said. "We're going to put a stop to this. But there's one other thing I have to ask you. I think I see a bad bruise on your left arm. When did that happen and how?"

Karen looked down at her arm, which was uncovered below the short sleeve of her blouse. There was an ugly black and blue mark between her elbow and the sleeve.

"Oh, that's nothing. I took a dumb fall the other day. It doesn't hurt now."

"But it's an odd place to get bruised in a fall. Are you sure you and Mr. Chambers weren't involved in some kind of fight — sure he didn't hit you or push you against something?"

Miss Lester, so composed as she had recounted Phil Chambers' unpleasant attentions, started to cry.

"He is the one who did it, isn't he?" Carol asked.

"Look, I don't want to bring charges against him. It wasn't a big deal. When he came over this weekend, I tried to push him out the door and he shoved me against the door frame. I guess it was a lot harder than he meant to."

"I doubt that, Karen," the sheriff said. "I'm sure he's very frustrated and he was taking out his frustration on you. If you wish, we can charge him with assault. Think about it."

She was certain that the young woman would not press charges. Miss Lester had reached the end of her tether with the stalking, but she was obviously afraid of Chambers.

They talked for several more minutes, discussing things that Karen should do to keep Phil Chambers out of her life. The sheriff said that she was prepared to see Judge Olcott about issuing a restraining order, but that she also intended to speak directly with Chambers herself. Put the fear of God in him, was how she put it.

And she would do just that. But what Carol planned to do first was revisit her thoughts about Chambers' relationship with Sandra Rackley. Maybe she had been too quick to buy into Kevin's theory about a Chicago connection. It was just possible that Phil Chambers, a man who didn't take easily to rejection by a woman, might have had more to do with Rackley's death than he had admitted.

CHAPTER 34

The man who wasn't Beckham turned his car off the Cumberland Road and drove leisurely down a back country lane that had no sign announcing its name. He was going nowhere in particular, and he wasn't in a hurry. After a couple of miles, he found himself in an area of abandoned vineyards. No grapes had been produced in this field in years. And as far as he could tell, no one lived anywhere in the vicinity. He could see no houses, no barns, and, with the main road now well behind him, no cars.

He pulled to a stop, shut off the engine, and climbed out of the car. It was early in the morning, and the birds of spring were making their presence known all around him. He took a deep breath, inhaling fresh air and enjoying the smell of grass still damp from an overnight shower. There was time in his day to find a place to sit, listen to the birds, clear his head. He had awakened early, earlier than usual, with a vague sense of unease. He had known that he would be unable to go back to sleep, that he would be better able to throw off that presentiment of trouble if he were up and about.

A cup of coffee had helped, but not all that much. And so he had decided to take a drive, get away from the lake and people. Maybe the *Today* show would have been better, but he had opted for the out-of-doors, even if it left him alone with his thoughts.

There was no specific reason he could think of why he was uneasy. He had gone over the situation many times, and each time he had concluded that there was nothing to worry about. Nothing had happened that might be a cause of alarm. The *Gazette* had stopped writing about the woman in the ravine, now known as Sandra Rackley, late of Chicago. Well, almost. The editor seemed to feel an obligation to tuck into the weekly edition a brief non-story just to remind readers that the cause of the woman's death had not been determined. But the most recent story had suggested that a fall resulting in her accidental death was beginning to look like the most probable explanation. Even gossip had largely dried up. Oh, there were still people who liked to talk about it. People who thrived on unresolved mysteries. But he had heard of nothing that even hinted at a truth with which he was all too familiar.

The field made for rough walking. He was glad that he had worn his old waffle-soled shoes. There was a small, slightly elevated spot ahead of him and probably a hundred yards from the car. It looked like it might be a good place to sit for awhile, so he headed for it. Someone had tried to clear the field of large stones at some time in the past, and a small cairn of those stones had been piled at one edge of the rise in the ground. He moved a couple of those stones and made a seat for himself.

And sat. And tried to enjoy the birds.

But mostly he thought about his needless worries. Maybe the problem wasn't that the sheriff's department could be gathering information which would lead to him. Maybe it was his conscience. Much as he wanted to dismiss the thought, it lodged in his mind and wouldn't go away.

Did he feel guilty about the woman's death? Should he feel guilty? The answer to the first question was easy. No. At no time had he felt guilty. The second question was harder. He was not a religious man, but he knew that one of the Ten Commandments was "Thou shalt not kill." But he'd heard somewhere that this commandment didn't necessarily mean what it said. Something about its original meaning in times long past that Jews had an obligation not to kill fellow Jews. Following the logic of this ancient proscription, one apparently got a pass if he killed someone other than a member of his own people or tribe. And Sandra Rackley had certainly not been one of his people. But who exactly were his people? What did the Bible mean? Could he be sure Rackley wasn't part of some larger in-group to which he also belonged?

These weren't things he thought about often. Often? In fact, he doubted he had ever given the matter any thought. He hadn't attended church in many years. He couldn't remember when it was that he had traded in the pew for the golf course on Sundays. It had been a long time ago. If he were completely honest with himself, he was agnostic. Maybe even an atheist. No, probably not an atheist. He would have to have given the matter much more thought to put himself in that category, and he just didn't think about it. What if he'd been a Catholic? Then he'd have to go to confession. Would he have confessed to killing Rackley? What would happen to him if he hadn't confessed? Would the priest somehow know? Probably not. But would God know? And if so, then what?

But never mind, he wasn't a Catholic and he didn't go to confession. He found himself becoming annoyed with these thoughts. Why should he feel guilty about the woman's death? He hadn't actually killed her. She had simply fallen, and the fall had killed her. Of course he had taken her to the top of the embankment. He had argued with her and they had started shoving each other. The rocks were slick, and she had lost her balance. But it wasn't intentional. Or was it?

What difference did it make? She was a threat to him, making demands which would change his life irrevocably. Change it for the worse. Whatever happened was a matter of self defense. He hadn't gone to the police to report her death because they would never have believed him. He had no choice but to leave her there in that pool of water.

The man who wasn't Beckham got up from his seat at the cairn and walked slowly down through the old abandoned grape arbors. He could justify everything he had done. At least to himself. And that was all that mattered. He would never have to justify what he had done to the police or a judge or a jury of his peers. No one from the sheriff's department had ever come knocking on his door, and as time went on it became less and less likely that anyone ever would. Or did it?

He had no idea what had come of his effort to link Rackley's wallet to the real Beckham up on the Turkey Hill Road. He was mildly disappointed that there had been no report that Dennis Beckham had been arrested or that he was being treated as a suspect in the woman's death. The sheriff or one of her officers would certainly have paid Beckham a visit after receiving the wallet in the mail. He had hoped the man would have been upset, and that in his confusion he would have behaved suspiciously. Perhaps he had. In any event, either the sheriff had decided to make no public statement about Dennis Beckham being under suspicion or she had concluded that he had had nothing to do with Rackley's death. The more he thought about it, the more he found reason to worry.

If the man he had tried to frame was under suspicion, why had the sheriff said nothing? The only explanation he could think of was that she was still unsure, which meant that he was still not safe. But if she had concluded that Dennis Beckham had not killed Rackley, he was equally unsafe. So no matter what the sheriff was thinking, he was not out of the woods. He could not afford a false step. Not that there had been any, but he had to remain hyper vigilant. Think through carefully everything he did. And said.

Most important was the fact that he could not take steps to get out of the area. His first thought after the discovery of Rackley's body was that he should pack up and slip away. But he quickly realized that that would only call attention to him, if not at first, then if and when the sheriff came to the realization that she was dealing with someone from Chicago. He had been in Chicago back around the time that Rackley had become pregnant, and he was sure that an autopsy would have revealed both that she was pregnant and approximately when she had become pregnant. He didn't know much about forensics, but he knew enough to know that unless this sheriff was a political hack, she would have put two and two together and started scouring the Crooked Lake area for men who had been in Chicago during those critical few days.

So he would have to stay put until the woman's death became one of those so-called cold cases. And that was an unpleasant prospect. Independently of the problem posed by the late and unlamented Sandra Rackley, he wanted to get away from Crooked Lake. He hadn't been here long, but it was rapidly becoming too long. The scale was wrong. Too small, too remote from the kind of place he was accustomed to. Damn it, he swore aloud, venting his frustration.

The man who wasn't Beckham turned and headed back toward his car. He no longer found pleasure in the clean morning air and the songs of cardinals and goldfinches.

CHAPTER 35

Doing his best to think about something — anything — other than his problem with Carol, Kevin decided to pursue the owner of *Second City*. It had been agreed that Phil Chambers, who worked on the boat, would pave the way for him by first speaking with Mr. Slavin. But Chambers had either chosen not to answer Kevin's phone calls or had taken a vacation from his duties at Cobb's Marina. No one at the marina seemed to know where he had gone. The proprietor denied that he had taken a vacation, and appeared to be as puzzled as Kevin was that he had not been around for several days.

"Probably doing something for Slavin, that's what I figure. The *Second City* has become sort of a full-time job for Phil. Still, it's funny, him not stopping by the office at all. Maybe Slavin has him on some job at his cottage."

Yes, Kevin thought, that's probably the way it is. He found the informal work schedule at the marina interesting. Chambers had obviously shifted from Cobb's payroll to some arrangement with the owner of *Second City*.

He decided to go down to the marina and make one more stab at finding Chambers, but concentrate on locating Slavin. As he expected, Phil Chambers was not around, but there was a man onboard *Second City*. Kevin assumed that the man was the owner, the Mel Slavin about whom he had heard much but whom he had never seen. He was tall and well tanned, and looked as if he worked out at a gym regularly. A formidable man, Kevin thought. He walked slowly down along the dock, rehashing in his mind the way he had decided to approach him.

Whatever the man was doing, his back was turned to Kevin so that he didn't see him approach.

"Hello," he said, getting the man's attention. "Is Phil Chambers around?"

Kevin had decided to talk with Slavin, with or without Phil's intercession, but he thought it a good idea to let the boat's owner know that he knew the man who was caretaking *Second City*. As it turned out, that was a miscalculation.

"No, he's not."

Kevin was surprised by the laconic answer to his question. No, Phil wasn't there. Nothing more. Slavin, if indeed this was Slavin, obviously had no interest in explaining Phil's absence, much less asking who Kevin was or why he was looking for Chambers.

If he was to have a conversation with Slavin and get aboard *Second City*, he'd have to take the initiative.

"I'm Kevin Whitman," he said. "I thought maybe Phil had talked to you about me and my interest in your boat. You are Melvin Slavin, right?"

The change that came over the man would not have been greater had Kevin announced that he had just won untold millions in the lottery. His face had been expressionless. Now it had acquired a look that said as clearly as words that the man was upset by what he had heard. No, not upset. Suspicious was more like it.

But what had he said? He'd introduced himself and mentioned an interest in the boat. And that had put the man he assumed was Slavin on instant alert.

"What's your interest in my boat?"

The tone of voice reinforced Kevin's impression. This man was suspicious of him, and his suspicion had something to do with Kevin's interest in the boat.

"I'm sorry," Kevin began, not sure what he should feel sorry about. "I should explain. I was down here at the marina one day and saw this boat. It's really impressive, and I got to talking with a guy who was working on it. That would be Mr. Chambers. Anyhow, I was admiring the boat and I asked him if it would be all right for me to come aboard and look around. He said he'd have to ask the owner for permission, so I told him that would be fine — that I'd appreciate it if he'd do that. Today I came by to see if he was here and find out if it was okay for me to see the boat."

The tall, well tanned, and physically fit man listened to this self-conscious explanation, his facial expression unchanged.

"I'm Mel Slavin, and I own the boat," he said in a monotone. "Chambers never mentioned you, so this is the first time I've heard about you or your interest in my boat. And Chambers isn't here. He doesn't work for me anymore."

No expression of pleasure that someone admired his boat. No invitation to come aboard. The man seemed intent on being unfriendly. Maybe he was just unfriendly by nature. Or perhaps it had something to do with Phil Chambers. Or with Kevin's interest in looking around the boat, although why that should bother Slavin, he could not imagine.

In any event, he had come to Cobb's Marina hoping to find Chambers and through him get to meet and talk with Slavin. The middle man was no longer necessary. He had now met Slavin and in a manner of speaking was now talking with him. However, the conversation was not going well.

Kevin wondered if it might be helpful to make it clear that Chambers was not a friend. Slavin had said that Phil was no longer working for him, and there had been no hint of regret in his voice. Either Phil had quit or been fired.

"I probably made it sound as if this man Chambers was doing me a favor — you know, talking to you on my behalf. Actually I don't know Chambers. Never saw him before that day when I was admiring your boat. Haven't seen him since. He volunteered to see if I could have a look around."

"Like I said, he's not working for me. Son of a bitch took advantage of me and I sacked him."

Taking advantage of Mel Slavin was clearly not a good idea, but for the first time he sounded animated. Kevin tried to use the change in tone to jumpstart the conversation.

"Sounds bad. What'd he do?" Slavin might well regard the question as none of Kevin's business, and that would be the end of his effort to get aboard the *Second City*. On the other hand . . .

"What he did was use my boat to make out with some woman. Can you imagine? I hire him to take care of it, let him keep it in good running order, and what does he do? He brings some babe aboard, takes her down to my cabin, and screws her, right there on my bed. Left a used condom on the floor beside the bed. Not neat, and not very smart. It takes a lot of cheek to pull a stunt like that. Well, as far as I'm concerned, your friend is finished. Paid him the month I owed him and told him I didn't want to see him again."

"He's no friend of mine," Kevin insisted. "Like I said, I just met him once."

"Yeah, you told me that. So what's your interest in my boat?"

Slavin still sounded suspicious, but he now seemed willing to talk to Kevin.

"It's hard not to be impressed. I mean, this boat is something special. You see the ones in the other slips here — they look pretty ordinary alongside yours. Anyway, I've been giving some thought to getting myself a boat. After seeing yours, it seemed like a good idea to talk to you. You know, get some information from an expert."

Kevin had no interest in buying a power boat. The canoe was good enough for him. But he hoped that Slavin would accept his explanation, dressed up as it was with a bit of flattery. If Slavin was flattered, he didn't show it.

"What've you got now?" he asked.

"What kind of a boat?" Kevin had seen his neighbors' power boats over several summers, but had paid little attention to names. He thought he remembered one that had the word "Nautique" displayed along the side. But he would only make a fool of himself if he tried to sound knowledgeable. Slavin would quickly realize that he knew as much about power boats as he did about quarks or black holes. "Actually, I don't have a boat. If I get one, it'll be a first. That's why I need advice."

"You've never owned a boat and yet you're thinking about getting one like mine?" Slavin's tone of voice made it clear that he thought Kevin was crazy.

"Maybe not just like yours. But I'm going to be doing some shopping, and I thought your boat would be a place to start — you know, give me some ideas."

Slavin stared at Kevin for a moment. When he spoke, a note of suspicion had crept back into his voice.

"Mr. Whitman, just look down the dock here. I count six boats, no two alike. Why is it that mine is so important? You could be talking to the owner of any of these other boats. Or what about your neighbors? You live on the lake, I assume."

"Sure. Well, at least in the summer."

Once again, Slavin was staring at Kevin as if trying to figure out just who he was. Or what he was doing talking to him.

"So?" The question was more like a challenge. "I repeat myself, but why this fascination with my boat?"

"I guess it's because it's what started me thinking about getting a power boat. You look at it and you start to think, hey, I'd like one of those."

Slavin shook his head, but said nothing more. It was obvious that their conversation was coming to an end, and Kevin had not even asked if he might come aboard the *Second City*.

"Would you mind if I took a look around?" he asked, choosing to be direct for the first time since he had introduced himself. He hoped that Slavin would do the courteous thing and invite him aboard. But he didn't.

"Look, Mr. Whitman, I have some things I have to do. I appreciate your interest, but . . ." He looked as if he were trying to think of a way to say "no" politely, but the words didn't come. After an awkward moment, he produced a half smile, shrugged, and headed back toward the cabin.

There was no point in pursuing the matter, so Kevin set off down the dock. As he stepped off onto the shore, he turned and looked back at *Second City*. Mel Slavin was standing on the deck of his boat, looking directly at him. He was no longer smiling.

CHAPTER 36

The search for a Chicago connection was not going well. Kevin had mixed a martini, put on his windbreaker, and settled into a chair on his deck, from which vantage point he looked out over the waters of Crooked Lake and took stock of what he knew about local residents who might have been in Chicago in December. The sun had disappeared behind the cottages on the west side of the lake, and within another half hour it would be too chilly to stay outside on this nippy June day, even in a windbreaker. But he was enjoying the view, as he always did, and he hoped that the brisk evening air would stimulate some creative thinking. It hadn't yet.

He had identified two people who had a Chicago connection. One owned a boat bearing the name *Second City*. The other drove a car with bumper stickers declaring him a fan of the Chicago Cubs and the Chicago Bulls. But he knew that if Carol were there on the deck with him, she would be saying "So what?" or something to that effect. *Second City* could refer to lots of places — the owner's private code for some place where he had once lived, maybe Oakland across the bay from San Francisco, or St. Paul rather than Minneapolis. No, that would be Twin City. This is a waste of time, Kevin thought. Why didn't I just ask Slavin where he got the name for his boat? Not that it mattered. In all probability, Slavin would not have answered the question. He hadn't been forthcoming. In fact, he had acted suspicious of Kevin. And what reason did he have for being suspicious? The only one Kevin could think of was that he was indeed from Chicago, had killed the Rackley woman, and would naturally be suspicious of a stranger who showed so much interest in him and his boat.

Kevin took another sip of his drink and turned his attention to bumper stickers. He had no idea who the man was who owned that car. A former resident of Chicago? A sports fan who just happened to root for not one but two Chicago teams? The driver of a used car who had purchased it from someone who lived in Chicago? Kevin had not made much progress with Slavin. He'd have to see if he'd have better luck with the driver of the car with

Chicago bumper stickers. Which meant he'd have to take another trip to the Hilltop, where he believed the man worked, or visit him by canoe at what he assumed was his cottage. He hoped the man would open up to him. Or did he? After all, if he'd had anything to do with Sandra Rackley, wasn't it likely that he'd behave much as Slavin had?

Then there was the letter from the Chicago Chamber of Commerce. To his great surprise, it had arrived in that day's mail. They had given him so much trouble over the phone that he had not expected to hear from them for a week or two, yet the information he had requested appeared in his box within 72 hours. Would wonders never cease.

He had torn open the envelope and read the message immediately. And been disappointed. None of the organizations listed by the Chamber seemed promising, so he'd set the letter aside and gone about the business of assembling things for a small casserole and popping it in the oven. Now he picked up the letter again and went down the list for a second time.

His first impression had been correct. These didn't sound like conventions or conferences that people from the Crooked Lake area would be likely to attend. But as he thought about it, he realized that he was being condescending to his summer neighbors. Why wouldn't there be teachers from the area who attend professional conferences? Or doctors? Or union members? Or vintners? People from many walks of life.

Kevin scrutinized the Chamber's list more carefully. There was something about an association of orthodontists. Surely there would be orthodontists in the Crooked Lake area. And apparently teachers of special needs children, children with ADHD, had had some kind of convention. Even relatively small rural schools would need specialists along these lines. There were a couple of other groups on the list that caught his eye, but he decided that he would make inquiries about special ed teachers and orthodontists first.

And so he did. He didn't want to hazard another visit with Slavin just yet. As for the man with Chicago bumper stickers, he decided he'd go back to the Hilltop and try to find out if the owner of that car worked there. And then he'd create an excuse for talking with him. In the meanwhile, he'd consult the local yellow pages and contact the area schools.

Kevin regarded the school taxes imposed on summer lake dwellers to be on the high side, but he himself was an educator, so he had never grumbled. But it quickly became apparent that those high taxes did not underwrite a sizable program for children with learning disabilities. Perhaps the local kids were, like those in Lake Wobegon, all above average. He did, however, get the names of two teacher/counselors whose job descriptions suggested that they might have had reason to attend a conference in Chicago in early December. He caught one of them between classes, and, no, she had never been to Chicago. The other called him back during the lunch break and simply chuckled at the thought she would have been able to afford such a trip, however helpful it might have been. Not that it mattered. Both were women, and hence certainly not Sandra Rackley's lover or murderer.

Orthodontists proved to be as much in short supply in the Crooked Lake area as special ed teachers. Three were listed in the yellow pages of the area's thin telephone book. One was a Linda Thurston in Cumberland, one a John Cleveland in Yates Center, and the third a Garrett Larrimore in Southport. There was no point trying the woman. Kevin dialed the number in Yates Center and found himself speaking to a man who proudly announced that he had just celebrated his 83rd birthday, that he was no longer taking new patients, and that he had no interest in attending any of those damned fool conventions. At 83, he was an unlikely candidate for Sandra Rackley's tryst in a Chicago hotel.

So Kevin turned to the other name in the yellow pages, one Garrett Larrimore. A recorded woman's voice recited Dr. Larrimore's office hours and suggested leaving a message after the tone. It was 12:45, and obviously lunch hour for the dentist and his receptionist. Kevin decided against leaving a message. Maybe if he drove down to Southport he'd be able to catch Larrimore after his lunch break. The drive would provide a welcome change of pace in a day that had so far produced no new candidate for the Chicago connection he was seeking.

He parked on the west side of the village square, where he watched the front of the building where, according to the yellow pages, Larrimore had his office. As he sat and waited, he found himself rethinking the way in which he was approaching these conversations. He had asked people whether they had attended a convention in Chicago in December. Such a straightforward approach had seemed like a good idea. People would not be expecting such a call, and before caution kicked in they would simply answer truthfully. But what if they had been in Chicago and met Rackley there? Wasn't it likely that they would be aware of the danger of admitting they had been there? And that could mean that they would deny it whether they had attended a convention or not. Kevin was beginning to have doubts about what he was doing. Not for the first time.

It was just after 1:30 by his watch when a man, presumably the orthodontist, entered the office. Kevin slid out from behind the wheel and walked around the square and up to the front door. The man who opened the door had put on a white coat of the kind doctors and dentists wear. He was obviously Dr. Larrimore.

"Hello. Sorry my assistant isn't back from lunch yet, but she'll be here any second. Please take a seat. Like some coffee?"

Kevin had never had a dentist offer him coffee just before examining his mouth. He smiled, said no thanks, and sat down to peruse an old copy of *Newsweek* as the orthodontist retreated down the hall. He was not Larrimore's next patient, and he might well not be seeing him again, depending on what his receptionist told him.

She walked in before Kevin had a chance to open the magazine.

"Oh, dear, I guess I'm late. You must be Mr. Slayton, right? Where's your daughter?"

Kevin explained that he was not the father of the next patient, that he only wanted to see about making an appointment. The woman, whose name according to a name plate on her desk was Betty Lansing, sat down and pulled out her appointment book.

The time had come to adopt a new approach.

"I seem to be having a problem with my bite," he said. "I tried to make an appointment back in early December, but the doctor was away. At a conference, I think. Anyway, I got busy and didn't follow up. But I was in Southport today and thought it'd be a good idea to get on his schedule."

"Sure. Let me see what I can do for you."

While Ms. Lansing was leafing through the appointment book, Kevin began to make small talk.

"I hope the doctor had a good conference. I've had to attend these things, and they're no fun unless you get to play some golf. Where did he go? Some place with golf, I hope."

Ms. Lansing smiled and shook her head.

"I have no idea. He made the arrangements himself, just said he was off to a conference. But regarding an appointment, I see there's a cancellation for this Friday. It would just be a consultation, right? Could you make it at 10:15?"

Kevin had had no problem with his bite, but it looked as if he'd have to go through with his make-believe dental problems if he was to learn where the orthodontist had been in December. He dutifully entered the date and hour on his Blackberry, thanked Ms. Lansing, and walked out the door just as Dr. Larrimore's first patient of the afternoon came up the steps in the company of her father.

For the first time since the letter from the Chicago Chamber of Commerce had arrived, Kevin was excited. On the drive back to Blue Water Point, Kevin reflected on what he had learned — and not learned — from Larrimore's secretary. He had pretended to know that the orthodontist had attended a conference in December, and the result was better than he could have hoped for. Yes, Dr. Larrimore had been away at a conference. If he had been up to no good, his receptionist had at least not entered into a conspiracy of silence with him. But she did not know where the conference had been held. Wasn't that odd? Wouldn't most people in his position have had his assistant make reservations for him? And wouldn't she therefore know where he had been? But by the time he reached his cottage, his excitement had waned. The orthodontist would not have known when the reservations were made that he would be meeting a woman named Sandra Rackley and would have reason to cover up such a meeting. Which made the fact that he had made the reservations himself and not told Ms. Lansing where he was going look far less suspicious. He was probably just one of those people who preferred not to use their secretary to take care of personal business. Kevin knew of a few of his colleagues who were only too ready to take advantage of their assistants, asking them to get lunch for them, pick up their dry cleaning, and otherwise do what used to be called scut work. Suddenly Garrett Larrimore looked like a much nicer human being than he did when Kevin had walked out of his office.

Still, there was the nagging question of where that conference had been held. He'd find out on Friday.

CHAPTER 37

"It's a woman named Karen Lester," Ms. Maltbie announced from her desk on the other side of the half open door.

Carol was not anxious to talk with the young woman, and was mildly annoyed that her secretary had not taken the message and said that the sheriff would return her call. But she was really upset with herself. She had promised the Lester woman that she would speak with Phil Chambers and tell him in no uncertain terms that he was to leave Karen alone or they would seek a restraining order from a judge. And she hadn't done so. She had been busy, but that was no excuse. What would she tell Miss Lester? That her problem was so unimportant that she hadn't been able to find five minutes to put a call through to Chambers?

She decided that it would be better to take the call and see what Miss Lester had to report.

"Hi," an effervescent voice on the phone greeted the sheriff. Before Carol had an opportunity to apologize for not having spoken to Chambers, Karen Lester explained her reason for calling. And made an apology moot.

"Thanks for getting that man out of my life. He hasn't bothered me for three whole days. I feel like I can breathe again. I'm not sure what you did, but it's working."

Carol briefly considered telling Karen that she had had nothing to do with Phil Chambers' decision to leave her alone. But she chose instead to thank her for the good news and to repeat the promise to seek a restraining order if Chambers started harassing her again.

Now why do you suppose he has suddenly stopped his pursuit of the young woman, she asked herself after hanging up the phone. Almost immediately she started thinking about Chambers' relationship, if there had been one, with Sandra Rackley. Which reminded her that there were still good reasons to talk with him. She reached for the phone.

Her conversation with the owner of Cobb's Marina was brief and disappointing. In fact, it was more than disappointing. It was worrisome.

What she had learned was that Phil had not been seen around the marina for over a week. While that was unusual, it hadn't set off alarm bells. He was probably off somewhere doing something for Mr. Slavin, the owner of *Second City*. But when his absence stretched into an eighth day, Cobb had spoken with Slavin and discovered that Phil had been sacked. He might have been expected to come by and see Cobb about resuming his regular duties at the marina. But he hadn't. He had simply disappeared. Carol tried to get specific dates from the owner, but had to settle for approximations. What was clear was that Chambers had been served his walking papers more than a week earlier and then vanished.

Cobb suggested that Chambers probably feared he would lose his job at the marina when the cause of Slavin's firing him became known. Would he, Carol wondered, simply have avoided that scenario by leaving the area? Or might there be some other explanation for what he had done? And what had he done? Perhaps he had disappeared because he feared that he might be tied to the Rackley murder. But that made no sense. After all, if he had had something to do with the woman's death, he could have flown the coop weeks ago. She didn't even know that he had left Crooked Lake. For all she knew, he was at his home, guzzling beer and watching TV around the clock.

Carol decided to do the logical thing and call Phil's home. No one answered at the house in West Branch, so she got in touch with one of her officers and asked him to stop at the house. Poke around, see what you can find out, was the way she put it. Half an hour later, Officer Barrett called back.

"No sign of him," he reported. "It appears that he lives with his sister and brother-in-law. They're not at home. A neighbor, name's Perkins, says he hasn't seen Chambers in a week. Doors are locked, but it shouldn't be too hard to let myself in if you want me to."

"No, Jim," Carol said, rejecting her colleague's suggestion. "Let's not get dramatic. It's likely that the brother-in-law and maybe the sister are at work. What I'd like you to do is stick around, talk to them when they get home. They'll probably know what he's doing. And where. We know he's been working at Cobb's Marina, then just dropped out of sight. Beyond that we know nothing, other than that he fancies himself as a ladies' man."

"Have we got a problem with him?" Officer Barrett asked.

"Not that I know of," the sheriff said, very much wishing she had tried to contact Phil right after her meeting with the Lester woman.

———

It took a couple of days before the Chambers file consisted of more than a few scribbled notes. Barrett, like Deputy Sheriff Bridges, made up for his lack of imagination with tenacity. Ms. Maltbie had typed up his report, and Carol took it home with her. She didn't expect anything out of the ordinary. Barrett would have told her had he found something interesting.

She opened a bottle of beer and sat down at the kitchen table to read the report.

Chambers' sister, now identified as Jean Kennedy, was the source of most of the information in Barrett's report. It appeared that Phil was unmarried, something of a lay-about, and a chronic source of trouble in the Kennedy household. Adam Kennedy did not like Phil and constantly badgered his wife to get rid of him. But his wife, in spite of promises to do something about the problem, had not had the courage to give her brother his walking papers. So Phil was still living in the Kennedy home, where he had what amounted to a two-room flat on the second floor. He had chipped in on the rent and, according to Jean, had been a responsible tenant. Adam's objection to Phil seemed to have less to do with his abuse of the Kennedy's house rules than with disgust that a healthy man in his thirties should still be acting and living like a teenager.

But neither Jean nor Adam Kennedy had any idea where Phil might be. They had paid little attention to his comings and goings, and it was not until Jean realized that he had not collected his mail for several days that it occurred to them that he had gone away. Jean was not worried about her brother, but thought it strange that he had said nothing to her about his plans. Adam regarded this as more evidence that Phil should be kicked out of the house.

Barrett had quizzed Jean about Phil's friends and habits, but she had been unable to shed any light on his whereabouts. He had asked for permission to take a look at Phil's rooms, a request which had been granted without protest, but he had found nothing that might explain where he had gone or when and why. His bed had been made up, the heat turned off under a half-full pot of coffee. Phil Chambers' digs offered no clues to what his interests were or what he habitually did with his life.

Conversations with the neighbors had proved equally unhelpful. Perkins, the neighbor with whom Barrett had first spoken, thought it strange that Phil was still living with his married sister, but had nothing to add to what the Kennedys had told him. No one recalled an occasion when a woman other than Jean Kennedy had been seen at the house, and Jean had been quite sure that her brother had never had a woman in his rooms. If Phil was the womanizer that Ginny Smith and Karen Lester thought he was, it looked as if he made out with his women in their own homes.

The sheriff put the thin file down and scowled as she did so. Where are you, Phil Chambers? And why have you so suddenly disappeared from your home and your job on Crooked Lake?

CHAPTER 38

Another bad night. And then a bad morning. Kevin peered into the refrigerator, looking for eggs that were not there. This on top of the empty bread box. He realized that he had done no real shopping since Carol had walked out on him almost two weeks earlier. At least there was coffee, so he poured himself a cup and headed for the deck where the fresh air might improve his mood.

He revisited the dream that had turned into a nightmare. He had been swimming, well out into the lake. But when he turned back, instead of closing the distance between himself and the shore he had found himself further and further from the cottage. The lake was calm, but hard as he tried he was making no headway. And standing there on the dock was Carol Kelleher, the sheriff of Cumberland County, watching him flail away. Watching and laughing. Kevin could even recall the sound of her laughter, growing fainter as he drifted toward the center of the lake.

He had awakened in a cold sweat, turned on the light, and gradually reoriented himself to the familiar sight of his bedroom. But while he had eventually dozed off, he slept fitfully and finally got up to face the day just after six o'clock. Only to find that the cupboard was bare.

It didn't take a psychiatrist to interpret the dream. His relationship with Carol was once again in trouble. Serious trouble. Kevin doubted that Carol was laughing at him, but he was sure she was angry with him. And there didn't seem to be anything he could do about it. Unless, that is, he could persuade Jennifer to tell Carol the truth. Or discover Sandra Rackley's killer.

Persuading Jennifer would be difficult in any circumstances. He couldn't do it over the phone, and inviting her to come up to the lake so that he could talk to her face to face seemed like a very bad idea. But if he went down to the city to see her, he would have to put his effort to establish the elusive Chicago connection on hold. Moreover, he didn't even know that Jennifer was still in the city. For all he knew, she might have gone to Europe.

Frustrated in his effort to think of a satisfactory way to coax a confession and an apology from his teaching assistant, Kevin turned his attention to the Rackley case. It was Thursday, and he'd have to wait until Friday to talk to the orthodontist who might have visited Chicago in December. He wasn't anxious to have another meeting with the owner of *Second City*. Not today, anyway. There might be other men from around the lake who had had some reason to visit Chicago, but the only one he knew of at the moment was the driver of a car with bumper stickers announcing an interest in two Chicago sports franchises. Kevin decided to make this man, name unknown, the focus of his day.

It was nearly noon when he pulled into the parking lot in front of the Hilltop restaurant. It was perched on a hillside above Crooked Lake. When the weather was clear, as it was this morning, the lake, which stretched out to the north in the valley far below, was a brilliant azure blue. It presented a picture worthy of a postcard, but Kevin's mind was on other things than the beauty of the lake and the surrounding hills.

A quick survey of the cars in the parking lot told him that the car with Cubs and Bulls bumper stickers was right where he had hoped it would be. Kevin was about to enter the restaurant and make what he hoped would appear to be an innocent inquiry into ownership of the car when its owner himself appeared. He came, as he had the other evening, not from the entrance to the dining room but from around the back. He went up to his car, opened the door, and leaned in as if to retrieve something. The something turned out to be a pack of cigarettes, and the man proceeded to light one and then leaned back against the car to smoke it. Another victim, Kevin thought, of the spreading phenomenon of smoke-free workplaces.

The man had either not noticed Kevin or didn't much care whether anyone had observed him sneaking out of the restaurant for a cigarette. As Kevin approached, the man turned slightly, acknowledging him with a nod of his head.

"Hi," Kevin said in a friendly voice. "I was noticing your Cubs bumper sticker, and I just had to say hello. I'm a Cubs fan, too, and you don't get to see many of them around here."

"Yeah," the man responded, "this isn't Cubs' territory. You from Chicago?"

"Not anymore," Kevin lied. "But you know how it is with the Cubs. Have to love the underdog. By the way, I'm Kevin — and you?"

"Tom Carrick. I'm the chef here at the Hilltop."

The two men shook hands.

"Well, then, I've got you to thank for a great dinner I had here the other night."

Carrick shrugged and said he appreciated the compliment.

Kevin was anxious that this parking lot tete-a-tete not end before he learned more about what really interested him — Carrick's whereabouts in early December.

"I see you're a Bulls fan, too. Must have lived in Chicago some time or other. Right?"

"It was a while ago," Carrick said, his tone of voice implying that he wasn't much interested in discussing his life history.

"But still a fan? It must be hard, you know, you being so far from Chicago. Same with me. Ever get back for a game?"

The Hilltop's chef now looked uncomfortable.

"Look, I've got to get back to the kitchen. Sorry. I don't mean to be rude, but —"

"Of course, no problem," Kevin interrupted. "I guess I miss Chicago. No one to talk with about those teams. Maybe I'll catch you sometime when you're off duty. Okay?"

"Sure," Carrick said as he put out his cigarette. "Nice meeting you."

And he was gone.

Damn, Kevin swore under his breath. What had he learned? Nothing. Well, maybe not nothing. The chef had acknowledged that he used to live in Chicago, and without actually saying so had seemed to confirm a continuing interest in the Cubs and Bulls. And he had been reluctant to be drawn into a conversation about going back to Chicago to see his favorite teams play. Kevin had no idea about the rules the Hilltop's owner imposed upon his staff, but he doubted that someone as important as the chef was limited to a five-minute break for a smoke. And their conversation had not even lasted five minutes. Kevin looked at the cigarette Carrick had tossed on the ground and snuffed out with his foot. It had been smoked no more than half its length.

Odds were that Carrick had never met Sandra Rackley, much less been the cause of her death. But Kevin was grasping at straws in his effort to establish a Chicago connection, and there weren't many straws. He'd have to pay Carrick another visit.

———

Kevin restocked his pantry and refrigerator that afternoon and took his first swim of the season. The lake was still cold and he was back out of the water within ten minutes. He checked his e-mail and voice mail, as he had done several times a day ever since Carol had stormed out of the cottage, but there was no word from her. Restless and disinterested in reading or working on the article he was supposed to be writing, he decided to vent his frustration on an overgrown forsythia hedge behind the cottage. It was while he was whacking away at the hedge that the older of Mike Snyder's daughters came out of the cottage up the road. She was wearing what looked like a uniform. Of course, Kevin thought to himself — that's the kind of uniform the waitresses at the Hilltop wear. And it was then that he remembered Mike telling him that his daughter waited table there.

He dropped his clippers and hurried across to his neighbor's yard. "Gail, wait a minute," he called out as she was sliding behind the wheel of the pickup.

"Oh, hi, Mr. Whitman." The young woman closed the door, but rolled down the window.

"Haven't seen you around since I came back to the lake," Kevin said. "How've you been?"

"Okay. Busy. I've got a job now, or didn't you know?"

"That's what I want to talk to you about. You're down at the Hilltop, right? I think that's what your Dad told me."

"That's right. I started after school last summer — just part-time, but they worked me into a full-time job in the fall."

"Well, that's great. Hope you're getting good tips. But I've got something I'd like you to do for me if you can."

"Sure. What is it?"

Kevin hadn't had time to prepare his proposal, and he knew she was on her way to work. He'd just have to make it up as he went along and hope it would sound like a reasonable request.

"Look. This may sound a bit funny, but I really do have my reasons. Trust me. What I'd like to know — what I'd like you to do — is see if you can possibly find out if the chef there, a Mr. Carrick, took leave back in early December. I don't want you asking him or making it obvious what you're doing. I just figured that maybe there's a chart or a book or something where you could find a record of who's taken time off. Not a sick day or something like that, but a vacation — you know, a week or so."

Even as he said it, Kevin was starting to have second thoughts about asking the young woman to do this. He didn't want to get her into trouble, but he might be doing just that. He needn't have worried.

"Oh, I can tell you about that," she said, obviously pleased to be helpful. "Mr. Carrick took a week off right after Thanksgiving. I don't remember the exact dates, but it was around the beginning of December. His mother was sick, and he had to go see her. I remember we kind of wondered how the kitchen would do without him — you know, supervising the staff and doing the stuff he does. But it worked out okay. I suppose he'd trained the others — that'd be Molly and Jimbo. They're sort of assistant cooks."

Kevin wasn't interested in Molly and Jimbo. But he was very much interested in the unexpected report that Carrick had been on leave from his duties at the Hilltop when Sandra Rackley had had her encounter with D.B. Beckham in Chicago.

"You've got a wonderful memory," he told Gail. "You wouldn't also happen to know where Mr. Carrick went, would you?"

"I'm not sure, but I think one of the girls said something about Chicago."

Thank you, thank you, Miss Snyder — you have made my day, Kevin said to himself. To Gail, he said something quite different.

"Please don't tell anyone at the Hilltop that we talked about this. Okay? It's no big deal, you understand, but I don't want any of the people at the restaurant to know that I asked about Mr. Carrick's leave. I'm not trying to make trouble for him. It's just a personal thing."

"Sure, whatever you say."

They waved at each other as she backed out of the driveway, and Kevin found himself hoping that Mike's charming daughter could be counted on to suppress her curiosity as to his reason for asking about the chef and keep their brief but possibly crucial conversation a secret.

CHAPTER 39

Kevin had never looked forward to dental appointments. But the one he had penciled into his calendar for a Friday in June was another matter. He had arranged a session with a Dr. Garrett Larrimore in Southport, ostensibly to obtain a professional opinion about his bite. Kevin was quite sure that the orthodontist would tell him what he already knew: that his bite was just fine. What Kevin wanted Dr. Larrimore to tell him was something he did not know: if the orthodontist had attended a professional conference in Chicago in early December of the previous year.

The clock on the wall behind Ms. Lansing's desk told him it was 11:23, which meant that Larrimore was running late. Few of the magazines in the waiting room looked interesting. Most were for young readers, kids who would be there to be fitted for braces. Instead of reading, Kevin killed time by going over in his mind the conversation he would be having with the dentist.

It was just after 11:30 when Dr. Larrimore himself came into the waiting room and addressed Kevin.

"I'm so sorry to keep you waiting, Mr. Whitman." The apology sounded genuine. "Can you give me another five minutes?"

Kevin said he could, trying to keep the fact that he was annoyed from showing. He wondered if Larrimore was chronically late, much like his own GP and dentist back in the city.

Finally, some 45 minutes after entering the orthodontist's office, Kevin was told that Dr. Larrimore would see him.

"Thanks for your patience. I had to do a bit of repair work on some braces that got mangled in an accident on the soccer field. Takes time, I'm afraid. But now let's climb into the chair and we'll take a look at your teeth."

Kevin dutifully assumed his place in the big chair next to what looked suspiciously like implements of torture.

"I wouldn't be here except my wife's been nagging me about fixing my teeth," Kevin began, thinking as he did so that he had become quite proficient at lying. "I think my bite's just fine. Don't know what she sees that I don't."

"We'll know soon enough, won't we?" Larrimore said. The orthodontist busied himself with preparations for examining Kevin's teeth.

"I tried to see you back in December," Kevin said, taking advantage of the fact that the orthodontist had not started to poke around in his mouth. "You'd gone to a conference, I understand. How's it work in your profession? You there to give a paper, or do you have to attend lectures to stay current in your field?"

Larrimore laughed.

"No, I don't do papers. Just stay in touch with colleagues, take a peek at the latest gizmos — new ways to run a painless practice."

"Get in any golf? In my field, we go to hear boring papers and then we play golf. At least we do if they don't do something dumb like schedule a meeting up north somewhere in the winter. They did that a few years ago — Chicago, if you can believe that. I skipped it."

Kevin gave Larrimore a chance to say something, but the orthodontist didn't oblige.

"How about you?" Kevin asked. "Your conference where you could get out on the links between meetings?"

Again, silence. Kevin could not see Larrimore, who had gone over to a cabinet behind the patient's chair. Maybe he'd stepped out of the room.

When at last the orthodontist spoke, he didn't answer Kevin's question.

"What's your profession?" he asked.

"I'm an academic. Teach, write articles, try to interest young minds in culture. Hate conferences, but I seem to go anyway."

Larrimore moved around to the side of the chair, and told Kevin to lean back and open his mouth wide.

For the next several minutes Kevin found it impossible to talk. Nor did Larrimore say anything. Unlike Kevin's dentist back in the city, he didn't seem interested in carrying on a one-sided conversation.

"Okay, you can sit up now." The search for evidence of a bad bite had obviously come to an end.

"What's the verdict?" Kevin asked.

"There's nothing wrong with your bite. In fact, your teeth are in excellent shape. Who's your dentist?"

"You wouldn't know him. He's down in the city — that's where I live much of the year."

"Well, he's damn good. Be sure to tell him I said so."

It looked as if Kevin would be ushered out the door without having learned whether Larrimore had attended the Chicago conference for orthodontists back in December. But the dentist surprised him.

"You know, I have a problem with winter conferences, too," he said as they shook hands. "Like you, I like to get in some golf."

They were now in the reception room. Ms. Lansing looked up from her desk and smiled.

"I'll let you in on a secret," he said, obviously unconcerned that his receptionist would hear him. "I had intended to go to my professional conference, but most of all I just wanted to take a break. So I changed plans at the last minute and went south for some golf."

"No kidding?" Kevin said, intrigued by the man's candor. "Where'd you go?"

"Florida. In December there's no point going to Hilton Head or one of those other in-between places. Can't count on the weather. And there's lots of good courses in the old Sunshine State."

"Where'd you play?"

"Several places. It's fun to move around, hit a course down in Dade, then hop over to Fort Myers. Not to mention Orlando. Like I said, golf is big down there — lots of challenging courses."

"Sounds great. I promise not to tell any of your patients that you took a golfing holiday," Kevin said, wondering what Ms. Lansing would think of what she had just heard.

Larrimore laughed.

"You don't look like the kind of patient who's going to spread gossip about their dentist. Have yourself a good day."

No, Kevin thought as he walked to his car. I won't be talking to your patients, whoever they are. But I'm not who you think I am.

As he drove back up the West Lake Road, he tried to recall just what the orthodontist had said. And what he had not said. Initially he had said nothing, even as Kevin tried to draw him out. And then, as they left the examination room and entered the receptionist's domain, he had become quite voluble, confessing in Ms. Lansing's presence that he had not attended a professional conference after all. Which suggested that the woman was loyal to him and that he could trust her to say whatever Larrimore wanted her to say.

If he had spoken the truth, he had substituted a week of golf in Florida for a week of conferencing in Chicago. But Kevin was not satisfied. Larrimore had barnstormed around Florida rather than settling into one city, one hotel. Or at least that is what he said he had done. Which made checking up on his story much more difficult. And as Kevin reconstructed what had been said, he realized that Larrimore had never said that he had not gone to Chicago. Perhaps he had done so and then flown from there to some place in Florida. Or perhaps he had not gone to Florida at all.

As he approached Blue Water Point, Kevin began to question his own assumptions. Why should he be suspicious of Larrimore? He knew absolutely nothing about the man. Was his desire to find a Chicago connection so strong that he was assuming guilty behavior where none existed? What were the odds, after all, that an orthodontist practicing in Southport, New York, had had anything to do with the death of Sandra Rackley? Or, for that matter, that the chef at the Hilltop or the owner of an oversize boat at Cobb's Marina were involved? Not for the first time since he had returned to the lake, Kevin had the feeling that he was on a wild goose chase.

He usually turned off of West Lake Road at the northern end of the point, simply because his cottage was much closer to that exit. Today, for no reason he could have explained, he turned off at the southern end of the point. He drove along the stretch of the road that skirted the wooded area which the late owner of the Silver Leaf Winery had planned to develop. This brought back memories of the previous summer. Many of the cottages he passed reminded him of one facet or another of that earlier investigation, but he was jolted out of these reminiscences by the sight of a familiar car behind a cottage whose owner's name was written large on the roadside mailbox. Wilder.

Kevin did not know the Wilders. But the presence in their driveway of a car with an Illinois license plate, a car belonging to Mel Slavin, made it incumbent on him to visit them, introduce himself, and hopefully learn something about the owner of the *Second City.*

As he pulled into his own driveway, Kevin knew that it was too soon for him to write off the search for the Chicago connection as a wild goose chase.

CHAPTER 40

It was to have been the day when Kevin dropped in on the Wilders, but it didn't work out quite as he had planned. He was just finishing dressing when he heard a knock on the back door. Probably a neighbor, one of the Brocks or Mike Snyder, he thought. He slid into his loafers and went to the door.

"Hi, it's me," Jennifer Laseur said, and threw her arms around him and kissed him. On the lips.

Jennifer was the last person he expected to see that morning, and her presence at his door came as a shock. He pulled away from her surprisingly tight grasp, his mind searching for the right words to say to her.

"What are you doing here?" was the best he could come up with.

"I had to see you. I need to talk to you about us. Can I come in?"

She moved around him and into the kitchen, not waiting for him to invite her in. Kevin followed her, now alarmed that she had so brazenly come to his cottage, kissed him, and seemed ready to make herself at home.

"Jennifer, there isn't anything to talk about. About us, I mean," he said as he watched her take a seat on the couch.

"Yes, there is, Kevin." It was the first time she had ever used his given name when talking with him. "Would you by any chance have coffee? I could use a cup. Black, no cream or sugar."

"Of course," he replied, his day spiraling out of control.

When he returned from the kitchen, she had moved to the end of the couch, a silent invitation for him to join her there. She had obviously gone to some trouble to make herself physically alluring. Kevin knew that she was an attractive woman, but this was the first time he had seen her in a dress rather than the jeans that were the uniform back on the Madison College campus.

"Look, Jennifer, I don't know what you're doing here. I have plans for the day."

She ignored that.

"Kevin, I love you. And I think you love me. We just never talked about it — about us. And I thought now that that sheriff person is out of the way, we could have that conversation."

If he had had any doubts as to who had written the letter to Carol "exposing" his fictitious affair, those doubts vanished. It was clear that Jennifer knew about Carol, and knew that she was no longer seeing him. This girl, this former teaching assistant of his, was one formidable woman.

"Are you telling me that you wrote the sheriff a letter, a letter that said I was dating somebody down in the city — dating, sleeping with, whatever?"

"I don't know anything about any letter. But I do know that you aren't seeing her anymore. It was just one of those things, wasn't it? You were alone up here, and I was a long way away. So I decided I'd fix that. And here I am."

Kevin didn't know whether to be angry with her or sad for her. But he would have to disabuse her of the idea that he loved her. It wouldn't be pleasant.

"You do know about the letter, Jennifer. You wrote it, and you hoped it would poison my relationship with the sheriff. Her name, by the way, is Carol. It was not a nice thing to do, and that's putting it mildly. You told her things about me that simply aren't true."

"Kevin. I like that name, it's so much nicer than Professor Whitman. Let's not talk about the past. We can start over. I'm no longer your assistant, so no one at the college can criticize you for an improper teacher-student relationship. We're free to love each other."

"No, we aren't," Kevin said, trying to sound as adamant on the subject as he felt. "You may think you love me, but what you're feeling isn't love. And I do not love you. Do you understand? I do not love you. You are an intelligent young woman, and you were a very capable assistant. But it was never more than that."

Jennifer Laseur had no intention of being rejected.

"I know how it is," she said. "We've never spent time together. You know, what people call quality time. I didn't expect you to confess your feelings for me just like that. It may take a little while. But you'll see how it is when I'm here for you."

Kevin got out of his chair, the chair he had chosen in order to be as far from Jennifer as the room's dimensions allowed. He turned his back to her, looking instead out the window at the lake.

"You aren't going to be here for me, Jennifer," he said, still with his back to her. "You are going to go back to the city, back to your violin. You are going to enroll at Julliard, and you are going to concentrate on becoming a great violinist. You have a wonderful gift. I look forward to the day when I can hear you play at Carnegie Hall. But I am not going to pretend that I love you. I don't, and that's the end of it."

Jennifer got up from the couch and came over to him, wrapping her arms around him. She didn't say anything, but he thought she might be crying.

Kevin turned around and pushed her gently away. Either her tears were genuine or she was putting on a good act for his benefit.

"There are some tissues in the bathroom, down the hall to your left."

It was almost five minutes before she returned to the living room.

"Do you mind if I go out onto the deck? I'd like to get a look at the lake."

"Of course not," he answered. He had a twinge of anxiety, worried that a neighbor might see her. But he brushed that thought aside. He figured that he could explain her — the story might even get a laugh or two. And then it occurred to him that he didn't want his neighbors laughing at Jennifer's expense. She had behaved badly, but she was really not a bad person. She had just let herself be carried away by an adolescent infatuation. Too bad she hadn't focused on someone other than him.

Jennifer stood at the deck railing for several minutes, probably trying to compose herself so she wouldn't start crying again in his presence. He watched her with a clinical curiosity. What would she do, now that her fantasy world had come crumbling down around her? And more importantly, would she agree to apologize to Carol?

When Jennifer came back into the living room, her eyes were red but she had stopped crying.

"I'm very sorry about this," Kevin said, aware that he meant it. "I know that this is hard for you. It probably doesn't help, but you should know that I am very much in love with the sheriff, with Carol. It's a long story. It began last August, and I'm sure you can appreciate how hard it was for me — and for her — over the long winter months. And then about two weeks ago, she received this letter that claimed that I had been having an affair down in the city. I want very badly for her to know that the story of the affair is not true. I want us to be together again."

Jennifer started to say something, stopped, then began again.

"I wish you loved me. You can't begin to know how I feel. But I —"

She paused, hunting for the right words. Tears were welling up in her eyes again.

Kevin would have liked to put his arms around her, to comfort her. But he knew that it was a bad idea, certain to be misunderstood. He also wanted to ask her how she knew that he and Carol were now estranged. He chose not to. It would only add to her humiliation. In all likelihood, she had been staying somewhere around the lake for days, maybe even a week. She would have been aware of his comings and goings, of the fact that he hadn't been seeing Carol. He realized that he really was feeling sorry for this woman who had tried to break up his relationship with Carol. But there was no reason to prolong an already awkward conversation.

"Jennifer, I want you to do something. For me. I think it will make you feel better, too. I want you to speak to the sheriff. No, that's asking too much. I'd like you to write to her, tell her that there is nothing to the story about me and some other woman. You can send the letter without a signature if you wish. She's a good person. She wouldn't hold a grudge against you. But she might let me back into her life. Can you do that for me?"

Jennifer dabbed at her eyes with what was now a much used kleenex.

"If you want me to."

Kevin had no idea how Jennifer would actually handle it. He wasn't even sure she would do what he asked. She might change her mind, and if she did, there wasn't much he could do about it.

He walked his former and now miserable assistant to the door and offered her his hand as she stepped out into the backyard.

"Goodbye, Kevin. Do you mind if I still call you Kevin?"

"Not at all. It sounds much better than Professor Whitman — besides, it's what all my friends call me. You have my best wishes, you really do. And remember what I said about wanting to hear you someday at Carnegie Hall."

She turned around halfway to her car, and for a moment Kevin thought that she was going to come back and — and what? Argue her case some more? Kiss him good-bye?

But she didn't. She managed a half smile and climbed into her car. He half expected her to burn rubber backing out of the driveway and onto the gravel road. But she didn't do that either. She simply drove slowly off in the direction of West Branch. Gone, he hoped, from his life. And Carol's.

It was still well before noon, but Kevin helped himself to a beer from the refrigerator and took it out to the deck. He was, he realized, actually shaking. The conversation with Jennifer, if it could be called that, should have occurred months earlier. Before she had had a chance to convert a romantic interest in him into an obsession. By pretending not to notice, he had only postponed the day when he would have to tell her what he had told her that morning.

What would she do? He rated the prospect of her writing or calling Carol at no better than fifty-fifty. If she were to get in touch with Carol, would she do it soon — even today — or would she sit on it for awhile, trying to find the courage to do what she must dread doing? And then there was the question of what he should do. Call Carol and tell her about the unexpected visit from Jennifer? Wait until Jennifer contacted her? But how would he know when — or whether — Jennifer had been in touch with Carol? Maybe he would have to wait for Carol to make a move. Yes, that was what he would do. For a while at least.

Kevin knew that he should be up and doing something like going down to the Wilder cottage to find out what Mel Slavin had been doing there, but he felt glued to his chair. The meeting with Jennifer had been emotionally exhausting. It had been almost as hard on him as it had been on her. What he really wanted to do was sit there on the deck until the phone rang and Carol's voice said "I love you."

"I can't do that," he said aloud to himself. So Kevin went back into the cottage, put the dishes in the dishwasher, and got ready to walk down the point to the Wilder cottage.

CHAPTER 41

As Kevin walked down the gravel road to the cottage where he had seen Mel Slavin's car, he realized that he didn't really know many of his neighbors. Other than the Milburns, who occupied the cottage at the place where the point bent sharply into Mallard Cove, he could not have identified any of the owners of the cottages to the south of his except for his next-door neighbors, the Brocks. Which reminded him that their grandsons, the boys who had discovered Sandra Rackley's body in the ravine, would soon be coming back to the lake for much of the summer.

But today he wasn't concerned with who lived in or rented which cottages except for the one with a mailbox proclaiming that it was the Wilders' residence.

Slavin's car was not in the driveway, but a well maintained black Cadillac was. Kevin rapped on the back door.

The woman who appeared at the door looked to be in her forties. She greeted him with the kind of half smile that said "I don't know you, but welcome."

"You're Mrs. Wilder, I presume," Kevin said.

"Right. It's Beth. Are you looking for Steve?"

"Well, maybe, but you might be able to help me. Mr. Wilder isn't here, I take it."

"No, he's up at the estate. I don't believe we've met."

"Oh, I'm sorry. My name's Whitman. I live in that white cottage with blue shutters up the point a ways. Actually, I only spend summers here. I assume you're year-round residents, is that right?"

"Yes, though we haven't been here all that long."

"I should have come by to introduce myself sooner," Kevin said, apologizing for his neglect of the social amenities.

"What can I do for you?"

Kevin had thought long and hard about this. He knew that a straightforward answer wouldn't do, so he launched into a rather convoluted — and not entirely truthful — explanation for his presence at the Wilders' door.

"It's about a man whose car I saw in your drive the other day. A car with Illinois plates. I only met him once, down at

Cobb's Marina. We had a pleasant chat. I found it interesting that he had put such a large boat on our lake, and he was going to tell me about it when we were interrupted and never finished our conversation. I haven't seen him since, but when I saw his car here, so close to my own place, I figured I might kill two birds with the same stone — introduce myself to you and resume my conversation with Mr. Slavin. Is he a friend of yours?"

"I guess you might say that. He's really a friend of my husband's. They went to school together. Actually, Mel — that's his name — he's been staying with us. Until recently, that is. He's living on his boat now, but it was too cold back in the winter for him to do that. And it's been a nasty spring, so he didn't move out until a few weeks ago."

There was something in Mrs. Wilder's tone that said almost as clearly as words that she was relieved her husband's friend had finally moved out.

"I'm sure Mr. Slavin has been grateful for your hospitality," Kevin said, hoping that she would elaborate on what sounded like an unusual living arrangement.

"Oh, he probably was, but he's been distracted — I guess that's how I'd put it. He brought his boat here from Chicago to keep it away from his wife, and I don't think he ever planned on staying so long with us. Steve's been too busy up at the estate to spend much time with him, and Mel and I don't really have much in common."

"How long was he with you?"

"He arrived about a week before Christmas. What's that make it — nearly five months?"

"Sounds right. Having a marital spat, was he?"

Mrs. Wilder suddenly looked uncomfortable.

"I really shouldn't be talking about this. Mel, he's a private sort of person. Talks a lot about boating, but almost never about his personal life. You'd better talk to him yourself."

"You're right," Kevin said. "Anyway, it's his boat that interests me. I'll look him up down at the marina, now that he's living there — on the boat, I mean. By the way, you said your husband was up at the estate. Sounds interesting. What's the estate?"

"Oh, that's Steve's new business. He bought that old Plantation place outside of Yates Center. You probably know of it — it's that big rundown building up on the hill, been unoccupied for more than a decade. Steve's at work turning it into a conference center or something like that. It's a big roll of the dice for us. I'm not as optimistic as Steve is, but he just keeps at it. You won't see much of a difference. Not yet. But Steve says to give him another year, maybe eighteen months at the outside. I'm keeping my fingers crossed."

"I certainly wish you well. The Plantation is a legend around here, just waiting for someone willing to tackle restoration."

"Well, we're the ones I guess. How about you?"

"Nothing much to tell. I teach at Madison College, spend my summers here on Crooked Lake. My cottage is just a few cottages up the point."

"Married? Or perhaps I shouldn't ask."

"That's okay. I'm divorced and living a bachelor's life." He wished he were able to say that he was planning a second and much happier marriage. "Look, I'm sorry to have bothered you, but I did want to extend a belated welcome to our little colony here on Blue Water Point. Please tell your husband that I'd like to meet him, too. And see Mr. Slavin again."

He now knew something about the Wilders. Not much, but then that had not been the reason for stopping by their cottage. He knew even less about Mel Slavin. The old college friend had been living with the Wilders since December, when he had moved his boat from Chicago to Crooked Lake. His move east from Chicago had had something to do with his wife. And that was it. What Kevin had learned was that Slavin had presumably still been in Chicago when Sandra Rackley met and slept with the man who claimed his name was Beckham. And he had told Mrs. Wilder that he had enjoyed talking with Slavin and wanted to resume their conversation. He felt reasonably certain that Mrs. Wilder would report to Slavin what he had said. How would Slavin react to the fact that Kevin Whitman was still interested in him — and in his boat?

———

Mel Slavin's reaction to the report that Kevin was asking about him came two evenings later. He had stopped by at the Wilders to ask a small favor of Steve, and in the course of a three-way conversation at the kitchen table, Beth Wilder brought up Kevin's visit.

"A neighbor of ours was asking for you just the other day. His name's Kevin Whitman. Says he had a pleasant chat with you down at the marina."

The way in which Slavin received this apparently innocuous piece of information came as a surprise to the Wilders.

"Damn him," he said, his voice strained and ugly. "Why won't he leave me alone?"

As he said it, Mel Slavin pushed his chair back away from the table and got up. Before either of the Wilders could say anything, he began asking Beth questions. It was clear that he was angry.

"What'd he say he wanted? What did you tell him about me? For that matter, how in hell did he know to ask you about me?"

"Goodness, Mel," Beth said, "it didn't seem like a big deal. He lives here on the point and wanted to introduce himself as a neighbor."

"He lives here? Which cottage, did he say?"

"No, just that it's up the point a ways, a white place with blue shutters. I think he's interested in your boat. What's the matter? He seemed like a nice guy to me."

"Yeah, he's a nice guy all right. He bugs me down at the marina, now he comes around asking you all about me. What's he want with me anyway?"

"Did I do wrong?"

Slavin frowned at the drink in his hand.

"Look, I'm sorry I sounded off like that. But I don't like the guy. He's a real nosy parker."

"Is he someone you knew from Chicago?" Steve Wilder joined the discussion of Kevin Whitman's interest in Slavin and his boat.

"No, never saw him until the other day down at the marina. Let's let it go. But do me a big favor, will you? If he comes around again, find some excuse not to talk to him."

When Slavin left, he didn't drive south toward the marina. He drove in the opposite direction the better to get a good look at the Whitman cottage. He slowed to a crawl as he passed the white and blue cottage, making a mental note of the license number on the back of Kevin's Toyota Camry.

CHAPTER 42

Carol had always prided herself on her ability to set priorities and stick to them. She had never been one to let personal problems interfere with her professional responsibilities. There had, of course, been the rare exception. The death of her father had led to a two-week leave of absence from her old law firm, and it had eventually led to her succeeding him as the sheriff of Cumberland County. But since becoming sheriff, she had never missed a day of work, which meant that she had toughed out a couple of terrible colds and sent her regrets when a close friend from law school had been married out in Oregon.

However, her estrangement from Kevin was putting her priorities to a serious test. It had been difficult enough back in the winter when their relationship was strained by the fact that their careers kept them apart, but there had always been the knowledge that he would come back to the lake when the school year ended. And so he had. She had been both surprised and relieved that they had quickly taken up where they had left off the previous summer. Carol thought that she had never been happier. She even managed to stop worrying about what would happen after Labor Day, when Kevin would have to return to the city.

And then came the letter. The letter and Kevin's unconvincing attempt to explain it. She had dealt with it by staying busy, but as the days passed, she had found it harder and harder to concentrate on Cumberland County law enforcement. Even Bridges, never a particularly observant man, had noticed it.

"Are you all right?" he had asked her one day in the squad room. "It's none of my business, but you seem to be preoccupied." .

"I'm okay," she had replied, doubting that she sounded very convincing. It would only be a matter of time before Bridges and the others figured out what her problem was. They would try so hard not to notice that it would be obvious that they had noticed. Carol wondered what her men thought of their boss dating a summer resident on the lake. Or dating at all, for that matter. She suspected that they talked about it among themselves. Had she been a man, their reaction would probably have been different.

They could then picture themselves in the sheriff's shoes. But not Carol Kelleher's.

In any event, she wasn't dating now. In spite of her problem, she found the thought of dating amusing. Dating is what teenagers and young twenty-somethings did. What do you call it when you are in your mid-thirties? When you share a bed? When you brainstorm together the mysterious death of a young woman from Chicago?

Carol had considered calling Kevin and asking him to try again to explain his theory that the letter had come from a love-sick teaching assistant. A teaching assistant whose gender he had misrepresented to her. But she couldn't bring herself to do it. Why? She had gone over the reasons in her mind several times. Was it because he had lied to her, and she could not love a liar? Or was it that the letter episode was one more piece of evidence that a relationship between two people who live apart for most of the year is ultimately impossible? Or maybe it was simply that it was Kevin who should make the first move.

She had tried to imagine why he had not called her. Initially she had assumed that he would persevere in his efforts to persuade her that it was all just a silly mistake. But he hadn't. Perhaps it was because what the letter writer had written was true, and he knew that he would never be able to convince her that it wasn't. Perhaps it was because he had never loved her as much as she had believed, and was using the letter as a means of ending their relationship. Carol did not like these explanations, both because she didn't want them to be true and because, upset with Kevin as she was, she still thought of him as a basically good man. As her man.

It was Saturday afternoon, and a few weeks earlier she would have been getting ready to meet Kevin. Maybe at the Cedar Post. Maybe at his cottage. She would have her small overnight bag packed and would be going through her modest wardrobe, looking for the slacks and blouse that would be most flattering.

Instead she was watching a baseball game on TV. Neither team was one she could call a favorite, but she had let herself be caught up in the excitement of a tense, well-pitched game. For the rare moment, Kevin was not on her mind.

Out of the corner of her eye, she saw the young woman who delivered mail in her neighborhood mount the front steps and deposit the day's mail in the box by the door. She was not expecting anything important, so she waited until the end of the inning before getting up to collect the mail.

It was, as she had expected, a lean mail day. The phone bill, a catalog that would be tossed out unread, and a letter with no return address. Carol opened it and found herself staring at a two line typed message, no salutation, no signature. The terse message read: "None of the things you read about Kevin Whitman in an earlier letter are true. I am sorry."

The ball game no longer held any interest for her. What mattered were those eighteen words. The letter accusing Kevin of an affair down in the city was a hoax. The writer of the letter regretted having written it. And was too ashamed of what she had done to divulge her name.

Carol's mood, increasingly bleak as the days had gone by, was suddenly transformed. She was now ebullient. She flicked off the television set and reached for her cell phone. She would call Kevin, tell him about the letter, and ask if she could come over for supper, or maybe go out to dinner.

She started to punch in his number, then stopped. An unpleasant thought had occurred to her. What if Kevin himself had written the short message she had just read? What if he had decided to get back in her good graces by pretending to be the repentant author of the letter that had so suddenly ended their relationship?

Carol's ebullient mood evaporated. She was once again suspicious of Kevin. Was he the sort of person who would do such a thing? Only a few minutes earlier she had been thinking of him as a basically good man. But she had to admit that she didn't really know him all that well.

She reread the note, but it didn't help. Those eighteen words revealed nothing about the person who had typed them. Even the "I am sorry" was at best a perfunctory apology. People were expressing regret for some action or other all the time, and wasn't it often because the apology was expected rather than that it was sincerely felt?

Carol decided not to call Kevin. She'd wait and see what he would do. She hoped he'd call her soon.

CHAPTER 43

While the sheriff was wondering what to make of the brief message she had just received, Kevin was communing with nature. It was not that he was less concerned with their relationship than Carol was. It had everything to do with burnout. He wasn't physically tired, but he was frustrated by his inability to make more headway in his pursuit of the Chicago connection. And he could think of no other way to bring Carol back into his life. He could, of course, simply confront the men he had decided might qualify as suspects in the Rackley murder. He could bluntly ask them if they had been in Chicago during the first week of December and whether they had met the Rackley woman at that time. But that approach would get him nowhere. Might as well come right out and ask if they had killed her.

Slavin, Larrimore, and Carrick had all put him off, each in his own way. Or had they? Perhaps it was just a figment of his imagination. Probably they were all innocent of any wrongdoing. On Sunday morning, he decided to give it a rest and take a hike up the ravine instead. There would probably be a variety of bird life in the woods. A lifelong birder, he would enjoy the possibility of spotting a few migrating warblers. Besides, this was where it had all started back in the late winter. In effect, he would be revisiting the scene of the crime.

Kevin had no intention of going farther upstream than the steep bank from which Sandra Rackley had fallen to her death. When he reached the place where her body had been found, he sat on a nearby rock and considered the pool. The water level had gone down a bit. The surface of the water was perfectly calm. The dead branch of a nearby locust tree lay across the corner of the pool nearest the bank. It was a peaceful picture.

He stared at it for awhile, then got up and knelt beside the pool. He put his hand in the water, gauging its temperature. It was considerably warmer than it had been in April. He went back to his rock, thinking of this secluded spot as his equivalent of Thoreau's Walden. He wondered why it had taken a tragic death to lure him to it.

It was while he was enjoying the peace and quiet of the ravine and trying to identify an unfamiliar bird call in the woods behind him that he realized that a man was approaching from the direction of the lake.

As he came closer, Kevin recognized him as Jim Stuart, a casual acquaintance who lived in the last cottage at the north end of Blue Water Point.

"Hi, Jim," he called out. It was obvious that Stuart didn't recognize him.

It was not until he was within a few yards of Kevin that a look of recognition crossed his face.

"Hey, Kevin, how're you doing?" Stuart said, his voice expressing his surprise to find his neighbor in the ravine. "Didn't recognize you. Damned cataracts, got to get 'em taken care of."

"I'm okay," Kevin said. "How about you? Haven't seen you since last summer."

"Well, that's because you insist on working, unlike us retired types. We're fine. Helen was laid up for a while with a sprained ankle. Tripped over our dog, if you can believe that. But tell me, what're you doing up here? Don't think I've ever seen you in the ravine."

Kevin was aware that Stuart spent a lot of time in the woods. Studying mushrooms, he thought. He didn't remember exactly what his field was — mycology or something like that. Or had been before he left the state's extension service. Whatever it was, the ravine seemed to be a good place to muck about, his vocation now his avocation.

"You're right," Kevin said. "I'd rather swim than hike. But, funny thing, this is my second time here in this ravine in just two months. Thought I might see a couple of migrating birds to add to my list. That and curiosity about the dead woman they found up here back in April. Do you know about that?"

Stuart had found a ledge across the pool from Kevin and taken a seat.

"Oh, yes, everybody's been talking about it. Hear she had a fall from up top of that bank there."

"And landed right there in that pool," Kevin added. "No one seems to know whether the fall killed her or she drowned."

Kevin could see no reason not to talk about his search of the ravine on the sheriff's behalf. Stuart would probably have heard that he and Carol were an item. Or that they had been.

"This is the first time I've been up here since right after they discovered the body. The sheriff and I talked about it, and she let me look around to see if I could find anything that might help explain how the woman ended up dead in the pool."

"No kidding?" Stuart said, sounding surprised to hear this.

"You probably remember that I was involved in that Britingham case last summer. Even a suspect for awhile. Well, the sheriff remembered, and was willing for me to do some informal looking around for her."

"You got something going with the sheriff?"

"Not really. Just friends. Anyway, I came up here one cold day, poked around for several hours, didn't find anything."

Kevin was aware that Stuart might think he was showing off. His story would sound even better if he mentioned the button and the boot prints, but he knew that that could compromise Carol's investigation. He'd already said enough.

While they were talking, Stuart had shifted his position on the ledge, sliding his legs out in front of him. Kevin found himself looking at a very familiar pair of waffled boot soles.

The first thought to come to his mind was that this neighbor on Blue Water Point might have been Rackley's killer. The second thought was that the first thought was ridiculous.

"I like your boots," he said. "If I'm going to become a ravine regular, I've got to find something better than beach sandals or these city shoes. Where'd you get yours?"

Stuart laughed.

"You can get 'em in just about any decent shoe store. They're common as dirt. I'd bet half the people on our point own a pair. Comfortable — good for walking on rough ground. Those loafers of yours are just a fall waiting to happen."

Kevin looked down at his shoes, shoes that announced that, even after several years on Crooked Lake, he was still really a city boy. Then he changed the subject.

"Do you do much climbing around here in the ravine in the winter?"

"Hell, no. Wrong season for us mycologists. Besides, it's usually icy. Good time to take a fall, break a leg. Or worse."

"So you didn't see any other hikers in the ravine back in March and April?" Kevin asked.

"I've seen a few people, of course. Not many. But I don't think I was in the ravine that early. Maybe once. There's one guy I've seen two or three times. Not in the last few weeks, though."

"Can you describe him for me?" Kevin asked, now more interested in the conversation.

"Ordinary looking guy. Probably about your age, give or take a few years. Only thing distinctive about him is that he's got a rather pronounced streak of white hair. Otherwise, hair's brown — like mine used to be. Why, do you think there could be a connection between someone I've seen here and that dead woman? Does the sheriff suspect she was killed? I thought she just did some stupid climbing and fell."

Kevin didn't think it wise to answer Stuart's questions, but he was excited by the information he had just obtained from his neighbor. Barring a highly unlikely coincidence, Tom Carrick had been a frequent visitor to the ravine at the north end of Blue Water Point.

"Truth is, Jim, I have no idea what the sheriff thinks. She keeps her own counsel. But I guess I'm naturally curious. Like you, only about different things — mushrooms for you, people for me."

"Fungi, Kevin. Fungi."

The two men chatted for another five minutes and then went their separate ways. Kevin knew what he would be doing that Sunday evening.

CHAPTER 44

Tom Carrick. Chef at the Hilltop Restaurant. Fan of the Chicago Cubs and Bulls. Sandra Rackley's killer? Kevin could hardly wait to see Carrick again, but he had learned enough about the man's schedule to know that he would not be home from the restaurant until sometime around 7:30. It appeared that he arrived at the Hilltop between nine and ten in the morning, supervised preparation of lunch and dinner menus, and then left the rest to his staff, leaving the restaurant in the early evening. Carrick might not go directly home, but Kevin thought that would be his likely destination after a long day. If he had a relatively early dinner and then set out in the canoe, he figured there'd be a good chance of catching Carrick during his dinner hour or, better yet, while he was enjoying a drink before dinner.

It was roughly fifteen minutes after seven when Kevin pushed off in his canoe. It was a beautiful evening, the sun lighting up the shore across the lake from his cottage, the water calm. He paddled out a dozen yards or so and turned the canoe toward the north. It would take him no more than ten minutes to reach the place where he had seen Carrick turn and drive to the cottages nestled against the bank below West Lake Road. He was anticipating the conversation he would have with Carrick. If the man had gone elsewhere after work today, he'd try again tomorrow. But Kevin was feeling optimistic, more so than he had at any time since he began pursuing the Chicago connection.

After passing Jim Stuart's place, the last cottage on Blue Water Point, he followed a short stretch of undeveloped shoreline before coming to a quartet of small cottages that had been constructed along a narrow beach below the road. One of these four cottages would be Carrick's. He knew this because Carrick had taken the steep road that led to the cottages the day he had followed the chef home from the Hilltop, and he had confirmed what his eyes told him by consulting the phone book.

From his vantage point in the canoe, Kevin saw no sign of activity in front of the cottages. He drifted for a minute, then did a U-turn and with a few strokes sent the canoe back along this mini-point. He decided to beach the canoe and knock on Carrick's door.

But just as he was about to turn the canoe toward shore, he saw a man emerge from one of the cottages. Kevin was too far from the shore to know whether it was Carrick or not. He paddled slowly in the direction of the dock in front of that cottage. The man had seen him, and had stopped to watch the approaching canoe.

It was not until he was less than fifty feet from the dock that Kevin recognized the man. It was indeed Carrick, and it was also clear that he did not recognize Kevin. He beached the canoe next to the dock and called out a cheery hello.

"Hi. I'm Kevin Whitman. Remember me? The Cubs fan — we talked in the parking lot at the Hilltop."

Carrick looked puzzled. Not because he still doesn't know who I am, Kevin thought, but because he can't imagine why I'm here.

"Not interrupting dinner, am I?" Kevin asked as he climbed out of the canoe. Whether he was or wasn't, Kevin intended to stay for a few minutes.

"No. Well, not yet." Carrick took Kevin's extended hand, but otherwise gave no indication of welcoming him.

"I was just out getting some exercise, enjoying the evening, when I saw you. Then I remembered we have something in common, so I thought I'd stop by and say hello."

Kevin had the fleeting thought that it was becoming too easy to lie. He wondered if people in the law enforcement business did it routinely. And with what results? When it became apparent that Carrick wasn't going to hold up his end of a conversation, Kevin plunged ahead.

"There aren't many baseball fans up this way," he said. "Much less Cubs fans. Do you get to see many games?"

"No. It's a long way to Chicago. Besides, the season was just about over last year when I signed on at the Hilltop. Maybe I'll get out there for a game before the summer's over. No plans right now."

"How about the Bulls? I see you're a basketball fan, too."

Kevin thought Carrick looked as if he were trying to decide how to answer the question.

"There was a time, back when Michael was playing. They've never gotten back to that level since."

Kevin had purposefully changed the subject from the Cubs to the Bulls, and he was determined to discuss the Chicago basketball team, even if Carrick was not. After all, Sandra

Rackley's tryst with someone from around Crooked Lake had taken place in December. The Cubs weren't playing then. The Bulls were.

"Michael — that'd be Michael Jordan, right?"

"Yeah. Best ever, better than Bird, Magic, all those other guys."

"I like basketball almost as much as baseball," Kevin said. Another lie. "Most of the year I'm down in the city, and that means the Knicks. I never saw Jordan, though. My loss, I guess. But I did see Kobe one night when he had one of those humongous 50-point games. Hard to forget nights like that."

Kevin had done his homework. After his conversation in the ravine with Jim Stuart, he had spent a good part of the afternoon on the Internet, searching for information about professional basketball, about which he knew next to nothing. He had discovered that the Bulls had played three home games in the first week in December. And he had made notes about those games, jotting down names of players he'd never heard of plus lots of statistics. One of the names he had heard of was Kobe Bryant of the Lakers, and he had discovered that in a game during that week in December Bryant had scored 53 points.

"Ever see Kobe play?" he asked, using Bryant as bait, hoping Carrick might come alive at the mention of his name.

A spark of interest showed in Carrick's eyes. But his answer to the question wasn't quite what Kevin wanted to hear.

"Yeah, I even saw one of those 50-pointers myself. But it was a few years back. When I lived in Chicago."

Kevin tried not to let his irritation show. Would he never get one of these men with a Chicago connection to come right out and admit he had been in the Windy City back in early December?

"I don't follow the Bulls much, but I get the impression they're getting it back together. Not like what they were with Jordan and Pippen and all those titles, but a real comer. What about that big guy from Africa?"

"You mean Deng. He's from Sudan, I think," Carrick offered, sounding more engaged in the discussion. "Amazing, isn't it? Players come from all over now — Nowitzki, and some guy with the Spurs. Funny name. Can't seem to think of it."

Kevin played his ace.

"Ginobili, you mean. He's from Argentina."

"Yeah, that's the one." It was a different Carrick. More animated, obviously eager to talk basketball with another fan.

Kevin was pleased with himself. His afternoon on the internet was paying dividends.

"Give Deng and those other young guys like Gordon a year or two, and I'll bet the Bulls take it all."

"Damned right." Carrick said it emphatically. "Just wish I could be there."

"It isn't that hard. You can get a flight from the regional airport by way of Rochester. I did it once for a meeting. Easy trip. I can't believe you haven't seen a game since you moved here."

"Well, I did make a —" Carrick cut himself off in mid-sentence. It was as if some inner voice had told him not to go there.

"Good for you," Kevin said.

"Not so good, I'm afraid. What I'm saying is that I tried once to get a ticket, but it was a sellout." The chef had shifted gears, and Kevin was sure he'd learn no more that evening about Carrick and the Bulls. But he was wrong.

"I guess I'm lucky. I doubt that my boss would have been pleased to know I'd gone off to Chicago for a ball game."

So that was how he'd done it, Kevin said to himself. Of course he couldn't be sure, but he'd be willing to bet that Carrick had in fact seen a game, going to Chicago because his mother was sick. That's what Gail Snyder had told him, and as he thought about it, it sounded like a perfect cover.

They talked sports for several more minutes, but Kevin let the conversation drift in other directions. He found it interesting that Carrick had never offered him a drink, or even invited him to sit down. He still hadn't mentioned the ravine, and he decided it was time to do so before Carrick told him he had to put dinner on.

"By the way," he began, "have you discovered that ravine just down the road from your cottage? It's a great place to get away. I took a hike up there this morning, felt like a new man. You ever get to spend time there?"

"I wish I had more time," Carrick said. "The owner over at Hilltop keeps me busy. Nice man, but my schedule doesn't leave me time for that sort of thing."

Great, thought Kevin. What do I do now, ask him point blank if he's been in the ravine in the last few months? Carrick hadn't answered his question, but Kevin chose to treat what he said as a denial. In view of what Jim Stuart had told him, that would constitute a lie. But why would the man lie about spending time in the ravine? Because he'd pushed Sandra Rackley to her death there?

When Kevin finally pushed off and paddled back to his cottage, he was inclined to view the conversation with Carrick with mixed feelings. He'd learned nothing specific that could link the man to Rackley, but neither had he heard anything that ruled out a relationship with her.

Only once had Carrick said something that could be proved — or disproved. He had spoken of seeing Kobe Bryant play on a night when he had scored more than fifty points, and had said that that game had taken place several years ago. When he got home, Kevin went at once to his computer. He thought it likely that something as rare as 50-point games would pop up on a Lakers' Web site, complete with dates and details. And so it did. The Lakers' star had indeed had such a game in Chicago, but only once, and that had been in early December of the previous winter.

CHAPTER 45

For a change, Kevin had slept well. He awoke to face a sun already well above the hill across the lake from his cottage. His thoughts didn't immediately turn to his problem with Carol as they usually did. Instead, he found himself thinking of Tom Carrick, accomplished chef and avid sports fan. He lay in bed and reviewed his conversation of the night before with Carrick and his discovery of the fact that the man had lied to him. Of course, he knew that he had seeded their conversation with several lies himself, but he had done so in order to get at the truth. Carrick, on the other hand, had lied to obscure the truth. The truth, Kevin suspected, was that Carrick had been in Chicago in December, ostensibly for the purpose of seeing his sick mother, but in reality to take in a Chicago Bulls basketball game.

If true, this did not necessarily mean that Carrick had rescued Sandra Rackley from a game of frisbee, slept with her, and subsequently killed her in one of Crooked Lake's many ravines. But it made all of these things possible. And that was enough to account for the smile of self-satisfaction that flitted across Kevin's face as he got out of bed.

Indeed, Kevin was feeling so pleased with himself that he decided to drive down to Southport and have breakfast at the diner on the square. It was because of this spur-of-the-moment decision that Kevin was pulling into a parking space in Southport at the very moment that Garrett Larrimore was stepping out of the door to his dental practice. Larrimore walked the short block to the diner; Kevin watched him with interest, then got out of his car and crossed the street, following the orthodontist into the diner.

Larrimore had taken a seat and was unfolding a newspaper when Kevin came up beside his booth.

"Dr. Larrimore, I believe. Mind if I join you?"

He didn't wait for an invitation, but slid into the booth across from the orthodontist. Nor did he wait for his startled companion to say anything.

"Didn't expect to see you again so soon," he said. "Much more civilized, don't you think, a booth in a diner rather than a dental chair? You having a midmorning coffee? I'm here for a late breakfast, treating myself, you might say."

Before Larrimore could more than mumble a weak good morning, Kevin had turned toward the counter and ordered two coffees.

"That's okay, isn't it? Coffee? It's on me — with thanks for giving me a pass on my bite."

Kevin was rarely so garrulous, but he knew he had the dentist at a disadvantage and wanted to keep him off balance. Carrick looked like the most promising Chicago connection, but there were others who couldn't be ruled out, Larrimore among them. Kevin had decided, the minute he'd spotted him, that he'd use this serendipitous meeting to question him further about his decision to play golf rather than attend a conference in the Windy City.

"Let's see, you're Whitman, right?" Larrimore said.

"That's me," Kevin responded. "You having anything else? I'm starved."

The waitress deposited the two cups of coffee on the table and took Kevin's order for a stack of pancakes. Larrimore waved her off.

"Coffee's all I want," he said.

"You know, I'm glad I ran into you," Kevin said. "We got to talking about our professional conferences the other day. And about Chicago — nasty, cold, old Chicago. Always glad to meet someone who likes golf and tries to avoid Chicago in the winter. Can't tell you how many times I've been stuck there. O'Hare closed because of a snowstorm. That's the story of my life."

As a matter of fact, Kevin had experienced a delay at O'Hare only once in his life, and that had occurred in July. Moreover, he'd been in Chicago only four times that he could remember, most recently when he'd searched the late Sandra Rackley's apartment.

"Not mine," Larrimore said. "Like I told you, golf comes first."

"I know what you mean. You were telling me about playing down in Florida back in December. I can't remember whether you flew to Chicago for the convention, changed your mind when you got there, and then went to Florida, or did you just go directly down there for some golf — you know, just said to hell with the conference?"

Larrimore had been stirring sugar into his coffee. He stopped, then resumed stirring. And kept it up long after the sugar had dissolved.

"Never did go to Chicago," he answered, his face expressionless.

"Probably just as well," Kevin said. "I can imagine it'd be hard to get a seat at the last minute, what with all those snowbirds heading south."

Larrimore had nothing more to say to this.

"I meant to ask you more about the golf," Kevin said, trying to put some life into the conversation. "I've been planning on going down to Fort Myers. Got myself a little real estate deal. I think you mentioned that was one of the places you played. Can you give me the name of the course? I'd like to try it."

Larrimore was once again slow to respond.

"Can't remember the name," he said.

"Was it on Sanibel?" Kevin asked, trying to be helpful.

"Sanibel? Where's that?"

"It's a chichi part of the area — just over the causeway from town."

"It's like I said, Mr. Whitman. I didn't expect to be playing those courses again, so I kind of forgot their names. I'm not in the habit of storing up useless knowledge."

The orthodontist's cup was still more than half full and Kevin's stack had not yet arrived. But the conversation was clearly over.

"Look, I've got a patient in five minutes. Got to get back to the office. Good to see you again."

Larrimore took his leave, depositing a buck and three quarters on the table. Whether he did so because he had forgotten Kevin's offer to pay the bill or because he didn't wish to be beholden to him was not clear.

The waitress put Kevin's order in front of him, swept the bill and change into her apron pocket, and moved on to the next booth. Kevin was indeed hungry, so he pitched into the pancakes. And reflected on the conversation — or lack of one — he had had with Garrett Larrimore.

Thinking back on what had been said, Kevin was actually surprised that he had been as direct as he had. If Larrimore had in any way been involved with Sandra Rackley, he could well have seen Kevin's questions as a not very subtle attempt to check up on his whereabouts in December. If, on the other hand, he had had nothing to do with Rackley, those questions would simply have looked like an attempt to establish common interests. Either way, the dentist had not been very forthcoming. He said he had bypassed Chicago, but couldn't remember details about his golfing trip to Florida.

Twenty minutes later and no longer hungry, Kevin left the diner and headed for his car.

"Whitman!"

The man's voice was deep, and his tone was peremptory. Kevin stopped in his tracks and looked around. Coming across the town square toward him was Mel Slavin.

When he caught up with him, the owner of *Second City* put a hand firmly on Kevin's arm. This was not going to be a pleasant chat, an invitation to come down to the marina and take a closer look at the boat. The expression on Slavin's face made that abundantly clear.

"What in hell do you think you're doing, asking the Wilders about me? If you want to talk to me, you know where to find me. Besides, there's nothing to talk about. I'm a private man, Mr. Whitman. My business is my business, and none of yours. Now I'd very much appreciate it if you would just leave me and my boat alone. Are we clear about that?"

Kevin, obviously taken aback by this outburst, tried to find words to calm the man down.

"I didn't think I'd done anything wrong," he began. "I just wanted —"

Slavin had no intention of listening.

"I'm not here to argue with you. Just stay away from the boat. You and Chambers. If you see him, you tell your friend that I'm upset — that I don't want to see him anywhere near my boat. That goes for you, too."

The man turned and walked away, but not before squeezing Kevin's arm as if to demonstrate that he meant what he had said.

It had been years since anyone had spoken to Kevin like that. No two ways about it, he had been threatened. It was a most unpleasant feeling, and it took him several minutes, sitting behind the wheel of the Camry, before he felt like starting the engine and driving back to the cottage.

In the short space of fifteen hours, he had talked with three local residents who might qualify as the Chicago connection he had been seeking. There could well be others, but for the moment Kevin was focusing on the day's trifecta. One of the men had been interested in seeing the Chicago Bulls play, and in discussing the matter had told at least one lie. A second was supposed to have attended a professional conference in Chicago, but claimed to have been playing golf instead on a course in Florida whose name he couldn't remember. The third had been living in Chicago prior to moving his boat to Crooked Lake, and had objected most vehemently to Kevin's interest in him and his boat. In fact, he realized, all three men seemed to object to his interest in them. Slavin had said as much, but Carrick and Larrimore, each in his own way, had been anything but forthcoming when Chicago came up in the conversation. Absolutely nothing had been said that hinted at a relationship with the Rackley woman, or even that any of the men knew who she was. The odds that any one of the three had killed her remained long. But Kevin had become obsessed with the idea that one of them probably had.

Why not simply ask them if they had known Rackley? They would, of course, deny it, but it was possible that one of them would give himself away by how he reacted to the question. He wasn't sure how Carol would feel about such an approach, but he was in no position to ask her. By the time he reached the cottage, Kevin had decided to talk again with each of these men with a Chicago connection, and to bring the late Sandra Rackley's name into the conversation.

CHAPTER 46

April had come and gone, the Memorial Day weekend was now history, and the calendar said that in less than a week the summer solstice would occur. Which meant that it was now more than three months since Sandra Rackley had taken her fatal fall in the ravine north of Blue Water Point. There was every reason to relax and assume that her death was officially being treated as an accident. It was no longer news, either on the radio or in the *Gazette*. The people he encountered here and there around Crooked Lake had stopped talking about it. The new sensation was the arrest of the mayor of Cumberland on a DUI charge.

Nonetheless, the man who wasn't Beckham was uneasy. The cause of his uneasiness was not the sheriff of Cumberland County or any other member of the law enforcement establishment. It was a man by the name of Kevin Whitman.

Until two weeks ago he had never heard of Whitman, much less met him. And then Whitman had come into his life. He was reasonably good looking and well spoken. In all probability, he was just what he appeared to be, a friendly guy who enjoyed engaging in small talk, even with strangers.

But there was something about Whitman that was troubling. He had been too friendly, too ready to assume an informal relationship within minutes of meeting a total stranger. It was as if he was searching for common ground, as if he was bent on insinuating himself into another person's life. Nor had it been confined to a single, casual meeting. Whitman had sought him out again, pursuing a line of questioning which, while superficially innocent, seemed to reflect a desire to know more about him. If there had been nothing to hide, Whitman might have been treated as a prospective friend, or alternatively as a nuisance. But there was something to hide. And what if the purpose of his sudden interest was to ferret out that secret?

Of course he had never mentioned the Rackley woman's name or talked about the circumstances of her death. But that didn't prove that Whitman wasn't interested in finding out whether he had had some relationship with her. It was entirely possible that Whitman's style was indirection, that he preferred to make his case by asking seemingly innocuous questions, the answers to which would put him and Rackley in the same place at a critical time. Whitman had seemed interested in Chicago and whether and when he had been there. Why this interest in Chicago? Because Sandra Rackley had lived there? And why Whitman's interest in where he had been in December? Because Rackley had become pregnant in December? There had been no official report that the woman was pregnant at the time of her death. But the inevitable autopsy would have revealed that fact and how far the pregnancy had progressed. Which would mean that the sheriff would be looking for a man who had been in Chicago in December and had met and had intercourse with Rackley there. In other words, the sheriff had probably figured everything out, everything, that is, except the name of the man whom Rackley was looking for when she came to Crooked Lake. And the sheriff would probably have concluded that that man had killed Rackley.

But it was Kevin Whitman, not the sheriff, who had been asking questions about Chicago and December. Why? Did Whitman have some interest in the matter that had nothing to do with the official investigation? Was he working for the sheriff in some undercover capacity? Whatever the explanation for Whitman's interest in him, the man who wasn't Beckham knew he might be in danger. He could not take the absence of media attention and gossip about the case as evidence that he was out of the woods.

The first thing he had to do was find out just who Kevin Whitman was. In one sense, this was not a difficult task. He had quickly located the cottage where he lived, found his phone number, and constructed a short bio with information as to his age, residence in the city, and profession. He learned that Whitman had been divorced for a few years, had no children, spent his summers at the lake, canoed and swam for pleasure and exercise, did not fish, had something of an obsession about opera, drank martinis, and was generally well regarded by his neighbors. Several people remembered that Whitman had become an overnight celebrity the previous summer when he discovered the body of the owner of Silver Leaf Winery dead on his dock. He felt reasonably certain that he had been able to acquire all of this information without arousing the suspicions of those with whom he had spoken.

It was also rumored that he might be in some kind of a relationship with the sheriff of Cumberland County, although no one seemed able to offer specifics. For obvious reasons, it was this information, vague as it was, that most interested him. The rumors proved nothing, of course, but they increased the likelihood that Whitman's interest in him had something to do with the death of Sandra Rackley. He tried to pin these rumors down, but it quickly became apparent that while the sheriff's car had been spotted at Whitman's cottage and the two of them had been seen dining together at a local restaurant, no one knew what they talked about, much less whether he was working for her. Nonetheless, the man who wasn't Beckham chose to believe that Whitman was a dangerous man. Everything they had talked about suddenly took on a different and more threatening meaning.

What should he do about Whitman? He had thought about this a lot. From the beginning he had been cautious about what he said to him. He had finally decided that he should simply refuse to talk with the man.

But he continued to worry. Had refusing to talk with him been wise? He had considered whether it might be better to try a totally different tack. Perhaps he should try to befriend him. Get to know him better. Cultivate a relationship, see if he could find out what he knows. Or what he suspects. Try to deflect his attention, much as he had with the sheriff when he sent her Rackley's wallet. Of course that hadn't worked out very well, but there might be other angles to play.

He had kicked this idea around for the better part of an evening before rejecting it. He had also downed four cold ones, and by the time he decided to pack it in he was still undecided as to how to deal with this dangerous man who was trying to coax him into some fatally damaging admission. His last thought before falling asleep was that the whole problem would disappear if something happened to Kevin Whitman.

CHAPTER 47

Kevin was tooling down the upper lake road between West Branch and Southport, enjoying the evening. He had no particular destination or timetable. He had simply felt the need to take a drive, to clear his head. Too much of his waking hours had been devoted to his pursuit of the Chicago connection. Too few of those hours had been spent in Carol Kelleher's company. In fact, it had been a matter of weeks since she had walked out of his cottage after the contretemps over Jennifer's letter. He had not spent a minute, much less an hour, with Carol since that unpleasant evening.

The sun had set, and the warm afterglow of sunset still bathed the hill across the lake. The vineyards that stretched out below him were now cloaked in the gathering dusk. One car had passed him a few miles back, but otherwise the road had been deserted. In spite of his worries about Carol, he was enjoying the drive. It had been good therapy. But now it was getting dark, and he should be heading home.

He decided to stop in Southport on the way and pick up a quart of ice cream. Funny thing, he thought. I almost never eat ice cream, or any other dessert for that matter, when I'm back in the city. But the lake had a liberating influence, a vacation from his diet regimen as well as from his classes at Madison College. The ice cream mission accomplished, he turned onto the West Lake Road for the last few miles back to the cottage.

By now, for all practical purposes it was dark. But Kevin knew every mile of the road from years of driving it to and from Southport, and had often joked about being able to make the trip blindfolded. His mind was on the prospect of a dish of ice cream with Mozart as accompaniment.

This pleasant thought gave way to mild annoyance about two miles north of the village. The car behind him had on its brights, and his efforts to adjust the rearview mirror to block out the harsh light were unsuccessful. Oh, well, he thought, it's only a few more miles. But the other car seemed determined to make those miles difficult. It closed the distance until it was less than a car length behind him.

231

"Damn fool!" Kevin said under his breath. The road was narrow, and for most of its length did not allow passing. They were now in a no-passing zone, and he knew it would extend almost all the way to Blue Water Point. He looked for a place where he could pull over onto the shoulder to let the rude driver pass, but found no such place. The road ahead curved sharply to the right, and as the two cars rounded the bend they were confronted with a short stretch where an earlier storm had washed out part of the highway. Orange cones had been placed there to steer cars away from the drop off on the lake side of the road.

Kevin had no choice but to veer to the left. That maneuver would have posed no problem had the following car not been so close. And had its driver not chosen that moment to try to pass. At that point, reflexes took over. To avoid being sideswiped, Kevin jerked the steering wheel sharply back in a clockwise direction. The result was inevitable.

The Toyota hit three of the cones. The right front wheel bounced off the broken asphalt and hit the soft ground a foot below. Kevin had been driving at the posted 35 miles per hour, which was fast enough to propel the car over the unprotected embankment. In the following seconds, the car half tumbled and half slid down the slope until it hit the narrow shale beach, stood briefly on end, and then toppled over into the shallows of Crooked Lake.

Had it been earlier in the evening and had anyone been peering down from the edge of West Lake Road, that person would have seen a car, upside down, its tires spinning uselessly in the air, some forty feet below. But it was dark, and the car was not visible from the road. Nor was anyone standing there, looking down. The only car within a mile of the scene was the one which had tried to pass the Toyota as the two vehicles came around the curve. That car had not stopped, but sped on its way north along the road toward West Branch.

Kevin found himself upside down, water from the lake lapping against the roof of the car. He was still held in place by his seatbelt, and was obviously in no danger of drowning. It took him nearly three minutes to disengage from the seatbelt and push the door open far enough to crawl out of the car. Those three minutes of effort were enough to tell him that he had a broken arm. He was probably banged up in other ways as well, but he knew he had been lucky.

The embankment down which the car had fallen ended in a beach not two feet wide. Had the lake level been much higher, there would have been no beach at all. From where he stood beside the car at the edge of the water, he could see no lights. The faint sound of music came from somewhere off to his right, but the curve of the shoreline and the bushes on the bank effectively blocked his view. Kevin was trying to imagine how he would get back up to the road to hail a passing car. It was then that he heard a voice. It came from above.

"Hello, are you all right?" It sounded like an elderly man.

"Yes and no," he shouted. Kevin had no idea who the man was; for all he knew, he was the driver of the car that had run him off the road.

"Your car went off the road," the voice said, stating the obvious.

"I know. I need help. Can you call 911? Tell them where I am, and that I'm hurt. Probably not too bad, but I know I've at least got a broken arm."

"What happened?"

Kevin wished the man would stop asking questions and place the 911 call. But the question suggested that the man was not the driver who had ridden him off the road.

"Another car passed me on that curve up there. Pushed me off the road. Look, please make that call. It's dark and I can't tell if I'm bleeding anywhere."

"Okay. It'll take a minute. I'll get Jake down here fast as I can."

The voice trailed off in the direction of Southport. It sounded as if he was calling out for the man named Jake.

Kevin ran his fingers across his face. There didn't seem to be any blood. And then, just as he was exploring his scalp, he felt a wave of nausea, a delayed reaction to the accident which had sent him down the bank. There didn't seem to be any place to sit, so he leaned against the car.

While he was waiting for the response from 911 and for Jake to appear, Kevin began to think about what had happened. His left arm wasn't working, but his brain was. And it told him that he had been run off the road deliberately. The driver of the car that was following him could have tried to pass at any time since they had left Southport. But the driver had waited until they were on a sharp curve. No matter how frustrated he had been about being stuck behind a man adhering to the speed limit, no reasonably careful driver would have chosen to pass on that curve. The more he thought about it, the more certain Kevin became that the driver was familiar with the road and knew that there was a washout which had not been repaired just beyond the bend. A minute before he had been shaking. Now he was angry.

The fact that the other car had not stopped was, in Kevin's mind, the clincher. Why would anyone pull such a dangerous stunt and then simply drive off? And how could the driver have been sure that the two cars would not collide? Had it not been for Kevin's reflexive correction to the right — the correction which had sent his car down the embankment, the other car would at a minimum have suffered damage to its passenger side.

So who was responsible? A drunken driver? A bunch of kids out for a joyride? While either was possible, even probable, Kevin was skeptical. What if it had been one of the men he had been thinking of as the Chicago connection? What if one of them had become so worried about Kevin and his questions, Kevin and his obvious interest in Chicago, that he had decided to — to what? Scare him off? Kill him?

Kevin didn't like where this was taking him. It was one thing to help the sheriff solve the mystery of Sandra Rackley's death. But it was quite another to become her killer's second victim. Better that the car crowding him off the road belonged to someone who had imbibed too much. Or to a bunch of crazy kids.

It was while he was thinking these thoughts that he suddenly felt dizzy. He had to sit down.

When he came to, he was in a strange bed. Standing at the foot of the bed was a woman in a white and blue uniform. He started to push himself into a sitting position, only to find that the nurse was faster. She moved to the side of the bed and gently restrained him.

"You shouldn't be sitting up. Dr. Gokhale wanted to see you as soon as you came to, and it looks like you're wide awake. You just stay right there — no, on your back. That's right. I'll fetch the doctor."

Kevin looked around him. He was obviously in a hospital, but not in a private room. There was no mirror, so he was unable to see how he looked. His left arm was in a cast. He could not recall coming to the hospital or having the arm set. He had no idea what time it was. His watch had been removed when the cast went on, and there were no windows in this corner of the emergency room. While waiting for the doctor, he began to reconstruct what he remembered of the accident. He got about as far as someone named Jake when the doctor entered the room.

"Hello, I'm Dr. Gokhale. How's your head? Headache? Double vision?" The doctor clearly did not belong to the "warm bedside manner" school of medicine. Right to the point, and the point had something to do with his head.

"Is my head all right?" Kevin asked.

"That's what I'm asking you, young man." Dr. Gokhale didn't look a day older than Kevin, and was probably younger. He raised an index finger and moved it back and forth across Kevin's line of vision.

"My head feels fine," Kevin said. "Maybe you can tell me what's wrong with me. Other than this arm, which probably wouldn't be in a cast if it wasn't broken. I gather I've been out of it for awhile. Can you fill me in?"

"You'll live," Gokhale said as he examined the chart at the end of the bed. Kevin figured that that was as close as the doctor would come to having a sense of humor.

"I thought I would, but I want to know what's wrong with me. Can I get out of here? I mean now?"

"Not yet. You've had a concussion to go with the broken arm. That and some scratches here and there that don't amount to much. I want you to stay here for a day, maybe two."

"Look, doctor, I don't know where I am or how long I've been here. I don't even know what time it is. And I've got a car to worry about, a few people I want to call. Is there someone around here who can fill me in on things? You know, how I got here, whether they got the guy who ran me off the road - things like that."

Kevin knew he sounded impatient. Which he was. And frustrated. He had said he wanted to call a few people, but the only person he really wanted to call was Carol. Depending on how long it had been since the accident, she probably already knew that there had been a case of hit-and-run on the West Lake Road. Odds were that she also knew who the victim was.

"There's a man named Corwin or Corman or something like that sitting in the waiting room. Maybe he can tell you. He's been here all night. Good Samaritan type. Tell the nurse it's okay to bring him in. Just don't get ideas about running around the corridors. Understand?"

With that, Dr. Gokhale opened the curtain that gave Kevin a modicum of privacy and disappeared.

Ten minutes later Kevin was chatting with Jake Corrigan. It appeared that Corrigan had made his way down the embankment, found Kevin unconscious, wrapped him in a blanket he'd thoughtfully brought from home, and escorted him to the Yates Center hospital along with the ambulance crew. He reported that the paramedics didn't think Kevin's condition was life threatening, but that he had felt responsible for staying with him until a proper doctor confirmed their on-the-spot diagnosis. Jake had no idea what had happened to the other car, although he did have quite a bit to say about the failure of the county to repair the West Lake Road at the site of the washout. It was obvious that Corrigan was pleased with himself, and that he would soon be telling all of his friends and neighbors about the important role he had played in rescuing the victim of this terrible accident.

Kevin was profuse in his thanks, and finally had to insist that he was well enough for Corrigan to go home. It then became apparent that the good Samaritan had no way to get home unless somebody else at the hospital drove him or he could prevail upon a neighbor to come for him. One of the hospital's custodial staff ultimately agreed to provide taxi service, but he wouldn't be leaving for another two hours. Kevin thought those two hours would never end, and he was feeling much less charitable toward Jake Corrigan when he finally left.

The nurse bothered him from time to time to check his vital signs and give him a painkiller, but she also located his watch and helped him put it on. Thus he knew that he had been in the hospital for close to nineteen hours when jell-o and other unappetizing things arrived on a tray from somewhere in the bowels of the hospital. To hell with Dr. Gokhale, he thought. I'm going to get up tomorrow morning, get dressed, and walk out of this place. And then Kevin fell asleep, his dinner untouched.

CHAPTER 48

"You have a visitor," the morning nurse said as she removed his breakfast tray. Kevin had been moved from the ER to a marginally better room, and through its window he could see a gray overcast. His watch told him that it was 7:40.

"A doctor, I hope," he said. "I want to get out of here."

"No, the doctor will be making his rounds sometime around nine o'clock. Your visitor said she was a friend."

She. It had to be Carol. Kevin instantly felt better than he had at any time since his car went off the road. Indeed, he felt better than he had in weeks.

The sheriff came into the room and, ignoring the patient in the next bed, hurried to Kevin's side and leaned over to plant a kiss on his forehead.

"Kevin, Kevin, Kevin!" she said in a soft but urgent voice that turned their weeks of separation into ancient history. "How are you? I couldn't believe it — that you'd been in an accident."

"I'm fine. Much better now that you're here."

The words sounded banal in his ears, but he had spoken the truth. Carol hovered over the bed, taking in the cast on his arm and searching with her eyes for other evidence of injuries.

"Can you straighten up? I want to plump up that pillow."

Kevin did as he was asked, all the time smiling at Carol and enjoying her bedside manner, so much more welcome than Gokhale's.

"I'd like to be more familiar," Carol said in a low voice, "but that man in the next bed —"

She gestured toward the other bed in the room. Its curtain had been drawn, but Carol guessed that its occupant might be awake and listening to their conversation. Her suggestion that she'd like to be more familiar stimulated Kevin's imagination, but he knew what she meant.

"Why don't you sit on the bed here," he said.

Carol was only too happy to do so.

"Now," she said, "let's hear how you're doing. They say you were brought in after an accident on the West Lake Road, that your car went down a bank that didn't have a guard rail. Aside from the arm, is the rest of you okay?"

"As far as I know," he replied. "The doctor comes by in a little more than an hour, and I'm assuming he'll let me go. They're worried about a concussion, but my head feels fine today. What's my face look like?"

"Pretty good to me," she said with a mischievous smile. "Actually, you've got what looks like a bump on the forehead, and your left eye is black. Not a bad shiner, but you obviously hit something with that side of the head. I'll still take you, just as you are."

"You can have me — how's that old chestnut go? — 'All of me, why not take all of me.' If it weren't for my roommate, I'd burst into song."

"The word we got was that you were run off the road by a drunken driver or maybe some crazy kid, and he would probably have been drunk, too. I've put a couple of my men on it. Did the other guy's car hit yours?"

"No, damn it. He got away clean, no dents or paint marks. But it wasn't a drunk who did it. Somebody was trying to send me over that embankment. It was deliberate, I'm sure."

"Whoa!" Carol said. "You were deliberately run off the road? How do you know that?"

The sheriff's surprise was understandable. Nothing she had learned since the call that there had been an accident pointed to anything or anyone but a drunken driver. She hadn't even heard about the accident until early that morning, when Bridges phoned her at around a quarter to six to tell her that her friend Kevin Whitman had had an accident and was in the hospital over in Yates Center.

"You want me to talk about it here? What about that man in the next bed?" Kevin whispered his question.

"I know, but who would want to send your car —" Carol stopped in mid-thought. "My God, you're saying someone was trying to kill you?"

"That's exactly what I'm saying, but I don't know who's in that bed and I don't think it's a good idea to share any of this with him. With anyone for that matter, not until I've had a chance to tell you what I think is going on."

It sounds like a lot has been going on, Carol thought. And all the while I've been behaving like an idiot, refusing to see you, refusing to talk to you. Refusing to have anything to do with you, and all because of a letter I never gave you a chance to explain."

She leaned over and this time kissed Kevin on the mouth.

"I'm so sorry," she said, and the way she said it made it clear that she meant it. "I just walked away, like some jealous teenager, didn't I? Can you forgive me?"

"Don't blame yourself, Carol. C'mon. We hit a bad patch. It's over. I love you, I've always loved you."

"Always? Kevin, we only met ten months ago. And, yes, I love you, too."

Carol looked at him, ruffled his hair, kissed him again.

"Do you know that only a few days ago I received a message from whoever sent me that nasty letter? This one wasn't signed either, but it said that it wasn't true, you'd never done the things you were accused of doing. The writer said she was sorry."

"No kidding?" Kevin sounded surprised. "The girl that sent you the letter surprised me recently. Came to my cottage door. She was still trying to pretend we were destined for each other. I talked turkey to her, she cried, said she'd apologize. Frankly, I doubted that she'd ever do it."

It was quite a few minutes before they got beyond reciprocal expressions of regret and vows of love and fidelity. A nurse looked in on them once and quickly backed out of the room, sure she had embarrassed them in mid-kiss. It was Kevin who finally changed the subject to his theory about the accident.

"It's important that you hear what I think happened over on the West Lake Road the other night. Can you take a peek to see whether that guy over there is asleep?"

Fortuitously, just at that moment an orderly entered the room, muttered an apology to Kevin and Carol, and went behind the curtain that gave Kevin's neighbor some privacy.

"He's getting some pictures taken," the orderly explained when he wheeled the man out into the corridor.

"How long do you suppose they'll be gone?" Carol asked.

"No idea, but if it's like everything else around here, they'll park him outside the x-ray room and leave him there for half an hour or so before somebody remembers that he's there."

"Then let's hear your idea about the accident," Carol said, looking nervously toward the corridor. "Just the essentials."

"Okay," he replied, voice still close to a whisper. "I'll bet this is related to the Rackley case."

"What gives you that idea?" she asked, looking highly skeptical.

"Well, it has to do with what I've been doing since we broke up."

"Kevin! We didn't break up, remember? And what have you been doing?"

Not for the first time since he had decided to pursue the Chicago connection as a way of getting back in Carol's good graces, Kevin was feeling uneasy about what he had been up to. Would Carol be upset? Would she feel that he had jeopardized her prospects of closing the case? If so, it was now too late. What had been done had been done.

"I've been looking for what we called the Chicago connection," he said. "I was convinced that the only way you'd forgive me was if I solved your case, so I've been spending my time trying to make book on people around here who have some tie to Chicago."

"Let me guess. You weren't having any luck, so you decided to crash your car. That way I'd be sure to forgive you."

It was the old Carol. Great sense of humor. Kevin wasn't so sure her sense of humor would survive his story about three men named Carrick, Larrimore, and Slavin.

"To make a very long story short," he began, "I've been spending my time learning who around here might have been in Chicago back in December. Back when the Rackley woman got herself pregnant. For all I know, there could be a dozen, but there are three men I think qualify as promising suspects. I've talked with all three, and I'd be willing to bet that one of them did the dirty deed."

"You're telling me that you've taken over my investigation," Carol said, her sense of humor on hold. "I hope to heaven you haven't done something — or said something — that will help the defendant if this case ever goes to trial. Are you going to tell me what you've done? All of it?"

He was, and he did. For the better part of an hour, Kevin recounted how he had become interested in Carrick, Larrimore, and Slavin, the conversations he had with them, and his impressions of the three men.

"So you see," he said, concluding his report, "why I suspect that one of these guys deliberately forced me off the road."

"It's possible, I suppose, but how would he have known that you were out taking a leisurely evening drive? That you'd be stopping for ice cream in Southport? And how would he know just when to pass you? That sounds like an awful lot of careful planning. You're talking about a premeditated attempt to kill you."

Kevin had had a lot of time to focus on just those questions. And it had led him to the conclusion that the man who had killed Sandra Rackley would have been willing to kill again if necessary to prevent his arrest and conviction for the first crime.

"I think our man was alarmed by my interest in him. Alarmed enough to want me out of the way. I'd bet he had been tailing me for days, and that he knew exactly where that washout on West Lake Road was."

It was at this point that Carol assumed her role as sheriff and started to talk about next steps. As she did so, a doctor — not Gokhale this time — walked in.

"Good morning, Mr. Whitman," she said, reading his name from the file on the clipboard in her hand. "How's the head today?"

"Fine. Just fine. I'm ready to leave, and I even have someone to drive me home."

Carol, who had become quite serious as she listened to Kevin's account of his unofficial investigation, smiled at this.

"That's right, doctor," she said. "I'm the sheriff, and Mr. Whitman has been telling me about his accident. I intend to take him back to his home as soon as you release him."

"First, let me see if he's in condition to leave," the doctor said, and proceeded with her examination. It went quickly, and he was given permission to get dressed. And told that he must stop at the office that handled hospital bills on his way out.

"What about my car?" Kevin asked en route back to the cottage.

"You won't be driving it again, I'm afraid. Bridges says it's in pretty bad shape. He contacted a company in Cumberland. I'm not sure how they'll get it out — probably try to pull it up the bank, but they may have to take it out by water. We're looking for any evidence it was sideswiped, just in case it was and you didn't feel it."

"Whoever it was, he didn't hit me. Which means there's nobody to collect insurance costs from unless we catch him."

"You could well be wrong about your Chicago connection, you know. I'm still interested in the drunk driver scenario. But odds are we won't be making any arrests at this late date. By the way, you could be without wheels for a few days. What do you say I loan you my Buick? It's just sitting in the driveway over in Cumberland."

"I'd rather take this one," Kevin said in jest. "I'd be a lot safer in an official car."

"No way," Carol laughed. "You're still a private citizen, even if you've been playing cop for the last few weeks."

At the junction in West Branch, Carol took the turn for Cumberland and the Buick.

"I know you want to take over the pursuit of a Chicago connection," Kevin said, "but I'd like to stay on it."

"No, Kevin." The sheriff was adamant. "You've almost gotten yourself killed, and we don't know yet whether you've screwed up the Rackley investigation. It's time the professionals took over."

"I don't think so. Let me tell you why."

Carol was a firm believer in the view that the driver should never take eyes off the road, no matter how interesting the conversation with a passenger. But this time she violated her own rule, turning to look at Kevin.

"I don't believe that these guys know about us," he said.

"Know about us? What are you talking about?"

"Just that. I'm the one who's been asking them questions. If they think somebody's on to them, it'll be me, not the sheriff. There's an excellent chance that they don't know anything about our relationship. You know, that I've been helping you. Pillow talk, stuff like that. Think about it. All three of them have only recently come to the Crooked Lake area. Why would they link me to you? Let me be the one to talk to them, worry them, keep them guessing. They'll think I'm just a busybody — that the official investigation doesn't even know they exist. They'll be a lot less careful if they think they're dealing with Kevin Whitman rather than Cumberland County's law enforcement machinery."

"But I do know about Slavin," Carol argued.

"Yes, but only because you were looking for that guy Chambers. You've never talked to Slavin. And you never even heard of Larrimore and Carrick until I told you today."

"Okay, and what about Chambers? He's still got my vote as the most likely suspect in the Rackley killing. Know why? He's vanished, disappeared. Been gone for a couple of weeks. Why do you suppose he did that? If he killed the Rackley woman, he just might figure that the best way to avoid capture is to go into hiding. Put yourself in his shoes. He fancies himself as a ladies' man. Rackley rebuffs his advances and he won't accept 'no.' He goes after her, they fight, he kills her. Then Slavin gives him a big paycheck when he fires him. So now, with that money to sustain him, he decides to run. Poof! He's gone and no one knows where. For all we know he's reinventing himself in some place where we'd never think to look."

"Do you believe that?" Kevin asked.

"I'm not sure what I believe. What I know is that the investigation is moving along in low gear, other things monopolizing my time. Maybe her fall was an accident after all. If not, why not Chambers?"

"There, you said it. You're busy. I'm not. Let me see if I can push the envelope a bit with one or more of these guys. I'll keep you posted."

"Now wait a minute, Kevin. Twenty-four hours ago we weren't speaking to each other. Now you tell me you'll keep me posted about what you're doing. Let's put it this way: we will discuss what you propose to do, I will decide whether and when you will do it, and then you will pursue your Chicago connection."

Kevin had known that this was the way it would be, the way he wanted it to be. They were once again a team. He would now even be driving the sheriff's car.

CHAPTER 49

"Guess what?" were the words that greeted the sheriff when she walked into the squad room the next morning. Officer Barrett, who had asked the question, gave Carol the kind of smile that says "I know something you don't know."

"Cindy had her baby?"

"Not yet," he answered. "How about Phil Chambers is back?"

"Really? How do you know?" Carol had almost given up on seeing Crooked Lake's missing womanizer again.

"Ran into him myself. Just this morning. He was going into the 7-Eleven over in West Branch."

"Will wonders never cease. You talk with him? Find out where he'd been?"

"I didn't know whether you'd want him to know we've been looking for him. Of course, his sister probably told him. Anyway, guy on duty at the store seemed to know him. They talked a bit, and I heard Phil say he'd been in Vegas."

"Vegas?" Carol was surprised, and then realized immediately that she probably shouldn't be. He'd been sacked by the owner of *Second City*, but had apparently gotten a sizable check for work he'd done on the boat. She'd figured him as a suspect in the Rackley case — as someone who might want to skip town. But wasn't it just as likely that he'd want to spend Slavin's money in a place where'd there be lots of women? That could be Las Vegas.

Barrett said that, no, he'd overheard nothing else of interest. But he was obviously pleased to have been the bearer of good news.

Or was it good news? Chambers' return had probably removed him from Carol's list of suspects. Which meant that she was down to Kevin's Chicago connection. Or connections. Three of them.

One of whom was Mel Slavin, the man who had moved his boat from Lake Michigan to Crooked Lake in December. On its face it had been a puzzling decision. And then Carol had an idea.

Why not try to take advantage of Phil Chambers' return to learn more about Slavin? After all, he had worked for the man for several months, and it was possible that he had learned something that would help the sheriff in her investigation. She could probably learn as much by talking with Cobb, but she didn't want the marina owner to start thinking negative thoughts about one of his best customers — a customer who in all likelihood was innocent of any wrongdoing. Chambers, on the other hand, might be pleased to volunteer information. But in case he wasn't, she had some leverage: the stalking case against him. Of course he hadn't harassed the Lester woman for several weeks, and maybe did not even know that she had lodged a complaint. But he was no expert on the law in such matters, and Carol was confident she could handle it in a way that would persuade him to help her.

When Kevin had driven off in her Buick the previous day, she had expected to spend the night at his cottage. But he had called in that afternoon to beg off, explaining that he was both very tired and very sore, much more so than he had expected to be. Carol would have preferred to discuss her plans for Chambers over a beer at the cottage, but had to settle for a phone conversation.

"It's worth a try," Kevin told her. "But I'd bet that Slavin hasn't shared much with Chambers. You'd learn more from the Wilders."

"I may have to talk with them," she said. "I think I'll start with Chambers, though."

With some help from his sister, the sheriff finally located Chambers and made an appointment for the following morning. The setting was her office, which she hoped would make his cooperation more likely.

"I understand you had a falling out with Mr. Slavin," she began. "What are you going to do now?"

"Who told you that?" Chambers asked.

"The sheriff is supposed to keep track of everything. And everybody," she said. "I've just been doing my job. But I haven't talked with Mr. Cobb. Are you planning on staying at the marina?"

"To tell the truth, I don't know. I'd like to. But he might be sore about my taking off like that. I mean my going to Vegas."

"Maybe he thought that was something you'd worked out with Slavin," Carol suggested.

"I don't think so. He didn't say so, but I think Mr. Slavin told him why he fired me. Probably wanted to get me away from the marina."

"I take it that you don't care much for Slavin."

"No, but I guess I can hardly blame him for being angry with me. I wasn't too smart."

"That's what I hear. Look, I didn't ask you to come over to Cumberland to discuss your situation down at the marina. I want to talk about Mr. Slavin. And it's very important that anything we say here stays here. Is that clear? Someone out in Chicago asked me for some information about him, and I figured you'd be the person to ask."

Chambers listened carefully, obviously wondering what the sheriff was up to — and what Slavin had done that was behind this hush-hush conversation.

"I'm not sure what you want," he said, feeling his way, uncertain whether the sheriff might really be interested in him, not Slavin.

"What I want is some factual information. Some answers to a few simple questions. Like when did Mr. Slavin first come to the marina? Mr. Slavin and his boat?"

"That's easy," Phil answered, pleased that he knew and relieved that the question didn't seem to have anything to do with his relationship with Slavin.

"I was in the office, sort of keeping an eye on things while Mr. Cobb was out. It was December 18th, just one week before Christmas. Mr. Cobb had one of those Advent calendars over the counter there, and I'd been looking at it. Mr. Slavin comes in with another man. They wanted me to come outside and take a look at something. What it was was that boat of his. It was on a trailer. They wanted me to tell them if we had a place for it, you know, winter storage. Well, we have those bubblers that keep ice from freezing around the docks, but mostly nobody keeps his boat in the water over the winter. So I said they could probably put it in that big storage shed of ours. But I had to see Mr. Cobb first. I mean I knew there was space, but I didn't do the business end."

It appeared that Chambers was not going to be reticent about talking. Nor could Carol see why he should be.

"Was there any discussion about why he was bringing the boat to Crooked Lake?"

"It struck me as odd. People don't usually move their boats in winter. And it didn't look like boats you see on this lake. Anyway, this other man — his name, I learned later, is Wilder — he said something like 'we did it' and Mr. Slavin said 'she'll never find it here.'"

Carol, of course, found the last comment especially interesting.

"Did he say who she was?"

"No, not then. It was some time later, maybe two or three weeks. By then, Slavin had worked out an arrangement with Cobb so I could help him with his boat. So I was on the boat one day and I heard Slavin and Wilder talking. Slavin kept saying something about the bitch. Never said it in so many words, but it sounded like he was getting a divorce and brought the boat here to keep his wife from getting it as part of the settlement."

Carol remembered enough from her law school days to think Slavin's chances of hiding the boat from his wife's lawyer weren't very good. If, that is, she had herself a good lawyer.

"Did he talk much about Chicago?"

"No, excepting that he was glad to be out of there. Funny thing, though, he kept going back to Chicago. Business, I guess."

"What was his business?" Carol asked.

"No idea. Something in finance. But like I said, he didn't like to talk about it. Or about his other life in Chicago. Most of what I know I just happened to overhear. When he and Wilder were together. I got the impression they were friends from way back."

"You wouldn't happen to know who was living in the house during divorce proceedings, would you? I assume that they weren't staying under the same roof."

"It was the wife. At least I think so, because I heard Mr. Slavin griping about living in a hotel. He spent most of the winter talking about how much he looked forward to moving onto the boat."

Carol was glad that Chambers was proving so voluble, but she wasn't sure she'd learned anything of significance. The fact that Slavin had apparently been staying in a hotel in December before coming to Crooked Lake might be important, however. Rackley had said in her diary that Beckham took her to his hotel room to put ice on her ankle. And have sex with her.

"Did he ever mention the name of the hotel?" she asked.

"I don't think so. Is it important?"

Carol ignored the question and asked another of her own.

"How about the marina out there, the one on Lake Michigan? Did you ever hear him mention it by name? Or maybe see something on the boat that said where he used to keep it?"

It had occurred to Carol that Slavin might have wanted a hotel near his marina. She knew nothing about Chicago, but if she had a name - of a hotel, of a marina - it wouldn't be that hard pinning down its location. For a brief moment, she imagined that both hotel and marina were within walking distance of Grant Park, then brushed the thought aside. For all she knew, Grant Park, where Rackley had met Beckham, was miles from Lake Michigan and bereft of hotels.

But Chambers knew no more about Slavin's Chicago marina than he did about the man's choice of a hotel. It soon became apparent that there was nothing more to be learned from him about his former employer.

————

Mulling over what she had learned from Phil Chambers, Carol was struck by the fact that nothing had been said about the divorce other than that the Slavins were getting one. How long do divorce proceedings typically last? she asked herself. Slavin had apparently moved the boat to keep it out of his wife's hands, and that had happened back in December. Which meant that the divorce had been in the works for at least six months.

Carol decided to start phoning Chicago. She wanted to know whether the divorce had been granted. And if so, what the terms of the settlement had been.

CHAPTER 50

It took Kevin only one look at his car to decide that there was absolutely no point in trying to repair the Camry. He'd enjoy the loan of Carol's Buick for a couple of weeks, and then he'd shop for a new car. In the meantime, he'd concentrate on finding whoever it was that had driven him off the road. It was really the sheriff's department's responsibility, and they knew a lot more about tracking down hit-and-run drivers than he did. But he was mad, and the search for the guy who did it was already taking on the aspect of a quest for revenge.

It was also something he could do from the cottage, at least the part of it that interested him most, which was finding out what Carrick, Larrimore, and Slavin had been doing as it turned dark the night of his "accident." He could do that as easily by phone as he could by car, and that was a good thing inasmuch as he still ached in places he hadn't expected to, including the shoulder that anchored his broken arm and his lower back. Those aches had been the reason for disinviting Carol the night before, something he couldn't have imagined doing when he was discharged from the hospital.

Kevin assumed that Gail Snyder could tell him whether the chef had been at the restaurant at the critical hour. Probably not, inasmuch as he normally left the Hilltop earlier in the evening. He wasn't sure what his next step would be, but he had first to rule out the possibility that Carrick had stayed through the dinner hour on Thursday night.

He realized that he was hoping that Carrick had an alibi. And he wasn't sure why he felt that way. Because Carrick liked the Cubs? That was patently ridiculous. He knew no more about him than he did Slavin and Larrimore. And he was the only one of the three who had clearly lied to him. If he had killed Sandra Rackley and tried to kill him, he was certainly entitled to no sympathy. Even if he did root for a perennial loser.

Waiting for Gail to come home promised to make it a long and frustrating evening. Kevin coped by calling Carol and playing some of the Mozart he had looked forward to the night of the "accident." Carol had filled him in on her conversation with Phil

Chambers and the loose ends it had not tied up. She had expressed concern about his condition and had offered to do anything that needed doing. The thing he needed most was for her to share his bed and he told her so. But they both knew they'd need to wait a few days for that to happen. The Mozart — a sublime recording of *Così fan tutte* — lifted his spirits as it always did, even though he had to abandon his couch seat in front of the speakers at intervals to look out and see if Gail had returned yet from the Hilltop.

It was on his fifth trip to the kitchen window at 9:05 that he finally spotted Gail Snyder's car. He turned down the music and went to the phone. It was Gail who answered.

"Hi, Gail. Kevin Whitman here. Do you have a minute?"

"A minute, yes, Mr. Whitman. But to be honest, I'm really ready for a shower. Hey, just listen to me, will you? I'm the one who's complaining, but Dad tells me you wrecked your car. That's a real bummer. How are you?"

"Oh, I'm okay. Look, I promise this'll only take a minute. Maybe less. Remember a while back, I asked you for some information about Mr. Carrick?"

"Sure, about his leave last winter."

"Right. Well, this is about him, too. Like I said before, I'd rather you not tell anyone that I asked. But I'd like to know when Mr. Carrick went home last Thursday evening."

"That's an easy night to remember. He didn't get ready to leave until I was punching out, and I didn't do that until close to ten. Molly had taken the day off for her daughter's graduation and Jimbo got sick, so Mr. Carrick had to stay through the whole dinner hour. It was a madhouse in the kitchen."

"I thought you served from five to eight on weeknights."

"That'll be the day," Gail said, implying that it rarely happened. "What we do is we don't seat people after eight. But we can't turn people away who come in at five to eight, and that's what happened that night. This couple showed up just before eight. And boy, did they stay. I think this man was taking his secretary out to dinner, kind of a celebration. He even asked for a special dessert — did we have like a cupcake we could put a candle on? I was their waitress, so that's why I got home so late."

Well, Carrick's eliminated, Kevin thought to himself.

"I'm sorry it was such a bad night," he said to Gail. "Customers aren't always as thoughtful as they should be. I'll have to try to be more considerate of the help."

"Oh, it wasn't as bad as I'm making it out to be. But I have to admit I was ticked. I made a note of his name on the credit card, just so I could let one of the other girls wait on him next time he comes to the Hilltop."

"Thanks a lot, Gail," Kevin said, pleased to have learned where one of the men with a Chicago connection had been when he'd been run off the road. "I'd better let you take that shower. And remember, please don't talk to anyone about this, especially Mr. Carrick. He's not in any trouble, but if you were to tell him we had this conversation he'd start to worry. There's no need. Okay?"

"I'm no gossip, Mr. Whitman. Anyway, Mr. Carrick, he's nice. Not like the cupcake and candle man with the fancy name — Garrett Larrimore his card said. Couldn't read his signature."

———

Considering all of his bruises and his broken arm, Kevin had slept reasonably well, even if Gail Snyder's report had come close to destroying his theory about a Chicago connection. Carrick could not have run him off the road. And in a totally unanticipated twofer, neither could Larrimore. That left Slavin. It'll probably turn out, Kevin fantasized, that Cobb himself had tucked the owner of *Second City* into bed at seven o'clock on Thursday.

He had started with Carrick because he knew that he could count on Gail Snyder's help. He hadn't been sure how he would learn where Larrimore had been and when, but Gail had fortuitously solved the problem for him. Slavin posed a more serious challenge. The obvious thing to do was simply to ask Cobb where the owner of *Second City* had been on Thursday evening. If he didn't know, he could obtain the names of owners of neighboring boats moored at the marina's docks and ask them. The problem with such a direct approach was that everyone at the marina would have heard of the accident. Asking when Slavin had come in for the night might suggest that Slavin was suspected of causing it. Carol or one of her men could get away with questioning Cobb or the other boat owners, but Kevin, a private citizen, would have a harder time justifying his questions.

He could see no way to do it other than leaving it to the sheriff, and that he was not ready to do. Slavin could well be innocent of any wrong doing, but he had been distinctly unpleasant to Kevin and there didn't seem to be any good reason for it. Unless, that is, the man resented his questions because he had something to hide. The hell with it, Kevin decided. What if I do stir up suspicions by asking about Thursday night? He already doesn't like me. Let me give him a good reason not to like me. If he wasn't the one who ran me off the road, the worst that can happen is that he'll threaten me again. It'll blow over. But if he did it, he'll know I'm onto him and why. I can take care of myself.

Which, of course, he had not been able to do the previous Thursday. A wrecked car and a broken arm were mute but compelling testimony to that. But what were the odds that Slavin would try twice to kill him? Kevin talked himself into believing that any slight risk was justified if it helped to capture Sandra Rackley's killer.

It was midmorning when he rang up the marina.

"Cobb's Marina," a voice said, "how can I help you?"

"Is this Mr. Cobb?"

"It is. What do you want?"

"My name's Kevin Whitman. I live two, three miles up the West Lake Road from you. I don't own a power boat, so I haven't done much business at the marina, but I've had a couple of pleasant chats with one of your customers. Slavin's the name, Mel Slavin. I'm the guy whose car went off the road just below here last Thursday. Somebody took me to the hospital, but I can't remember much else about that night. I thought maybe Mr. Slavin could help me. Do you happen to know when he came into the marina that night? I know he's staying on his boat, but I can't remember when we parted company that evening."

It was, of course, a phony story, but hopefully just complicated enough that Cobb wouldn't think the question odd.

"No idea. Don't pay attention to things like that. Stan was in the shop evenings most of last week, I'll ask him."

Kevin was surprised that Cobb had neither commented on the accident nor asked how he was doing. He waited while Cobb located Stan. It took all of long minute.

"Hi, this is Stan Ross. What is it you want to know?"

"I'm calling about one of your regular customers, the man who owns that big boat — *Second City* I think it's called. I'm trying to remember what happened last Thursday night. That was when my car went over the embankment down the road from here. It sort of messed with my short-term memory, but I think I'd been with Mr. Slavin. You wouldn't happen to know when he came back to the marina that night, would you? Doesn't have to be exact, just a rough estimate — early, say seven, seven thirty, or was it later, after dark?"

"You were driving the car that got wrecked?" Ross sounded incredulous, as if he didn't think the driver would still be alive, much less talking to him on the phone. "I guess you're a lucky man."

"That's what the doctor told me. But I asked about Mr. Slavin."

"Oh, yes, Slavin. Let's see. I was here all right, just checking up on things down at the docks. And I think — no, I'm sure about it. Mr. Slavin drove in around nine. Can't be a hundred percent sure, but it had just gotten dark. I saw his headlights as he came into the marina, so I walked back up to the parking area to see who it was. It was Slavin. He said hello when he saw me, went on to his boat. We didn't hear about your accident until the next morning."

So, Kevin thought, it could have been Slavin.

He thanked Ross, said something totally unscientific about accident victims having amnesia, and let the conversation drift into talk about how slow the county fathers were to get area roads repaired.

It was not until later, after lunch, that Kevin began to think about the probable consequences of his conversation with Cobb and Ross. For surely Slavin would hear that he had called them, identified himself, and inquired into Slavin's whereabouts on the night when he had had his accident. He wondered how long it would be before his next encounter with the owner of *Second City*.

CHAPTER 51

Kevin was sitting at his desk, still in bathrobe and slippers, when he heard the sharp knock on the back door. He looked at his watch. Barely seven o'clock. He was annoyed to be bothered so early in the morning. His initial reaction was that Mel Slavin had heard about his conversation with Ross and was coming to threaten him again. He headed for the kitchen, coffee cup in hand, thinking what he would say to him if it was Slavin.

To his great surprise, the person standing on the back porch was not the obnoxious owner of *Second City* but the very lovely sheriff of Cumberland County.

"Not dressed yet, I see," she said. "Does this mean that you were expecting me?"

"Carol! I feel better already." He took her in his arms, only to release her quickly when he felt a stab of pain in his shoulder.

"You're still hurting, aren't you?" she asked, although it was more of a statement than a question.

"A little, but only when squeezed," he replied, anxious not to sound like a poor patient.

"How about a kiss, then?" she asked, demonstrating what she had in mind.

"That's the way I like to start the day. Come on, don't just stand there. Coffee pot's hot. Let's go sit down so I can look at you for awhile."

By the time the coffee cups were empty and small talk about his physical condition had been exhausted, Kevin and Carol turned their attention to the Rackley case. It soon became apparent that she had invested little time on it during the days after the blowup over Jennifer's first letter.

"I don't believe I realized how necessary you are," she said. "And this time I'm not talking about us personally. I mean about the Rackley investigation. It was just impossible to get going on it. My men are too busy, and besides, they aren't brainstormers by temperament. Fact is, nothing has happened. It's fast becoming a cold case. I need your help, just as soon as you feel up to it."

"How about today?" Kevin suggested.

"Do you feel up to it?"

"You bet I do. I don't know what your day's agenda is, but I think we should do some of that brainstorming you say Bridges and the others can't do. Compare notes. Talk about what we've been thinking. I know I've got some things you ought to know about. Shall we start there?"

"Sounds good to me," Carol said. So after she had used her cell to give Bridges some instructions, they tackled the Rackley case, the sheriff in her uniform and Kevin in his pajamas and bathrobe.

An hour and change later, they were, in a manner of speaking, on the same page. Kevin had done most of the talking, reviewing again what he had learned about a chef, an orthodontist, and a financial wizard. Carol had never met Carrick and Larrimore. She knew a bit more about Slavin; in fact, she probably knew more about him than Kevin did, thanks to her conversation with the recently returned Phil Chambers. So they turned their attention first to the owner of *Second City*.

"It's pretty obvious," Carol began, "that Slavin and his wife are involved in a contentious divorce proceeding. Chambers may not be the most reliable source, but I think he's got it right. You tell me that Mrs. Wilder didn't want to talk about the Slavins' personal life, and I suspect the reason is that it's a mess. After all, here's Slavin, living on Crooked Lake for six months, while his wife stays in Chicago. Not exactly a scenario for connubial bliss. Chambers thinks that the sticking point in the divorce — or one of them — is *Second City*. She wants it as part of the settlement, he's determined to hang onto it. Why did he lug it all the way out here to Crooked Lake, a boat designed for Lake Michigan, not our little pond? He probably thinks it's safe from her clutches down at Cobb's Marina. And why not? Put yourself in her shoes. Is this likely to be a place she'd think to look for it? I don't think so."

"But if she wants the boat that badly, wouldn't she hire an investigator to track it down?"

"Of course. She's probably got a whole firm of big-time lawyers working for her, and they'd be derelict in their duty if they hadn't paid somebody a whopping big retainer to find that boat. But the divorce hasn't been finalized. It's taking a long time to come to closure, and one reason could well be that her lawyers haven't located the boat. These nasty divorces can drag out forever, both parties' heels dug in, nobody willing to give an inch."

"Okay, you're probably right," Kevin said. "But what does this have to do with poor Sandra Rackley?"

"Maybe nothing, and that's the point," Carol replied. "What if Slavin's never even heard of Rackley? He's obviously been suspicious of you. He's threatened you. If your hunch is right, he may even have tried to kill you. What if it's because he suspects that you're somebody his wife hired to find the boat? Not someone he thinks can tie him to Rackley's death, but someone who can get the boat away from him for the lady he so gallantly calls 'the bitch.'"

"Interesting theory, but it doesn't make sense. What if I were the gumshoe who was hired to find the boat? Okay, I found it, great big letters on the stern telling me that it's *Second City*. Don't ask me how I traced it all the way to Cobb's Marina. Just say that somehow I did. Then why in the devil would I hang around, asking all kinds of stupid questions of Slavin and Beth Wilder? Why not get on my cell and alert the lawyers back in Chicago that their boat is right here, snug in its berth on Crooked Lake? Let the money boys decide what to do instead of mucking things up all by myself."

Carol had to acknowledge that logic was on Kevin's side. But what if Slavin hadn't behaved logically?

"You're logical. Maybe Slavin isn't. Maybe he's so riled up over his divorce that he's not thinking straight. Or maybe he figures that his plan, bringing the boat to Crooked Lake, is so foolproof that the wife and her lawyers will never find it. But then this guy named Kevin Whitman comes butting in, asking questions, sounding interested in the boat. Whitman doesn't know anything about the divorce, but Slavin worries that his meddling could somehow screw up his plan. Not sure how, but he thinks he may be losing control. So he lashes out at Whitman. At you."

"You're not suggesting that we rule Slavin out as Rackley's killer, are you?"

"Of course not. But what evidence do we have that he killed her? That he was in Chicago in early December and here on Crooked Lake three months later? Pretty thin, don't you think?"

"There's that and the fact that he tried to kill me," Kevin said defensively. "Maybe his motive was the divorce and the boat, but it could just as easily have been that he thought we suspected him of killing Rackley."

"I know. By the way, he may have thought you suspected him of killing Rackley. I doubt that I've ever shown up on his radar screen. In any event, I'll keep an eye on him. I should be able to locate the hotel where he was staying in December and where he stays when he goes back to Chicago. Let's hope it's near Grant Park."

"Moving on, how about Larrimore?"

"Well, you suspect him of having been in Chicago in early December. That suggests checking airline flight manifests. Trouble is, we don't have a very strong case. We're not the feds seeking possible terrorists. What are we going to say — that maybe he attended a professional conference for orthodontists in Chicago, that he's a long-shot suspect — a very long shot — in a crime committed here in upstate New York? Privacy, Kevin. I can't imagine any airline being very cooperative. What's more, they may not even have those records anymore. I can try, but I'm not optimistic. Same with the conference hotel. We can probably find that out, but why would they give us the names of their guests of six months ago, assuming they keep them, just waiting for our call? Even the police can't just bully airlines and hotels without probable cause. And what is probable cause in Larrimore's case?"

Kevin had to admit that Larrimore was a suspect in his mind only because he had planned to go to Chicago for a conference, had said he changed his plans, and didn't offer much in the way of detail about those changed plans.

"Don't worry," Carol said. "I'll push all the right buttons. But I'll be very surprised if I learn anything helpful. No, make that anything at all."

"That leaves Carrick," Kevin said, "and I may be in the best position to push buttons in his case."

"How's that?"

"His mother, remember? He admits to taking leave from the Hilltop in early December to visit an ailing mother. I'll find her phone number and come up with some excuse to call her. You know, pretend I'm a friend of her son or something like that. And I'll get around to asking if he took in a Bulls basketball game while he was there. And where he stayed."

Carol looked depressed.

"We're just going through the motions, aren't we? I mean, what difference does it make whether he went to see the Bulls play? Would that move him up from party of interest to suspect? I don't see how."

"It might. Remember, he lied about when he saw a Bulls-Lakers game, the one when Kobe Bryant scored 50-some points."

"You know what, Kevin? I think we'll end up calling Sandra Rackley's death an accident. She fell from a steep bank in that damn ravine of yours. It was an accident. Case closed."

"Could be," Kevin said, "but I don't believe it for a minute, and neither do you. There's the car, carefully hidden in an abandoned barn. What did Rackley do, hide it before she went rock climbing in the ravine? And what about the wallet? You don't believe she lost it while admiring the scenery on Turkey Hill Road, and neither do I. Somebody from around here has been trying to cover up a crime and put the blame on that Beckham guy you've been talking to. Maybe that somebody isn't Slavin or Larrimore or Carrick. But at the moment that's all we've got, so let's treat the three of them as suspects."

CHAPTER 52

The first real heat wave of the season arrived on a Tuesday morning in late June. It was the kind of day, hot and humid, that sent Crooked Lake residents into the cool lake water or kept them inside where they could enjoy the air conditioning. Kevin Whitman would have preferred the lake, but the cast on his arm kept him inside. Sheriff Carol Kelleher's responsibility for preserving law and order in Cumberland County dictated that she, too, would spend the day in the air-conditioned comfort of her office. Their brainstorming session of the previous morning had ended on a note of pessimism, although both had agreed to soldier on in their quest for a solution to the problem of who had killed Sandra Rackley.

Carol's expectation that it would be difficult to obtain information on who flew when and stayed where on what dates proved to be accurate. Some of the people she spoke with were pleasant, others less so. But the result was almost invariably the same. The major exception was a woman at the nearby small regional airport. This woman, a Brenda Selwyn, knew who Carol was, and she had no reservations about helping the sheriff. She may not have had records, either on computer or in a paper file, but she had a good memory.

"I'm interested in whether you can possibly remember whether a man named Garrett Larrimore flew to Chicago in December," Carol asked.

"Yes, I'm quite certain he did."

This was the kind of information Carol had been seeking, but it came so quickly and easily that she was taken by surprise.

"How can you be sure? I mean, that was six, almost seven months ago.

"I don't have any records, Sheriff," the woman said. "But I know Mr. Larrimore. Not well, you understand, and I doubt that he would know who I am, but he flies out of here a lot. I'd say at least once a month on average. Never a nonstop flight, of course. You can't do that to many places from here. He sometimes leaves with a golf bag, and he goes south. Florida, the Carolinas. He either doesn't care for the courses around here or he hates our cold weather. Probably both."

"I don't follow you," Carol interrupted. "I asked whether he flew to Chicago in December, but you're telling me he flies south to play golf."

"That's why I remember that December flight so well. I can't remember him ever flying to Chicago other than that day. And he didn't have his golf bag when he checked in."

Carol was impressed with the Selwyn woman's recall, but forced herself to be skeptical.

"It's my understanding that Mr. Larrimore hasn't lived in this area very long, probably no more than a year and a half. So he couldn't have taken that many trips before December. How can you be sure about his flight habits?"

If Ms. Selwyn was annoyed that the sheriff might doubt her memory, she didn't say so, nor did she sound annoyed.

"I guess I just pay attention to things like that. And Mr. Larrimore, he'd already used us a lot."

"I really appreciate this," Carol said. And she meant it. "You don't happen to remember the specific date of that flight he took to Chicago, do you?"

"That's a little harder, Sheriff. It was early in the month, I'm sure of that. But date? No, I can't be that specific."

"One final question. Was his flight ticketed through to any place in Florida? I mean, say, Fort Lauderdale, Orlando?"

"I'm pretty sure it was just a round trip to Chicago. Like I said, he didn't have his clubs with him. Of course, he could have gone from Chicago to someplace down there and then back to Chicago, but I wouldn't know about that. But why do that and not take his golf bag?"

Good question, the sheriff thought.

"Ms. Selwyn, I'm grateful for this information. I'm sure you can understand that you're not to talk to anyone about our conversation."

"Of course. Is Mr. Larrimore in some kind of trouble?"

"Not that I know of. That's why I don't want you to talk with anyone about this."

If Larrimore had remained in Chicago and not, as he had told Kevin, gone golfing in Florida, he had presumably stayed at the Fairmont Hotel, which they had identified as the place where the meeting of the American Association of Orthodontists had been held.

Carol visited its Web site and found that the Fairmont was conveniently located at the northern end of Grant Park, within easy walking distance of places like the Art Institute and Orchestra Hall. But when she consulted a guide book of Chicago, Carol discovered that Grant Park covered some 220 acres. Unfortunately, Rackley's diary did not specify where in the park she had met D.B. Beckham. It could have been near the Fairmont, in which case she could have hobbled there on a sprained ankle. But it was equally possible that they had met many blocks to the south, and nothing in the woman's diary suggested such a long and arduous walk to the hotel.

———

Carrick was Kevin's responsibility because he had convinced the sheriff that he had a plan. But when it came time to put his plan into effect, he was less confident that it would work. It all depended on Carrick's mother. Could he locate her, and if he did, would she be able to answer his questions? She had not remarried and changed her name, so locating her turned out to be relatively easy. So now Kevin was on the phone, explaining the reason for his call.

"Mrs. Carrick, I know your son, Tom, from work at the Hilltop restaurant on Crooked Lake in upstate New York. We're very proud of him. He's really turned the restaurant around. What we want to do is give him a present to show our appreciation. We know he's a great fan of the Chicago Cubs, so we'd like to give him a weekend in Chicago, including a Cubs' game. What we don't know is the name of the hotel he prefers when he comes to visit. We could ask him, but that would spoil the surprise. Can you help us?"

"Well, now, aren't you kind? I'm so pleased that he's doing well. A mother loves to hear things like that. I keep telling him he can stay with me, but he's always been independent. Won't hear of it. Anyway, he likes the Blackstone. I think an old friend of his works there."

"The Blackstone, you say," Kevin said, pretending to write it down.

"Oh, dear," Mrs. Carrick interrupted, "you didn't say when he's coming. I'll want to see him."

Kevin explained that no date had been set, which was, of course, something of an understatement. No one at the Hilltop knew anything about this plan to send its chef to Chicago for a weekend, complete with a Cubs' game. If Carrick turned out to be Rackley's killer, there would be no such trip. If it turned out that Carrick had had nothing to do with her death, Kevin would have to busy himself turning a make-believe trip to Chicago into the real thing. Doing so might prove difficult. He'd think about it later.

"I understand that Tom visited you back in December," Kevin said. Carrick had not admitted doing so, but Kevin chose to treat Gail Snyder's report as fact.

"Yes, he did," Mrs. Carrick said. "Truth to tell, I think he came out here to see a basketball game or two. But he's a good son. We did get together — I made him lunch one day and we had a nice visit."

"And I assume he stayed at the hotel you mentioned. The Blackstone, wasn't it?"

"Yes, that's it. When you see him, why don't you tell him that his mother would love to have him stay with her, not some dingy downtown hotel."

Kevin had no idea whether the Blackstone was a dingy hotel, but he promised to do as his mother had asked, said good-bye to her, and turned to the task of pinpointing the location of the Blackstone Hotel. The small map that popped up on its Web site provided the information that it was just across Michigan Avenue from Grant Park. Kevin had known, as Carol had not, that the park was extensive. But like her, he had no idea of where in the park Sandra Rackley had been knocked down by frisbee players and rescued by a man who called himself D.B. Beckham. What he did know was that Carrick was still a suspect in her murder.

———

The third member of Kevin's Chicago connection, Mel Slavin, proved to be a more difficult case than either Larrimore or Carrick, and this in spite of the fact that both Kevin and Carol knew that he was still living in Chicago when Rackley met the man who would one day kill her. The problem was that he was going through a messy divorce and had moved out of the apartment on swanky Lakeshore Drive where he and his wife had lived in happier times. But where had he moved to? Almost certainly to a hotel, but Chicago had hundreds of hotels. Probably a first class or luxury hotel, given his economic status. It was hard to imagine Slavin hunkering down to wait out the divorce in a Motel 6 or Econolodge.

The sheriff had briefly considered calling Mrs. Slavin, who was likely to know where her husband was staying. But she decided against such a direct approach, inasmuch as it might necessitate explaining her interest in the Slavins' marital relationship and giving away the *Second City*'s whereabouts. So she assigned one of her men to the task of contacting every hotel with a four-star listing in Chicago and environs, starting with those nearest to Lake Michigan and its marinas.

It was Officer Barrett who hit the jackpot. It came on his fourth call, and the hotel that acknowledged that Melvin Slavin had a room there was the Fairmont. Carol was excited, although she had herself entertained the possibility that the Fairmont might be where Slavin was staying when he was not sleeping on the *Second City* or staying with the Wilders. After all, it met the criteria she had used in giving Barrett his instructions. It was a luxury hotel and it was very close to Lake Michigan and hence to Chicago's marinas. But what interested her most was the fact that all three members of Kevin's Chicago connection almost certainly occupied rooms on the edge of Grant Park in December, two of them in the first week of the month. For the first time since the discovery of Sandra Rackley's body, Carol felt cautiously optimistic about closing the case.

Of course, she didn't know whether Slavin had been in Chicago on December 2nd, the night of Rackley's ultimately fatal encounter with D.B. Beckham, but he had not yet moved his boat to Crooked Lake. And from what she had learned about the divorce proceedings, he had, in all probability, already settled into the Fairmont.

It was 4:30 in the afternoon when Carol and Kevin had their third phone conversation of the day. They agreed that they had good reason to celebrate.

"Do you mind spending the night with a guy whose arm is in a cast?" Kevin asked.

"Not at all. It might be an interesting experience," Carol told him.

"Okay, what do you say we do the Cedar Post again? And then back to the cottage for dessert."

"You're on. I'll pick you up at six."

CHAPTER 53

Ms. Maltbie was turning the calendar on the wall from June to July when the sheriff arrived on Thursday morning.

"I almost hate to see June end," she said.

Carol knew what her secretary meant. The Fourth of July weekend marked the end of the relatively slow first month of the lake's summer season. Now, with school over and vacations underway, the lake would not experience another quiet week until after Labor Day. Not that June had been an easy month. But demanding as it had been for the sheriff's small staff, the weeks ahead were sure to be even more hectic.

"Let's just hope that we make it through the weekend without any drownings," Carol said, reflecting on the fact that there had been three the previous year, two of them over the weekend of the Fourth.

"Don't know why people lose their common sense when they go on vacation," Ms. Maltbie said, her tone of voice suggesting that she didn't much care for the influx of summer residents.

"I'd like an uninterrupted hour," Carol said, changing the subject. "Unless it's really important, say I'll call back. Or see whoever it is later today."

She closed her office door behind her, and settled down with the Rackley case file and her recollections of her conversation with Kevin the day before. They had both been upbeat about the case, but in the bright light of a new day, Carol was less certain that they were closing in on Rackley's killer.

She removed her uniform jacket and was in the process of hanging it on a hook in the corner when she spotted a button that had come loose and was hanging by a thread. It reminded her that Kevin had discovered a button in the ravine many weeks earlier. She had been doubtful at the time that the button was of any importance, and had nearly forgotten about it.

The button, together with casts of two boot prints, had been tucked into a drawer in a small filing cabinet. Carol opened the cabinet and removed the button, less because she now thought it might be important than because she had largely exhausted her review of where the case stood.

It was an unusual button. Unlike most buttons, which are round, this one was shaped like a hexagon. It was of bone-like material, and measured just under an inch across. Carol studied it for a minute, shook her head, and returned it to the drawer.

She had gone on to other things, when an idea struck her. What if the owner of the jacket had discovered that the button was missing and had sought to replace it? It was unusual enough that replacing it might not be easy. Which could mean that whoever had tried to find a matching button might remember doing so. And that person might remember the owner of the jacket with the missing button.

Carol retrieved the button from the filing cabinet again, as if to confirm her judgment that it was indeed an unusual button which would be difficult to match. Her train of thought ran into several obstacles. The button, in spite of its shape, might be more common than she knew. The owner of the jacket might never have noticed that a button was missing, or, if he had, he might not have bothered to replace it. And of course she had no idea who might have been asked to replace the missing button. The owner of the jacket himself might have done so. Or he might have enlisted the help of any number of dry cleaners or clothing stores.

What decided her to pursue the matter was the fugitive thought that all three members of Kevin's Chicago connection were bachelors, two of them recently divorced and the third in the process of obtaining a divorce. Carol realized that she might be guilty of reverse sexism, but she thought that the odds were that any sewing of buttons in the Carrick, Larrimore, and Slavin families had been done by the wives. By the ex-wives.

Carol decided to check with area dry cleaners first, a choice dictated by the fact that she had sought the service of a dry cleaner whenever she need alterations to any of her own clothes. There were apparently four dry cleaners in the immediate area, one in Southport, one in Yates Center, and two in Cumberland. She found Officer Grieves in the squad room, entrusted him with the button, and instructed him to be polite but tenacious.

Five hours later, Grieves was back from his circuit of these establishments. He explained that it had taken him that long because he'd stopped for lunch and had to visit two of the places twice and one three times.

"Why two or three times?" Carol asked.

"When I went to Kim's Cleaners in Yates Center, the woman on duty seemed to know nothing about such things. She suggested I should come back when Mr. Kim himself was there. That got me thinking about the other places I'd visited, where the people I'd talked to were obviously young summer help. I figured maybe I should speak to the managers, so I went back until I'd seen the head guy in all the places."

"Probably a good idea," Carol said. "So, did you learn anything?"

"Not enough to be of much help to you."

"But it sounds as if you learned something though. Let's hear it."

"Came up blank at all but Kim's place, the one over in Yates Center. Everyone else said they couldn't remember a customer making such a request."

"But Kim was different?" Carol asked, trying to get her colleague to the point.

"Yes, in a way. He recognized the button, said a customer had come around looking to replace one that he'd lost from his sleeve. But Mr. Kim didn't have any luck matching it. He said he offered to replace both sleeve buttons, but none of the ones he showed pleased the man. He left, and Mr. Kim never saw him again."

Carol was impatient and it showed.

"Did he give you the name of the man?" she asked.

"No. He said he took the man's number so he could call if he found a match. But he wasn't successful, so he invited the man in to look over other buttons. Nice offer, but no sale."

"I don't suppose Kim could find the telephone number."

"No, he couldn't. Well, actually he didn't even try. Said he was sure he'd tossed it out when the man said he wasn't interested in any of the buttons he'd showed him."

It looked as if what might have been her best lead yet had disappeared along with the phone number. But Carol pressed on, now annoyed with herself for farming out to Grieves an assignment which she should have handled.

"How about a description of the man? I'd think Kim could have remembered something about him."

"I asked him that, but he didn't help much. Average height and weight, not much more. Oh, yes, fairly light hair. But I wouldn't put much stock in that. What he said was something about the man not being as dark as him, which I guess means not being as dark as a Korean."

Carol realized that she was in no position to contrast her suspects with Kim. She'd never seen any of them.

"When did Kim first discuss the missing button with this man?"

"He said he couldn't be sure, but he knew it had been sometime in late March."

Well, at least that's good news, Carol thought. It was after the time when they believed Rackley had met her death, but not that much.

After Officer Grieves had left, Carol silently berated herself for being impatient with him. He had done all he was asked to, and she doubted that she could have done any better. She might still make a follow-up visit to Kim's Cleaners to press Mr. Kim for a better description of the man who had lost a button off his jacket. The man who had probably killed Sandra Rackley. But it was unlikely that Kim would be able to add to what he had told Grieves.

She wished that she could arrange a lineup, consisting of Tom Carrick, Garrett Larrimore, Mel Slavin, and, for good measure, Phil Chambers. Maybe Kim would be able to pick out the button man. But she knew that such a lineup was but a pipe dream. It happens all the time on cop shows, but it had never happened in her experience and she doubted that it ever would.

CHAPTER 54

For as long as anyone could remember, the denizens of Crooked Lake had on Labor Day participated in a tradition known as the Festival of the Lights. Based on an old Indian legend, it called for every cottage to place flares on the shoreline and light them precisely at nine o'clock. The result was a spectacular sight, a ring of fire extending all around the lake. In effect, it was something of a farewell to summer. Not surprisingly, some lake residents decided that the Festival of the Lights was such a wonderful experience that it should be repeated on another milestone date, the Fourth of July. The result was another ring of fire, accompanied on this occasion by displays of fireworks by many of the cottagers.

With the Fourth of July only two days away, Kevin stopped by the hardware store in West Branch to buy eight flares. He had usually lighted only six, but this year he decided to light even more in celebration of the fact that Carol had come back into his life. He had a brief but pleasant chat with the proprietor, and was in the process of paying for the flares when an idea struck him. Why not use the Festival of the Lights, when virtually everybody is at home and in a celebratory mood, to turn up the heat on the men he considered to be the prime suspects in the Rackley case?

Kevin was so excited by the idea that he used his cell phone to call the sheriff's office while driving back to his cottage. Carol happened to be out of the office, so he left a message for her to call as soon as possible. It was while he was making himself a sandwich for lunch that she called back.

"I've got a great idea," he began. "It might be a way to smoke out our man — you know, Rackley's killer."

"You're telling me that now, after nearly three months of an on again, off again investigation, you're going to solve the case — just like that?"

"Yes. Well, maybe. But hear me out."

"Do you want to do this over the phone?"

"If necessary, but I was hoping you could meet me."

Carol had learned that Kevin's ideas, while sometimes far-fetched, were worth listening to. So she consulted her calendar and agreed to meet him at the cottage in an hour.

Kevin wasted no time with preliminaries.

"You know what's coming up this weekend, don't you?"

"Of course," Carol said. "It's the Fourth, and all my officers will be on duty. I just hope it's a safe and sane Fourth."

"And what happens on the Fourth?"

"Kevin, I didn't come over here to play twenty questions."

"What happens is the Festival of the Lights. That means that there'll be a lot of drinking through the evening hours. People doing stupid things with fireworks. Too many boats on the water, watching them. It must be one of the busier nights of the year."

"I know. I dread it. But you didn't ask me to come over so you could commiserate with me about maintaining law and order on the busiest night of the summer."

"No, of course not. But I think we can use the occasion to catch our murderer," Kevin said.

"What are you proposing that I do?"

"That's the point. You should do just what you would be doing on any Fourth of July. It isn't what you should do, but where you should do it. Look, you and your men will be cruising around, stopping to check out places where things may be getting out of hand, urging the good people of Crooked Lake to be careful. It's like the presence of police cars on the highway. Even if they don't arrest anybody, they tend to make drivers slow down."

"Yes, that's what we do, but what does it have to do with the Rackley case?"

"Let's say that while you're making your rounds, you stop off at Carrick's. You're just the friendly sheriff of Cumberland County, sharing the fun of the Festival, letting him know that his tax dollars are being well used."

"You're suggesting that I make it a point to visit with Carrick and Larrimore and Slavin, is that right?"

"Exactly. And they won't be alone. This is one of those nights when people congregate, mixing with their neighbors. That way Carrick and the others won't think you've come just to see them. You'll act natural, congratulate them on a great beach fire, enter into their small talk. You can do it, I'm sure."

"Thanks for the vote of confidence," Carol said. "But what am I supposed to accomplish?"

"Now comes the good part. At some point you mention their name. Only it won't be Carrick. It won't be Slavin or Larrimore. It'll be Beckham. You'll say something that sounds like it's just part of a good-natured conversation, like 'How long have you lived here, Mr. Beckham?' or 'Isn't this a great tradition, Mr. Beckham?' You'll think of something. But what matters is how they react when they're called Beckham. They won't have expected it — it'll catch them off guard. I'll bet one of them will give himself away."

Carol considered the scenario Kevin had described. It was bold, no question about it. Was it a good idea? Would it work?

"It's an interesting idea," she said, obviously not yet convinced she should try it. "You're gambling on all three of your men being on the beach. What if one of them, even all three, chose that night to go to a movie?"

"On the Fourth of July? It's possible, I suppose, that one or more of them won't be there. So what? We pull the same stunt at another time. You spot them on the street and call out to them using Beckham's name. There'll be other opportunities."

"If it's so easy, why don't you do it?"

"Wouldn't work. They all know me, know that I know their name isn't Beckham. You've never met them. And you're the law."

"What happens when I use Beckham's name?" Carol wanted to know. "That should be a conversation stopper."

"No idea," Kevin said. "They'll probably tell you it isn't their name, treat it as if you'd gotten misinformation from somebody. My guess is they'll all say pretty much the same thing, but in one case it'll ring false."

"Really?" Carol asked skeptically. "What if one of them is our killer, but is also a talented actor? Do I keep up our little charade? I can't very well start telling him why we think he's been using the name Beckham. He might not be our man, and I don't want to think about the consequences if he isn't."

Kevin's enthusiasm for his brilliant idea had begun to fade.

"I don't think any of these guys could fool you, but let's assume the worst. Then I'd just apologize, say something vague about mixing him up with somebody else."

"There's just one other little problem," Carol said. "How am I supposed to know these men? Can you give me a good description? I mean a very good description. Of all three of them. I sure wouldn't want to ask some perfectly innocent neighbor if he's Beckham."

"That won't be a problem," Kevin said.

They kicked the idea around for another hour, with Kevin supplying what he thought were persuasive profiles of Carrick, Larrimore, and Slavin. They knew that a confession was extremely unlikely, which meant that there would be no arrest on the Fourth of July. They considered the possibility that the guilty man, if indeed there was a guilty man among the three, might flee the area at the first opportunity. Carol, who had gradually and reluctantly decided to try Kevin's plan, said that she would assign one of her men to each of the three suspects with instructions not to let him out of sight. Until, that is, she had come up with plan B.

———

The nation's birthday rolled around two days later. Carol had committed to memory Kevin's description of the men who made up his Chicago connection. She had driven past the cottages where she hoped they would be spending the evening of the Fourth, making mental notes of where she could park. Slavin posed the biggest problem. He might be on his boat or he might be at the house of his friends, the Wilders. If the former, they agreed that it might be better to seek him out in some other way at another time. They had decided that she should start her rounds close to eight o'clock, at which time there would still be enough light for her to identify her targets. Too early for the flares, but well into the twilight time when people would be gathering on the beach and building their fires. The sheriff had also tapped three of her officers and given them orders to keep close tabs on these three murder suspects.

Carol still had an uneasy feeling about Kevin's plan and her pivotal role in it. She was reminded of the night the previous August when she had reluctantly consented to another of his plans, one in which he was to coax a confession from the man who had killed John Britingham while she waited anxiously in his car. Her memory of that earlier night did little to quiet her nerves; this time she was to be the stalker while Kevin stayed at home. She wasn't sure whether he would be having a beer or toasting marshmallows, but either way he would not be near at hand if things went wrong. But what could go wrong? Carol tried to reassure herself that the worst that could happen was that all three of the men she was hunting would pass the "Beckham test" with flying colors.

Her first stop of the evening of the Fourth was at the Wilders. It was as Kevin had expected. Slavin was there, as were several other neighbors. They were sitting on the front porch when Carol came around from behind the house.

"Hi," she said, mustering a cheerful voice to allay any suspicion that her sheriff's uniform signaled trouble.

She was invited to join them and proceeded to announce that it was her habit to drop in on people on the occasion of the Festival of the Lights. Beth Wilder introduced the other people on the porch, something the sheriff and Kevin had not taken into account in laying their plans for the evening. After a brief moment of panic, Carol saw how she could handle the problem. She expressed her hope that there wouldn't be any drownings to mar the festivities this year, and then segued easily into small talk. There had been no chair unoccupied next to the man who had been introduced as Mel Slavin, but from her seat across from him she thought she could have a good look at his reaction to what she said next.

"Funny thing, Mr. Slavin. I saw you recently in Southport, and somebody told me your name was Beckham."

Carol willed her brain to take a snapshot of the man. His face never changed expression, but she could have sworn that his body tensed for a brief moment. He might have been expected to act surprised, or to brush off the matter as a simple case of mistaken identity. But after a pause of several seconds, he merely said that, no, he was indeed Melvin Slavin.

When Carol left the party on the Wilder porch, she had the impression that Slavin was following her carefully with his eyes as she descended the steps and headed for her car.

Working her way north, Carol followed Blue Water Point, passed over the culvert that carried water down from the ravine where Sandra Rackley had met her death, and came to the pull-off that led to Tom Carrick's cottage. Once again she was in luck. This time a small knot of people were standing around a pile of firewood that had just been lighted. She gave them her excuse for dropping by, hurrying the conversation into other things so that they would not feel a need to introduce themselves.

These people, some seven of them, were more nearly Carol's age, and it was only a minute before three kids in the 10 to

12 age range came running out of one of the cottages, slamming the screen door behind them. There were expressions of disappointment that the fire was not ready for roasting marshmallows, but the overall mood of the group seemed light and unburdened by problems. Carol waited until one of the women made a comment about bumping into an old acquaintance in Cumberland, then jumped into the conversation.

"By the way, which of these cottages is yours, Mr. Beckham?" she asked the man with the streak of white hair.

"Who, me?" Carrick said, sounding surprised.

"Yes," the sheriff said, "you seem to be the only one here whom I remember seeing around the county."

"My name is Carrick, Tom Carrick. You must have me mixed up with someone else."

There was no point in pursuing this line of conversation, Carol thought. What was important was that Carrick had clearly acted as if he had been puzzled to be called Beckham. He had not looked anxious or annoyed, just surprised. But feigning surprise would be a good way to react to a troubling question. Carol found herself thinking that knowing when people are dissembling is not always easy. More like a polygraph test, the accuracy of which is notoriously unreliable.

The discussion drifted on to other things, and Carol said all of the proper things and left after about ten minutes. She had no idea whether D.B. Beckham and Tom Carrick were one and the same person.

It was now too late to give up the chase and tell Kevin that his plan was fatally flawed. Instead, she drove on up the West Lake Road for another half mile until she approached the Larrimore house. It was now beginning to get dark, which would make it harder to recognize the man she was looking for. As she started to pull the car onto the shoulder of the road, she saw a man emerge from the house carrying what looked like a sack of garbage. As he reached the side of the road, Carol realized that he looked very much like Kevin's description of Larrimore.

Carol cut the engine, got out of the car, and walked over to where he was depositing his sack in a trashcan.

"Hello. I'm the sheriff," she said, extending her hand. "Great evening, isn't it?"

Larrimore agreed that it was a nice evening, but he was clearly puzzled by the sheriff's presence beside his house.

"Is there something wrong?" he asked.

"Not at all," Carol said with a smile. "My men and I make it a habit to cruise around the lake on the Fourth, say hello, warn people about how dangerous fireworks can be."

"There won't be any fireworks here," Larrimore said. "Fact is, I haven't even started a beach fire."

"Well, there's still plenty of time. By the way, haven't we met? Isn't your name Beckham?"

Carrick had acted surprised when he was called Beckham; Slavin had seemed tense. Larrimore's reaction was harder to describe. For an instant she thought his expression reminded her of a deer caught in a car's headlights on a dark country road. Momentarily frozen, uncertain which way to jump. But the moment passed, the man relaxed, and then made the predictable response.

"Beckham? You must have me confused with someone else."

"I'm sorry," Carol said.

"Nothing to be sorry about. I don't think we've ever met, but I know how it is. I'm an orthodontist down in Southport, and there are times I can't seem to remember a patient I run into on the street."

Carol had done what she had come to do, so she steered the conversation to other things and after a few minutes made the excuse that she had to be on her way to see how other lake residents were doing on this glorious Fourth of July. One of three men might be Beckham, she thought, but she was damned if she knew which one.

CHAPTER 55

When Carol discussed her impressions of the three men with Kevin later in the evening, after the fireworks, she could not know that the situation was going to change dramatically the following morning. Her first intimation that the Rackley case had taken a sharp turn came at 8:30 the next morning when, still in her pajamas and robe, she was finishing breakfast in Kevin's kitchen. The call came from Bridges, who had been given the assignment of keeping track of Garrett Larrimore.

"Sorry to bug you so early," he said, "and at the professor's cottage, but I know you're going to want to hear this."

For all the deputy sheriff knew, his boss was still in bed, doing what he did not know, so he paused, giving her time to shift her attention away from Whitman and focus on what he had to say.

"What's up?" Carol asked.

"I'm at the airport. Larrimore arrived about twenty minutes ago, carrying a small suitcase. He's obviously going somewhere. He bought a ticket, but I'm not sure where he's going or when. My guess is he's taking the 9:15 to Washington. It's the first flight out of here."

Carol was now wide awake.

"Has he seen you?"

"I'm afraid so. I followed him from the lake, but stayed well back. I figured he was going to the airport when I saw him putting the suitcase in the trunk of his car back at his house. I didn't want him to see me, so I used that old by-pass road around the terminal. Lot of good that did. I had to be in the terminal to see what he was doing, and what he was doing was buying a ticket. He knows I'm here, right out in plain sight. The uniform's a dead giveaway."

"What's he doing now?"

"Just sitting and waiting to board. Drinking coffee."

Well, Carol thought, the pace quickens. Is our friend Larrimore the man who pretended to be Beckham? Maybe it doesn't matter how these men reacted to being called Beckham; maybe what's important is what they do now that I've called them

Beckham. What Larrimore seems to be doing is running. And if Bridges is right, he's running to Washington. Or some place via Washington.

Kevin had been mouthing silent questions at Carol from across the kitchen table. She held the phone to her chest and quietly told him that she was talking to Bridges and that Larrimore looked as if he were fleeing town.

"You can't let him go," Kevin said under his breath. "Tell Bridges to find a way to keep him off that flight."

"You know that's impossible," Carol said. "We don't have any grounds for detaining him."

She turned her attention back to Bridges.

"Look, Sam, try to act as if you're not interested in him. You know, read a paper, get a cup of coffee, pretend you don't know who he is and could care less. Then when he's boarded his plane, talk to the person who checked him in and find out everything you can. You know, where's the flight to, does he have a return ticket. If so, when's he coming back."

"Coffee, Carol, coffee!" Kevin interrupted the sheriff. "Find out if Larrimore's drinking coffee."

"Bridges already told me that he is," she responded.

"Good," Kevin said, getting up and coming around to Carol's side of the table. When he spoke again, it was clear that what he had to say was for Bridges' ear as well as for Carol's.

"We need that coffee cup. When he leaves, grab his coffee cup. We don't care whether he leaves it by his seat or drops it into a trashcan. Just be careful not to touch the rim of the cup. And first chance you get, if anything's left in the cup, make a hole in the bottom so it can drain out."

"Did you get that?" Carol asked the deputy sheriff.

"Yes, but I don't understand what —"

"Never mind. Just do it."

Thirty seconds later, the phone was back in its cradle and Kevin and Carol were discussing this latest wrinkle in the Rackley case.

"Why don't you tell me who's in charge here?" the sheriff wanted to know.

"Sorry. But I was afraid you'd lose Bridges before we got in that bit about the coffee cup."

"Before you told him what to do, you mean. How am I supposed to make my men believe that I'm the sheriff? I can hear it now, back in the squad room: 'First she's sleeping with him, and now he's calling the shots.' If I wasn't nuts about you, I'd be tempted to swear out a warrant for your arrest."

"On what charge?" Kevin asked.

"I'd think of something," she answered. "I take it you think we'd get Larrimore's DNA from the saliva on the cup."

"Right, and we wouldn't have had to do anything illegal to get it. I've been wondering how we might get any of these men to give us a sample of their DNA. We couldn't ask them for the usual cheek swab, and I didn't think there was much chance of a blood or semen sample. I'd even considered sneaking a peek at Slavin's garbage some dark night. And then when you said Larrimore was drinking coffee out at the airport, it just popped into my head. The cup. Chances were he'd either leave it where he'd been sitting or drop it into a trashcan. An abandoned cup — abandoned DNA, right there for the taking."

"I had no idea you'd become an authority on DNA," Carol said.

"I'm not, and to be honest I haven't given it much thought. But I saw one of those cop shows on TV recently — back when you weren't speaking to me and I had a lot of time on my hands. The good guys solved the crime by a DNA match. Somebody had the good sense to put a used condom to another use."

"Okay. Bridges will get the cup, and I'll see what Doc Crawford can do with it and the tissue we have from the fetus Rackley was carrying. But Larrimore will be gone, and if he's our man, how do we get him back here to face the music?"

"Do you think he's on the run? If he is, you must have really scared him last night. You drop the magic word, Beckham, and they're heading for the hills."

"I don't know about that," Carol said. "In the first place, he didn't head for the hills. Bridges said he's off for Washington. But why should he run? It just makes him look more suspicious."

"True, but suppose he thinks your office is closing in on him. Maybe he's gone into panic mode, isn't thinking straight."

"I'd say the man who killed Sandra Rackley isn't too likely to hit the panic button. He's lured her into a ravine and up a dangerously steep bank. He's hidden a rental car that took weeks to find. He's used Rackley's wallet to send me after that other

Beckham. He's managed to maintain a very low profile for months. Not the profile of a jumpy guy."

"Tell you what," Kevin said. "Why don't you call Larrimore's office, speak to his receptionist, see what he has scheduled for today. I'll bet he's skipped out on appointments. No, wait, I should make the call. Better a patient than a sheriff. No point worrying the Lansing woman."

The phone in the orthodontist's office was busy, and continued to give out a busy signal the first three times Kevin tried it. He was luckier on the fourth try.

"Hello, Ms. Lansing," he said, "this is Kevin Whitman. Remember me? I saw Dr. Larrimore a couple of weeks ago. I was wondering if he could possibly fit me in sometime today."

"Oh, I'm so sorry, Mr. Whitman. Dr. Larrimore had to leave town unexpectedly at the last minute. He called me this morning and asked me to cancel his appointments. Even if he were in today, he probably couldn't have seen you. He was booked right up to five o'clock."

"Well, that's what I get for waiting until the last minute," Kevin said. "By the way, did he say when he'd be back?"

"Not exactly. He said to cancel appointments through Wednesday, but leave those for Thursday and Friday unless he called back."

"My bad luck. It looks like I'll be away the latter part of the week. I hope everything is all right. I hope it wasn't a family or medical crisis."

"He didn't say," Ms. Lansing said.

Poor woman, Kevin thought. She must spend much of her time juggling the orthodontist's schedule and his impromptu trips out of town.

———

Carol and Kevin had agreed that Larrimore's cancellation of his appointments through the middle of the week constituted no proof that he had decided to skip town out of fear that the sheriff's net was closing around him. But neither did it prove that he was merely doing what he seemed to do frequently, which was to put a private agenda ahead of his professional one.

Deputy Sheriff Bridges did as Carol and Kevin had instructed him to, and reported back to the Cumberland office before lunch with details of Garrett Larrimore's travel plans and a used coffee cup. He had indeed taken the flight to Washington, but was not ticketed beyond that destination. He had made no return reservation, which resulted in a somewhat more rigorous trip through the airport's security system than would otherwise have been the case.

Larrimore had apparently not been taught to pick up after himself, because he left his coffee cup at his seat in the terminal. Or had he been careless because he was distracted, his mind on the possibility that the sheriff knew that he was the man who had pretended to be D.B. Beckham.

Before the afternoon was over, the coffee cup had been placed in the good hands of Dr. Henry Crawford, whose practice not only helped sustain life among the citizens of Cumberland County, but, thanks to an earlier incarnation, enabled him to serve as the area's forensic pathologist. He promised the sheriff that he would pursue the possibility of a match between the DNA from Larrimore's saliva and the DNA from the tissue sample taken from Sandra Rackley's three-month-old fetus. He set Thursday as the day when Carol could expect his report. Thursday, the day Garrett Larrimore was still scheduled to see patients.

Carol got in touch with her men who had drawn the assignments of tailing Tom Carrick and Mel Slavin. But if the fact that those two men had been called Beckham by the sheriff the previous evening worried them, it had not precipitated any change in the pattern of their lives. The chef prepared a dinner featuring rack of lamb at the Hilltop. Slavin gassed up the *Second City* and took her at a leisurely pace for a tour of the lake's eastern arm.

Phil Chambers quite accidentally bumped into Karen Lester on Main Street in Yates Center. He quickly apologized and set off for some business he had at the local hardware store. Whether he did this because he was trying to reform or because he thought a more gentlemanly approach might be a better way to entice her to bed, is not known.

CHAPTER 56

Crooked Lake is not the longest of the Finger Lakes. Nor is it the deepest. But for those who live or vacation on it, it is the most beautiful. From the hillsides above, it offers a gallery of attractive views of the vineyards and the blue waters that lay below them. From the shoreline, it draws one's eyes up to the crest of the heavily wooded hill which bisects the lake, giving it its fascinating Y shape. There are those who prefer the colorful palette of reds and golds that burnish the landscape in October. Others favor the white silence of January following a morning snow. But the favorite season for most is at its peak in July. It is then that the hills are at their darkest green, the lake waters at a temperature that invites swimming and boating, the air alive with hummingbirds at feeders, orioles in the treetops, and dragonflies skimming over the lake's surface.

While most lake residents were thoroughly enjoying this Friday in July, there were undoubtedly a few who were less happy because they were suffering from allergies, coping with failed air conditioning, or fretting about the weatherman's prediction of thunderstorms. The lake resident who was arguably the least happy had only recently returned to his home on the West Lake Road after a short visit to the nation's capital. The reason for his unhappiness had to do with the fact that the county sheriff was standing at his back door, a search warrant in her hand.

"What is this all about?" Garrett Larrimore asked, his voice betraying the fact that he was both irritated and anxious.

"Please step aside, Mr. Larrimore. My men have orders to search the house and we'd very much like to get started."

"What are you searching for?"

"It's all right there in the warrant," the sheriff said.

What was there in the warrant reflected developments in the Sandra Rackley case over the three days since the nation's holiday had been celebrated on Monday.

The first thing that had happened was that Larrimore had left the lake on an early flight on Tuesday morning, heading for Washington.

The second thing that had happened was that the deputy sheriff had picked up a coffee cup that Larrimore had carelessly left by his seat in the airport terminal and brought it back to Cumberland.

The third thing that had happened was that the forensic pathologist had examined the coffee cup and taken from it a DNA sample, which he had compared with the tissue taken from the fetus discovered in the womb of the late Sandra Rackley. And there had been a match. Voila! Garrett Larrimore was the father.

Carol Kelleher, the sheriff of Cumberland County, knew better than to jump for joy or otherwise celebrate the end of her three month long pursuit of the Rackley woman's killer. But she also knew that the case was no longer in stasis. The coffee cup had seen to that. The coffee cup and Doc Crawford's reading of the message encoded in the DNA of Garrett Larrimore's saliva.

"I've got what I'm sure you will see as good news," Crawford had said on the previous day when he walked into Carol's office.

"There's a match?" she said, rising hopefully from her chair.

"No doubt about it. I did most of my forensic work back in the day before DNA became big. But even an old school doc like me could see that we had a match."

"Which means," Carol said, "that the man responsible for that tiny fetus we found in Rackley's womb was the same man who drank out of that coffee cup."

Carol sounded as if she had to spell it out in layman's language for it to be true. Doc Crawford assured her that she was right.

The tale of the DNA made Larrimore the prime suspect in Rackley's death. But Carol knew it didn't prove that he was her killer. They would have to obtain more evidence if they were to take him to court and obtain a conviction.

Carol had wanted to search the homes of Carrick and Larrimore, as well as Slavin's boat, ever since Kevin had steered her attention to the three men who constituted his Chicago connection. But she had known that no judge with even a passing knowledge of the law would grant her a warrant. All she could say was that the three men had been or might have been in Chicago in early December, that they had been evasive when questioned as to their whereabouts by a citizen with no legal training, and that they lived within walking distance of the glen where Rackley's body had been found. And she would have been laughed out of his office, her reputation in tatters.

But now, she thought, a judge might look upon a request for a search warrant differently. Larrimore may be a respected professional, but we can prove that he knew Rackley, that he had slept with her and left her pregnant, and that he had not come forward when the fact that she had lost her life right here on Crooked Lake had become general knowledge.

And so the sheriff had gone to visit Judge Olcott, the member of the bench whom she knew best, and laid out her case for a warrant. It appeared that Olcott hadn't paid much attention to the Rackley matter, and had assumed that the absence of news about it in recent weeks meant that the sheriff was treating it as an accidental death. The judge had not known Larrimore personally, but knew that two of his own grandchildren wore braces courtesy of the orthodontist. He was obviously worried about the damage that might be done to an innocent man's reputation, but Carol ultimately convinced him that fathering a child out of wedlock, while not uncommon, was not the best evidence of a good reputation, especially when the mother turned up dead when the fetus was but three months old.

And so it was that Carol and two of her officers marched into Garrett Larrimore's West Lake Road home early on Friday morning. It was immediately apparent that theirs would be a sizable task. To say that Larrimore was disorganized or messy would not do justice to the scene that greeted them. The entranceway was partially blocked by several boxes, overflowing with newspapers and old magazines. To their right in the kitchen both drain rack and sink were full of dishes, and the counter was cluttered with cereal boxes, a sugar bowl that had been tipped over, and what looked like the remnants of a rather large breakfast. Ahead of them, through a door to what was presumably the living room, they could see more evidence of the fact that Larrimore was not a good housekeeper.

"Mr. Larrimore, I'm not going to ask you to leave your own house, but I am going to ask you to find someplace — how about the kitchen table? — where you can sit down and stay out of our way. Have another cup of coffee or something. Better yet, go and take care of your patients."

"But this is outrageous," Larrimore protested. "I've never been treated like this, ever, in my whole life."

Carol ignored the objections to her search and chose not to engage Larrimore in a discussion of what he was alleged to have done. He knows, she said to herself. Let him stew.

The search was thorough, but when they were through they had found no physical evidence that Sandra Rackley had ever been a part of Larrimore's life. Unless, that is, one were to count a pair of waffle soled shoes and a winter jacket which was missing the cuff button on the left sleeve. Moreover, the button on the right sleeve looked very much like the one that Kevin had found in the ravine. Neither shoes nor missing button proved that Larrimore had been in the ravine with Rackley, but the missing button made it all but certain that he had visited the ravine at some time. The sheriff could hardly be blamed for thinking that that sometime had been in March, and that he had been accompanied by Rackley, en route to her death.

The only thing that had not been closely examined by the sheriff and her men was Larrimore's computer. Over his vigorous protest, they took it with them, along with the jacket and the shoes, when they left.

Carol gave Officer Byrnes the task of working with the computer. He was known as the most computer savvy member of the team, and she figured that if the computer contained any evidence that Larrimore had had a secret life involving Rackley, he was the one most likely to find it. However, it didn't take someone with Byrnes' know-how to find what the sheriff was referring to as the smoking gun. Any one of her officers could have done it, for all it took was patience. The computer, like the house, was a mess. It didn't look as if the orthodontist had deleted any document or weeded out any file in many weeks. No reference to Rackley could be found, but there amidst the hundreds of things that Larrimore had saved was a brief two paragraph statement addressed to whom it may concern.

Carol looked over Byrnes' shoulder and read the following document.

> I do not know whether your department handles lost-and-found inquiries, but I am sure you will know what to do about this wallet I found last night.

I was driving on Turkey Hill Road when I suddenly had to take a leak very badly. I know it isn't nice to do it by the side of the road, but it was an emergency. Anyway, this wallet was lying there in the weeds by the roadside, right where I stopped the car. As you can see, I did not remove anything from the wallet. It is just as I found it. I hope you are able to find the owner.

A conscientious citizen.

Carol recognized it immediately as the note that had accompanied Rackley's wallet when it arrived in her office weeks earlier. Larrimore had obviously typed it out, printed a copy, and mailed it to her along with Sandra Rackley's wallet. If only he had deleted it, really wiped it off his computer, he might still be able to wiggle out of his predicament. But he hadn't. His bad habits had finally done him in, she thought.

———

Kevin was just finishing lunch when the phone rang.

"Hi, it's me," Carol said. "I think we've got him."

She filled Kevin in on the search of the house and the computer. Carol could not see his face, of course, but she could imagine his look of smug satisfaction when she reported finding the jacket with the missing button and the waffle-soled shoes. Larrimore might come up with a story that would explain the missing button, but they were in agreement that it would be almost literally impossible for him to deny having typed the message about the wallet — typed it and mailed it to the sheriff, for that copy was safely tucked away in her file on the case.

The computer had also given up the information that Larrimore was involved with a woman named Ellen Noyes of Washington, D.C., where he had apparently lived prior to moving to Crooked Lake. Indeed, it was probably to see her that he had flown to Washington on Tuesday morning. Carol read to Kevin the message that Larrimore had sent to Noyes late in the evening of July 4th.

Ellen — Coming to see you tomorrow. We've got a problem and I need your help. Tell

you about it when I see you. Looking forward to
Labor Day. Love, Garrett

In fact, Byrnes had found numerous e-mail messages from
her to him and from him to her, beginning back in the winter. This
e-mail correspondence made it clear that they were planning to
wed, with the Labor Day weekend the projected date. Inasmuch as
this was apparently a second marriage for both, they seemed to
have settled on a small wedding, even a private one.

Kevin was intrigued by the news of the pending Larri-
more-Noyes nuptials, and told Carol that he'd like to have a look
at the e-mail correspondence between them. Pursuant to her
instructions, Byrnes met him that afternoon in Cumberland and set
him up at Larrimore's computer.

For the next hour and a half Kevin played voyeur, following the conversation that Larrimore and Noyes had carried on
electronically. At the end of this trip through their private lives,
Kevin was left with two impressions. The first was that Larrimore
seemed to be very much in love with her, and anxious to redeem
the disaster of his first marriage with a "'til the end of time"
relationship with Noyes. Larrimore was known to have taken leave
of his practice on several occasions, and the impression he had left
with Kevin was that he spent most of those days on golf courses.
But the e-mail dialogue made it clear that he spent much of the
time away from his practice with Ellen Noyes in Washington.

The second impression was that Larrimore's messages
changed in tone on two occasions. Back in the winter he had
written in considerable detail about his professional meeting in
Chicago. He devoted two messages to the meeting, stressing the
panels he had attended and the knowledge he had gained.
Moreover, there were repeated assurances of his love for Ellen.
Knowing what he knew now, Kevin thought those messages read
like a conscious attempt to convince Noyes — and himself — that
he was both a conscientious orthodontist and a man deeply in love
with the only woman in his life. It was almost as if he were trying
to erase the fresh memory of the one-night stand with Sandra
Rackley.

The second change in tone came around the second week
in March. It lasted for two or three weeks, then resurfaced from
time to time right down to the present. These messages were still
full of expressions of love and anticipation of the September

wedding, but the dominant theme was worry. He was not sleeping well. When he slept he was troubled by unpleasant dreams. He had tired of Crooked Lake. He had decided he would never make real friends up here. Once he had even posed what was obviously meant to be a rhetorical question: can we ever really escape from our pasts? The message in which Larrimore had raised this question was uncharacteristically introspective.

How strange it is, Kevin thought, that this man has been using an e-mail correspondence with a fiancée he obviously loved to work out a personal crisis, a crisis which went from an evening's sexual pleasure with a stranger to the murder of that woman and then to chronic anxiety about the consequences of her murder.

———

That evening, Kevin and Carol met for dinner at the Cedar Post. Carol had spent most of the afternoon with the prosecutor, providing him with all she knew about the Rackley case and mapping strategy for what would arguably be the most important trial held in Cumberland County in many years. Her people were keeping close watch on Larrimore, both at his home on Crooked Lake and his office in Southport, as well as points in between. This time they would not hesitate to step in aggressively if he tried to skip town.

Kevin listened attentively, offering his opinion when it seemed warranted. But he was also very much interested in discussing with Carol the e-mail correspondence between Larrimore and Noyes. By the time they got to dessert and coffee time, Carol had said most of what she had to say, so Kevin took over.

He gave her an overview of what had been said in the e-mails, and went on to offer the theory that what Larrimore had to say in his messages to Noyes more or less followed the evolution of the Rackley case. Of course, Larrimore had never mentioned Rackley, but to Kevin his choice of words seemed to reflect the fact that she was on his mind. Kevin tried to present his argument by sketching the shifts in focus and tone of Larrimore's messages on the paper tablecloth. Carol paid Kevin the compliment of close attention. She had learned not to dismiss his ideas out of hand. He was usually right. But this time she had serious reservations.

"Kevin," she said, "you may be onto something, but you're no more a psychiatrist than you are a detective. Wait. I'll take that back, because you show signs of becoming a pretty good detective. But what if you're right? I can hear a defense attorney saying 'so what.'"

"Do you know any psychiatrist around here? Wouldn't it be a good idea to let him see the e-mails, tell us what he thinks? I may be all wet, but maybe a professional expert could help make it a stronger case."

"I'll take it up with the D.A.," Carol said, "but I think we've got a pretty good case, with or without somebody trying to deconstruct Larrimore's messages. Tell you the truth, I'm more worried that in the end our guy will try to get out of it by telling us he was with her when she accidentally fell. It was just an accident. 'We were discussing what we would do regarding the pregnancy,' he'd say, stressing the we, 'and she just lost her footing on the slippery bank. I'd warned her not to get so close to the edge.' And he'd tell us he was just so distraught he didn't know what to do. Say he blamed himself for not pulling her back from the edge of the bank. Say he was afraid he'd be accused of causing her death, so he didn't dare come forward. Tell us it's still eating at him inside — can't sleep, you know, blah, blah, blah. I can hear him now."

"But remember," Kevin argued, "he's going to get married, has been since before he met Rackley. How can he possibly deal with a pregnant Rackley, demanding that he marry her or help her and the kid financially? With her in the picture, he'd always be afraid that she'd show up one day, ruining his life with Noyes. The Noyes woman would probably leave him. She'd sure never trust him again. So what does he do? He silences Rackley by pushing her off the cliff in the ravine. Tell you what. I think you scared him out of his wits when you called him Beckham. He figures you're on to him. First thing he does is fly off to Washington to see Noyes, making up some story that he hopes will guarantee her loyalty if and when he goes to trial."

Carol was nodding her head in agreement.

"That's the way the prosecution will present it," she said. "Let's hope the jury goes along. That way he'll serve a long stretch in one of New York's not-so-cozy jails."

The hour was getting late, and Carol had to look forward to an unusually busy day on Saturday, starting with Larrimore's arrest. There was still too much to do that evening for the sheriff to spend the night, as she would have liked to do, at Kevin's cottage.

"We're in good shape," she said as they walked to the cars. "But I'm tired. Glad that somebody else will be prosecuting."

"Really?" Kevin asked. "I'd love to be doing it."

"Kevin! Do you think standing up in front of a jury is just like standing before a class in music history? While you're at it, you might consider trying to get yourself named to the jury — I'm sure you could talk them into making you their foreman."

"Can you be put on a jury if you're not a full-time resident?" he asked.

"No, you can't. The jury pool comes from among registered voters, and last time I looked you weren't voting in Cumberland County."

"Damn! Another plan foiled." Kevin smiled at Carol, threw his good arm around her and gave her a kiss before heading for the borrowed Buick.

"Tell you what you can do, though," Carol said. "Come by my office in the morning and I'll let you draft the news release on Larrimore's arrest for the *Gazette*. Maybe you'll win a Pulitzer."

Kevin slid behind the steering wheel, now an awkward move because of the cast.

"That'll be the day," he said, shaking his head. "My dean would much rather I got a rave review for a new book.

"Come on over anyway. You can be a fly on the wall, just watching us law enforcement types at work. It's going to be a big day."

"Arrest Larrimore, then what?"

"He'll be released on bail, of course. And then the fun begins — impaneling the jury, planning strategy, lining up witnesses, staying one step ahead of the defense, keeping the process moving."

"Witnesses. You said witnesses. Will I be expected to testify?"

Carol had worried about this. She would have to be prepared to explain how it happened that Kevin Whitman, a college professor on summer vacation, was the one who had found the button from Larrimore's jacket. Or, more importantly, that he had searched Sandra Rackley's apartment and found her revealing diary.

"I don't know, but yes, in all probability you'll have to testify."

Kevin started the car, then put another question to the sheriff.

"How long do you think the trial will last?"

"I'd be surprised if we get a verdict before Halloween, maybe November, probably later. Our case against him is entirely circumstantial. It'd be nice if the D.A. could produce a witness who saw what happened up on that bank, but we know that won't happen. Which means he's going to have to spend a lot of time convincing the jury that the facts he lays out add up — that considered together they tell us that Larrimore is guilty. Beyond a reasonable doubt."

"So what do you think? Does what we've got add up? Is he guilty?"

"I think he's guilty. Very guilty. But what I think doesn't count. It's what the jury thinks."

"And we won't know that until this fall, you say. Which means I won't be here to see it."

He didn't want to add what was now uppermost in his mind, that he and Carol would once more be living in very different parts of the state, pursuing their different professions. The sheriff knew what was on his mind. It was on hers as well.

CHAPTER 57

Kevin pulled himself up onto the dock, toweled off, and looked out across the calm and vivid blue waters of Crooked Lake. The sky was cloudless. It was the kind of day that inspires those who write tourist brochures. But much as he treasured days like this, Kevin's mind was on a woman he had never met and a man whom he had known for barely more than a month. The woman was Sandra Rackley, the man Garrett Larrimore. Rackley was dead, had been dead for nearly five months. Larrimore was about to be put on trial for having killed her. Indeed, he had been arrested and charged that very morning, and Kevin had been a witness to the process. True to her word, the sheriff had allowed Kevin to draft the news story of Larrimore's arrest for the *Cumberland Gazette*. She had even allowed him to accompany her and Bridges when they made the arrest, Kevin having assured her that he could write a better story if he were present when Larrimore was taken into custody.

Things had moved swiftly after that. Larrimore's lawyer had appeared, as if by magic and certainly by prearrangement, at the West Lake Road address, and in just a bit over two hours they were all present in Judge Findlay's chambers to argue about bail. The D.A., whom Kevin was to get to know better when he was called as a witness, had argued passionately that Larrimore was a flight risk and that bail should consequently be set at a million dollars. The judge had not been persuaded, with the result that bail was nominal and Larrimore's attorney, one Lawrence Hackett, was admonished as to his responsibility for his client's presence when the trial began.

By noon, it had been obvious to Kevin that he was not needed in Cumberland and that there was nothing further to be gained by hanging around the sheriff's office. Somewhat reluctantly, he headed back to the cottage. Three hours later he had eaten lunch, taken a swim, and puzzled over the fact that Carol had not called. He knew she was busy, but as the hours went by he found himself increasingly worried that there had been some hitch in her plans for putting the wheels of justice in motion. He had promised himself that he wouldn't bother her, but when his watch told him it was now close to four o'clock, he pulled out his cell phone and called her.

"Look, I can't talk now, but give me ten more minutes," she said. "You can't believe what's been going on over here. I've got one more call to make and then I'll be over."

"Great. That'll give me time to get dressed and start organizing dinner."

"Let's put dinner on hold for an hour or so. I want to take a swim first. Can you believe I haven't been in the lake once all summer? Not once. Anyway, I'm bringing my bathing suit. See you in thirty-five, forty minutes."

Kevin realized that he'd never seen Carol in a bathing suit. The prospect was pleasing. Dinner could wait.

Carol's forty minutes turned out to be closer to forty-five, and much of Kevin's dock was in the shade by the time she pulled up to the cottage, dashed inside, and reappeared in a flattering two-piece suit.

"Now give me a few minutes more," she said, as she balanced on her toes at the end of the dock and dove into the lake.

Kevin watched her surface and set out in a surprisingly strong crawl toward a neighbor's float. A beautiful woman, he thought, and followed her into the water with a dive that wasn't quite up to the standard she had set.

Ten minutes later they were sitting at the end of the dock, breathing hard from this burst of activity.

"I needed that," Carol said, leaning over and giving Kevin a kiss. "Let's do it more often."

For a fleeting moment, Kevin forgot all about Garrett Larrimore and Sandra Rackley. All that mattered was that he and Carol were alone in the world, feeling more like a couple of kids on summer holiday than the sheriff of Cumberland County and a professor of music at Madison College. It mattered not at all to either of them that five people on the decks of nearby cottages were observing them. And smiling at what they saw.

"Who gets to break the spell?" Carol asked.

"I guess it'll have to be you," Kevin said as he pulled away from her. "Okay, back to the chase. What's happened? You said I wouldn't believe it."

"And I don't think you will. Two things happened after you left, both out of the blue. First, this woman barged into my office, ignoring Maltbie's effort to announce her first. Turned out she was Ellen Noyes, Larrimore's bride-to-be. She didn't introduce herself, not at first. Nor did she take a chair. She just stood there across the desk and told me I had to release Larrimore. Just like that. He's innocent, she kept saying — had nothing to do with the death of this Rackley woman. She went on at some length, got herself all worked up about it."

"Did she ever tell you why she knew Larrimore was innocent? I mean, she wasn't up there in the ravine with them, was she?"

"No, of course not, but she insisted that her dear Garrett could never kill anything, much less a human being. Anyway, get this: she said that if we didn't let him go, she'd have her father do something about what she called 'Crooked Lake justice.' And she didn't mean that as a compliment."

"Her father?" Kevin sounded as if Miss Noyes must be some kind of a nut case.

"Yes, her father, who happens to be a member of the House of Representatives. According to Noyes, he's represented some district in Tennessee for decades, heads up some powerful committee, has lots of clout."

"So daddy's a VIP. So what? We're talking about a crime committed in New York, not Tennessee. I can't imagine a congressman getting involved in a murder case, especially a murder case about which he knows nothing."

"That's pretty much what I told her," Carol said. "But she claimed that he'd see to it that funds for projects in our district — 'earmarks' is what she called them — would be cut out of the federal budget."

"All this because this man is marrying his daughter? Does Noyes know that Rackley was carrying her fiancé's child when she died?"

"I think so, but it looks like Larrimore fed her a line on that issue and she bought it. Apparently she's prepared to forgive him for having sex with Rackley. You know, everyone does it, no big deal."

Kevin shook his head, as if to say he doubted that it was no big deal.

"In any event, we're not going to throw in the towel just because the Noyes woman wants us to. I think it's all bluster. This congressman didn't win all those elections to the House by doing stupid things like interfering in criminal cases on behalf of a family member."

Carol got up and stretched a leg to get the circulation flowing again.

"Now about that other thing that happened this morning," she said. "It's about Phil Chambers."

"Chambers?" Kevin was obviously surprised. "I thought we'd narrowed our focus to the men who'd been in Chicago back in December."

"We had. Well, more or less. I've never been able to get him off my mind. Not completely. Anyhow, I got a phone call from Cobb, the guy who runs that marina on this side of the lake."

"Is Chambers in some kind of trouble at the marina?"

"Not that I know of. Cobb must have heard somehow that we were interested in somebody named Beckham. That wouldn't surprise me. Anyway, Cobb wanted to pass along the information that Slavin had stopped by to give him a work shirt that belonged to Chambers. It seems that he left it on the boat when Slavin fired him. Cobb was going to tell Chambers to stop by and pick it up, when he discovered that there was something in the breast pocket. Being naturally curious, I suppose, he looked at it. He says it was a bank deposit slip, and that on the back was scrawled the name and address of Dennis Beckham. Now what do you make of that?"

Kevin was as puzzled by this piece of information as the sheriff had been when Cobb called her. Carol had sent Barrett down to the marina to collect the shirt and note, and was now trying to make sense of the fact that Phil Chambers was apparently involved in some way with Dennis Beckham.

"Maybe Chambers and Beckham are friends, or at least acquaintances," Kevin suggested.

"That's possible, and it should be easy to prove or disprove. But why would Beckham's name and address be written on the back of a deposit slip? Not what you'd expect if they know each other. If the note had read something like 'Call Dennis Beckham,' that's one thing. But what it suggests to me is that for some reason Beckham's name comes to Chambers' attention, and he reaches for the handiest piece of paper to make a note of it. Maybe it has absolutely nothing to do with the Rackley case. But both Chambers and Beckham are what might be called parties of interest in the case, and I think we should take the note seriously, don't you?"

"Yes, and what about Slavin?" Kevin asked, his mind now fully engaged. "Slavin brings the shirt, together with the note, to Cobb. Suppose he didn't do it out of the kindness of his heart. Suppose he wanted to make trouble for Chambers. Maybe he wrote the note himself, making it look as if Chambers and Beckham had some sort of relationship. What if Slavin is Rackley's killer, the man who called himself Beckham? At the very least, he would have complicated your search for the murderer. And hasn't he done just that?"

It was now Carol who was shaking her head, signaling her objection to this line of reasoning.

"Sorry, but I got Barrett busy on the note right away. It was easy to put our hands on several copies of his handwriting, and I'd swear that the name and address on the deposit slip were written by Chambers. Slavin may be a bastard, but he didn't try to frame Chambers."

"Are you sure?" Kevin was now excited, thinking like a detective, or so he imagined. "Even if Chambers did write the note, putting it in Cobb's hands pretty much guaranteed that it would get to you and that you'd be doing just what you're doing today, trying to make sense of a Chambers-Beckham relationship."

Suddenly, Carol's face broke into a big smile. And then she started laughing.

"Did I say something funny?" Kevin asked.

"No. Well, maybe yes," Carol managed to say, even while laughing. She tried to suppress the laughter, only to start giggling.

The laughter was infectious, and Kevin found himself laughing. too, even if he didn't know what was so funny.

"Just listen to us, will you," Carol said. "Here we are, on the day Garrett Larrimore has been charged with having caused Rackley's death, and what are we doing? We're having a serious conversation about the possibility that our friend Chambers knows Dennis Beckham. Pretty soon we'll be speculating on the possibility that Cobb is the killer, or Ginny Smith, or who knows."

"Ginny Smith?"

"We need to take a deep breath. Why wouldn't Chambers be interested in Beckham? What was Rackley doing the night Chambers met her at the Cedar Post?"

"Tossing a drink in his face," Kevin answered.

"Yes, but more importantly she was asking around if anyone knew a man named Beckham. Chambers, our local womanizer, is trying to get something going with Rackley. It doesn't work, but he remembers that she was looking for Beckham. So what does he do? He starts looking for Beckham, too. Maybe that way he'll find Rackley, maybe have better luck the second time. And here we are, making a mountain out of the proverbial molehill."

Kevin started to protest, but an awareness of the absurdity of it all won out.

The neighbors, had they been watching, would have been treated to the sight of two people rolling with laughter on the Whitman dock until one of them, the professor, fell into the lake. The other, the sheriff, promptly dove in after him.

After a bout of good-natured horseplay in the water, Kevin and Carol dried off and retreated to the cottage, dinner on their minds. By the time they had dressed, enjoyed a glass of Crooked Lake's finest wine, and eaten a rather pedestrian meal, they had reassured themselves that the case against Garrett Larrimore was airtight. It might not lead to a conviction for murder, but it would surely, at a minimum, result in a conviction for manslaughter.

Both Carol and Kevin were well aware that their summer was almost over, which meant that there would only be a few more nights like this at the cottage before he packed up and returned to the city. But neither of them wanted to talk about that, and so, by tacit agreement, they didn't. They left the dishes in the sink and retired to the bedroom at an early hour.

EPILOGUE

"Hi, it's me," Carol said, sounding breathless at the other end of the phone line. "Guess what? It's over."

"What's over?"

"What's over? Come on, Kevin, where were you all summer? The trial's over. It's the Rackley case. The jury just came in."

Kevin spun around in the swivel chair at the desk and looked at the Sierra Club calendar on the wall. The date was December 3rd.

"How about that — almost exactly a year since Rackley met the man who killed her. So what's the verdict? No wait — let me guess. Innocent on all counts?"

"When did you become such a pessimist? Look. I'll fill you in as soon as I see you. That's why I'm calling. Is there any way you can get yourself up here for a day or two? And I mean right away. I need you all the time, you know that, but this is a special occasion. This was *our* case. I can't celebrate alone."

Kevin reached for his pocket calendar, fumbled for the December date, and started to read off his schedule for the next day. There was one 75-minute class, plus office hours in the afternoon and a reception for a faculty candidate.

"I didn't think you'd just be twiddling your thumbs," Carol said as he read off his obligations at Madison College. "But can't you scrub those things?"

"Most of it won't be a problem. The class is tricky, though."

Carol interrupted his explanation as to why the class would be a problem. "What about your assistant? You have one, don't you? Can't you let her — or is it him this time? — why not let her meet the class?"

"It's a her, and it's not Jennifer Laseur. Peggy — that's her name — she's engaged to a marine, and it just so happens that he's in town briefly before shipping out to Iraq. I can't possibly mess up their time together."

Kevin paused briefly and then told Carol he'd be there.

"I'll do it," he said. "I want to see you and hear about it. To hell with the class. I'll have a note put on the door saying class canceled, professor ill. No, I'd better not do that. I'll just say it's a personal emergency."

"Great! When you've made the reservation, let me have your flight info and I'll pick you up at the airport. Can you stay over, you know, not go back tomorrow night? When I say I want to celebrate, I mean celebrate. You haven't shut the cottage up for the winter, have you?"

"Sort of, but we can build a fire, snuggle up — what did they used to call it, bundling?"

"Sounds wonderful. I'm an expert at bundling."

"You never told me what the verdict is. I think I'm entitled to that."

"Do you ever watch *Law & Order*? If you do, you've probably heard McCoy talk about 'man one.' Well, that's what we've got here — Larrimore is guilty of manslaughter in the first degree."

"You pleased with the verdict?"

"That's one of the things we'll talk about while we're bundling."

Kevin collected his bag from the overhead bin and made his way up the aisle and down onto the tarmac with the handful of people who had made the flight to the airport that served the western Finger Lakes. As planned, Carol was waiting for him inside the terminal. The kiss with which she greeted him was the first since the Columbus Day weekend, when they had enjoyed a few days of Indian summer, complete with a beautiful display of autumn's colors. Before that, back in September, he had returned to Crooked Lake to testify for the prosecution. But now that the trial was over, he would no longer be able to use civic duty as an excuse for cutting classes and going back to the lake.

Carol's situation was no better. Her plan to spend the Thanksgiving weekend with Kevin in the city had fallen through at the last minute for the simple reason that crime doesn't take a holiday. And she knew that Ms. Maltbie's decision to retire at the end of the calendar year meant that she would be spending more, rather than less, time on the job.

They walked through the largely empty terminal and out into the parking lot, which was covered with a light dusting of snow.

"You should have worn a warmer coat," Carol said as she unlocked the Buick.

"Not to worry. I've got my love to keep me warm." As if to demonstrate the point, he turned her to him and kissed her again.

"All kidding aside," she said, "you're going to be cold in that windbreaker. Do you have something back at the cottage you can put on?"

"Could be. Let's go find out."

The drive to the Crooked Lake cottage took close to forty minutes, during which time they chose to talk mostly about how much they had been missing each other. Carol had to push Kevin's hand away from her knee several times.

"Later," she said as his fingers began another slow trip up her leg. "One accident on this road is enough. I don't drive very well when I'm distracted."

"Me either. I'll try to be good."

They picked up a few groceries in Southport and arrived at the cottage shortly before five. The absence of good insulation meant that the cottage was almost always too hot in summer and too cold in winter. But today, when the thermometer on the porch announced that the outside temperature was only eight degrees above freezing, the cottage was warmer than Kevin had expected. Two space heaters were plugged in and purring away in opposite corners of the living room. Carol had obviously been there earlier in the day.

When Kevin ducked into the bedroom to deposit his suitcase, another piece of evidence that Carol had stopped by the cottage confronted him. Her overnight bag lay open on the bed. She had stayed overnight with him on numerous occasions over the summer, but the sight of her bag, with its neatly folded blouses and underwear, still prompted a broad smile.

"You look happy." Carol was standing in the doorway, wearing a smile of her own.

"I am," Kevin said, "but it's all your fault."

"You make my tummy tickle," Carol said as she walked into his embrace.

Kevin raised an eyebrow.

"Sorry," Carol explained. "It's an old family line. When I was a little girl, my mother used to tell me that I made her tummy tickle. That made no sense to me — I think I had too literal a mind at that age."

"Most kids do, I suppose. Anyway, I like it — you know, the idea that I'm a tummy tickler."

Carol backed away, as if afraid that Kevin would start tickling her.

"You haven't said anything about my cast," Kevin said. "Haven't you noticed? It makes kissing a lot easier, now that it's gone."

"Does it still hurt?" Carol asked, now concerned that she hadn't mentioned it.

"No. I'm fine. So, what's our agenda?"

"I want to tell you about the Larrimore trial," Carol said. "But not on an empty stomach. And not without a fire."

Kevin laid a fire in the fireplace while Carol located a warm blanket and spread it out in front of the hearth. Neither was in the mood to cook anything, so Kevin opened a couple of beers and brought out the crackers and cheese they had picked up en route to the cottage.

"Now this is what I'd call cozy," Carol said as she stretched out on the blanket.

"Agreed," Kevin said. "But you were going to tell me about the trial."

"Right. First things first. I can't remember just what you know and what you don't know."

"You've told me the outcome, but I still don't know how the jury reached its verdict. We talked about my testimony when I was here last month, and you assured me I'd made a good witness."

"All I said was that you hadn't screwed up the prosecution's case."

"Okay, whatever. But Larrimore's attorney was surely doing his damnedest to make me look like an amateur interloper."

"Which you were." Carol's smile canceled any impression that she was critical of his role in the investigation. "No point in my reviewing the trial, day by day," she said. "Just say that Hackett was a pretty good defense attorney. He got about as much mileage out of Larrimore's position as he could. But in the end it just wasn't good enough. And I was proud of Stokes. He did a darn good job for an inexperienced small-town prosecutor, wouldn't you agree?"

Kevin nodded in agreement.

"Anyway, I think Hackett's biggest mistake was trying to make the jury believe that Larrimore wasn't there in the ravine when Rackley died. Or that he knew Rackley had come to Crooked Lake. If he could have made that stick, her fall from that bank would have been either an accident, pure and simple, or the doing of someone else."

"Meaning Chambers, I assume."

"Right. The defense had done its homework. They knew about the episode with Chambers at the Cedar Post. Not sure how they did it, but they'd even found out about his stalking Karen Lester. They weren't trying to pin the blame for Rackley's death on Chambers, just trying to establish a reasonable doubt about Larrimore's guilt in the jury's mind. After all, if the prosecution was going to use Rackley's pregnancy as Larrimore's motive for killing her, why wasn't the bruised ego of an angry stalker like Chambers as likely a motive?"

"So why do you believe Hackett made a mistake in arguing that Larrimore hadn't been with Rackley in the ravine?"

"Remember that we half expected Larrimore to claim that her fall was an accident, that he had been afraid to report it because it would only make me suspicious of him? Well, looking back at it, that would probably have been the better approach. Most of the things that the killer did after we discovered Rackley's body point to Larrimore, not Chambers or X. I suppose that someone other than Larrimore could have hidden the rental car, but it is impossible to believe that that business about the wallet being found on Turkey Hill Road wasn't Larrimore's doing. More than that, Larrimore had to have been the one to tell Rackley that his name was Beckham. So he'd have been quick to see the possibilities of leaving the wallet beside the road where the real Beckham lives.

"Anyway, if the defense had admitted that Larrimore had been with Rackley in the ravine, it could have explained everything else as the behavior of an innocent man who was scared that my investigation would target him. And why not, in view of the fact that he knew he had impregnated Rackley."

"I assume that the DNA evidence was crucial," Kevin said.

"It was. Hackett certainly tried to get it excluded. He argued that taking that coffee cup amounted to illegal search and seizure. Even cited some case law. But the preponderance of case law seems to go the other way — Larrimore had abandoned his coffee cup, threw it away. The judge was on our side on that one."

"And Noyes wasn't bothered by any of this?"

"Well, it turned out that she was. Not at first. It was pretty obvious that Larrimore had told her about his one-night stand with Rackley. Not in the beginning, of course, but when it became clear to him that his paternity had been established beyond a doubt, he didn't have much choice. He probably manipulated the facts a bit, doing his best to make Rackley the aggressive one that night in Chicago. I'm not quite sure how he would have done that, but Noyes was very much in Larrimore's corner in the early going. She made a powerful witness for the defense — you know, 'He's a wonderful man, my Garrett, and no, I don't hold that little indiscretion against him — he'll be a faithful husband, I know.' Or something like that."

"So what happened to change her mind?" Kevin asked.

"You could see it coming as the trial went on. Her face betrayed her growing doubt that Larrimore had told her everything. But I'm doing what Doc Crawford always does, God bless him. He leaves the most important news for last. Noyes abandoned her fiancé when she found the keys to the rental car."

"You're going to tell me that she found them in Larrimore's house," Kevin interrupted.

"Exactly. And instead of discussing her discovery with Larrimore, she came straight to my office, keys in hand."

"I thought your people had given the house a thorough search back in the summer."

"I thought so, too. In fact, I was there, helping with the search. Obviously it wasn't thorough enough. Noyes found them because she found the bed uncomfortable. So one morning she rotated the mattress and turned it over. And there they were, under the dust ruffle."

"I take it that it was obvious they were the keys to Rackley's rental car."

"Yes. The prosecution had already brought up the fact that when the car was found there were no keys in it. So I'm sure Noyes would almost immediately have suspected a connection. Besides, who keeps his keys under his mattress? When Noyes came in that day, she was mad. And I mean smoking mad. She assumed that they belonged to the rental car, that Larrimore had hidden it, and that he had then hidden the keys. It wouldn't have taken much of a leap in logic to conclude that her fiancé had killed Rackley. So all of a sudden it was the prosecution's case, not that of the defense, that rang true to her. She had no problem throwing Larrimore to the wolves. One thing to excuse the man's one-night stand in a strange city, but quite another to love and plan to marry a murderer."

"So the keys were the clincher."

"Well, it certainly punched a hole in the theory that Chambers or X killed Rackley."

"That's almost too bad," Kevin said. "I suppose it means that my contribution — the jacket button — was irrelevant."

Carol knew that he wasn't serious about his disappointment, but she hastened to tell him that finding the button had not been entirely irrelevant.

"As it happens, the button strengthened the prosecution's case. Not so much finding it as when it was found. They admitted that Larrimore had been in the ravine and had lost a button off his jacket. But they claimed that it had happened long before Rackley's death, soon after Larrimore had moved to Crooked Lake. But Kim, the dry cleaner, testified that he hadn't been asked to locate a replacement button until this spring. Even more important, my man Byrnes found the date when the jacket was purchased and paid for when he gave Larrimore's computer a thorough going over. He had bought it at a fancy men's shop in Washington in February of this year, less than a month before Rackley's death."

"So Larrimore was done in by his sloppy lifestyle, his inability to get rid of stuff. The keys, those damning entries on his computer. Funny, though. He was very careful to wipe out fingerprints — on the car, on the wallet."

"I know," Carol said. "Being human means being inconsistent. We were lucky that Larrimore was all too human."

"And so we get a manslaughter verdict. Why not murder?"

"Supposedly, the difference between murder and manslaughter is that murder requires malice, manslaughter doesn't. In both cases, killing is unlawful and intentional, but manslaughter lacks malice. Back in law school, I had a hard time seeing the difference, even with all that case law we had to struggle through.

Anyway, I think the 'man one' verdict reflects the simple fact that the jury believed Larrimore felt he had to get rid of Rackley, but wasn't sure just what was going on up on that bank. Manslaughter in the first degree looked like a way to hedge their bets."

"I don't get it. Pushing her off that ledge looks pretty malicious to me."

"I know, but we still don't know for sure — probably never will — exactly what happened. If she fell accidentally, he sure never tried to help her. Anyway, I'm pleased with the verdict. He'll get a stiff sentence, and eventually Southport will get itself a new orthodontist."

"Won't Larrimore appeal?"

"He'll be sentenced first. But, yes, I'm ninety percent certain he'll appeal."

"What's happened to the rest of my Chicago connection?" Kevin asked.

"Carrick's still filling the tables at the Hilltop. I've only talked to him once since we arrested Larrimore. Pleasant, informal chat one day over in Cumberland. He'd heard about the trial, but didn't seem to have paid much attention to it. Frankly, I'm not sure he'd ever heard of Sandra Rackley."

"I don't think he had. His problem, I'm pretty sure, was that he took a week off back in December to see some basketball games out in Chicago. He told his boss he was going to visit a sick mother, but he was afraid the owner would find out that it was basketball, not momma, that accounted for his leave, and that he'd be fired for it. I feel kind of guilty for hounding him like I did. I must have made him pretty nervous."

"Do you think his job's in jeopardy?"

"Can't see why. I'm certainly not going to share my theory with the owner of the Hilltop. What I think I'll do, though, is use a friend who works there to help me plan a trip to Chicago for Carrick. We'll find a way to get him out there for a couple of Bulls games. I'll ease my conscience by footing the bill."

"Going to be mister nice guy for a change, huh?"

"Have I ever been anything else?"

"Yes, at least once. In Slavin's case."

"No tears shed there. What's the latest on his divorce? "

"It's not going well for him," Carol said. "The wife's attorney was down here recently. Looks like the jig is up with

Slavin's little hide-the-boat maneuver. You knew it would be, didn't you?"

"Let's say I hoped so. I know he wrecked my car, nearly killed me, but no way I could prove it. So, like I told you back in October, I called his wife, told her where the boat was. She'd have found out about it in some other way, I'm sure, but she was grateful, thanked me profusely. I like to think of it as Kevin's revenge."

"Slavin's madder than a hornet about the boat. He actually came to see me and demand that I do something about it. I'm glad I was able to say I was powerless to interfere."

Kevin got up and poked at the logs in the fireplace. The suddenly brighter flames lit up their faces. Carol's was wearing a smug smile.

"Would you like to know about our other suspect, Phil Chambers?"

"As I remember it, he was your candidate as Rackley's killer, not mine."

"If you say so, but you should hear this. A few days ago, I was having an early dinner at the Cedar Post. Just me. I kept myself company by rereading an old Agatha Christie mystery. Anyway, this man came up behind me and asked if he could get me a drink. He saw the empty chair across the table and was obviously thinking about joining me."

It was clear that Carol relished the story she was telling, and was looking forward to Kevin's reaction to it.

"Of course it was Chambers. Coming up behind me like that, he didn't recognize me. Even when I turned around, it didn't look like he knew who I was. He'd only seen me in my uniform, and that night I was wearing slacks and a wooly sweater. Earrings, too. Anyway, I had the distinct impression that he was looking to pick me up. I wish you had been there to see the change that came over him when it dawned on him that he was talking to the sheriff."

"Backed off, did he?"

"Not exactly. Much to my surprise, he sat down across the table and started to give me a line about how much he respected me. You could almost see the wheels at work in his mind as he tried to turn a failed effort to pick me up into a tribute to all of my many talents. It was all I could do not to roll my eyes. But the fact that I didn't immediately tell him to get lost seemed to encourage him, and he repeated his offer to buy me a drink. He almost got back into pick-up mode before I called a halt to the whole charade."

This time it was Carol who got up to tend to the fire.

"At least his taste is improving," Kevin said. "The way I remember it, last time it was a girl just out of high school who worked the checkout line at the supermarket."

"Come on, Kevin, I don't find Chambers' attentions the least bit flattering. I probably should have thrown my drink at him, just like Rackley did."

"Too bad you didn't. Can't you just see the headline in the *Gazette*? 'Sheriff in Altercation with Local Stud: Beer Flies at Cedar Post.'"

Kevin found Carol's encounter with Chambers amusing. The man posed no threat to his relationship with Carol. But what about other men, now only shadowy figures in his imagination, who might suddenly walk into her life while he was occupied with teaching his students about opera down in the city?

The thought triggered a familiar feeling of anxiety, which brought him up off the couch. Carol turned and stepped back from the fireplace. Their shadows merged on the cottage wall behind them, and the words from the immortal Rodgers and Hammerstein tune "Some Enchanted Evening" ran through his mind: *Once you have found her, never let her go.*

No, he thought as he gathered Carol into his arms, I'll never let you go. Never.